Bella Osborne has been jotting down stories as far back as she can remember but decided that 2013 would be the year that she finished a full-length novel.

In 2016, her debut novel, *It Started at Sunset Cottage*, was shortlisted for the Contemporary Romantic Novel of the Year and RNA Joan Hessayon New Writers Award.

Bella's stories are about friendship, love and coping with what life throws at you. She likes to find the humour in the darker moments of life and weaves this into her stories. Bella believes that writing your own story really is the best fun ever, closely followed by talking, eating chocolate, drinking fizz and planning holidays.

She lives in the Midlands, UK with her lovely husband and wonderful daughter who, thankfully, both accept her as she is (with mad morning hair and a penchant for skipping).

A Walk in Wildflower Park

Bella Osborne

avon.

Published by AVON
A division of HarperCollins*Publishers* Ltd
1 London Bridge Street
London SE1 9GF

www.harpercollins.co.uk

A Paperback Original 2019

1

A catalogue copy of this book is
available from the British Library.

ISBN: 978-0-00-825822-1

This novel is entirely a work of fiction. The names, characters
and incidents portrayed in it are the work of the author's imagination.
Any resemblance to actual persons, living or dead, events or localities
is entirely coincidental.

Typeset in Minion by Palimpsest Book Production Limited,
Falkirk, Stirlingshire
Printed and bound in UK by CPI Group (UK) Ltd, Croydon CR0 4YY

MIX
Paper from
responsible sources
FSC C007454

This book is produced from independently certified FSC™ paper
to ensure responsible forest management.

For more information visit: www.harpercollins.co.uk/green

For Patty – with love.

Prologue

Three months earlier

'Happy pre-versary!' Anna called from the kitchen.

'What?' asked Liam, screwing up one side of his face as he removed his coat. He walked through to where Anna was bouncing on her toes with excitement.

'One year today will be our wedding day. So, I made you this. Ta-dah!' Anna stepped away from the table and kissed Liam lightly.

Liam pulled away. 'Right,' he said, rubbing his neck. His eyes alighted on the amorphous brown mass behind Anna. 'What the hell is that?' He took a hasty step back and stared. 'It looks like some sort of . . . demon? Have you been binge watching *Game of Thrones* again?'

Anna was hurt. She'd spent hours carefully crafting something special for him. 'It's a hedgehog.'

'Made from what? Poo?'

'It's chocolate cake.' Anna put her hands on her hips but, remembering they were covered in chocolate icing, she wished she hadn't.

'It's got teeth?' he said, peering closer.

'Hedgehogs have teeth,' said Anna, feeling defensive.

'O-kay.' He didn't sound convinced. 'Anyway, I wanted to talk to you.'

'What about?' asked Anna, turning her attention to aligning the hedgehog's wonky eyes.

'Those teeth are like my granny's dentures.'

'You wanted to talk to me about dentures?' She smiled at him.

'No. I think we need to take a break.'

There was a pause as Anna frowned. All she could focus on was that maybe she shouldn't have used glacé cherries for the eyes. They *were* demon-like. Chocolate buttons would have been better.

'Anna?' prompted Liam.

'Yes, fine.'

'Really? You agree?'

'Yes. I think it's a good idea,' she said, over her shoulder. 'You've been working crazy hours recently and I could do with a break too. I've always wanted to go to New York but I don't think I could cope with the flight.' She turned around to see Liam was staring hard at the floor. 'Did you have somewhere in mind? It'll be cold and wet wherever we go in this country at this time of year.'

Liam's eyebrows inched higher with her every word. 'I don't mean a holiday, Anna.' Beads of sweat were forming on his top lip. His voice was gentle, his expression pained. 'I mean a break from each other.'

And that was it. Her engagement, her future, her neat little life unravelled by one sentence. She hurled the hedgehog cake at Liam's face and truly wished it had been made of poo.

Chapter One

'Are you sure about Majestic Mayonnaise?' asked Sophie, brandishing the tester pot.

'Well, obviously.' Anna playfully waved her loaded paint roller at Sophie.

'Hey, I'm pregnant!'

'Barely.'

'Ten weeks actually, which means it's the size of a large green olive.'

'Which apparently means you can only supervise the decorating, rather than provide any actual help,' said Anna, smudging paint across her cheek as she attended to an itch.

'I'm sorting this out.' She pointed at the box in front of her, the words 'Random Crap' emblazoned on the side in Anna's handwriting. 'I'd love to help with decorating but this is about you starting a new chapter without Liam and I don't want to intrude.'

'Two years I wasted on him. What is it with me always picking the same sort of commitment-phobe? Liam makes it four in a row. *Four!*' said Anna, emphasising her point by holding up four fingers. She was beginning to think she was either a serial monogamist or she was destined never to find *the one*. She unceremoniously dropped the roller into the paint tray.

'You're not entirely over the anger phase yet then?' said Sophie, blowing out her cheeks.

Anna's flash of fury waned. 'That's two years of my life I'm not getting back. What sort of person dumps someone four months after proposing?'

'A prize plughole?' offered Sophie, who only ever used what she felt were child-friendly swear words and frequently resorted to making up her own versions. 'You need to think about you now. Not him.'

Anna took a deep breath. Sophie was right. This was her new start. She needed to leave Liam in the past and concentrate on her future. She was more cross than she was upset. In fact, she probably should be more upset than she actually was. She spotted one of his books in the random crap box, snatched it out and slammed it into the box labelled 'Arsehole's Stuff'. Perhaps it would take a little while longer for the anger to abate.

'You're right. A new start in my new flat.' She wasn't sworn off men forever; she needed to prove to herself that she didn't need one, prove she could manage perfectly well on her own. Then maybe if the right person came along she would consider a relationship on her terms, but given how many times she'd been bitten, it would be a long time before she'd feel ready to do that.

'Have you got any biscuits? I'm Hank Marvin,' said Sophie.

'Top cupboard, Hank,' said Anna, pointing behind her. It felt like a good time to have a break. She'd been decorating the kitchen all morning and the thought of a cuppa and a Hobnob was now dominating her thoughts. She was pleased with how the little flat was shaping up but it would be a while before it'd really feel like home. Anna had been moved in a week but with her dad's help she was already putting her own stamp on things.

A few minutes later Sophie was thoughtfully dunking her third biscuit in a large mug of coffee.

'You okay?' asked Anna.

Sophie pursed her lips as she appeared to carefully consider her answer. 'I don't like to complain about this, considering what you're going through, but I can't shake the feeling that I'm hurtling towards thirty and I've not done any of the things I thought I would have by now. I'm fed up with being a general skivvy. I'm bored of having virtually no life outside the kids. I'm sick of washing, ironing and clearing up – it's relentless. And I'm feeling a bit useless at work too . . .' As if highlighting her gloomy state her biscuit dissolved into her tea. 'Bumfuzzle!'

Anna handed her friend a teaspoon. 'I meant the pregnancy.'

Sophie briefly screwed her eyes up and then opened them particularly wide. 'Right. Sorry about the rant. Of course, I'm thrilled. We want lots of kids. The first two took ages to conceive so we thought we had plenty of time but this one must have been the Usain Bolt of sperm.'

Sophie's husband, Dave, was the polar opposite of Usain Bolt. Dave was to speed what crayons were to fine art – simply not cut out for the job. He was the sort of person most labelled as 'a nice guy' but he was a constant source of irritation to Sophie.

'Still, a new baby will be lovely and now I live seven doors away I'll be able to help.'

'Thanks. I'm going to need it.' Sophie fished out another Hobnob.

'It'll be fine. You're glowing.' Wasn't that what you were meant to say to pregnant women?

'I don't feel glowing. I feel tired and a little nauseous most of the time. And I'm spotty and fat already! All the pregnant celebrities look stunning and I look like this.' She pointed in turn at her limply hanging hair, pimply chin and lumpy midriff.

'I keep telling you the magazines you read are full of rubbish. The celebrities are all airbrushed and styled so much they'd make the Gruffalo look like Kim Kardashian. In fact, who knows for sure that the Gruffalo *isn't* Kim Kardashian, I've never seen them together.' Sophie gave a weak attempt at a smile. 'You're naturally beautiful.'

Sophie didn't seem convinced. 'I'm bloated and I've not lost my baby weight from the first two yet. And I really miss proper coffee.' She peered accusingly into her mug.

Anna wasn't sure what to say; instead she opted for squeezing Sophie's shoulder. She didn't like to see her like this but she knew her well enough to know jollying her out of it wasn't the answer. They sipped their drinks in silence.

'Come on,' said Anna. 'Let's go for a walk in the park.' The novelty of having a private park literally on her doorstep was going to take a long while to wear off. The park was in an area called Walmsley but was known as Wildflower Park because of the many varieties of wildflower that grew there. The history of the park had fascinated Anna when Sophie had first moved there a year before. The old manor house had been demolished during the Industrial Revolution leaving its grounds isolated but surrounded by other large houses, the owners of which were not keen to have their view spoiled by cheap workers' housing or worse still a factory. They'd clubbed together to buy the gardens and turned them into a private park accessible only by those who had a property backing onto it. Even now keys were held by a select few who had an adjacent property. Anna was incredibly lucky to have been able to buy one of the flats in the small 1970s' block, which was somehow allowed to be built, backing onto the park and therefore qualified its occupants for access.

'Okay,' said Sophie with a groan although Anna knew she loved a stroll around the park too.

Sophie zipped up her hoodie and Anna grabbed her coat and keys. It was early April and the signs of spring were becoming evident as the temperature was starting to feel warmer. Daffodils were everywhere and things were generally greener. As times had changed Anna no longer needed an actual key to open the gate to the park, just a special key fob. She pressed it to the gate, which buzzed in recognition and she pushed it open. Anna felt like she was being transported into the secret gardens of her favourite childhood books.

The park was a good size and must have been magnificent gardens in its day. Now a team of volunteer residents cared for it. A few years ago a community project had set about focusing on the reintroduction of wildflowers to help support bees, butterflies and other wildlife, and it had been a huge success.

Where Anna entered it was sheltered by some conifers, which hid what was once the rockery. A neat path wound its way through budding trees, past some newly sprouted crocuses and down to the pond. Everyone called it a pond, but to Anna, who had been brought up in the city, this was more than a pond. A pond was a thinly disguised plastic shape about four foot round you bought from the garden centre and filled with a few buckets of water; what they had here was more of a lake to Anna. It took up about a fifth of the park and must have been 250 metres across at its widest point. She loved the little island in the middle where the ducks seemed to take refuge at night in case any foxes came looking for an easy meal. But most of all she loved the areas that were given up to wildflowers – they were her favourite.

Sophie glanced at her phone as they walked side by side.

'Are you going to check they're all right?' asked Anna.

'Who?'

'Dave and the kids?'

Sophie did some gurning followed by a long drawn-out sigh. 'If I call I'll hear chaos and get stressed out and I'll have to go home and shout. It's best if I don't know.' She gave a wistful glance in her house's general direction.

'Dave's not that bad.'

'Don't get me wrong, I love him to bits. He's just totally useless with the kids . . . And the house. And the garden.' Sophie rubbed her middle and sighed.

'You any nearer to agreeing names for number three?' asked Anna, keen to cheer up the plunging mood.

Sophie put her phone in her pocket. 'No, it's the usual battle. Dave wants something traditional and I want something distinctive. And now we have the added pressure of getting something that works with Arlo and Petal. You know when you send cards and it says "Love from Dave, Sophie, Arlo, Petal and Moby."'

'Moby? As in Dick?'

Sophie rolled her eyes. 'Don't say that. Moby's my favourite but I also like Enoch and Thaddeus.'

Anna failed to hide her flinch. 'So, you're counting on a boy this time?'

'No, we've already agreed what she'll be called if it's a girl – Darby.'

'As in Derby County Football Club?'

'No, with an "a", you muppet.'

Anna nodded her understanding. 'Still, Dave won't be happy when he goes to work on a Monday and someone says, "I see Derby got stuffed at the weekend."'

Sophie took her hand out of her pocket to give Anna a swipe. They walked past the pond with the tall swaying reeds at its edge and headed up towards the largest of a series of oak trees. Anna decided to change the subject completely.

'I've met Mrs Nowakowski,' she said, with a raise of her eyebrows.

'Did she ask you millions of questions?'

'It was like completing a questionnaire.'

'At least we don't need surveillance cameras with Mrs Nowakowski about. She's got more nose than Pinocchio – she doesn't miss a thing,' said Sophie.

'She was disappointed I was single but thrilled I didn't have a dog or a parrot. She seemed all right though.'

'She's not a fan of animals. She's always reporting dog walkers who don't pick up their poo.' Anna gave her a quizzical glance. 'Not their own poo, the dogs'.'

'Oh dear. I'm thinking of getting a kitten.' Anna bit the inside of her mouth.

'Is this the start of your mad cat lady phase?'

'No. I've always wanted one and Liam was never keen, so this is my opportunity. At least talking to a kitten instead of to myself won't make me look quite so bonkers and it'll be company.' The thought of coming back to the empty flat bothered her. This was the first time she'd lived alone. At university she'd shared with friends, but her time there had been cut short and she'd moved back in with her parents. From there she'd rented places with her first fiancé and subsequent boyfriend with brief stints back home in between. After that she'd bought the cosy two-up two-down she'd shared with Liam for the last two years.

'Kittens are manic and there's the cost of stuff like vet's fees and injections. It'll wreck your curtains and scratch your furniture,' said Sophie, with a knowing look. 'But then the kids cost us a small fortune and they pretty much wrecked all our furniture. I've never been able to fix the bathroom blinds after Arlo used them as a parachute. On the plus side, I guess you don't have to potty train a cat.' Sophie looked thoughtful. 'Maybe we would have been better off with kittens instead of kids . . .'

'No, way. Your kids are gorgeous,' said Anna and Sophie tilted her head questioningly. 'Okay, they're both proper bonkers but they're still gorgeous.'

'I know, but I feel like I'm doing a rubbish job in the office and a rubbish job at home. I can't win.'

'I don't know how you do it all,' said Anna. She was knackered when she got in from work and some nights was barely capable of heating a ready meal; how Sophie turned around and took care of three other people amazed her.

Sophie shrugged. 'Anyway, how are you feeling about tomorrow?'

Anna gave a pout worthy of a sulky teen. 'It's not ideal, but I guess it'll be okay.' Anna and Sophie worked for the same insurance company who had recently taken over another company and Anna had banked on getting the job of managing the integration. However, the other company had negotiated hard and she now found herself in the odd situation of having to jointly manage the project with whomever the other company appointed. 'To be honest, as they're integrating into our processes I'll be leading it by default.'

'As long as they see it like that,' said Sophie.

Anna badly wanted a big project on her CV, and she was willing to ruffle a few feathers to get it. 'Yeah, let's hope they're a reasonable sort of person. But before that I've got Liam coming round to collect his stuff.'

Sophie pulled a face. 'You know it's times like this you really should give alcohol another go.' Anna chuckled but there were too many demons guarding the reasons why she would never touch a drop again.

They followed the path silently until they reached the furthest oak and then turned around. From here they had a great view of all of Wildflower Park. There were a few dog walkers crisscrossing the large expanse of green in the middle and a jogger in a bright orange top circling the pond, but other than that it was just them. The sky was the palest blue edged with pearly grey clouds – like a scene escaping from an open book. It was the prettiest place and a stone's throw from Birmingham, making it an oasis of colour on the edge of the Black Country. Anna felt a sense of calm wash over her and she knew moving here had been a good decision.

Chapter Two

Liam was never going to be her first choice for a fun evening but he needed to pick up his stuff and she would be as amicable as she possibly could. She plonked the box marked Arsehole's Stuff onto the sofa and noticed the velvet ring box perched on the top. She gave it a hard stare before picking it up; it had promised so much and then let her down so badly. She thought of the moment when Liam had unimaginatively pushed it across the breakfast table to her. At the time she'd hoped it would be a story she would tell her children and grandchildren – how she'd asked what it was but secretly had guessed, and how she told him he needed to be on one knee and he'd laughed at her because that was what they did in the schmaltzy films she watched but he'd done it anyway. She now remembered the begrudging look in his eyes as he did so and the lack of any romantic precursor to his offer of 'Let's get married.'

She realised now it hadn't even been a question. He hadn't asked her as such, just merely suggested it as he would a casual trip to the cinema. Yes, this box had a lot to answer for. Anna didn't open it; she knew the ring inside. It was the classic claw setting – the ring she had always wanted, the one she had dropped into conversation with Liam many times. Seeing it again was not going to help.

Seven o'clock came and Anna checked her mobile. She wanted this to be over. She wanted Liam to come in, take his things and go with as little small talk as possible. She was moving on with her life and this was a key milestone along her journey. The knock on the door made her jump and she shook her head at her own silliness.

'Hi,' she said, opening the door. Liam appeared relaxed and casual, the polar opposite of how she was feeling. 'Come in.'

They walked through to the lounge and Anna pointed at the box of random items. 'Here you go. I think that's everything.'

'This is nice,' said Liam, having a good gawp around the room.

'Thanks,' said Anna. She wanted to pick the box up and thrust it at him but she wouldn't be so rude.

'So,' said Liam, rubbing his hand across his chin. 'Have you been okay?'

'Yes, terrific, thanks.' She said it too enthusiastically and Liam looked a little taken aback. Or was that hurt?

'Oh, that's good.' He pursed his lips. Liam wasn't paying attention; he was still inspecting the room and it annoyed her.

She wondered why he wasn't just taking the box and leaving. He sat down on the sofa. Her sofa. Anna folded her arms. 'Did you want a coffee or something?' she asked out of politeness, which irritated her further. She was so British.

He smiled and she wondered why. 'A coffee would be great – or something stronger. Have you still got the bottle of Châteauneuf you took?'

Anna knew her annoyance was disproportionate but really – how rude was Liam to walk in and think he could dictate to her in her new home! 'No, I gave it to Dad. I'll get you a coffee.'

Anna was standing next to the kettle and boiled inside as the plumes of steam escaped around her. She only put one sugar in his coffee when she knew he liked two – it was a silly thing but it made her feel a little better, until he tasted it and asked for more. Then she really could have screamed at him.

Finally, they were sitting next to each other – well, on separate ends of the sofa, which showed how much things had changed, and how uncomfortable they both now felt. Anna looked at Liam in a similar way as she had the ring box. He had once held so much promise too. Everybody liked Liam with his boyish good looks and confident air. Her mum had been particularly fond of him. Who could have known that proposing was going to be the trigger to make him question their whole future?

'I wanted to talk to you about how we decide who gets which of our friends.' This was all he said that started it off. Such a simple sentence, and yet two hours later they would still be locked in a head-to-head battle . . .

Anna looked up. 'I'll give you Tom and Alice for Darnell and Shanice.'

Liam shook his head. 'Tom was my friend from uni and you never really liked Alice, so that's not giving me anything. How about Matthew and Matt for Darnell and Shanice?'

'Don't be ridiculous. No way! The two Matthews are worth ten Darnell and Shanices. And you hate it when Matt beats you at Ping-Pong – you get all stroppy,' said

Anna, knocking back another gulp of coffee. It had taken a lot of caffeine to get through this evening and she knew she'd have even less chance of sleeping tonight now.

'It's called table tennis. Only children call it Ping-Pong.'

She liked it when he got all picky because it made her loathe him a little bit more, which made things easier. 'The two Matts are non-negotiable.' They had been totally brilliant since the split and were definitely in her camp. Camp being the operative word.

He sighed deeply and crossed them off his list. 'Any other non-negotiables we should get out of the way?'

Anna scanned her list quickly. 'Stacey and Paulo?' She bit her lip because they were the coolest couple they knew, and she knew Liam would want them. They had the best jobs, the jet-set lifestyle and the most amazing dinner parties. It wasn't so much that she didn't want to lose them as friends but as the antidote to her small simple life they were an addiction she wasn't ready to kick.

He shook his head and gave her a pitying smile. 'Yeah, okay. Tabitha isn't keen on them anyway.' As soon as the words were out Liam looked like someone had stuck a pin in his genitals, which was something Anna would have relished doing at that precise moment.

Before she could stop herself, she'd already asked the obvious question. 'Who's Tabitha?'

Liam rubbed his chin again. 'She's just someone I've started seeing.'

Anna felt her stomach drop and started to bob her head far more vigorously than was necessary. 'Right. Good. That's good. I'm pleased for you.' No, she wasn't. She was wrong-footed, vexed and, above all else, hurt.

An hour later they had been reduced to pulling the

final few names out of a mixing bowl. There had been no other way when they had reached a stalemate. Who knew dividing up eleven couples could be so hard?

'Yes! Charles and Lydia,' whooped Liam, as he opened his piece of paper.

'Crap,' said Anna with feeling. She loved Lydia, so maybe she could find a way to see her on the sly. Getting up off the sofa, Anna held her head high. 'Now bugger off out of my life . . . Please.'

She glanced at the list of rules they'd created. Despite it being a difficult moment, Anna smiled to herself, thinking: 'This is what happens when you get two change professionals together.' Liam stood up and pulled his box of stuff up into his arms. 'You have to be proactive with those on your list and contact them. No need to tell them about the segregation,' he said, letting himself out.

'Shit weasel,' said Anna, and she had another large mouthful of cold coffee.

Walking into the office, Anna thought about how Liam had annoyed her on two levels the previous evening: one with the whole dividing up their friends, and secondly by the mention of Tabitha. Not the mention of her alone but the fact he had moved on so effortlessly. Anna was a long way from moving on – she was still at the licking her wounds stage, which was why she was sworn off men for the time being. Perhaps men were designed differently? Maybe they were meant to switch to the next available female. It didn't seem right that she had been so easily replaced. She hoped that said more about him than it did about her or their relationship, but she wasn't sure. When Liam had dumped her she'd thought her world was caving in but she'd quickly realised her relationship with him had been much like Gruyère cheese – harder than it needed to be and full of holes.

It worried her that she'd not noticed how Gruyère he was before this point. What she needed was something more reliable. Cheddar, perhaps? She wanted something a bit more exciting than Cheddar. Cheshire? Too flaky. Maybe she'd hold out for a nice Brie: soft on the inside with a touch of decadence. But Brie could be smelly and a little crusty. She'd got it! White Stilton with apricots: simple but interesting with an edge of sophistication, which always felt special. How had she got on to cheese? All she'd done was make herself hungry.

When she was a little girl she remembered telling everyone she was going to marry her daddy. Her mother had had to sit her down and explain it really wasn't an option and she had been quite upset at the time. Her very first life plan had been blown out of the water with one easy strike. She knew she had her parents up on a pedestal; their relationship wasn't perfect but it was one born out of total love and care for each other and had stood strong for almost thirty years. Perhaps she was searching for a man to love her the way her father adored her mother – but was that so wrong?

Anna knew she had partly ignored the niggles in her relationship with Liam because, at twenty-eight, she was worried about veering off her life plan. But now they'd split up, she was totally off plan and way out of her comfort zone. She hadn't only lost Liam; she'd lost her wedding day and her beautifully mapped-out future too.

Anna had always been conscientious and focused in every job she'd had since university; she was keen to establish her career before she started a family. She had always expected to have been married with children and well settled by the time she was thirty, based on the fact her parents had married quite young and she'd been born within the year. Her sister had followed shortly afterwards.

Anna's thoughts were miles away as she pulled her security pass from the side pocket of her bag. It caught on the zip and she stopped to try to free it. Someone appeared, as if from nowhere, at her side.

'Hi, can I get in this way?'

'Ooh, you made me jump,' she said, catching a quick look at the man. 'You'll need one of these,' she said, wrestling her lanyard free, which bungeed the pass card out of her bag and whipped into the face of the stranger.

'Ow!' He clutched at his eye. 'Damn it.' He couldn't have sounded more American if he'd tried.

'I am *so* sorry,' said Anna, profusely British and mortified at what she'd done. He staggered a little on the steps, his eyes tight shut. 'Come over here,' she said, taking his arm, noting the muscle definition through his jacket sleeve, and guiding him away from the flow of people coming up the steps. 'Are you okay?' she asked, hoping he was going to say yes.

'Do I look okay?' he snapped but at least he opened his good eye to survey his aggressor. He definitely had an American accent.

Anna gave an apologetic smile. 'I am really very sorry. Shall I take a look?' She pointed at his eye and he flinched.

'No, thank you. Can you just tell me how to get inside the building?' He gave her a look that implied he doubted she had the ability.

'This is a staff entrance. You need . . .' she thought better of showing him her pass again '. . . a staff security pass to get in this door. Shall I show you?'

'No, I think you've done enough.' His sarcasm wasn't lost on her.

'Okay, right, yes.' You couldn't help some people. 'Have a nice day,' she said, and she waltzed up the steps. There were a few people in front of her. When they shuffled forward she swiped her card and followed them into the revolving door. She glanced over her shoulder. He was still watching her. Perhaps he was trying to get in illegally, although she couldn't think why. Suddenly the door stopped revolving but Anna carried on, banging her head on the glass. 'Ow!' She rubbed her forehead. That'd be a bruise later. The door then proceeded to go in reverse and spat her out into a queue full of tutting people. This happened every so often when your card hadn't registered properly. Anna apologised to the queue, firmly reswiped her card and gave a quick glance at the American who was smirking broadly with his eyebrows raised in amusement. Great.

She took the stairs to the second floor and scanned the office for any new faces in their area; she was keen to meet the person who she'd be working closely with over the next year. The company operated a hot-desking policy, which was a bone of contention with everyone. A few people had allocated desks for a variety of valid and spurious reasons, leaving the rest of them to fight on a first-come, first-served basis. Anna was in luck as her favourite desk was free. It was a little like an old folks' home in that they didn't have their own seat but they all liked to sit in a certain one – and woe betide anyone who sat in a different seat.

She plugged in her laptop and while it fired up she went to get coffees for her, Sophie and their lead designer, Karl. Anna, Sophie and Karl had met when they'd been put on the same special project a few years ago and had quickly bonded over long days, a shared sense of humour and a love of good coffee. When she returned, Sophie and Karl were behaving like a pair of snooping meerkats, both on tiptoes peering over the filing cabinets towards their boss's office.

'What's going on?' asked Anna, handing out the coffees.

'Venti, Americano, with hot milk?' asked Karl, not averting his eyes from his surveillance operation as he took the cup.

'Yep,' said Anna, trying to see what they were watching.

'With an extra shot?' added Karl.

'Yes, of course. What's going on?'

'And the cute brunette's phone number?'

'Y . . . No!' Anna gave him her best withering glare and he replied with a wink. Karl was incorrigible; one of the last non-PC people she knew and also the gayest straight man she'd ever encountered.

'We think Roberta's meeting with the project manager from West Midlands Insurance,' said Sophie.

Anna went up on tiptoes herself but it did no good – she was already in very high heels and still too short to be able to see anything. Her mobile trilled into life: it was Roberta.

'Anna, could you come to my office right away? I'd like you to meet the new PM.'

'On my way,' said Anna, but Roberta had already ended the call.

'Cover me, I'm going in,' said Anna, picking up her trusty project folder and coffee.

Anna knocked on the glass office door. Office was too grand a term for the small corner sectioned off with boards and a sliding smoked-glass door but Roberta was very proud of it, having battled tooth and manicured false nail to get the 'office' she deserved.

'Come in,' said Roberta. 'Ah, Anna. You took your time.' Anna ignored her. Roberta was an odd sort and it was best not to challenge her. 'I'd like you to meet Hudson Jones.' What sort of name was that?

The person sitting with their back to the door stood up and turned around. Anna noticed he was rather tall and slim in his trendy suit, good-looking in an obvious way, and unnervingly familiar. When she saw one of his eyes was swollen it all clicked into place.

'Hudson, this is Anna Strickland, our lead PM.'

'You?' said Hudson, blinking with his good eye, which she noticed was a beautiful shade of blue.

She gave a nervous laugh and extended her hand. 'Yes, it's me. Lovely to meet you. *Again.*' She gave a little nod with the last word but had no idea why.

'Oh, you already know each other. That should speed things up. Hudson has some excellent suggestions for project team structure, operational integration and . . .' Roberta was checking her notes.

'Project approach,' said Hudson, sounding confident.

'That's terrific,' said Anna, thinking the opposite. 'I'll walk you through what I *already* have in place.' Hudson didn't look pleased. They had both quickly picked up on the other's frostiness.

'Anna will bring you up to speed. I have a very important meeting to go to,' said Roberta, squeezing her ample form from behind the largest desk the company could provide.

'I think we're all in that meeting,' said Anna, giving her printed calendar a quick check.

'Then I'll follow you,' said Hudson. 'From a safe distance,' he added for Anna's benefit.

Chapter Three

It was a day of back-to-back meetings, never her favourite thing and even less so as she'd found herself going head-to-head with Hudson in the last two sessions. He was overconfident – or cocksure, as her grandad would have called it – and so far he had challenged everything Anna had raised. He had a bunch of ideas he seemed to think he could apply without knowing the first thing about their company processes and it was already starting to infuriate her.

She had a long list of things she would need to explain to him when she got the chance. The next meeting was with Karl, so Anna hoped that would offer a little light relief. She headed off to the room she'd booked, which she knew was barely more than a cupboard. When she got there the blind was down and the 'In Use' sign was on, so she waited. She was mulling over what to have for tea when she recognised the voices giggling inside as Karl and Sophie. She opened the door expecting to be greeted by friendly faces rather than a shifty duo caught in the act of something they shouldn't have been doing.

Anna stared at the small table where Karl had two teaspoons and a small pile of white powder. She gazed disbelievingly at the guilty-looking pair and hastily shut the door behind her. 'What the hell are you doing?' asked Anna. Sophie stepped forward but erupted into giggles. 'OhMyGod. Have you taken some of that?' Anna was beyond shocked. She looked to Karl for an answer. They would all be instantly dismissed if anyone saw this.

'It's not what you think,' said Karl, before joining Sophie in hysterics.

'For goodness' sake – shhh. And pull yourselves together,' snapped Anna, anxiety coursing through her at the thought of being caught in this situation. 'Get rid of it!' Anna stabbed a finger at the white powder.

Sophie paused her giggling to sweep the white powder into a plastic cup of what looked like water. The liquid fizzed. Sophie gave it a swirl, lifted it to her lips and to Anna's horror drank it down. Anna dropped her notebook and papers as her hands flew to her head. Was Sophie trying to get rid of the baby?

'Whoa. It's okay,' said Sophie, seeming to realise Anna's distress was very real. 'It's only paracetamol.'

Anna didn't believe her. Paracetamol came in tablets not white powder. 'You're mainlining paracetamol?'

She glared at Karl. 'Sophie's got a headache and I read somewhere it acts quicker if you crush the tablets and take them in lemonade,' he said.

Sophie was nodding. 'I had a wicked headache and I don't like taking anything when I'm pregnant. I thought I'd try a single crushed paracetamol and see if it worked. It's probably hokum.'

Anna was shaking her head. 'I thought it was . . . It looked like . . . Bloody hell, you scared the life out of me.'

'Did you think we had a crack den going in here?' Karl looked amused.

'No . . . well, possibly. What on earth was I supposed to think?'

'This was totally innocent. If you're after the real crack den, it's in the stationery cupboard up on the fourth floor,' he said, with a tap of his nose.

'You are a pair of idiots. Anyone would have thought the same as me. Now clear away any trace of that stuff,' said Anna, picking up her things from the floor.

'Sorry,' said Sophie. 'We didn't mean to freak you out.'

'We'd have been snorting it through ten-pound notes if we did,' said Karl, with a chuckle.

'I hope your headache goes,' said Anna, as Sophie left the room.

'Right, Karl, let's talk Design Architecture,' said Anna, turning back to him.

Karl narrowed his left eye and pouted. 'I'm guessing you've not spoken to Hudson then?' Of course Hudson had jumped the gun and spoken to Karl already, without her. Anna felt an involuntary sigh escape. She was feeling less and less guilty about whacking the guy in the eye.

After the day from hell Anna was in need of a strong coffee and a good old moan but what she opted for was a trip to the cat rescue. She didn't like going home to an empty flat and it was a small stand for something she wanted and Liam had never let her have. And moaning to herself was never any fun, but with a cat at least she'd feel like someone was listening. As she had suspected they had lots of kittens and any one of them would have been perfect. They were all cute and all she had to do was choose one. She liked the one with the black patch over its eye and the one who looked like it was wearing a dinner jacket.

A young couple with two small children were looking at the same litter of black and white splodges. There was only one volunteer who was clearly rushed off her feet and was being continually harassed. Anna moved out of the way and went to peruse the pens at the other end away from the kittens whilst she waited for her turn. Each cage had a jolly write-up of its occupant. A very noisy Burmese called Sasha focused his elongated meow at her until she spoke to him. Anna moved out of Sasha's field of vision and was watching Bill and Ben, two ginger and white males, who were peering over a sign on their window that said 'reserved' when there was a thud behind her. Anna turned around to see an exceptionally large tabby cat with both paws on the glass window of his pen. Clearly happy he'd attracted Anna's attention, he started to parade up and down in front of the glass with his fluffy tail held high. Anna smiled and went over.

His bio said his name was Maurice and he was nine years old, though when Anna peered closer, he didn't look like an old cat. The dark, long-haired tabby was now sitting, staring directly at Anna. He seemed to fill most of his pen. Anna didn't think she'd ever seen a cat that big before that wasn't in a zoo.

'Sorry, were you next?' asked the volunteer.

'Yes,' said Anna. 'Is he really nine?'

'Maurice? Yes, he is, but there's plenty of life left in him,' said the volunteer, reaching to open the pen so Anna could meet the cat.

'It's okay. I was really after a kitten.' Anna felt instantly guilty. She sidled away so Maurice wouldn't hear, which she knew was a bit crazy.

'We have plenty of kittens. Let's fill the form in and you can tell me which one you'd like.' Anna relaxed and followed the volunteer back to the kitten section. She glanced over her shoulder. The big fluffy cat was watching Anna intently. The volunteer went through the questions but Anna's mind kept going back to Maurice.

'Has Maurice been here a long time?'

'A couple of months. He's got a lovely nature but very few people want the middle-aged ones. Is your property rented or owned?'

'It's owned. Where did he come from?'

The volunteer stopped filling in the form and looked at Anna. 'It's a bit sad really. His owner had a fall and had to go into a nursing home and they couldn't find anyone to take Maurice so he came here. He's struggled to settle into life at the centre. He's been used to the same lap to sit on for nine years and a garden to wander around in, so it's a bit of a shock for him. That's why he doesn't interact much.' She sighed. Back to the form: 'Any other pets?'

'Err, no. Poor thing, he seemed quite friendly.'

'Did he? You should be honoured. He ignores most of us.' She scribbled her initials at the bottom of the piece of paper. 'Right, we'll pop over one evening and do your home check, and then you'll be able to come and collect your kitten. Which one was it?'

'It was . . . um . . .' Anna had to think hard as both the kittens she'd liked had slipped from her mind and all that was there was a picture of Maurice. 'Actually, could I have another look at them please?'

Sophie kissed Arlo's forehead and smoothed his hair to one side. It was wayward like his father's. 'Night, sweetie. Straight to sleep now.'

'I don't see why I should when Petal is still up,' said

Arlo, folding his arms indignantly over his Star Wars pyjamas. 'She's younger than me!'

Tiredness had claimed most of Sophie's body and it felt like she was sinking. Sophie sighed and adjusted the grumpy jiggling mass on her hip that was Petal. She'd forgotten how tired she got when she was pregnant. It went beyond the usual levels of yawning and looking forward to bedtime and was more a sensation closer to lapsing unconscious.

'Sweetie, Petal's going to bed now too. Night, night.'

'But it's not fair!' he said, his bottom lip starting to quiver.

'Sweetie, please, Mummy is tired. Please go to sleep.'

'Everyone in my class stays up late. Why can't I?'

I can't have this conversation now, thought Sophie as Petal's wriggling increased and was now accompanied by whining.

'We'll talk about it tomorrow. Night, night.' She switched the light out and shut the door.

'I don't like the dark!' shouted Arlo. Sophie closed her eyes, and tears tumbled silently down her cheeks. The clunk of the key in the lock announced that Dave was home.

'Hiya,' he called into the hall. Sophie briskly wiped away the tears, sniffed and headed downstairs.

'Hello, gorgeous,' said Dave to Petal who reached out for him. 'You should be in bed by now – it's late.'

'Give over, Dave. I've not stopped all day so please don't walk in and start criticising my parenting.'

'Hey, it wasn't a criticism. Tell me what you want me to do and I'll do it for you.'

Sophie huffed. 'But that's the thing, you're not doing it for *me*. These are your children too!'

'Blimey, who's upset you today?' He headed upstairs with a happily dribbling Petal.

'You,' said Sophie, but he was out of earshot. 'It's always you.'

When Dave came back downstairs Sophie was plonking dinner on the table.

'This looks great. I think I'll have a glass of Merlot with it,' said Dave, diverting to the wine rack. Sophie glared at him. She needed a glass of red wine far more than he did but she wasn't allowed one – pregnancy was so unfair.

Dave merrily loaded his fork with spaghetti bolognaise and took a large swig of wine as he read an email on his phone. Sophie sipped her glass of water and stared at him. He'd hardly said anything since they'd sat down to eat aside from imparting that the irritating dry skin patch had returned to his elbow.

'Dave, I want to go on holiday.'

'Hmm.' He eventually pulled his eyes away from his phone. 'Maybe next year.'

'Next year we'll have three kids to contend with. That's no holiday, plus it'll cost more.'

That seemed to grab his attention. Dave loved to save money. 'I guess we could take Arlo out of school, which would make it a lot cheaper. It's a right rip-off that the travel companies hoik up the prices because of the school holidays.' He shook his head.

'Okay, great.' This was a lot easier than she'd anticipated. Of late Dave seemed to be displaying many Scrooge-like qualities so this was a pleasant change. 'I'm thinking some-where in the Caribbean. Nothing too touristy but somewhere like Anguilla might be nice.'

'We can't afford . . . where was it again?'

'Anguilla. Beyoncé and Richard Gere holiday there.'

'Together?' asked Dave, through a mouthful of spaghetti.

'Don't be daft. Or Bora Bora, that looked amazing on *Keeping Up With The Kardashians*.'

'Sophe. That sort of holiday costs thousands and the kids would be a nightmare on the plane. How about a few days at Butlins?'

'Butlins?' Sophie almost shouted.

'What's wrong with Butlins? The kids would love it.'

Sophie was shaking her head. 'Plugging hell, Dave. I don't work my bum off to have a few crabby days in Butlins. I thought it might be nice to have some time just the four of us before the new baby arrives. Have a proper family holiday.'

'I had proper family holidays at Butlins as a kid and loved it.'

'Your mum went to Butlins?' Sophie found this hard to believe as her mother-in-law, Karen, was the stuck-up sort. She was also a force to be reckoned with, which had earned her the nickname the Kraken – though it was mainly Sophie who called her that.

'No, our grandparents took us. But we had the best time. I think it'd be great. We could do a weekend and see what we think?'

'I am not going to fuzzing Butlins.' Sophie went to pick up her glass but realising it contained water she slapped her hand on the table, making them both jump.

Dave's mouth drooped at both edges. 'Sophe, do you remember the conversation we had when we bought this place?' Sophie gave a twitch of her head and tried hard not to pout. 'We agreed this was our forever home but to be able to afford it we had to give up all the other stuff for a while, including big holidays.'

At the time Sophie would have agreed to anything.

She'd fallen in love with the house and Wildflower Park, and she knew she had to have it. Even if it had meant selling a kidney, she would still have given it serious consideration.

'And you'll get a break when you're on maternity leave,' he said, spearing his dinner with his fork. Sophie had to stop herself from spearing him with hers.

Chapter Four

Sophie was deep in conversation with Roberta's PA, Priya, when Anna emerged from the stairwell soaked to the skin and thoroughly fed up that her bus had been late and she'd got caught in a torrential April shower. She scanned their area but all the best desks were occupied.

'Where can I sit?' asked Anna, trying to avoid looking at the dark side of the office.

'Peter is out today, you can sit there,' said Priya, pointing at the desk behind her that was strewn with photographs of two small blonde children and a selection of pictures of stick people. Anna dumped her stuff on the desk and instantly felt like a squatter as she moved the 'Best Daddy in the World' mug to one side.

'I think he must have had his teeth whitened,' said Sophie, running a tongue over her own.

'You'd be able to find him in the dark,' giggled Priya. 'He is gorgeous though.'

'Who's this?' asked Anna, switching on her laptop.

'Hunky Hudson,' said Sophie, widening her eyes.

Anna's interest waned. 'Do you have to call him that?'

'He's gorgeous! How can you not fancy him, Anna?' asked Priya, looking genuinely surprised.

'Meh?' was all Anna could manage. His domineering attitude had completely deleted any alluring quality he may have displayed.

'I think he's totally fit and—'

'Who's fit?' asked Roberta, emerging from the lifts and Anna made a mental note that she clearly had bionic hearing.

'Hudson,' said Priya, as she shuffled some papers to make herself appear busy.

'Fit and very gay, I'm afraid,' said Roberta. Anna and Sophie became interested again.

'He never is?' said Sophie dismissively.

'I think his life partner would disagree with you,' said Roberta, radiating smugness as she took her list of meetings from Priya.

'His shirt yesterday *was* very fitted,' said Priya, emphasising it by running her hands over her own body.

'Have you met his other half then?' Anna's usually strong gaydar abilities had been called into question.

'I spoke to him on the phone when I rang to discuss the job with Hudson.'

Priya looked thoroughly disappointed 'That's ruined my day that has.' Roberta headed off to her first meeting and Priya followed at a trudge.

'Because otherwise, she would have been well in there,' whispered Sophie to Anna who shooed her back to her own desk. The last thing Anna needed was to get into office backbiting. She checked her watch: two minutes to the start of the project meeting and no sign of Hudson or Karl. She gathered up a pile of Post-it Notes and a roll of brown paper from the stationery cupboard en route, and felt a spring in her step as she strode off to the meeting. This was where she took control and Hudson would have to acknowledge her project management prowess.

Anna heard laughter as she approached the room and tried hard not to look shocked as she saw Hudson, Karl, and a variety of others sipping coffee and munching on croissants.

'Morning, Anna! Help yourself to breakfast. We're about to kick off,' said Hudson, taking off his jacket to reveal a distinctive pale pink shirt with shiny spots woven into the material, which was a perfect, although somewhat snug, fit.

'Nice shirt,' said Sophie, taking a seat and giving Anna a knowing look. Anna offloaded her stationery cargo to the floor. She decided she would see what he had planned before she dived in.

Sophie leaned over conspiratorially. 'I don't care if he is gay, he's still gorgeous.' Anna shook her head at Sophie, who stuck her tongue out playfully.

'Our goal today is to get a common understanding of the project end state,' announced Hudson. 'You are all absolutely key to its success but only if we are all focusing on the same thing.' She had to admit he was quite charismatic but already she hated herself for being passive and letting him lead. This was exactly what he wanted and she needed to fight back.

'If you're ready to map out that end state and how we get there, I've brought the tools,' said Anna, casually indicating the brown paper and sticky notes.

'Thanks, but the whiteboard will be fine,' said Hudson, barely glancing over.

'But you can move the sticky notes about . . . and there's a different colour for each workstream.'

Hudson's expression was disparaging. 'I prefer the

whiteboard and I can just take a photo at the end when we're happy with it. Anyway,' he said, clasping his hands together and focusing on the smiling Sophie. Traitor, thought Anna. 'I'm really keen that we work together as a cohesive team.' Sophie nodded vehemently and Anna rolled her eyes.

'In which case we need to be clear on roles and responsibilities within the programme,' stated Anna, leaning forward in her chair and starting to feel ready for a fight.

'I disagree,' said Hudson. 'We don't need defined roles, we just need to utilise everyone's skills.'

Anna felt as though she were on the centre court at Wimbledon as the heads spun back in her direction in anticipation of her response. She wasn't backing down now. A voice in her head said 'Deuce'.

'And the easiest way to understand each other's skills is to assign everyone a specific role on the project . . .' Hudson opened his mouth to butt in but Anna continued, 'to ensure we maximise resources and don't have any duplication of effort.' *Advantage Strickland.*

'I really don't want to waste anyone's time this morning, so let's focus on the end state for now and we can have a discussion later about roles and responsibilities. *Offline.*'
Deuce.

Anna hated office speak or Corporate Bollocks and she had a feeling Hudson was going to be fluent in it.

'Okay,' said Anna, and Hudson let out a sigh. 'But we are all going to have a slightly different view of what the end state is—'

'Which is the whole purpose of this meeting,' said Hudson, the agitation in his voice apparent. 'Let's spend what's left of this session coming to a consensus on what that end state looks like.' *Advantage Jones.* 'Is everyone happy with that approach?' Everyone nodded except for Anna. *Game Jones.*

Hudson swept away the writing someone had left on the whiteboard with a few broad strokes of the board rubber, his toned muscles flexing under his well-fitted shirt. He had no need to go up on tiptoes to reach the top edge or jump up and down like an untrained terrier as Anna always had to do. She was really beginning to dislike him.

Anna was beavering away at her computer, trying to ignore the laughing coming from the other side of the office. She gave a cross glance in their general direction and paused. Hudson was sitting nonchalantly on the corner of his desk holding court as the others all gazed at him adoringly. Anna slumped back in her seat – it was like being back at school and being up against Chloe Buglioni for Head Girl all over again. Just like Chloe, Hudson was taller, more attractive, funnier and more confident than her. Unlike Chloe, he wasn't promising to kiss anyone who voted for him, although from the looks on their rapt faces they would probably have liked him to. Another guffaw of laughter and head-shaking seemed to signal the end of Hudson's story and everyone started to disperse. Anna gritted her teeth – he wasn't Chloe, and this time, she wasn't going to lose.

'You coming to the pub?' asked Sophie.

Anna stretched her neck and it clicked. She checked her watch. 'Yeah, go on then – just for half an hour and then I need to get home for my home inspection from the cat rescue place.'

'Hudson's paying,' added Sophie, turning to watch him bend over to pick up his laptop bag.

Anna was instantly no longer keen. 'Actually, I'll finish this.' She angled her head towards her screen.

Sophie pouted. 'Come on, don't be like that. It's not his fault you're doing a job share.'

'He could back down.'

'But you're not,' said Sophie, with a knowing look. She had a good point.

Anna was trying to think of another excuse when Hudson strode over with his bag slung casually across his body. 'You coming, Anna?' He had one of those smiles she'd only seen previously on film stars. All perfect white teeth and twinkling eyes.

'Yes, she's just packing up,' said Sophie, before Anna could form her excuse.

'Awesome, see you both over there,' said Hudson, and he strode off.

Anna slumped back in her chair. 'What did you do that for?' Her voice came out whinier than she'd have liked.

'Because you and Hudson have to find a way to get on and if this is him offering an olive branch . . .'

'I'd like to shove it up—'

'Uh-uh,' said Sophie leaning over and unplugging Anna's laptop. 'Play nice.'

The pub was noisy and busy and Anna was regretting agreeing to go but she had a plan: she'd have one Coke then she'd slip away without anyone noticing. She spotted the usual suspects at the far end of the bar, and with lots of apologies she weaved her way through.

'Anna,' called Hudson, beckoning her over.

As she and Sophie reached him, he produced two filled champagne flutes. 'Here you go, ladies.'

'Thanks, but I'll just have a Coke,' said Anna, getting out her purse.

'Me too,' said Sophie, gazing longingly at the glass of fizz.

'Come on, who doesn't like champagne?' asked Hudson, raising both the glasses temptingly.

'I don't,' said Anna.

Hudson proffered a glass to Sophie. 'I'm on antibiotics,' she lied. She wasn't ready to share her baby news yet.

Hudson insisted on paying for their soft drinks and they moved away from the bar to a marginally quieter corner. 'I need the loo,' said Sophie and she selfishly disappeared, leaving Anna with Hudson. As if I don't get enough of him at work, Anna thought.

'I'm excited about working with you Anna.' He actually sounded genuine but Anna's bullshit monitor went into overdrive anyway.

'Why's that?'

'You know so much about the company. You know the right people to engage with and they like you.'

He had clearly been doing some snooping around to find out about what people thought of her. She wasn't sure if she felt flattered or intruded upon, but she definitely didn't want to talk shop at the pub.

'Thanks. Let's not talk about me. What's your story?'

He took a slow draw of champagne. He had attractive lips, plump and pink.

'My dad's American, my mom's British. I was born just outside New York in a village called Port Chester. My dad worked in Manhattan. Shortly after 9/11 we moved to England. I went back to the US for university and I've been working in the UK for a few years now.'

He had a way of holding her attention and she wanted

to know more but didn't want to appear keen. 'You've not lost the accent.'

'I'll let you in on a little secret.' Without realising it she was leaning closer. She detected a hint of aftershave. 'I think it's *you* who has the accent.'

'Ha, ha. You're hilarious.' She sipped her Coke.

'Roberta said you're local. Have you lived here long?' he asked.

'All my life.' She had always been quite proud of the fact she was a Brummy although her short stint at university had watered down her accent a great deal. He held her eye contact and did a good job of appearing interested. 'My mum and dad live in Hockley.' He looked impressed, which meant he clearly had no idea where it was.

'You've only worked for the one company then?'

'In project management, yes.' He didn't need to know about the earlier roles as a filing clerk and a serving wench at Warwick Castle.

'This is my fourth.' He seemed proud of this. 'It gives you a breadth of experience you can reapply elsewhere.'

More corporate bollocks. 'I think loyalty to a company pays off.'

'I think that's naïve.' How had they ended up talking about work again? And why was she getting annoyed with him?

Anna made her excuses and disappeared to the toilet. She had a quick word with herself. She needed to focus on the big issues; getting caught up in petty power struggles was a waste of time and energy. At the end of the day, Roberta was going to judge them both on what they delivered. She redid her lipstick, pulled back her shoulders and went back to the group.

'. . . cacky pants,' said Sophie through hysterical giggles.

'What's so funny?' asked Anna, feeling left out already.

'It's a quirk of American pronunciation,' said Hudson, changing into an English accent. 'You'd say everyone at the programme board meeting wore khaki trousers but to us they're—'

'Cacky pants,' repeated Sophie and she doubled up again.

'In my experience people often leave board meetings with cacky pants even if they didn't arrive wearing them,' said Anna. 'Apart from me.'

Hudson's eyebrows twitched. 'I don't doubt that for a second.'

A few days later, with approval from the cat rescue in the bag following their home visit, Anna drove her beloved Mini to the rescue centre. It had been a difficult decision choosing a pet and she hoped she'd made the right one. For the first time in her life she was going to be a pet owner, assuming the time she briefly had a goldfish didn't count. She'd built him a lovely Lego home, but unsurprisingly the house move didn't go well for the goldfish. Anna had only been four at the time.

She followed the volunteer past the many cats and tried hard to ignore their sad faces and the guilt she felt for not being able to choose all of them. All the cats at the rescue needed homes but she knew the older ones would always find it harder than the cute mewing kittens. The volunteer stopped at a cage with a sign covering the bio, which read: 'I'm going to my forever home.' The cat inside glanced up.

'Hello, Maurice,' said Anna. 'I've come to take you home.' Maurice became very interested when his pen was opened but less so when he was bundled into a cardboard cat carrier scarcely big enough for him.

'Is that secure?' asked Anna, as the carrier lurched about.

'They're very sturdy. Don't worry, he won't be able to escape. Here's all his paperwork,' said the volunteer, handing a bundle of papers to Anna. 'His last owner usually calls once a week. It'll be nice to tell him that Maurice has a new home.'

Up until then Anna hadn't thought much about Maurice's previous owner and she didn't have time now either as the heavy cat carrier was starting to bounce around worryingly.

Anna put it on the front seat of the car and set off. It was twenty-five minutes to home. She started talking to the box each time it began to jiggle or meow. The meows got more desperate and the box's movement got more vigorous. He didn't have much room inside. She was expecting to see a leg burst from each corner, cartoon style, and start marauding around the car. Anna stopped at the traffic lights and pulled on the handbrake.

'Now listen, Maurice, we're nearly home. It's not far away and when we get there I'll let you out.' But Maurice had other ideas and, with a startling bang, the top of the carrier burst open and out jumped Maurice. Anna squealed involuntarily and the traffic lights changed. She crunched the gears and the car lurched forward as she set off again gripping the steering wheel tightly. Maurice disappeared over the passenger seat and Anna tried to keep an eye on his manoeuvres through the rear-view mirror.

'Maurice!' She was trying to keep one eye on the cat and the other on the road.

Maurice appeared at her headrest on cue but after a brief sniff he quickly disappeared. At the next set of lights

Anna turned around to see what he was doing. Inside the small car it was even more apparent that Maurice was a lot bigger than the average cat. He had his paws on the glass and was rubbernecking at the cars queued next to them, in a similar way to how he was at the rescue centre. The people in the car next to them did a double take when they saw the cat staring at them. The lights changed and they were off again. Maurice was keen to investigate the front of the car and slid down Anna's side and became particularly interested in the pedals. Anna had to push him gently to the side for fear of an accident, but his response was to jump onto her lap, filling the space between her and the steering wheel. Anna could barely see over him and had to drive the last few minutes with a furry head checking the road ahead for her.

She pulled up into her designated parking space and once the engine was switched off she could hear Maurice purring; he was almost as loud as the engine had been. At least one of us is happy, she thought.

She gave him a tickle around his ear and he pushed his head hard into her hand. 'Welcome home, Maurice.' All she had to do now was work out how to get the large fluffy cat from the car to the flat.

Maurice was more relaxed on her lap so with one hand she manoeuvred the cardboard cat carrier nearer to her and opened the lid wide. She lifted Maurice up but as soon as he sussed what was happening he appeared to expand in all directions and started to wave his legs about wildly. Getting a large star-formation cat through the broken box lid was not going to happen.

A quick call to Sophie with a request for something she could use prompted Sophie's arrival at the driver's window a few minutes later with a sling-style baby carrier.

Anna buzzed the window down a fraction: she daren't let it open fully in case he escaped. 'Seriously?' She nodded at the baby sling.

'I figured transporting kids and pets was kind of similar.' Sophie studied the harness and glanced inside at the large cat filling up more than half of the back seat. 'He's huge. You didn't say it was a baby sabre-tooth.'

Anna shot a glance over her shoulder. 'One of the volunteers thinks he's a Maine Coon.' Another American who's got one over on me, she thought, uncharitably.

'He looks like he's mainlining steroids,' said Sophie, waving the baby sling at her.

'I couldn't get him in a box, so I have no hope with that,' said Anna. She didn't want to distress Maurice any further. As if sensing something was afoot he retreated to the back parcel shelf and hunkered down.

'Try this,' said Sophie, feeding a large pillowcase through the gap in the window.

Anna held up the pillowcase; it had a giant picture of a pug's face on it. The inappropriateness seemed lost on Sophie. Anna turned the picture of the dog away from Maurice.

'Here,' said Anna, passing Sophie her door keys. 'You open up and I'll . . .' she lowered her voice '. . . bundle him up and make a dash inside.'

Anna needed to get in the back of the car but didn't want to risk Maurice escaping so she daren't get out of the car. Instead she squeezed herself slowly between the seats all the while uttering what she hoped were reassurances. Maurice watched her intently from the relative safety of the parcel shelf. She took a deep breath and, gripping the edge of the pillowcase, firmly swooped upon him and tried to scoop up the cat like a fisherman trapping his catch.

Maurice began to yowl and tried to reverse out of the pillowcase but Anna was already gathering up the ends and gripping them tightly together. She opened the car door and scrambled out holding up the squirming protesting bundle. Anna made a dash for the flats as Mrs Nowakowski came out wearing fluffy orange slippers. Maurice let out an ear-splitting cry and the older woman's eyes pinged wide open like a bush baby.

'Hello again,' said Anna, holding on tight to the wriggling pillowcase as the pug face on the front distorted and bulged. 'Sorry, I have to dash.' She didn't want to appear rude.

Mrs Nowakowski's mouth opened and closed like a goldfish's but nothing came out. Sophie held the door open and Anna and the dissenting pillowcase shot inside.

Chapter Five

The next morning Anna left Maurice curled up on her most expensive cushion. He seemed to have claimed it during the night and she hadn't had the heart to take it from him. He had spent most of the previous evening hiding under furniture, which probably wasn't surprising given his pillowcase ordeal, but this morning he seemed calmer, if still a little wary. She'd left him food, water and a clean litter tray and locked him in. The rescue centre said he had to stay inside for at least three weeks – and preferably longer – so he knew where to return to when he was let out. Maurice was on her mind as she walked through the office, and up ahead she could see Sophie. Anna checked her watch, as it was unusually early for Sophie to be in.

'Morning,' said Anna, scanning the holiday chart on the wall and trying to work out whose desk might be free for her to squat at today.

'Hi,' said Sophie, giving her a shifty glance.

Anna paid attention to what Sophie was doing. 'Are you moving desks?'

'It's temporary so Hudson and I can be together. *Sit* together,' she hastily corrected.

'Just be careful, Sophe,' said Anna. She didn't trust Hudson and Sophie seemed to be getting hooked in very fast.

Anna settled herself down in a nearby desk and moved the usual occupant's clutter to one side. Really, who kept a potato clock and a pink toy troll on their desk? She had a friendly email from a member of her old team, which she replied to, and told her about Maurice. Anna opened up a new email and added in the names for the board and all senior people on the programme. She and Karl had made good headway on the project scope and she wanted to share that work ahead of the big meeting they had later. Her friend sent a message demanding a picture of Maurice. Anna was happy to oblige as she'd already taken quite a few of him looking rather handsome curled up on that cushion. She sent them from her phone to her work email address, copied the pictures over and pressed paste as she was interrupted by Hudson.

'Anna, did you say you were issuing the deliverables paper first thing?' he asked, his tone reasonable but the words instantly making Anna feel defensive.

'I'm literally sending it now,' she said, as she huffily stabbed at the send button. In the very same millisecond her brain registered what she was sending and where. 'Nooooo!'

She had attached the many pictures of Maurice to the deliverables email and now it was zapping its way through the ether to all the great and the good on the programme.

'What's up?' asked Hudson.

'I've sent . . .' Anna couldn't believe what she'd done. It felt like her stomach had dropped to her toes and bounced back up again. She ran her palms down her face. 'Wrong email...' Her fingers jabbed at the keyboard; embarrassment swamped her. She'd never live this down. She tried to remember how to recall messages. 'Nightmare . . .'

'Anna? What is it?' His voice was surprisingly gentle.

He would think she was a total idiot but there was no point in lying – he was on the distribution list too. She swallowed hard. 'I've sent pictures of my cat to almost everyone on the programme.'

His eyebrows jumped but he recovered his expression quickly. 'Budge up,' he said, shoving her wheelie chair and making her collide with Sophie like an errant bumper car. His fingers whizzed across the keys as her heart thumped at an unnatural speed. She'd never done anything quite so stupid before. There was the time she left her egg salad on a sunny windowsill and went to a workshop, stinking out the office . . . but this beat that hands down.

Hudson stood up straight. 'Okay. Recalled successfully—'

'Thank you so much,' said Anna, relief swamping her.

'—with the exception of Roberta. She's already opened the email,' he added, wincing and scrunching up his shoulders as if waiting to be thumped.

'Bugger,' said Anna, with feeling. That was going to be a fun one to explain. Anna twisted around. Roberta's office was empty and her laptop wasn't there – she liked to take it to meetings to make herself look extremely important.

'Don't worry, I'm sure it'll be fine,' said Sophie, 'I mean Catwoman was a feminist right? And so is Roberta so . . .' She gave Anna's arm a pat whilst she and Hudson exchanged knowing looks.

A meeting reminder popped up, jerking her back into action. She had precisely five minutes until the big meeting. She dashed to the printer to collect her handouts but the printer was lit up like Las Vegas with warning lights and had not printed anything. She checked all its paper trays, she rummaged around in the middle bit and nothing appeared to have been chewed up, and as a last resort she switched it off and on again. She was now ready to give it a thorough kicking.

'Is there a problem?' asked Hudson, who must have crept up behind her.

Anna spun around and leaned back against the printer to put a little space between them. 'No, I'm fine.' She tucked a piece of stray hair behind her right ear in a jerky movement. She wasn't fine but having him see that wasn't going to improve things.

'Can I help at all?' he asked, peering past her to the myriad flashing lights on the printer's panel.

'I doubt it,' said Anna, before running him through all the things she had tried. She checked her watch – she needed to leave or she'd be late. Hudson leaned towards her and she wondered for a second what he was going to do. He pushed the toner door slightly and it clicked shut. The whole machine whirred into life and Hudson gave her a nonchalant rise of his shoulders. She hated it when that happened.

'Thank you.' She managed to say it without gritting her teeth. She gathered up her papers and scuttled off.

Anna's day proceeded to go from bad to worse; Roberta was not impressed with the photos of Maurice and had a rant at her in front of everybody over an entry on the risk log, which she clearly didn't understand, only to apologise later in private and explain away her behaviour as a result of her imminent period. Karl was stressing about lack of data – he really did put the anal in analyst, and Hudson was being perfectly efficient, which was always irritating. She was glad to escape at the end of the day, even if the sight that greeted her was perplexing . . . Maurice was still asleep on her expensive cushion and appeared to have not moved all day, but the entire contents of a man-size box of tissues had been shredded and liberally scattered around the living room making it look like an indoor snowdrift.

The fact Maurice had slept all day unfortunately meant that he was awake and meowing for most of the night; evidently he didn't feel quite at home yet. Anna went for a jog first thing, though after very little sleep, it was like sticking her head in a washing machine during spin cycle – neither was a great idea, but at least she was out in the fresh air and enjoying the park. It was Saturday morning and she was keen to leave her work frustrations behind her. The steady rhythm of trainer on path consumed her body while her brain could focus on what was troubling her.

Anna realised what had started out as a jog had been speeding up and her lungs were burning with effort. She slowed down and stopped near a bench, holding on to the back of it while she caught her breath, admiring the row of grand houses that circled the park. They all had gardens that gave them exclusive access to the park on their doorstep, and she could see Sophie's house from here – or rather, her back gate. Sophie's house had a very long garden, which led to a lovely family home, and without even realising what she was doing, Anna had given up on her run and was walking towards it. It was time for a cuppa and a serious bitching session.

Anna wasn't surprised to find the gate was locked but a quick phone call to Sophie had Dave sent down to let her in.

'Welcome to the madhouse! You okay?' He was his

usual upbeat self. Nothing seemed to faze Dave, he bobbed along happily as the rest of life's shit flew around him. Sometimes literally, if Petal was in a nappy-diving mood.

'I'm good, thanks. Settling in to the neighbourhood.' She felt the need to pre-empt the next question.

'We knew you'd love it here. Sophie's in the utility wrestling with sheets. Arlo was sick last night. He'd sneaked a box of Maltesers and eaten the lot.'

As they neared the house the noise of shouting children increased. Arlo was running around the kitchen wearing a sieve on his head and waving a pirate sword, his latest obsession.

'Hiya, Arlo,' said Anna, intercepting him and the plastic sword neatly. 'How's school going?'

'Rubbish. Willoughby Newell keeps getting me into trouble.'

Anna mouthed the name at Dave and he shook his head. Kids who were given names like that were always going to have problems, thought Anna. 'What does he do to get you in trouble?' she asked.

'He cries when I hit him,' said Arlo, a deep frown burrowing across his perfect skin.

'Do you think maybe if you didn't hit him, that might help?'

Arlo pondered this for a moment, his wavy baby blond hair swinging about his head as he shook it vehemently.

'Shitake!' Sophie's voice came from the utility. Anna left Dave to explain the laws of cause and effect to his son.

Anna popped her head round the door. 'Mushrooms as swear words – that's a new one. What's up?'

Sophie hugged Petal to her hip. She was surrounded by a rainbow of laundry; brightly coloured baskets overflowed with clothes all around her. '*This,*' she said, waving

49

her one free arm in a chaotic fashion. 'I swear the kids get through three outfits each a day. It's like painting the Forth Bridge but at least doing that you'd get some fresh air rather than being stuck inside all the time. Why isn't being naked socially acceptable?' Her eyes told Anna this was a genuine question.

Anna studied the piles of dirty clothes. 'How do they wear this much?'

'These people are experts. They train hard. They're at the peak of their performance. I have bred Olympic mess makers.'

'Takeaway coffee and a walk round the park?' suggested Anna with a weak smile.

Sophie decided to bring Arlo because Dave was complaining he couldn't do what he needed to and watch both the children.

Arlo had found a giant stick and like an overenthusiastic Labrador was attempting to drag it along with him, but at least he'd tire himself out and Sophie might even be in for the rare treat of an undisturbed night's sleep.

'You okay?' asked Anna, sounding tentative.

'My eyes have more bags than a schoolkid with PE and Food Tech on the same day, my husband is as useful as go faster stripes on a tortoise, my children act like they've been raised by hyperactive wolves and I haven't slept properly since the millennium.'

'Same as usual then,' said Anna.

'You know, I actually fantasise about sleeping for a whole uninterrupted eight hours.' Sophie stared off into the distance and sipped her coffee thoughtfully. 'Sleep is my fantasy. It used to be Ryan Gosling, and before him it was Robert Pattinson.'

'I thought it used to be David Beckham.'

Sophie nodded. 'Him too. Oh, who am I kidding? I couldn't be bothered even if he turned up on my doorstep. I'd end up getting him to play with the kids while I went for a nap. Victoria Beckham's very lucky. Her David is a real family man, he's loaded, has world-renowned dress sense and he's gorgeous. In life's lottery I got my David. He's a real ale man, all his money goes on the mortgage and bills, most homeless guys are better dressed than he is and he has the kind of face that perfectly describes the word "gormless".'

'Ouch, that's harsh.'

'I don't mean it to be. But when you step back and examine the decisions you made that brought you to where you are now. It makes you question and compare.' She paused. 'Arlo, the stick won't go through that gap. It's going to snap in half and hit you in the face if you're not careful!' Sophie threw her hands up in despair. 'It's non-stop. This week I've got loads to do at work for this big meeting. It's Kraken's birthday so Dave slipped into conversation that it'd be nice if the kids made her a card and Arlo needs some cakes for school because they're celebrating VD Day.'

'Blimey that's fully inclusive for you.' Anna laughed but Sophie didn't join in. 'Do you mean VE Day?'

'Hmm?' Sophie was deep in thought. 'I don't know if I can do this any more, Anna.' Sophie stopped walking and Anna patted her arm.

'You don't mean that.'

'I do. I really do.'

They walked in silence for a while. Sophie took in great lungfuls of fresh air. Sometimes it made things seem a bit better. She liked to imagine the park was all hers. It was looking a luscious green in the intermittent May sunshine. There were some welcome splashes of colour thanks to the pretty pink flowers of the red campion and the last of the blossom on the hawthorn. The bluebells were carpeting the small wooded area and she had to shout at Arlo not to destroy them. Instead, he started a solo game of fetch with his stick.

A bouncy Labrador joined Arlo and took hold of the other end of the stick. 'Hey! That's mine,' protested Arlo, but the dog was already winning the tug of war.

'Why is everything a battle?' asked Sophie, with a deep sigh, and she went to intervene.

Chapter Six

Anna was pleased with the letter she'd crafted. All she needed now was an address for Maurice's previous owner and her good deed would be done. His old address, from Maurice's vaccination records, was her starting point. Hopefully the new occupants would have a forwarding address, or at least know the name of the nursing home he was in, if it was local.

She pulled up in front of the neat row of terraced houses and went in search of number 55. She spotted the for sale sign before the house number. Anna rang the bell just in case, but there was no answer. Now what? Number 57 looked like number 55's glamorous friend with its double glazing and shiny front door, so she decided to knock there. No answer. She was about to admit defeat when the door of number 53 opened and Paddington Bear reversed out. At least it looked like Paddington Bear from the back – the duffel coat and hat were spot on but if the wearer had hairy toes they were secreted inside a pair of sensible brogues.

'Excuse me,' said Anna. 'I'm trying to find where Mr Albert Freeman has moved to. Can you help me?'

Paddington checked the door was secure for the third

time then slowly turned to face Anna. Under the fancy dress was an elderly lady who looked Anna up and down and blinked a lot. 'Who's asking?'

A little surprised by the gruff voice, Anna paused. 'Sorry, I'm Anna. I've a letter for Mr Freeman.' She held the envelope aloft as evidence and Paddington was distracted by it.

'He's moved away.'

'Yes, I know,' said Anna and Paddington seemed intrigued. 'I got a cat from the rescue and it's . . .'

'Maurice!' exclaimed Paddington as she put her bony hands to her mouth in surprise.

'Yes,' said Anna, with a smile. 'I thought Mr Freeman would like to know he's got a new home.'

Paddington drew closer as if about to share a secret. 'I can take you to him, if you'd like? Is that your car?' Paddington pointed to Anna's Mini.

'It is.'

'Good. Let's go then. I've not got all day.'

Anna learned that Paddington was a Mrs Temple and she'd lived next door to Mr Freeman for forty-four years.

'Pull up here,' instructed Mrs Temple after a ten-minute drive. 'That'll do me lovely. Thank you.'

Anna leaned forward and surveyed the row of shops. 'Um, this doesn't look like the nursing home?'

'No,' said Mrs Temple with a chuckle, and her many chins jiggled happily. 'This is my optician. You want the turning back there on the left – it's just up there. Bye!' And Mrs Temple slammed the car door.

Anna smiled – she had to admire her cheek. She turned the car around and followed Mrs Temple's directions. A large painted sign informed her she had arrived at The Cedars although there were no trees in sight.

Stepping inside it was as she'd expected: homely with a strong smell of detergent. Nobody seemed to be manning the reception desk so Anna felt it was acceptable to have a little wander about. She figured it was okay as she just needed to hand the letter to someone and she'd go. She was drawn to the sound of a television and as she reached the door, an efficient-looking woman wearing some sort of uniform was coming out. 'Hello there. Are you looking for someone?'

'Yes, Mr Freeman,' said Anna, 'but I just need to hand in . . .'

'You're in luck,' she said, reopening the door. 'Bert, you've got your first visitor.' Anna wanted to explain to the carer that she was delivering a letter, but she was gone.

An elderly man turned his head half-heartedly towards the door. Bert didn't appear thrilled to have a visitor. If anything, he looked quite concerned. He was sitting in a large wingback chair and he leaned forward as Anna entered the room, narrowing his eyes sharply as he scrutinised her. It was a large square room with high ceilings and a long redundant fireplace. Too many armchairs had been squeezed in and all were attempting to point at the television. Each chair was occupied, mostly by a sleeping resident, but those who were awake watched Anna with great interest.

'Hello, I'm Anna.' She moved nearer to Bert and wished there was somewhere for her to sit down and be slightly less conspicuous. Bert didn't take his eyes off her. 'I popped in to give you this,' she said, presenting him with the letter.

'I don't know anyone called Anna,' said Bert, ignoring

the letter in Anna's outstretched hand. She placed it on the arm of his chair.

'No, you don't, but the letter explains everything.'

'Seeing as you're here, why don't *you* explain everything?' asked Bert, sinking back into the armchair, his face dour.

'Okay.' Anna took a breath. 'I just wanted you to know that Maurice has got a new home and he's very happy.'

Bert sat forward abruptly. 'Are you from the cat prison?'

Anna was taken aback by Bert's turn of phrase. 'No, I'm not from the cat *rescue*. I'm the person who's given Maurice a new home.' Anna finished with her warmest smile. The old woman next to Bert had woken up and she was leaning forward too as she fiddled with her hearing aid.

'You took my cat?' Bert's voice was rising.

'Well, I chose him,' said Anna, struggling to maintain her smile. This was uncomfortable and unexpected.

'They had no right to let you take him. He's my property!' Bert's pale face swiftly coloured up as his volume increased.

Within seconds everyone in the room was awake and a whistling broke out from another nearby hearing aid. Anna felt the elderly eyes all fixed on her. 'But when you moved in here, you signed him over to the rescue.' Anna liked to stick with the facts; it was frequently the best policy and she hoped it would work now.

'This is temporary. I'm not staying here. When I go home, Maurice is coming with me.'

'Who's Maurice?' asked the old lady next to Bert.

'My cat,' said Bert and Anna together. Bert ground his teeth together and Anna suspected they weren't his own.

Anna reached for the envelope. 'There's a photo of Maurice I thought you'd like to see. He's in his favourite place on the . . .'

'His favourite place is with me,' said Bert, folding his arms very deliberately and glowering at Anna.

She thought for a moment. For one thing, she didn't know if Bert had all his marbles, but what she did know was that his house was up for sale and the cat was legally hers. 'Okay, how about this? I'll look after Maurice at my place until you're ready to go home?'

Bert squinted at her and she wasn't sure if that was progress or not. 'What will that cost me?'

'Nothing. He was unhappy at the rescue centre and he's happy now. It doesn't make sense to move him again. Agreed?'

'How will I get in touch with you when I want him back?'

Anna fumbled on this question and blurted out, 'I'll come back and see you, and you can tell me then.'

'Hmm,' was all Bert muttered. He broke his stare for the first time and looked around the room. 'What are you lot gawking at?' There was lots of shuffling and one loud fart before most of the residents pretended to go back to sleep. Bert's tone changed. 'And you promise you'll come back . . . Anna?'

'Cross my heart, Bert,' said Anna, and she meant it.

One sunny morning Sophie joined Anna for her walk across the park to the bus stop. 'To what do I owe this pleasure?' asked Anna, pleased to see her friend.

'The Kraken is having the kids because it's a teacher training day and I thought I'd avoid the hellish parking for a change . . . oh, and I'd like to spend some time with my best friend.'

'Excellent,' said Anna, breathing in the May air full of the dewy scent of the lilac bushes.

'And I wanted to have a chat.' Anna wondered where this was going. 'I think I have a crush on Hudson,' said Sophie.

'What?' asked Anna, with a half laugh.

'Don't laugh, I mean it,' said Sophie, getting teary. 'I'm thinking about him all the time. If he talks to me I get all hot and flustered like I did when I was fourteen and Stephen Bethel used to sit next to me in Geography.'

'That's your hormones playing tricks.'

'But it's all the time, Anna. And I keep dreaming about him.' Her eyes wandered off to somewhere near the pond. 'It's great stuff. Really sexy. If I could film my dreams I'd make a fortune . . .'

'La, la, la, not listening,' chanted Anna, putting her fingers in her ears until Sophie stopped talking.

'I thought you'd understand.' Sophie's bottom lip wobbled.

'Really? Me? I can't even bring myself to like Hudson, let alone drool over him. Plus, he's a gay man in a committed relationship.'

'But you're my friend.' Sophie coughed to disguise the choke of emotion.

Anna gave her arm an affectionate pat. 'Yes, and you are mine. Though Dave's my friend too. How would he feel if he knew about this?'

'I can't help my dreams. And even if I told Dave that I fancy Hudson, he wouldn't be bothered because who's going to fancy me.'

'You're gorgeous.'

'So's Hudson. He's perfect, isn't he?'

'I'm not keen and he definitely doesn't like me. Yesterday he did a coffee run and I swear he missed me out on purpose. And then he didn't tell me the risk review meeting was cancelled . . .'

'It's just you. Even the witches like him,' said Sophie. Silvie and Janey were renowned for their bitchy comments and therefore known as the Witches of East Wing.

'I heard he brought in Marks and Spencer's biscuits. They're easily bought that pair.'

They walked up the path to the main park gates and the bus stop and Anna noted the multitude of dog roses in bloom, as they passed. She let out a giant yawn.

'Don't,' said Sophie following suit.

'Sorry, someone kept me awake playing with his balls half the night.'

'Tell me about it. Dave's the same,' said Sophie and they both burst out laughing.

After a good natter to Sophie on the bus Anna was feeling optimistic, but the sight of Roberta at her desk diluted her cheerfulness somewhat.

'Morning, Roberta,' she said as she approached.

'Are you a feminist, Anna?'

Anna sensed a trick question but could only answer honestly. 'Ye-es,' she said cautiously.

'You don't sound very sure?'

'I believe in people being treated as individuals regardless of gender.'

Roberta's nodding indicated she approved of this response. 'Apparently someone has complained that the central heating is set at a sexist temperature.'

Anna blinked slowly. 'And what temperature would that be exactly?'

'Cold enough for things to be noticed through material,' said Roberta, her demeanour and voice mimicking a schoolteacher.

'Nipples,' mouthed Karl behind her back and Anna had to concentrate hard not to smirk.

'I see. I guess it can be a bit chilly but I wouldn't have called it sexist,' said Anna, hoping that would suffice.

'Okay. If you're sure it's not an issue,' said Roberta. 'Ladies don't start fights, but they can finish them,' she added, with a tip of her head. Anna was squinting with the pressure of trying to work out what the hell she meant. 'It's a quote,' explained Roberta.

'Right.' Anna had no idea which feminist icon would have said that but thankfully Roberta was about to enlighten her.

Roberta leaned in close. 'Marie.' Anna was still looking blank. 'From *The Aristocats*.'

'Of course,' said Anna, trying hard to ignore Karl's huge grin.

It was another quiet night in for Anna as, now Maurice's period of confinement had ended, she found she was often on her own once it got dark. He was a proper night owl and the living room window was working well as his exit route. It was too small for a human to fit through, and meant she didn't need to get a cat flap fitted until it started to get colder. She flicked through the telly channels again but decided there was still nothing worth watching so she switched it off. She may as well go to bed and read. She had settled into life without Liam but it didn't mean she had got used to being on her own.

Anna picked up her mobile phone and jumped slightly as it sprang into life. She was a little embarrassed about how pleased she was to get a message, whoever it was from. She looked at the screen in anticipation. It was a number she didn't recognise, so she flicked to the text expecting to see some random marketing message but she was wrong.

It read: **Can't wait to get down and dirty with you tomorrow. Looking forward to catching up over lunch too. C.**

Anna stared at the message; clearly it was a wrong number. She crafted what she hoped was a suitable reply: **Hi, C. Thanks for the offer but I think you've got the wrong number.**

Anna was sitting huddled over the phone waiting for a reply. She'd had wrong phone calls before but never a text. It was quite funny really – she wondered how much the other person would cringe when they realised their mistake. After five minutes she felt ridiculous for sitting with her phone in her hand, waiting for a reply from a wrong number. Why would they respond? They'd resend the message to the right person and be a little more careful when texting next time. Then the familiar little beeps came and she hurriedly opened the message: **How embarrassing. I'm so sorry, please forgive me. I hope I've not offended you. C.**

Anna wondered if C might actually be a girl, because how many men would bother to respond? She suspected not very many. But seeing as they'd been nice enough to reply, she sent them another text: **Not a problem, I'm pretty resilient. Enjoy your date tomorrow.**

A response came straight back this time: **Pretty and resilient is an interesting combination. Tomorrow not as exciting as it sounds. Helping a friend clean their patio. C.**

It was a comedy text to a friend, a clever play on words, not a sexy text to a lover as she'd first thought. She was intrigued as to who this mystery texter was. Though she was keen to text straight back, she calmed herself down and went and put the kettle on and did a little bit of analysis. She really did need to get out more if this was

61

the most excitement she'd had in her life since they'd added Peanut KitKats to the vending machine at work. Anna still didn't know if the mystery texter was a man or a woman – or worse still, a teenager. Loads of kids had mobiles these days. She gave a little shiver; that was a creepy thought.

Part of her mind had already wandered off in the opposite direction and conjured up a tall handsome stranger, sitting in a large glass-fronted office laughing at the text exchange. He had no wedding ring and bore a striking resemblance to Ryan Gosling – well, it was her fantasy after all.

Anna was cupping her tea and thinking about whether she should reply when another much longer text appeared: **Hi Tim, just did something funny – texted wrong number and got cute messages back. Worried it's a big hairy bloke! See you at 10 tomorrow, mate. Text me postcode for your new place. I don't know my way around Selly Oak. Did you get the festival tickets? C.**

It was as if he'd read her mind, as she could now safely assume he was male and clearly not ancient if he was going to a festival. And he'd called her cute – well, he'd called her texts cute. *And* he was most likely local if he was going to Selly Oak tomorrow. This was getting interesting. She had to reply to this message, because surely it would be rude not to. After all, she had to inform 'C' that Tim wouldn't have received his text . . .

Hi, C. Sorry, you got the wrong number again. Nice to text with you though, and enjoy the patio cleaning. A. There. That was okay – informative, and not too forward.

By the time she'd brushed her teeth there was another message: **Dear A. Once again, soooo sorry. I am clearly**

62

a sausage-fingered idiot. Apologies! I'll let you know how the patio cleaning goes. C :-)

Anna placed her phone on the bedside table and turned off the light. She quickly drifted off to sleep with the tiniest of smiles on her lips, a large cat on her feet, and just the faintest glimmer of something in her heart.

Chapter Seven

Anna had a spring in her step the following morning as she picked up her things and went in search of the room for her first meeting of the day. At least she wouldn't be alone with Hudson; she was able to handle him better if other people were involved. Maybe she needed them there to help her keep her annoyance levels in check. She knew she sometimes overreacted but it was only because she was passionate about getting it right. She found the room and checked it was the right one because it was really small. She knew there were loads of people on the invite list. Her smugness blossomed at the thought of Hudson having to apologise to everyone for the tiny room as they all tried to cram inside. She was going to enjoy this meeting. She picked her spot on the far side of the table so she could see his reaction when he came in, and settled herself down.

She was making some notes when Hudson arrived. 'Hey, Anna. How's your day going?'

Why did Americans ask that? Nobody did in this country. At best you'd ask someone at the end of the day, but never earlier – and who was interested anyway?

'Great thanks.' About to get a whole lot better when

everyone sees your room cock-up, she thought. 'How about yours?'

'Swell, thanks. Right, let's get started.'

Anna did a double take as Hudson started tapping on the large telephone in the middle of the table. Anna scrabbled through the meeting notes. It was a bloody conference call; she hadn't spotted that. If she'd realised, she could have dialled in from her desk. Now she was stuck in a broom cupboard with Hudson for the next hour, but her resolute Britishness meant that she wasn't going to leave. She'd have to stick it out. 'Hudson and Anna,' said Hudson, when the system prompted him for his name. As he was opening the call there was a rush of everyone's name and Anna didn't have time to tick everyone off the invite list.

'Hey, everyone, thanks for joining us this morning. Is Todd on the call?'

There was a very long pause where they could hear breathing, general office background noise and the odd cough. 'Okay, no Todd, let's—'

'Yes. Hi, Hudson. I'm here,' said Todd, rather belatedly. Hudson and Anna both looked skywards.

'Great. Thanks, Todd. Can I ask everyone to go on mute to cut out the background noise?' There was a series of clicks and the phone went eerily quiet.

'Raj, please can you give us an update on the finance meeting you attended?' asked Hudson. He looked over at Anna who was jotting notes. She paused and they waited for Raj to speak. Nothing. Total silence. Anna checked the names she had managed to tick off: Raj was ticked off. He was definitely on the call. She shrugged at Hudson. He unmuted their end and started to speak. 'Raj, are you okay to give us an—'

'Sorry, I must have been on mute,' said Raj, followed

by an embarrassed chortle. Raj proceeded to run through far too much detail about the very dull finance meeting he'd attended, which had no consequences for their project at all. When Raj finally stopped talking Hudson thanked him and moved on. 'Carol, Programme Office update please.' Hudson muted their phone and leaned back.

A loud bark came from the phone making them both laugh nervously. 'Buster! Quiet. Mummy's on a conference call,' said Carol, who was working from home. 'Hi, everyone, yes. We've set up the filing system on the shared drive . . .' But Buster was determined to be heard and continued to bark all the way through her update. The only pause was when 'Todd has left the meeting' was announced by the automated call system and closely followed by 'Todd has joined the meeting.'

'You okay, Todd?' asked Hudson.

'My phone keeps cutting out. I don't know what . . .'

'Todd has left the meeting.'

'Does anyone have any questions or anything they'd like to add?' asked Hudson.

A jumble of voices all spoke at once, followed by a round of apologies and lots of people politely repeating, 'No, after you.' When everyone did exactly the same again Hudson stepped in. 'Okay. Steve, you had a question?'

'Yeah, hi, Hudson. The workshop next week, is lunch provided?'

Anna slapped her forehead with her palm and Hudson spontaneously laughed at her. 'I'm not sure Steve, but I'll check and get back to you.'

'Who else had a question?'

There was a long pause. 'Hi, Hudson, it's Paul. It's okay, I was going to ask about lunch too.'

'Okay, any questions that weren't about lunch?' asked

Hudson and was met with a bark from Buster. 'Okay, if there's nothing else. We'll catch up again on Wednesday. Thanks, everyone. Bye.'

A series of disembodied voices said bye in quick succession.

'Todd has joined the meeting.'

Hudson hit the end-call button and let out a sigh as he slumped back in his seat. 'Sometimes, things are a lot harder than they need to be,' he said and Anna had to agree.

'Night night, Mummy,' said Arlo, looking perfectly angelic. Sophie's heart melted with love for her first born. He was a monster sometimes but she loved every inch of him more than she could ever explain.

'Night night, darling.' She kissed the top of his head and reversed from the room. She'd almost made it to the door when he spoke and her heart sank. All she wanted was to sit down and put her feet up. She'd had a crappy day at work as she'd managed to forget to go to a meeting and send out the wrong documents twice.

'Mummy?'

'Yes,' she said, being as patient as she could be when she'd been on the go for fifteen hours, her back ached like she'd been carrying cement around all day and her feet were feeling puffy.

'I'm looking forward to animal day tomorrow. Night night.'

Sophie froze. 'Animal day? What's that?' It couldn't be World Book Day – they'd done that a few weeks ago.

'I need a costume of my favourite endangered animal. Can I be a dinosaur? They're endangered aren't they?'

'Costume? Animal?' said Sophie, struggling to form a sentence.

Arlo giggled. 'Mummy, you're funny. Costume. Animal,' he mimicked. His expression changed to deadly serious. 'It has to be better than Willoughby Newell's. He's coming as a turtle.'

'You get some sleep. Mummy will sort it out.'

Within minutes Sophie was rifling through Arlo's school bag. At the bottom was a screwed-up piece of paper smeared in mud and some unidentifiable sticky substance. She unfolded it and speed-read the letter. 'Argh!' Arlo was right. He needed to wear a costume to school, a costume that represented one of the many endangered animals on the planet as part of Climate Change and World Awareness Week. How could schools do this to parents? Where was she meant to get an endangered animal costume that was better than Willoughby sodding Newell's turtle at this short notice?

Dave's face peered around the living room door. 'You all right?'

'Arlo needs to go to school as an animal tomorrow.' The fight was fast ebbing from Sophie as her body gave way to exhaustion and fatigue.

'How about a monkey? He goes as that every day,' said Dave, with a big grin. Sophie wanted to slap him.

'It's serious, Dave. He needs an outfit and it's . . .' she checked her watch '. . . a quarter to nine at night.'

'Ah, don't worry about it. I bet most of them won't have a costume. He'll be fine without one.'

'He can't be the odd one out!' Sophie was outraged. Pictures of poor Arlo dressed in his school uniform danced through her mind, alongside ones of all his friends and Willoughby Newell sporting the best endangered species outfits money could buy. 'You could help more, Dave.'

'Okay. What did he wear for Halloween? Could he wear it again?'

'He was a zombie pirate.'

Dave pulled a face. 'Sorry. Dunno then.' And he disappeared back to watch the television. Sophie sat on the stairs, clutching the school note, and felt like crying.

The next morning Sophie came flying into the office; her wild hair matched her eyes and the buttons on her cardigan were done up out of sync. 'You okay?' asked Anna, already knowing the answer.

'No. I have been up half the night sewing.'

Anna did the thing where you open your mouth to speak but your brain is going 'Nope, I've got nothing of any use in this situation.' 'Sewing?' said Anna.

'Yes, sewing. I made a polar bear costume out of an old sheet, a cardboard box and a weird furry scarf thing Kraken gave me for Christmas, which I'm sure was something she was regifting.'

'You are such a good mum. Any photos?' asked Anna.

Sophie fumbled with her phone and passed it to Anna. Anna studied the picture of a white mass with drawn-on claws in black Sharpie and a conical-shaped head with yogurt pots for ears. It did resemble an animal of some kind but she would have struggled to identify it as a polar bear. More like a ghostly aardvark. 'It's amazing,' she said, in what she hoped was an encouraging voice.

'I thought so,' said Sophie, her voice changing into something akin to Linda Blair's in *The Exorcist*. 'It's not rubbish, is it?'

'Nooooo,' said Anna, shaking her head firmly.

'What's this?' asked Hudson, popping up at Anna's shoulder. He started to laugh and Anna gave him a

Paddington Bear stare. He turned his laugh into a cough. 'Wow, that is the scariest Ku Klux Klan member I've ever seen. His hat's slipped a bit.'

Anna failed to stifle a splutter of a laugh. 'It's a polar bear.' Hudson almost pushed his face into Sophie's phone for a second look.

'Arlo refused to wear it. He said it was the worst polar bear in the world and it deserved to be endangered.' Sophie looked glum.

'Kids can be harsh critics,' said Hudson.

'Dave agreed with him.'

Anna feared for Dave's safety. 'And where is Dave now?'

'He merrily trotted off to work leaving me with a completely naked Arlo who refused to wear anything unless it was an endangered species. I was tempted to tell him to go as he was because his life expectancy was diminishing with every second.'

'Here, have my coffee. It's decaf,' said Anna, passing it to Sophie.

'Thanks.' She didn't look like she meant it.

Anna hardly dared to ask how it all ended but she had to know. 'So, what happened?'

'He's gone to school dressed as the Pink Panther. It's the costume he wore for World Book Day last year. It's too small. I had to slit the legs and arms so he looks like he's had an Incredible Hulk moment.'

'As long as he's happy,' said Anna, trying to ignore Hudson who was still chuckling behind her.

'He freaked his teacher out when he pulled the long pink tail between his legs and waggled it at her.' Sophie gave a weak smile. 'That was almost worth it.'

'Brilliant.' Anna giggled as she pictured the scene.

'What's brilliant?' asked Karl, arriving at his desk.

'They've decided to introduce my idea of Naked Thursdays?' he offered. 'The next team event is mud wrestling? Roberta's been abducted by Aston Villa supporters?'

'Nope, sorry. Sophie's son went to school as the Pink Panther,' said Anna.

'I already knew about that,' said Karl, plugging his laptop back in. Both the women looked confused. 'It's front-page news everywhere. Bloody hell, your lives are riveting.'

'Shut up, Karl,' they chorused.

He held up his hands in defence. 'Okay, okay.' He turned to Sophie. 'I read your outline paper. It's really good. When this syncs . . .' he pointed at the laptop '. . . there's some feed-back coming your way. Then you can update and issue it.'

'Thanks,' said Sophie, viewing him as if he were an unexploded bomb.

'What? Don't look at me like that. I can do a good impression of a sensible person, you know. I've got a certificate and everything.'

Silvie wandered over and they all tried to appear as if they were busy. 'Can we move our three o'clock to four?' she asked Karl.

He checked his diary.

'Have you lost weight?' Silvie asked Anna.

Anna was standing next to Sophie and she immediately straightened. 'Um, no. I don't think so.' Anna's size was fairly static thanks to her running.

'Actually, I think it's just where you're standing,' said Silvie, eyeing Sophie.

Karl coughed. 'Yep, no problem moving the meeting. I'm loving your tan, Silvie.' Silvie beamed at him and sauntered off.

'You are such a liar,' said Anna, once Silvie was out of earshot.

'What? It's not a lie. Orange happens to be my favourite colour,' said Karl, putting his hand to his chest as if saying an oath.

Sophie was looking puzzled. 'Did that cow imply I was fat?'

Chapter Eight

Roberta managed to intercept Anna first thing by thrusting a scribbled note at her and demanding she and Hudson organise a team event, and that it should be treated as their absolute priority, thus sending Anna's day immediately into a tailspin. Despite her best efforts she had failed to track Hudson down, which was typical, so she had ended up doing most of the legwork herself.

Anna checked her phone whilst walking back to her desk after lunch and found a text: **Hi, A. How is your week going? Any more texts from strange men? C.** It made her smile involuntarily.

She replied: **Hi, C. Week going okay. How about yours?** pressing send and then instantly regretting it. His text had been witty whilst hers was simply dull – and who was she kidding anyway? Her week wasn't okay, it was utter rubbish.

As she sat down her phone pinged again: **My week is going great, just bought a new car.**

Anna replied without engaging her brain: **Exciting! My week has been rubbish by comparison.**

The response was almost instant: **You need cheering up. Anything I can do? C.** Anna smiled again. He was quite sweet really, for a total stranger.

No, but thanks for asking. Got to go, I'm at work.

Anna was aware someone was watching her and she looked up suddenly. Hudson was right behind her. 'Did you want something?'

'Nope.' Hudson slunk back into his desk and started to work. Anna slid her chair over to him.

'Actually, Roberta was looking for you.'

Hudson glanced over his shoulder in the direction of Roberta's office.

'On top of this project we're also managing a team event – like an away day thingy.'

'Another clear brief from Roberta I'm guessing,' he said, with a wry smile. It was a lovely smile, warm and reassuring.

Anna blinked and pulled her concentration back to the matter in hand. 'Yep, there's virtually no budget and she's expecting lots from it. I'm thinking something outdoors and a hostel in the Peak District.'

'Sounds perfect.'

'Really?' Anna couldn't read if he was serious or not.

He nodded. 'I've been once for a wedding but the scenery was beautiful and who doesn't like bunking up?'

Anna's eyebrows did a little jump. 'Some people object to . . . bunks.'

'Not me.'

No, she thought studying his perfect bone structure, your partner is a very lucky man. 'There's not much choice as it has to happen next week apparently. Roberta's usual forward-planning skills.'

Hudson's expression had changed. 'Or it's just been dumped on her.' He narrowed his eyes. 'Did she give any clue as to what had triggered it?'

Anna thought for a second. 'Came from above she said.'

Hudson pouted. 'I'm sure you've thought the same but I'll voice it anyway. Sounds like something might be going on. Why would you suddenly send the whole team out of the office when they've just started a critical project? Makes no sense.'

Anna was nodding. She hadn't queried it at all, but now she was. He was right, it was very odd. She tried to put it to the back of her mind and fired off an email to Roberta with the details of what she'd discovered.

Anna was mentally planning what she was going to have for dinner when Roberta appeared at her desk. 'Bunk beds in Derbyshire – is that the best you could do?' Anna felt something deflate inside and took a deep breath to try to pump it back up.

'On this small a budget and at such short notice, yes, it is. But it will provide us with a series of team challenges, which I believe will help us to bond as a team and it's not too far away, which is a bonus.' Anna's voice went up at the end. She waited for Roberta's reaction.

Roberta snorted her derision. 'I'm not sleeping in bunk beds.'

'Ah, no, but . . .' She hated herself for stumbling over her words. 'You didn't say you were coming.'

'Aren't I part of the team? Aren't I, in fact, an integral member of the team?'

It was hard to disagree without it being a career-limiting conversation. 'Of course you are, but I assumed you'd be too busy.'

Roberta's perfectly pencilled eyebrows moved up a degree. 'A fair assumption but no, on this occasion, I will be there. I'm keen to see how everyone performs.' Things were getting more bizarre.

'Great, there's a pub in the village. I'll book you a room there.'

'En suite,' said Roberta, and she strode back to her office.

Anna's instinct was to run to Hudson and share what she'd learned as it added more fuel to his theory that something didn't add up about the team event but that would make her look desperate to please him and she wasn't.

It was warming up outside and Anna and Sophie decided to take their lunch in the square. A simple sandwich seemed better when eaten in the fresh air as long as you could keep the pigeons away long enough to enjoy it.

'Here,' said Anna, handing Sophie her phone. 'This guy sent me a text by mistake.' Anna wasn't sure what the sensation was in her gut as she watched Sophie's expression change as she read the series of messages from the mystery person known only as C. There was definitely a hint of excitement and more than a smattering of intrigue about him and the fact he had bothered to message her again.

'Bloody hell, Anna. Who is it?'

'I don't know.'

'But who do you think it is?'

'It's a random stranger.' Anna ate the last of her sandwich.

Sophie tilted her head. 'Or it could be a celebrity who wants to remain anonymous.'

'Not likely,' said Anna. 'And if it is, knowing my luck it's one of the Jedwood twins.'

'No, think about it. It could be a famous actor or reality star.'

'Who happened to stumble across my number because it's like their friend's? I think it's just some guy. But he seems kind of sweet.' Anna felt a flutter of something and almost rolled her eyes at herself. What was she doing? She was sworn off men. Especially ones she'd never met and who were incapable of sending a text to the right person. The last thing she needed was to get caught up in another fruitless relationship. She needed to focus on being an individual, not part of a couple, and on furthering her career because she knew that wouldn't let her down. She had a plan and she was going to stick to it, but there was no denying that with a mystery texter and some innocent flirtation, she could do both. She was keeping her promise to herself and she also had the opportunity for safe flirting by text. Did it even have a name? Flexting perhaps? And if at any point she wanted to stop she could block his number. Yes, it was the best of both worlds.

'What if it's someone you know?' said Sophie.

Anna considered this. 'I don't think Liam's that creative.'

'Mystery admirer?'

'Possibly.'

'Are you going to meet him?' Sophie looked keen.

'No. It's just a wrong number.' But there was something fun about having a little fantasy about who C was and what he might be like, though that was as far as she was prepared to go because this was all from the safety of her own home and she could block him at any point it felt like he was getting serious or turned out to be a crazed lunatic.

'What if it's fate?' Sophie went all gushy.

'You think C is short for Charming, as in Prince Charming?'

'You never know. Stranger things have happened. You read about things like this all the time in magazines. People who meet the love of their life in the frozen fish section of the supermarket or get run over by them.'

'Really?' Anna was pulling a disbelieving face. She wouldn't be keen to marry someone who had attempted to run her over, even if it was accidental.

'Oh, yeah. It's quite common,' said Sophie, taking a chunk out of her sandwich. Anna doubted that was true. 'What if he's this gorgeous millionaire who wants to whisk you away on his private jet to his castle?'

'Then I'm wondering what he's doing cleaning his mate's patio.'

Sophie openly huffed and handed Anna her phone back. 'True. Shame. It would be nice to have someone take you away from all this.' She gestured randomly.

'How're things with Dave?'

'He's still Dave.' She said it like she was apologising. 'He thinks he's dying because he's got a cold at the moment. Last night it was like trying to sleep next to someone experimenting with a chemistry set. And he managed to sleep through Petal having two night terrors and Arlo coming into our bedroom at four to ask how many sleeps until Santa comes. Then he woke me switching on the bathroom light too loud this morning.'

'How do you switch a light on too loud?'

'I don't know, but he does it all the time. Then he's in there for ages and afterwards it's like sleeping in a public toilet.'

They both pulled faces as if they could smell something unpleasant. 'Not nice,' said Anna, who had long wanted an en suite but was filing this for future reference.

'He said he'd book the train tickets for our trip to

London on Saturday but he forgot. He promised to start sorting the garden out. But apparently some new shooty killy game came out, which has kept him busy. Still, I'm looking forward to getting away for a couple of days on the team jolly. Dave won't know what's hit him.' Sophie seemed to perk up.

'Don't get too excited. There wasn't much available at such short notice. I've found a farm who have converted a barn into hostel-style accommodation and they teach dry-stone walling but I think we can make the best of it.'

'Sounds like fun.'

Anna felt they would have to add quite a bit of alcohol to get it to that level but she was willing to give it a go, though she was more concerned about the motivations of senior management in sending them all off on something like this – now Hudson had sown that particular seed.

'I hope I can cope with being in a confined space with Hudson,' said Sophie, looking both worried and dreamy-eyed.

'You still having improper thoughts?' Anna tried hard to hide a smirk. It was funny to think of her having a crush on someone at her age.

'Stop it.' Sophie gave her a playful swipe. 'All the time. If anything it's getting worse. I can barely take in what he's saying because I'm concentrating hard not to grab him and snog his face off.'

Anna's expression conveyed her alarm. 'Bloody hell. Really?'

'Really,' said Sophie, sounding miserable. 'I wish I could stop it but I've tried and I can't. I've tried imagining him sitting on the loo and kissing his partner . . . not at the same time . . . but *even* at the same time, nothing works.

Whenever I'm near him there's this electricity, this magnetic attraction. He helped me put my coat on the other day and I was actually aroused.' Sophie was deadly serious.

'You poor thing. Did you go home and shag Dave's brains out?'

Sophie recoiled. 'Goodness, no. Why would I do that?'

'Because he's your husband.'

'But it's not him who's turning me on,' she said and her face returned to its disappointed resting state.

Anna went off to visit Bert. She stopped at the paper shop on the way to pick up some toffees and a big Sunday paper; she wasn't sure if he was a broadsheet kind of person but she didn't want to look like a cheapskate.

'Hello again,' said the carer, coming through reception. 'Bert's in his room.' She pointed back up the corridor.

Anna walked past the television room, past two closed doors with the number five and six on before coming to one with an open door. She gave a quick squiz round the door, unsure of what she'd find. Bert was sitting in an armchair staring out of the window.

'Hello, Bert, I brought you a paper,' said Anna, walking in and plonking the paper on his lap and herself on what she supposed was a footstool.

Bert glanced at Anna and then at the paper on his lap. 'Didn't think I'd see you again.'

'I said I'd come back. And I got you these,' she said, putting the toffees onto a small table in front of him. He squinted at them and then returned to looking out of the window.

'How's Maurice?'

'He's great,' said Anna with gusto, 'but he's still missing you,' she added hastily.

80

Bert's shoulders jumped as he gave a short laugh. 'I bet he's forgotten me.'

'I doubt it. Maurice forgets nothing. I gave him his food on a saucer because his two bowls were both in the dishwasher and now he expects every meal on a china saucer. You do something once and that's it.'

Bert chuckled. 'You're right. If he likes something he expects it all the time. I once left a cardigan on the sofa and that was his bed for weeks.'

Anna got out her phone. 'I've got some more photos of him,' she said, flicking to the right pictures and handing the phone to Bert. He returned to looking out of the window. 'It's all right, I'll remember him how he was.' Anna switched off her phone and put it back in her pocket.

'Has he brought you any presents yet?' asked Bert. There was a twinkle in his eye.

'No. He's not a bird catcher is he?' Anna was enjoying watching the birds flitting in and out of the park while she had her morning coffee; she didn't like the thought of having to deal with any in kit form.

'No, he doesn't catch birds. He brings in other things. The occasional mouse.' Bert looked off into the distance again and Anna checked her watch; it was too soon to leave without seeming rude. She surveyed the room. It was nice enough but there didn't appear to be anything personal in it. The picture she had given him of Maurice was propped up on his bedside cabinet next to a black and white wedding photo. 'Is that you?' she asked, nodding at the photo.

'Is what me?'

Anna got up to have a closer look. 'This photo of a strapping young groom and his beautiful bride.' She studied the two beaming faces staring back at her. From the style of clothes they were wearing she guessed it was probably the Sixties.

'Me and my Barbara. Tenth of July nineteen fifty-nine.'

'She's beautiful, Bert.'

Bert sniffed. 'She was that. No one like her.'

'Can I ask what happened?' asked Anna, replacing the picture and sitting back on the stool.

'Barbara died four years ago. We were doing the washing up and she said she had a headache. I teased her for trying to shirk doing the drying up – she hated doing the drying. She went for a lie-down. I finished off and made her a cup of tea and when I took it into her . . . she was gone.' Anna swallowed and Bert let out a sigh. 'Massive brain haemorrhage apparently – she wouldn't have known much about it.'

Anna reached out and patted Bert gently on the hand. He flinched at the touch but let his hand rest beneath hers just for a moment, before pulling it away. 'I'm sorry,' she said, meaning it.

'Our Maurice called for her for days, wandered the house making this pitiful meow, because he couldn't understand where she was. He was her cat really. She was a big Bee Gees fan you see,' he said, glancing at Anna, his eyes weighed down with sadness.

Anna nodded. 'Maurice Gibb.'

'Yes,' said Bert, revealing a proper smile. The stories of Barbara, him and Maurice flowed until Anna checked her watch and an hour had gone by.

'Bert, I need to make a move, but I'll see you next week. Is there anything in particular you'd like me to bring? Different paper, biscuits?' She almost offered something alcoholic but guessed that wouldn't be allowed.

'Assuming you can't smuggle in a Guinness, I'd love a

proper coffee. Americano with hot milk they call it. Sounds fancy but tastes bloody marvellous. They have instant here and it's not the same. Here, let me pay you for it.' He put his hand onto the table next to him and picked up a coaster and then put it down again quickly. 'Now, where did I put my wallet?'

'It's okay, Bert, you can pay me when I bring it. Take care of yourself.'

'Say hello to Maurice for me.'

'I will,' she said and she left. Bert had another feel about on the table for his wallet; he reached a bit further forward and his fingertips touched the familiar soft worn leather. He moved it to where he wanted it, folded the newspaper and put it in the bin next to him.

'Bert,' said Anna as she put her head back around his door. 'Do you take sugar?' She spotted the newspaper in the bin.

'Uh. No, thanks,' said Bert, clearly taken by surprise.

Anna paused for a moment, thinking. Pieces of a puzzle she had spotted before slotted into place. 'You can't see, can you?'

Bert sighed and continued to stare towards the window. 'Nope, not much. I'm not totally blind but it's not far off.' His voice hardened. 'That's why they put me in here, said I wasn't coping.'

'And were you?' asked Anna, returning to the footstool.

'I like you; you ask the questions others want to avoid. And, no, towards the end I had a couple of falls. But one of those was because some stupid home help cleaner put the kitchen bin in the wrong place. That was not my fault . . . And I fed Maurice a tin of beef casserole.'

Anna laughed and Bert joined in. 'No wonder he's a fussy eater,' said Anna, leaning over and picking the newspaper out of the bin. 'I can stop a bit longer. Shall I read you the good bits out of the paper?'

Anna wondered if Bert's pride would kick in but his mouth lifted at the edges. 'That would be lovely, thank you.'

'Headlines or sport first?'

'Always the sport,' said Bert, getting himself comfortable.

Anna went home smiling and feeling like she'd made a friend. Probably the oddest friendship on the planet after the lion who made friends with a baby gazelle, but a friendship all the same. She liked Bert and, since her beloved grandad had passed away a few years ago, there was a vacancy in her life for someone like him. Her mobile signalled the arrival of a message. She took a quick peek when she stopped at the traffic lights: **Hiya, A, How's your weekend going? C.**

Anna texted a quick reply: **All good thanks :-) A** and she pressed send quickly as the lights changed. Just as she was about to berate herself for not asking a question back, the phone started to ring and Anna felt a rush of excitement and something else: was it trepidation? She hadn't banked on C calling her. She pressed the button on her steering wheel so she could answer and drive at the same time. 'Hello,' she said, her voice uncertain and cautious.

'Hi, Anna. We thought you'd emigrated.'

'Hi, Dad.' Relief mixed with a little disappointment washed over her. 'How are you?'

'We're fine apart from your mum spending all her time on Facebook. She says you haven't done much recently.' They were stalking her again.

'I've been busy at work.' Anna indicated and went around the traffic island.

'Could you not just make some stuff up? Your mum worries.' Anna shook her head. She loved her parents but sometimes they were a bit overwhelming.

Chapter Nine

Sophie found herself sitting outside Arlo's classroom with mounting dread creeping up her spine. She'd had a phone call shortly after lunch asking if she could come in to discuss Arlo's behaviour. They didn't give her any other details and now she had gone over about eighty different scenarios in her head, each one more serious than the last. Arlo was sitting at her side swinging his legs and despite a thorough grilling, it appeared he genuinely didn't have a clue as to why they were there either.

The door opened and Mrs Armitage beckoned her inside. 'Arlo, please wait quietly whilst I speak to your mummy. We won't be long.'

Sophie gave Arlo *the* look and followed the teacher inside.

'Thanks for coming in at short notice but we felt we needed to nip this in the bud quite quickly.'

Sophie took the stupidly small child-sized seat that Mrs Armitage offered her and wondered if teachers did that on purpose to put you at a disadvantage. 'Okay. What's the problem?' Sophie was already feeling defensive. Arlo was cheeky but it was part of his character, his interminable spirit. He wasn't a bad kid.

'It's Arlo's language. He's been shouting swear words.'

Bollarding Dave, thought Sophie. She was careful to moderate her language around the children but Dave wasn't as good. 'Okay, I'm sorry. What's he been saying exactly?'

As if on cue Arlo began running up and down outside the office shouting what sounded a lot like 'Waaaaa-an-ker!'

And the teacher gave a curt nod at the door. 'This is what he's been shouting at the top of his voice for most of the day.'

Sophie had never felt this smug in all her life. 'He's into pirates so we went to London to see the *Cutty Sark*. One of the volunteers was quite theatrical and they told him what they used to shout and one of those things was *weigh anchor*.' Sophie emphasised the last two words.

Arlo bellowed from the corridor. 'Waaaa-an-ker!'

'I think that's fairly clear. Don't you?' Sophie raised one eyebrow and waited for Mrs Armitage to respond. She turned the colour any tomato would be proud of whilst Sophie revelled in her discomfort.

'Oh, I see,' said Mrs Armitage at last. 'I'm sure you can see our confusion and . . .'

'No,' said Sophie, forcing herself to keep a straight face. 'What else could a five-year-old possibly be saying?'

Mrs Armitage narrowed her eyes and Sophie wondered for a moment if perhaps she shouldn't have backed her into this particular corner. 'Arlo is a boisterous child who needs firm boundaries and . . .'

'You shouldn't jump to assumptions about him. Whilst he can be boisterous, on this occasion I think I'm right in saying he's done nothing wrong.'

'Indeed, Mrs Butterworth.' Mrs Armitage dropped her head in defeat.

'And if he starts saying something that sounds like Big Hairy Sex . . .' she paused and Mrs Armitage tried to control a facial tick '. . . he's talking about the film *Big Hero Six*. It's his favourite at the moment.'

'Of course,' said Mrs Armitage, letting out a long breath. 'Sorry to have wasted your time.'

Sophie was happy with the apology. 'That's fine. We'll speak to him about being boisterous.'

'Thank you.' They both stood up and Sophie was thrilled that the little chair wasn't stuck to her bottom as she'd feared it might be. She failed to hide her smug grin as she exited the room. Arlo was hurtling towards her and came to an abrupt halt.

'Calm down now, Arlo, time to go home.'

'Mummy, today I learned a new word and that word was . . . fuck.' Sophie rushed him away from the classroom without a backward glance.

It wasn't just raining, it was a torrential downpour of biblical proportions – a somewhat fitting start to the work bonding session. Anna was unhappy at going away and leaving Maurice but her mum had promised to call round twice a day to feed him and give him a cuddle. Anna had decided she wouldn't mention the two mice he'd brought round for a play date, which she'd had to catch and release into the park. She had suggested her mum might want to have a chat to Maurice as he was probably used to the conversations Anna had with him daily. Her mum had then proceeded to question her mental health, which was thoughtful but a little unnecessary.

After the short ride from the station the taxi deposited Anna and Sophie at the farmhouse where they were welcomed by a tall, ruddy man in a well-worn green jumper. Anna was pleased to discover they were the first to arrive. The farmer strode off to show them the barn and Sophie dragged her wheelie case across the muddy puddled ground with gusto, mud splashing up the sides. Anna was glad to get inside and dropped her bag by the door.

'Toilets and showers here,' he said, gesturing to the left. He opened a door to their right where there was a wood burner in front of three large sofas. 'Kitchen at the back, that's it downstairs. Two dorms upstairs. Here's a key. Lunch will be up at the farmhouse at 1 p.m. I'll do the health and safety briefing after lunch and then we'll head off to the top field and show you the ropes with dry-stone. Give us a shout if you need anything else.'

'Thanks,' said Anna, taking the key and shutting the door behind him as he strode out into the rain.

'I like this place. It's rustic,' said Sophie, shaking off her wet coat and hanging it up by the door where it liberally dripped onto the flagstone floor.

So far, so good, thought Anna, picking up her bag and heading upstairs. The two rooms were identical with three sets of built-in bunk beds each, open shelving and views across rolling countryside crisscrossed by pale-coloured dry-stone walls. Anna laid claim to a top bunk near the window. She'd briefly had bunk beds when she was a child but a change in circumstances had seen her room redecorated and the bunk beds had disappeared. Sophie flopped down on the bed underneath Anna's and stretched out.

'Ooh, comfy bed. I might not move from here. Two days of sleep should just about catch me back up. I'm fed up of being tired all the time. It's really tiring.' There wasn't even a hint of irony in her voice.

Anna turned and spotted herself in a large wood-framed mirror. She looked a fright. The rain had made her straight dark hair limp and her make-up had run.

'The caught-in-the-rain look is always attractive.' Anna wiped away the dripping mascara from under her eyes.

Sophie joined her at the mirror and studied herself. 'My neck's gone all red and blotchy.'

'Another lusty flush and Hudson's not even here yet.'

Sophie opened her mouth to speak but the sound of the door opening downstairs stopped her.

'Hey, anyone at home?' came Hudson's dulcet tones.

'Bugger,' said Anna with feeling, giving her eyes one last sweep with her fingers before she headed downstairs to meet him, zhooshing up her hair as she went. She found him hanging up his coat. His hair was wet but it seemed a quick headshake and a rough comb with his fingers was all it needed to have him pristine again. Something else to add to the long list of things she didn't like about him.

'Hey, Anna. This place is great. Shall we go and explore?' He reminded her of someone from the Famous Five, but in a good way.

'Yes, let's,' came the equally Enid Blyton response from Sophie who was now barrelling down the stairs at speed.

'Hey, Sophie, you look amazing.' He kissed her cheek lightly and Anna tried not to frown at the difference in warmth level of the greetings. But why did she care? She didn't.

'Aww, you're just saying that. Come and pick your bed,' said Sophie, turning around and heading back upstairs. For someone who was tired out a few minutes ago she'd made a remarkable recovery. Hudson definitely had a confidence-boosting effect on Sophie, although given the reaction of all the females in the office, she wasn't alone.

* * *

While Sophie was showing Hudson around, the door opened and pretty much everyone else arrived, instantly filling up the small space and creating a large puddle in the hallway. It didn't take long to sort out who was sleeping where and for opinions to be shared on the mixed shower and toilet situation. Anna tried to point out that if they were staying at someone's house it would be the same but with four showers and three toilets they were fairly well covered.

Anna was handing out a quiz to help everyone relax when she spotted a taxi pull up outside. Roberta got out and headed towards the farmhouse. She was hunkered down due to the rain. Anna was watching her as a second person with their head covered by a hoodie got out from the taxi and ran to join her.

'Right, everyone. Looks like Roberta's arrived. We'd better head over to the farmhouse. You can complete the quiz over lunch.' She was still speaking as she shrugged on her coat. She was interested to find out who the other person was – everyone she had been told to invite was here. The rain lashed at her as she opened the door and she wished she'd brought a coat with a hood. She turned up her collar and jogged across to the farmhouse with the others trailing behind her. The farmer opened the door and ushered everyone inside where they made more puddles with their wet coats.

They gathered in a very large conservatory where Roberta was waiting for them and she went straight into corporate mode and gave them a pep talk. Anna was only half listening. She was squeezing rain from her hair and trying to work out where the other person had gone and who they were. Anna tuned back in again.

'The question is: who's in my canoe?' asked Roberta. She was deadly serious.

A few hands started to go up and Anna joined in. Karl leaned over. 'Heading for shit creek without a . . .' Anna nudged him because Roberta was glaring at them. Roberta went on to explain that she wouldn't be taking part in the dry-stone walling as she had to get back to the office for important meetings.

'This project is paramount to the company and to that end we have a consultant joining us for the next three months to ensure that we maximise its potential,' said Roberta, gesturing to the back of the room. Everyone turned in unison to see the figure standing in the doorway. Anna tried to swallow but her throat was bone-dry.

'This is Liam Tinch. He has extensive experience in Lean Methodologies and is so excited to be part of the team that he volunteered to start early and join you for the next couple of days.'

Liam made his way to the front whilst Sophie repeatedly patted Anna's arm as if trying to alert her to what she could see very plainly for herself. At no point did his eyes alight on Anna. She was standing with her mouth open until she realised and shut it hastily.

'Thanks, Roberta. No speech from me. I'm thrilled to be here. Please treat me like one of the team. I can't wait to get started.' Anna stared at him. Too many questions were flooding her mind as well as a number of expletives. A clammy sensation drifted over her and she tried hard to distil all the hurt into anger.

'Of all the—' started Sophie.

'Arseholes?' offered Anna in a low voice. 'What the buggery bollocks is he doing here? He bloody well knows I work for this company.' She was upset but she wasn't going to let him see it.

'Enjoy lunch, everyone, and we look forward to hearing

all about it when you're back in the office on Monday,' said Roberta. Anna noted the look she gave Liam but couldn't read it entirely. Was this Roberta's hire or had it come from above? Either way something was going on and she didn't like it. Everyone greeted Liam warmly apart from Anna who wanted to make him feel as wretched as he had her and then drown him in the nearest puddle. Some people filtered through for lunch and Anna spied her chance.

'Well, this is a . . . surprise,' she said, attempting a smile but it was a grimace at best.

'Anna, I only found out a couple of days ago and—'

'Doesn't matter to me,' she said with a twitch of her shoulder.

'Really? Because I was worried it'd be awkward.'

'Not at all. Let's have lunch,' she said, offering for him to go first and resisting the urge to trip him up. Perhaps he'd choke, she thought hopefully and was disappointed to see soup was on the menu.

She was grateful to Sophie for saving her a chair at the other end of the table so she didn't have to sit next to Liam. Everyone tucked in and the chatter was noisy. Office-bound workers tended to get a bit overexcited when they were released from the confines of the workplace. Anna tried not to watch Liam but it was hard not to: he was right in her eye line. She noted his hoodie was new with large lettering on the front declaring it was a souvenir from the Grand Canyon. It appeared that now he was no longer engaged to an acrophobic, he was clearly making the most of being able to fly and travelling further afield. He looked up and she began paying attention to her soup. His hair was cut differently, nothing drastic but still notably different. It made his head look sort of square.

'You okay?' asked Sophie.

'Fine. I'm fine.'

Sophie gave her a shrewd look.

'Okay, I'm not fine. I want to murder him with a soup-spoon. But I will be fine.' She gave a firm nod and returned her attention to her soup and tried to ignore the gnawing sensation in her stomach which had nothing to with hunger and everything to do with the man who had so suddenly trampled on her heart and destroyed her well-made plans.

Chapter Ten

A couple of hours later, the rain had abated and the farmer had walked them up to the top field telling entertaining farming stories on the way. They were now working in two teams having been shown the basics of dry-stone walling. They were repairing a damaged wall rather than starting from scratch and Anna was pleased with how her little team were working together, not to mention thrilled that Liam was in the other group with Sophie, who would report back in detail later. It did, however, mean Anna was with Hudson, but it was a cross she was prepared to bear.

'What are your thoughts on the consultant?' asked Hudson, handing her a large stone.

Anna studied the wall, gave the stone the once-over and handed it back. 'Small one.'

'What?' asked Hudson with a quizzical expression.

'Stone. I need a small one first to fit in the gap.' She pointed at the wall.

'Okay,' he said, rummaging in the pile behind him and handing her another. 'Do you think he's here to undermine us?' She'd not seen Hudson this serious before.

'No,' she said and he seemed to relax a little. 'He's an

optimisation consultant and he's here to map out a full-scale reorganisation with redundancies.'

Hudson's face registered his alarm. 'How did you figure all that out?'

'He's my ex-fiancé and that's what he does.' Anna jiggled the small stone into the gap and gave it a tap to ensure it was secure.

'Wow,' said Hudson. 'You okay about him being here?'

'It's not the nicest surprise I've had but we're all professionals.' She pointed to the big stone and he passed it to her. She paused for a moment and watched Liam. He was standing back ordering about the others in his team. He was wearing the latest in hi-tech sports gear like he was about to run the London marathon, not do a bit of team building in Derbyshire. She noticed Hudson was watching him too.

Hudson leaned in to her shoulder so the others wouldn't hear. 'I'm no cactus expert, but I recognise a prick when I see one,' he said, his American drawl suddenly strong.

Anna burst into giggles and Liam turned abruptly in their direction. Anna and Hudson looked away and tried to appear as if they were concentrating on the wall. 'Your observation is spot on,' she said to Hudson with a smile.

'Great. But if you wanted me to draw on his face with a permanent marker while he's asleep you only have to say,' said Hudson, with a tip of his head.

'Thanks, I'll bear it in mind.' Maybe he was starting to grow on her.

Building the wall was hard labour and took a lot of time. The farmer kept moving between the groups to check on their progress and give helpful advice. He seemed pleased with what they had achieved when he declared it was time for some team games back at the farmhouse. As they walked back Hudson pulled Anna to one side.

'This was a good shout. Thanks for organising it,' he said.

'We made a good team today,' said Anna.

'Who knew?' said Hudson, with a cheeky raise of his eyebrow.

She knew they had to move on and stop fighting if they were to stand a chance against Liam. She feared he would be after any opportunity to rationalise the project. It wasn't a vindictive thing – she knew he was just doing his job. Well, she at least hoped that would be the case.

'You think we could transfer this new truce to the office when we get back?' she asked.

'I know things have been a little uncomfortable between us these last couple of months. I know I've not helped that. So, if I've been an ass I'm sorry.'

'You were both an ass and an arse, and I accept your apology. I could have behaved better, so I'm sorry too. And if you're saying we need to stand united against Liam then I completely agree.'

'That's exactly what I'm saying.'

'Then welcome to Team Strickland,' said Anna with a cheeky grin. Hudson laughed and gave her a high five, which Liam turned around in time to witness.

Sophie caught up with them. 'I can't believe Liam took the job.'

'Yes, you can,' said Anna. 'If the money was right he won't have thought twice about me.' She narrowed her eyes as the men in front laughed in unison. It was hard not to imagine they were laughing at her, especially when Liam glanced over his shoulder to see if she was watching.

'Thank goodness he's only here for three months,' said Sophie.

'After which we'll probably all be gone,' said Anna bitterly.

'I'm glad I'll be on maternity leave, but I need a job to come back to.' Sophie's expression was thoughtful. 'We need the money.'

'Don't worry. I'm sure it'll be fine.' Platitudes were all she had.

'I forgot my toothpaste. Can I borrow yours?' asked Sophie.

'Sure, it's in my washbag.' The one Liam bought me for my birthday, she thought.

There was a knock at the door while they were eating dinner and a laminated sheet was pushed under the door. Karl went to retrieve it as he'd already bolted down his food. As everyone else continued to eat, he read it out.

'Hi Team, this is your last challenge for the day. Write everyone's name on a slip of paper, put them in a bowl and draw one at random. On the other side you write down one question you want to know the answer to. Answer honestly and share with the group.' He put it down and started writing out the slips. 'To save time: I am available for sex tonight, for a small fee, and it's about eight—'

'Get on with it, Karl,' said Sophie.

'I bet that's what they all say,' added Priya.

'You have a lot of confidence for someone with a face like that,' said Sophie, tapping his cheek gently.

'Beauty is but a light switch away,' he said, pretending to flick a switch.

'There is no room dark enough,' said Sophie and

everyone laughed. Karl stuck his tongue out, tipped the remaining salad from the bowl onto Sophie's plate and dropped the folded slips into the now empty bowl.

As the bowl was passed around everyone took one and the group hushed as they mulled over who they had picked and what question they wanted to ask them. Glances shot around the table, each wondering who had them and the mood became a little tense. When everyone had refolded and replaced their slips Karl handed them out. He returned to the instruction sheet. 'Read your question and then give an honest and full answer to the group before revealing what the question was.'

'Interesting approach,' said Hudson, the only one of the group who was sitting back in his chair. Everyone else was either bolt upright or leaning over their slip.

'Right, I'll go first,' said Karl, unravelling the paper. He nodded as he read it. 'Okay. The answer is yes. It was behind a beach hut . . .' Everyone groaned and he waved a hand to settle them. 'In a lovely little place in Devon. Her name was Melanie and it felt amazing.' There was lots of eyebrow twitching round the table. 'And the question was – Have you ever fallen in love? And I forgot to say I was seventeen at the time.' For once Karl looked contrite. The colleague on his right gave him a pat on the back and Anna smiled at him from across the table. Perhaps there was a heart under all the bravado, after all. 'And she gave the most amazing blow job,' he added with a grin and everyone groaned. Maybe not, thought Anna. 'I nominate, Priya,' said Karl.

Priya read hers and her eyes darted to the ceiling as she thought. 'Right. My answer is – the ability to make all gorgeous foods calorie free so I could stuff my face and not put on an ounce. The question was – If I was a superhero, what would I want my superpower to be? I nominate Anna.'

Anna was stunned by the speed of Priya's answer and she grabbed up her paper slip. Anna wasn't fazed by the exercise – she'd done similar things before – as long as she didn't get Karl asking her what her favourite position was. He was giving her a lascivious look, which was par for the course with Karl. Anna unfolded her slip and read the question. An icy chill ran through her. She gripped the slip of paper, unable to pull her eyes away from the words.

'Come on, hurry up,' said someone. 'I need another drink.'

'I . . . I . . .' Anna swallowed hard, aware her palms had begun to sweat. 'It wasn't my fault,' she said, suddenly looking up and scanning the mix of eager and bored faces around the table. Hudson sat forward. 'What wasn't your fault?' he asked, his voice sounding loud in the now silent room.

'I can't do this,' she said in a hurry, pushed back her chair, which made an unpleasant scraping noise, and rushed from the room.

Priya leaned over and picked up the piece of paper. 'The question was – What did you do at university?'

Chapter Eleven

Anna was pacing the yard as the last of the evening sun hunkered down for the night. This wasn't how she had expected the team event evening to go. She hadn't meant to make a scene and was annoyed with herself for reacting, although the truth was she wasn't able to control her emotions that easily. It must have been Liam who had written the question, which had freaked her out. His attempt to wind her up, no doubt. At least now she knew what she was dealing with.

The door clicked open and she spun around to see Liam's face peering round the edge.

'Can I have a word?' he asked, still using the door like a shield.

Anna crossed her arms in front of her. 'What about?' She'd give him a chance to come clean before she tore him to shreds.

Liam gestured for them to walk a bit further away, perhaps anticipating an explosive response. 'You okay?'

'Fine. Why?'

Liam tilted his head to one side and scrunched up his features. 'I'm really sorry about the question.'

Anna pulled back her shoulders. She was right – of

course it had been him. A flash of temper and hurt coursed through her. 'I didn't think you'd stoop that low.'

'Hey, you have to believe me. I thought of the question before I pulled a name out. I just went with something generic: *what did you do at university*? I didn't think you'd think . . . You know. Sorry, it wasn't meant to upset you.'

Anna didn't believe him for a second but she also didn't want him to think he'd got to her. 'Okay. Apology accepted. Let's go back inside.' The breeze was making her shiver.

Liam touched her arm to stop her. 'Are you sure you're okay with me taking this job?'

'Yes. It's fine.' Anna spoke deliberately as if addressing someone a bit simple.

Liam gave a brief headshake and Anna straightened her back. 'Because every time I look up you're staring at me and I wondered if you still had . . . feelings. It's quite understandable if you do. I mean I—'

'No, Liam. I don't still have feelings for you.' Only murderous ones, she thought. Although saying it out loud had her brain ticking double time. It was hard to erase all they had shared; it was like their entire history had been buried underneath all the anger and sadness. Did she still care for him?

'Right. Because I want you to know that I still love you, Anna.'

She stepped back as if physically stunned by the statement. A million questions swamped her brain and she tried to order them. 'What about Tabitha?'

'She isn't you.'

It was a cheesy line and it should have made her loathe him a little more but there was a voice in her head saying: 'He's not the worst man on the planet. You invested a lot

102

in him. Is it worth giving things another go?' She hated that voice but it was a hard one to ignore.

The door opened and out strode Hudson. Anna was relieved to have had her villainous thoughts interrupted. Taking Liam back was a bad idea, and deep down she knew it.

'Hudson,' she said abruptly holding out her arm to halt his path to his car.

Hudson grasped her hand and she froze. She wasn't expecting that or the accompanying electricity shooting violently up her arm. They both stared at their clasped hands for a fraction longer than was necessary.

'Are you all right?' asked Hudson, his voice soft and full of concern.

Liam forced a cough and they both looked in his direction.

'I didn't realise you two were . . .' He pointed at their entwined fingers.

Anna's eyebrows shot up and she opened her mouth to protest but something about Hudson's expression stopped her. He gave a tiny shrug. 'I'll let Anna explain,' said Hudson, giving her hand a squeeze and keeping hold of it. He let their clasped hands drop down between them. Was it some sort of code? Did he want her to say they were in a relationship? It would stop Liam coming on to her, which would be a bonus. It would stop her making a knee-jerk decision to take Liam back too. In her foggy brain it seemed like a good idea. She wanted to know what Hudson was thinking; did he have a plan?

'No no, you explain,' she said.

He twitched his head. 'Err. Okay. Let's just say it's very early on in our relationship.' He eyed Anna as if seeking approval. Her mouth twitched in response. 'We'd really appreciate a bit of discretion,' said Hudson, slinking an arm around Anna's shoulder. She faltered for a second before she realised what he was doing and awkwardly snuggled into him.

Liam stared at them for what seemed like ages and Anna could feel herself heating up. For once Liam actually looked hurt. At last he seemed to snap himself out of his trance. 'Mum's the word,' he said, tapping his nose. He clapped his hands together. '*Die Hard* on DVD in five minutes.' He pointed inside before turning and heading back.

As the door closed behind Liam Anna let out a giant breath and Hudson removed his arm. 'Are you sure this is a good idea?' said Anna, spinning around to face him.

'I don't know. I'm not even sure what just happened. You grabbed my hand and then—'

'*I* grabbed *your* hand?' Anna was indignant.

'Err, yeah.' Hudson threw up his palms.

'No, *you* grabbed *my* hand.' She had to physically stop herself putting her hands on her hips.

'This is getting us nowhere. Whatever happened, we ended up holding hands. I thought you were trying to make him jealous or something. I don't know.' Hudson seemed flustered.

'No, I just wanted a distraction.' And to stop me doing something ridiculous like taking him back, she thought. It worried her how easily she had come to almost cracking. She thought she was stronger.

'Great. You could have said that because I can juggle you know. That would have been a much better distraction,' said Hudson, giving a small shake of his head.

'Sorry.' She felt stupid.

'But now we've said we're boyfriend and girlfriend I guess we'll have to keep it going.' He scratched his chin and she noticed it was a little stubbly.

'Or we could say we were joking.' They both pulled faces knowing this would make them look ridiculous.

Hudson seemed to be thinking. 'You never know. Now he thinks he knows secret information about us it could put him on our team, give us a chance to find out what he's going to do to our project.'

'Or he'll try to blackmail us,' said Anna. Knowing Liam, he was more likely to think it gave him some sort of advantage. Anna realised she was asking a lot of Hudson as someone who was already in a relationship. 'I'm sorry, I didn't think about your personal situation. In fact, I didn't think at all. If this makes you uncomfortable, I'll put Liam straight.' She shoved her hands in her pockets and turned to go.

'Hang on,' said Hudson and Anna spun around. 'It is crazy but I'm guessing you'll feel better having shown your ex you've moved on and maybe made him a bit jealous too.' He gave a cheeky pout and Anna brightened.

'I can't lie, it would be a bonus.'

'Then if you're happy to pretend to be my girlfriend, I'm happy to be your boyfriend.'

She gave a slow nod. 'I'd be honoured.' Her voice held a hint of sarcasm.

'Hey, I'm a very good boyfriend.'

'I bet you are.' A few unhelpful thoughts crossed her mind and she banished them. She felt like she was cheating on Sophie. It was bonkers.

'Then let's slay him,' said Hudson, and he followed her back inside.

* * *

105

Anna was in her sleeping bag when she was disturbed by the sound of distant screaming and the light going on, which woke her with a start.

'Anna, calm down, you're having a nightmare,' said Sophie, in her left ear. Anna turned to see her friend's tired face. Anna's pulse was racing and she could feel her hair was damp with sweat.

'Sorry,' whispered Anna. 'Was I shouting?'

'Yes,' came Priya's disgruntled voice.

'Ignore her,' said Sophie. 'You okay now?'

Anna nodded. 'Careful going back down the ladder.'

Sophie disappeared, the light went out and Anna settled herself back down. It had been a while since she'd had a nightmare. It was always the same one. And she was always too late to save them. She closed her eyes tight and tried to think of something else. Thanks to Liam stirring up long-hidden memories, it would likely be a while before she got back to sleep.

The next morning, she wanted to be one of the first in the showers as she didn't want anyone to see her with dark circles round her eyes and mad post-nightmare hair. And she wasn't keen on going in after Karl – she didn't want to think about what he might have been up to in there. Anna crept down the ladder, grabbed her washbag and reversed out of the room.

'Hey,' said a hushed American voice behind her. She shut the door and turned to face Hudson who was wearing a bath towel tied around his waist. Her breath caught in her throat and she started to cough. 'You okay?'

Anna took a deep breath and got her coughing under control. 'Fine thanks,' she said, trying hard not to stare at Hudson's impressive physique. She knew gay men often looked after themselves but this was a whole new level in body workout. She'd only ever seen carved abs like his on male models.

Hudson ran his fingers through his wet hair and his muscles rippled, which was very distracting.

'You sure? Only in the night I heard . . .' Hudson tailed off.

Anna gave a phoney chuckle. 'Yeah. I think I was dreaming about *Die Hard*.' She broke eye contact. She was a bad liar, and she knew people could always tell.

'As long as you're okay.'

'I'm fine. Are you acting the caring boyfriend?'

'Absolutely.'

There was an awkward pause. 'I thought I'd jump in the showers early,' she said, waving her washbag as evidence and they both watched as a stream of tampons tumbled from the open zip.

'Bugger,' she muttered, whilst scrabbling to gather them up.

'See you at breakfast,' said Hudson, failing to hide his amusement as he slunk into the men's bedroom. Anna hung her head. Sophie must have left the bag open after she'd returned Anna's toothpaste. Thanks a bunch, she thought.

Chapter Twelve

After a hearty farmhouse breakfast, the farmer announced the morning's exercise was at a nearby reservoir, which received a mixed response. When the minibus pulled up Hudson was quick to jump in and take the seat next to Anna and she was pleased to see Liam had spotted the gesture. Sophie had also noticed and was giving Anna pleading looks to swap places.

'I get sick if I don't sit near the front,' said Sophie, and she pointed at Anna's seat.

Anna's shoulders sagged. Sophie wasn't helping herself with the Hudson crush if she was going to seize every opportunity to be near him. Although Anna had to admit he did smell mighty fine this morning.

'It's okay, I'll move,' said Anna, seeing the plea in Sophie's eyes.

Sophie was about to sit down when Karl stuck his head inside the van. 'Can I sit at the front too? I hate these things and I might have overdone it on the wine last night. Gippy tummy,' he said, giving it a rub.

'Sure,' said Hudson, and he followed Anna to the back seat where they giggled like love-struck teenagers until Sophie spun around and glared at the pair of them. Anna clamped her lips together to try to stifle the giggles. She glanced at Hudson and he winked at her. For a moment she forgot they were pretending.

Carsington Water was impressive and the weather was far kinder today with a light breeze and a little sunshine glinting off the water making it sparkle and look more inviting than it should. They were introduced to Canadian canoes and got into teams of three while Karl perfected his impression of Roberta by asking 'Who's in my canoe?' Anna was with Priya and Hudson and they had to work together to keep in rhythm.

'Priya, you don't need to keep swapping sides with your paddle,' complained Anna when a trail of water splashed across her back for the umpteenth time.

'Sorry. But I want to beat Karl,' she said, lifting her paddle out of the water to point and inadvertently splashing Anna again.

The purpose of the game was to retrieve different-coloured buoys via the shortest route whilst heading off other canoes. Most went for the nearby markers meaning they all squabbled whereas Anna steered them towards the middle-distance ones to avoid bumping into other teams, enabling them to collect their buoys and return victorious. As they were making their final turn she heard a war cry nearby and a canoe came towards them at speed. She wasn't surprised to see Karl, Liam and Raj from Finance all with clenched teeth and paddling hard.

'Heads down, and paddle as hard as you can, team,' said Hudson. 'Go, go, go!' which was exactly what they did. Hudson was at the back, his powerful strokes doing the lion's share of the work. They sailed over the finish line with the other canoe on their tail. Hudson turned the canoe at speed and with a few neat flicks of his paddle soaked the occupants of the other one. Karl stood up to protest, wobbled dramatically and in an attempt to right himself, lost his balance further and fell in. Liam threw down his paddle in temper. It bounced off the canoe and into the water, making him swear.

Once out of the canoes there was lots of congratulatory blokey back slapping, a few playful remonstrations and lots of Karl shaking his wet head over people like a naughty puppy. When he knew Liam was watching, Hudson leaned into Anna's ear. 'Nice job, honey,' he whispered, making her shudder. She hoped Hudson assumed her squirming was all part of the act. If you weren't gay, you would make an excellent boyfriend, she thought. If she wasn't careful she'd soon be suffering from Sophie's complaint.

As the victors they were first to eat lunch, which was a barbecue by the water's edge.

'You okay?' Anna asked Sophie who was munching down a large hamburger overflowing with salad.

'Starving and a bit knackered but I had fun this morning and the lie-in was bliss. It's lovely not to be woken by someone jumping on your bladder.'

'You should stop Dave doing that,' said Anna drily and Sophie gave a smirk.

Sophie's gaze drifted over to Hudson in his tight white T-shirt. 'Do you think if I paid him he'd re-create the Mr Darcy scene from *Pride and Prejudice* for me?'

'You are aware you said that out loud?' said Anna, rolling her eyes. 'He's gorgeous but you know he's gay. You need to have a word with your hormones.'

'I noticed you two seemed a bit cosy on the bus earlier,' said Sophie, with a suspicious look in her eye.

Anna checked around her like an amateur spy. 'I was going to explain on the way home away from the others, but Hudson is pretending to be my boyfriend so we can . . .' Why were they doing this again? Anna was no longer sure. 'Get closer to Liam.'

Sophie frowned hard and inclined her head. 'Makes no sense to me.'

'I'll explain later,' said Anna, as Liam strolled over.

'Hiya, Sophie, how's Dave and the kids?'

'Great, thanks. How are your scruples? Oh, I forgot you don't have any,' said Sophie, and went to get another burger leaving him somewhat shell-shocked by the snub.

Anna avoided eye contact and followed Sophie into the salad queue. 'Don't piss him off, Sophe, he has the fate of our jobs in his hands.'

Sophie shrugged. 'I'm not sure pretending you're Hudson's girlfriend isn't going to do that anyway.' Anna could already see she wasn't happy about it but they could hardly backtrack now they'd come this far.

The afternoon whizzed by and Anna was thrilled that, with a bit of help, both teams managed to complete their sections of dry-stone wall and have their photographs taken next to their masterpieces. She was pleased Roberta bothered to show up for a final wrap-up and motivational send-off liberally scattered with feminist quotes. After everyone had dispersed Roberta took Anna to one side.

'Nice job with this team event, Anna, I'm impressed.'

'Thanks.' Anna was quickly buoyed by a little praise.

'I've just found out about you and Liam. I'm not sure what to say. Obviously, he didn't mention it otherwise I would have objected.'

'So, you didn't hire him?' said Anna, her left eye twitching slightly.

Roberta shook her head. 'No, this has come from on

high. But I'm fully supportive obviously.' She gave an expression that said she wasn't.

'Obviously. Thanks for the heads-up, I'll make sure he only sees what he needs to but to be honest I think Hudson and I are working far better together now than we were. There are no holes for him to pick on the project.'

'If you want something done, ask a woman. That's what the late, great Margaret Thatcher told us,' said Roberta. She straightened her dress and went to speak to someone else.

Hudson sauntered over and made sure his bicep brushed Anna's shoulder. 'Hey, girlfriend, how you doing?'

'Really?' said Anna in a mocking tone but the truth was she was enjoying their play-acting. She was seeing a whole new side to Hudson and it was one she liked.

'I forgot I don't need to try to win you over, you're already dating me.' He gave her another nudge.

'Careful or you'll be filed in the same section as Karl.' They both watched as he chased after Priya whilst swinging his wet T-shirt around his head. Roberta was looking unimpressed.

'I was wondering if you fancied grabbing something to eat?' he said. Anna stared at the hot dog she was holding. Hudson seemed to go a little pink. 'I figured we'd be hungry again later and I'd like to hatch a plan of attack now we have Liam snooping around the project.'

'Good call. And it'd be a chance to get our whole girl-friend, boyfriend story straight. I'm not sure I feel like going out though.' Anna was looking forward to a shower and an early night but Hudson's suggestion made sense and she liked to be on the front foot. 'How about a take-away at mine?'

'Takeout? Great. About seven thirty?'

'Perfect. Here's my address,' she said pulling a Post-it Note pad and pen from her bag and jotting it down.

'Always prepared. You'd have made an excellent Scout.'

A few hours later Hudson and Anna were sitting at her small dining table munching pizza. They had drawn up a list of everything they needed to check to ensure Liam couldn't find fault with the project governance and had now moved on to their fake relationship.

'We know how we met,' said Hudson.

'At work. Very clichéd but also very common.'

Hudson nodded. 'I asked you out and—'

'I could have asked you out.' Anna was slightly put out because she wasn't keen on gender stereotypes.

Hudson's mouth tweaked at one corner. 'Okay, but I warn you, I play hard to get. How would you have got me to say yes?'

Anna's smile reached her eyes. She liked him challenging her. 'There's my cute British accent.' She started to tick things off on her fingers.

He screwed up his nose. 'Everyone here has one of those. Even Karl.'

'Fair enough.' Anna had a think. 'You were missing America and I invited you to a breakfast meeting with . . . Pop Tarts, bagels and syrup.'

Hudson was giving her an odd look. 'It's a nice thought but Pop Tarts?'

'Yes. Pop Tarts, you thought it was adorable and we laughed about it and I promised to make you a proper breakfast next time we went out.' She gave him her best flirty expression.

Hudson nearly choked on his drink. 'You floozy. But you've got yourself a date.'

This was fun – all the flirting with none of the consequences. She thought to herself that she should probably date gay guys more often. They clinked glasses and got back to demolishing the pizza. Anna put a few more turns of black pepper on hers.

'You like black pepper huh?'

'On everything.'

'I make a mean pepper sauce to go with steak.'

'Mmm, sounds good. Old family recipe?'

'Err, yes and no. My ex's old family recipe actually.' Hudson broke eye contact and seemed to be studying her laminate flooring in great detail. The mood had changed quickly.

'Bad break-up?' She had to ask.

'You could say that. I got unceremoniously dumped by someone I thought was the one.'

It was oddly reassuring that he too had been in Anna's situation – both dumped by a man. 'You want to talk about it?'

He pursed his lips and shook his head. 'All water over the dam now.'

'Still hurts though, doesn't it?' She reached across and gave his arm a squeeze.

'Sure does. Now tell me about this Bert character, he sounds awesome.' And just like that the smiles were back.

After the meal Hudson dutifully helped her clear the table and they settled on the sofa with coffees. The door swung open and in marched Maurice. He loved to make an entrance.

'Are you okay with cats?' she asked as Maurice made a beeline for Hudson.

'I love cats,' he said. 'And aren't you a beauty?' he added, turning his attention to Maurice who responded by swishing his tail in a diva-ish manner.

'The rescue centre think he's a . . .' She had to think of what breed they'd called him. 'A Maine Coon I think.'

'He looks like it. We used to have one when I was a kid. You know they're an American breed, right?'

Anna rolled her eyes. 'I'm surrounded.'

Hudson gave a cheeky smile. 'You're a lucky lady.'

'I think Maurice is officially a Brummy now. You've got a bit further to go.' Maurice jumped up and made himself comfortable stretched out on Hudson's lap, staring up at him adoringly. Goodness, was nobody immune to his charms?

'Anything I should know to avoid Liam catching me out?' asked Hudson as he fussed Maurice and Maurice lapped it up.

Anna had a think. University shot into her mind and she instantly dismissed it. 'You know about my black pepper addiction.'

He nodded sagely. 'And I know you're a control freak.'

'You say it like it's a bad thing.'

'Not at all. What else?'

'I'm afraid of heights and I don't like mustard.' She pulled a face like she could taste it burning her tongue.

'Any brothers or sisters?'

Anna nearly gave her automatic answer but something stopped her. Her spine stiffened. 'I had a sister.' Hudson appeared shocked and intuitively reached out and laid his hand on hers. It was a tender and emotionally intelligent gesture. 'Her name was Lynsey.'

'I'm sorry, Anna.' She could see the genuine concern in his eyes.

'She was fourteen when she had a seizure. It was undiagnosed epilepsy . . .' Anna started to tremble. This was something she was sure she had dealt with years ago but right now it didn't feel that way at all.

She could sense Hudson's empathy. 'I can't imagine how awful that was for you and your folks.'

Anna tried hard to be positive. 'I think it brought us closer together. Makes you realise how precious the people you love really are.' She was surprised to hear her voice crack. It had also made her feel a great responsibility to do well in life but he didn't need to know that.

Hudson reached for her hand. 'I'm sure there are easier ways to find that out.' Anna nodded; she was scared of disintegrating into full-on blubbing mode.

'We've all moved on.' He removed his hand and Anna was keen to push the spotlight off her. 'What about you?'

She didn't expect to be questioned at length by Liam – she wasn't applying for a green card – but just in case it happened she didn't want the humiliation of getting caught out. Anna also realised their fake relationship was a great way to satisfy her curiosity and find out more about him.

'No siblings. Nothing much to tell.'

'Come on, Hudson. What do you like?'

'I run – a lot. Not like I used to but I try to keep my fitness levels up. I love music. Justin Bieber's my favourite, which is why I got the tattoo.'

'Okay . . .' She had to admit she was surprised, but she wasn't going to judge.

A grin spread across his face. 'I'm jerking around. I like a mix of stuff from Bowie to Red Hot Chili Peppers to Bruno Mars. Not Bieber.'

'Very eclectic.'

'How about you?' He leaned forward and watched her closely.

She thought for a moment and sipped her coffee. 'I like old films.'

'What are your favourites?'

She had a think. 'I love the Ealing Comedies.'

Hudson pulled a face. 'Never heard of them.'

'They're black and white, classic comedies. Very British, like me. You'd love them.'

'What other films do you like?'

'*Léon*.' She noted his nod of approval. 'And I absolutely love *You've Got Mail*.'

'One of my favourites too.'

'You're winding me up again.'

He shook his head.

'Really?'

'Yeah. Joe Fox is my all-time hero. All his references to *The Godfather*. Sure, it's classified as a chick flick, but it's a great film.' He was full of surprises.

Chapter Thirteen

Sophie came back to find her home ransacked by marauding savages, or worse still it appeared the children had managed to cover every surface with unidentifiable sticky substances. Anna didn't have to put up with this; she only had herself to think about and Sophie envied her. She could barely remember a time when she hadn't been running around after someone else. Sophie meandered through the house surveying the devastation. She'd only been gone for forty-eight hours. Hurricanes did less damage than her children. She retrieved a Peppa Pig sock from the goldfish bowl, pushed the pizza box to the floor and slumped onto the sofa and crumpled into tears. This was her reality – her life – and she didn't want it any more.

An hour later her distress had morphed into fury and with the children occupied by the television she was washing the kitchen floor with vigour. She didn't know what Anna was doing right now but she knew she wouldn't be washing a kitchen floor that looked like the England rugby team had been wrestling in treacle on it. She reckoned Anna was most likely mulling over all the men she had to choose from. She had Liam virtually begging her to take him back, she had a fake relationship with the most gorgeously sexy man on the planet and a mysterious texting admirer. Life wasn't fair. A key turned in the door and her hackles rose.

'Hiya, Sophe,' came Dave's familiarly jolly call. 'You won't believe the day I've had . . .' he began as he flung his coat on the stairs and Sophie met him in the hall, Marigold-clad hands held aloft like a surgeon.

'There's a hook for that,' said Sophie, pointing into the downstairs loo. She cringed at the thought of what she'd found in there earlier.

Dave twitched before giving her a fleeting kiss on the cheek. 'You okay?'

'I'm a bit plucked off to be honest. Did you not notice the state of the house before you went to work?'

Dave threw up his hands. 'Come on, Sophe. I've been a single parent for the past few days. Trying to keep ahead of the devil monkeys is really hard.' He actually looked serious, like he was telling her something she didn't already know.

'One night. It was just one night! I have the terror tots twenty-four seven. How do you think I cope?' She could feel temper bubbling up inside her.

Dave was pulling a questioning face. 'They're at school and nursery most of the day so technically—'

Sophie's exasperation level hitched up a notch. '*Technically* when they're in school and nursery I'm at work, just like you. What do you think I do there? Curl up for a nice sleep?'

'No, but you're better at all this than I am.' His expression changed to conciliatory. 'It goes to show you how much we need you. We're lost without you.' He tried to pull her into a hug and she pushed him away, her expression stony. He wasn't going to get around her that easily.

'Dinner will be ten minutes.' She could barely say the words for the tightness of her jaw.

'Great, I'm starving. I couldn't get Petal to eat anything while you were away but I think she may have eaten a sock. I couldn't find it anywhere.'

'Fish tank,' said Sophie, and she went to check on the veg.

Anna had been for a run, done all her washing and ironing, caught up on her work emails and now she was very bored. Everyone else had a life and here she was treading water, waiting for what exactly? She had no idea. She knew she wasn't making the most of the gloriously bright sunshine streaming through the flat. She could hear families having fun in the park and she wished she was part of it. It gave her an idea.

'Hiya, Sophie. Have you got plans for this afternoon?'

'There's a football match on, which means Dave is busy.' She huffed her frustration down the phone. 'Me and the kids are going to make and ice cupcakes then we're going on a wildflower hunt.'

Anna raised an eyebrow. 'They don't take much hunting.'

'Ha, ha. We've got spotters' sheets and we're trying to tick off all the wildflowers, which should keep them out of mischief for a while. Why?'

'Can I come too?' asked Anna, feeling as pathetic as she sounded.

'Err, of course. I mean it's not exactly riveting. But I'd love the company.'

'Great. Call for me. I'll bring a picnic.'

Anna needed to be kept busy. She was the sort of person who struggled to relax. She liked her mind to be fully occupied. A quick trip to the local shop and she was making healthy snacks and rustling up homemade hummus.

Sophie knocked as planned and Anna bounded outside with a cool box and a picnic rug. Sophie had the look of the perpetually harassed about her.

'Hiya, kids.' Petal launched herself at Anna, puckering her lips for a kiss, and Anna obliged. Anna gave Arlo a kiss on his forehead and he rubbed it off quickly. 'You okay?' she asked Sophie.

'We made cakes,' she said by way of explanation.

'Ah. With blue icing.'

'How'd you know . . .' began Sophie as Anna fished a lump of blue icing from Sophie's hair and presented it to her.

'Next time you need your kitchen redecorated invite my kids round to make cakes.'

Inside the park was a hive of activity with a group of teenagers playing a game of Frisbee up by the oak trees, a number of families picnicking on the benches and a variety of people and dogs all out enjoying the sunshine. But the park was so large everyone had plenty of space. They walked past the pond where a fisherman was packing up his tackle and a gang of small children were feeding a family of ducks.

They decided on a spot near the children's swings, under the dappled shelter of a large tree, and set out their wares.

'Cupcake!' shouted Arlo.

'Carrot stick,' offered Anna and Arlo screwed up his nose.

Sophie gave him a bottle of bubble mixture and he and Petal began happily making and chasing the bubbles.

'What's up?' asked Sophie, scooping up a dollop of hummus with a celery stick.

Anna took a deep breath, letting the tranquillity of their corner of the park engulf her. She watched Arlo and Petal chasing after bubbles before being distracted by trying to catch the tiny pink blossoms as a breeze tickled the trees. 'I'm off plan and I don't like it.'

She could see this had grabbed Sophie's attention. 'Off plan? I'd love to be free as a bird like you.'

Anna had seized her independence and was settling into life on her own terms but she was still very much outside her comfort zone. 'I don't want to moan but where am I going in life?'

'Wherever the hell you want to. Anna, you need to stop moping and give yourself a shake.' Anna was taken aback. 'I don't mean to be unkind but lots of people would kill to be in your situation with no ties or responsibilities. You could literally do anything you want to.' She pointed a celery stick at Anna. 'Yes, you've had a shock with Liam messing everything up but much better to find out now than eight years and three kids down the road.'

'You're right.' There was possibly a gentler way of saying it but whilst Sophie was blunt she was honest too. Anna narrowed her eyes. Was there another message in there somewhere? 'Are you okay?'

'Arlo! Don't feed duck bread to your sister.' She turned back to Anna. 'I'm on a treadmill and I can't get off but if I stay on it I'll die of exhaustion anyway.'

'Is it really that bad?' asked Anna, watching Petal giggling as she chased after her brother.

'Yes, it is. There's no excitement in my life. When I was younger I was wild and free. I thought that side of me would always be there. But Dave has worn it down. I should have married someone like Hudson.'

'He's off the market for you in more ways than one.'

'I said *like* Hudson. As in a non-gay, free and single version. Someone who makes my insides feel like stirred jelly with one look, who notices if I've made an effort and makes me feel special.' Anna knew what she meant, although she didn't like to admit it. 'Is that too much to ask?'

'No. It's not.' Anna had to agree that on occasion she'd felt the same. Hudson seemed to have that way about him. 'But it doesn't make Dave a bad person because he doesn't do those things. And it doesn't mean he doesn't love you.'

'Okay. Who would you pick? Dave or Hudson? Go on.'

Telling her she'd pick Hudson wasn't going to help. 'At least you have Dave. And he might not be exciting but he is reliable and he loves you. What do I have to come home to? An empty flat and a giant cat who thinks I'm his personal slave.'

'Most men are like that too. There aren't many Hudsons around.' They both sighed. 'You need to get out there and find yourself a non-gay Hudson.'

'It's not that easy when you're handling more baggage than Heathrow on a bank holiday.'

'We all have baggage, Anna. You need to find someone you trust enough to help you unpack.' Sophie's attention was drawn to the children. 'Arlo! What are you doing?'

'Watering the wildflowers,' came his giggled reply.

'Why does he think the world is his urinal?'

Another evening stretched before Anna. She'd enjoyed her afternoon in the park with Sophie and the kids. Although Sophie hadn't totally understood her issues, she had helped her see things from a different perspective and she'd learned the names of more wildflowers than she ever knew existed. After her chaotic, but fun, afternoon, tonight

Anna was particularly lonely. Curled up on the sofa with Maurice she stared into space and stroked him absent-mindedly. Maurice was so chilled out he looked drunk but then it occurred to Anna he was basically getting an all-over body massage and they made her zone out too.

Perhaps it was the contrast after being surrounded by people for a couple of days making her feel alone. It was silly but she was enjoying her fake relationship with Hudson. She liked him as a person but the fake relationship was like a shield, protecting her from her own mutinous thoughts about taking Liam back. Liam had caught her off-guard when he'd told her he still loved her but now he thought Hudson was on the scene hopefully he'd keep a respectful distance. Despite her desire to be a fiercely independent woman perhaps she was one of those people who needed someone else in their life. If that was the case, and it pained her to admit it, she needed to be very clear on what terms she would set out for future relationships. For now, a fake one with a gay man was more than enough.

She checked the television and when a documentary about people falling from holiday balconies came up she quickly switched it over but found nothing interested her. She picked up her book and put it down again and wondered if twenty to nine really was too early to go to bed. The documentary picked at her thoughts. Pandora's box of archived memories was not one Anna wanted to open. Once opened, even a fraction, a wisp of a memory could escape and rapidly snowball into an overwhelming avalanche of guilt, sadness and regret.

Anna's phone pinged and Maurice eyed it with disdain. 'Could it be?' she asked Maurice. Anna jiggled the mass of cat to one side as she reached for it. It was a message from her mystery man.

Hi, A. Did your week get any better? C.

She was smiling as she replied: **Yeah, a bit. You know, when life gives you lemons . . . A.**

. . . pretend they're hand grenades and lob them at whoever is pi**ing you off. C.

Anna laughed out loud and Maurice jumped off her lap and exited via the open window. 'Sorry, Maurice,' she called after him.

Not for the first time she wondered who C really was. Could it be someone she knew, as Sophie had suggested? There had been no texts while she'd been away on the team-building event, which made her think Liam, Hudson and Karl could all be possibilities. She shook the thoughts from her mind. Nonsense. It was just a random stranger – and a nice one too. She'd heard all the warnings but for someone to bother to keep in touch they must have benevolence at their core. She liked the mystery of who it might be. Perhaps someone like her – a little bit adrift in life, searching for an anchor.

She picked up the phone and started typing: **How's the new car? A.**

Car is excellent. Been driving Mum round all day. C.

She was quite surprised he'd admitted that but she really liked that he had. If a man cared for their parents it was always a good sign in her book. Especially as she was close to hers – not everyone understood the bond she had. It had puzzled Liam a few times; in fact she'd thought, on occasion, he'd actually been a bit jealous of their relationship.

She typed: **That's nice**, and then deleted it. Nice – she couldn't say nice. She tried again: **I bet she really appreciates it. A.** She pressed send.

It's the least I can do after all she's done for me and my sister. C.

125

Are you a mummy's boy? ;-) A. She put the winking face because she didn't want to offend him. They'd been messaging for a while now so it seemed okay to tease him a little. She had to wait for the reply.

Totally! Have a good night. C.

You too. A. She was a little disappointed that he'd ended the conversation so quickly.

It was an odd thing to be exchanging messages with someone she didn't know but he was starting to feel less of a stranger. She tapped out another message.

Maybe it's time we got on to first-name terms? I'm Anna. She reread it before pressing the send button. It was only her first name; he could hardly trace her from that alone. She wasn't totally irresponsible.

Her phone pinged back a text: **Hi, Anna, nice to meet you. I'm Connor :-)**

Now she had a name to go with the texts and a picture started to develop further in her mind. She tried to picture someone who didn't look like Ryan Gosling and she got Hudson Jones so she stopped trying. Connor. She liked the name and she was starting to like the idea of him a little bit too because a relationship by text was also a safe one.

Sophie had finally got the children to bed – technically they had just stopped climbing out of bed, which didn't mean they were asleep, but she was still counting it as a victory. She flopped onto the sofa, her face a shade of pink bordering on fuchsia and glowing with a sheen of sweat. Dave was playing his latest war game on the telly. Sophie watched it for a bit; bullets rained down on some sinister unshaven character. She let out a deep sigh and mentally prepared a list of things she still had to do. She decided she'd tackle the ironing first before it completely engulfed the utility room and they all had to go naked. She shut her eyes for a moment.

'Mummy. I need a drink!' called Arlo from upstairs. Sophie didn't move. She opened one eye to see Dave's reaction. Arlo called again. At last Dave speed-glanced in her direction, his thumbs still launching an onscreen attack.

'You okay?' he said, his eyes now back on the screen.

She studied him. His mid-brown hair was in need of a cut. His work shirt was open at the collar and his tie hung loose around it.

'I'm tired,' she said. It was more than that but she couldn't put it into words.

'You want me to get Arlo a drink?' asked Dave.

Why did he have to ask her? Why couldn't he just go and get it? She needed him to take the responsibility away from her sometimes. 'Yes, please.'

'Okay. Just let me finish this level.'

Sophie blinked. He was unbelievable. She waited for a moment and Dave continued to play. She silently stood up, got a beaker of water from the kitchen and went to settle Arlo. Afterwards she would take her frustration out on the ironing. She didn't expect to hear anything further from Dave.

Next morning Sophie feared she was going to be late for work. She'd slept through her alarm and overlooked Dave waking her up twice. She was exhausted. It was partly due to the team event, and the sort-out of the whole house that had followed but mainly it was the pregnancy. Each time she was pregnant she went through periods of extreme tiredness, where she could easily sit down wherever she was and go straight to sleep. When she was pregnant with Arlo she'd fallen asleep trying on shoes in Sainsbury's. Today was going to be one of those days. She'd almost nodded off in the shower.

She halted in the doorway and surveyed the kitchen. She had left it clean and tidy – pristine white cupboards had been washed down, the worktops had gleamed and the slate floor had been scrubbed and disinfected. Today it should have come with a warning and probably a welder's helmet and some industrial ear protectors.

Sophie believed a special circle of hell should be reserved for parents who put kazoos in party bags. Arlo was simultaneously playing a kazoo whilst tipping up a large container whooshing milk into an empty bowl, although his cereal was liberally scattered across the worktop and she heard it crunch underfoot, as a harassed Dave frantically searched the room for something whilst his coffee sloshed out of his travel cup. He was also trying to shrug his shoulder into his suit jacket. Petal was shouting happily in her high chair as she mashed a banana into oblivion, and Sophie watched as Petal studied the resulting goo on her chubby hands. Apparently she'd decided it would make excellent hair gel and started running it through her fine baby hair, making it stick up like she'd encountered a high voltage. Sophie took a deep breath and went in.

'Stoooooop!' she yelled and Petal's bottom lip started to wobble. Sophie quickly sponged her hands clean and released her from the high chair. 'I am not sorting this out.' She glared at Dave in challenge.

'I'll sort it when I get home,' said Dave, giving her a furtive glance. He pulled a folder from under Arlo's Lego box and headed for the door.

'No, Dave. I need to leave now and I'm not facing a shizzel tip like this again. The thought of it'll wind me up all day.'

'But I have to go too.' He checked the kitchen clock.

Sophie shook her head. It was time she made a stand. '*I'm* leaving now. This needs clearing up. The stuff from last night's bolognaise needs to go in the dishwasher, your daughter needs taking to nursery and your son needs to be dropped off at school.'

Dave opened and closed his mouth and she pictured ramming a Peppa Pig sock in there. Maybe Petal had thought the same. Sophie didn't wait for him to reply. She thrust Petal into his arms, crunched across the cereal-strewn floor and out to freedom. It felt surprisingly good.

Chapter Fourteen

Anna found herself in one of those meetings where despite a couple of emails and an agenda, you're still not entirely sure why you're there. Hudson had very smartly ducked out of this one saying they didn't both need to attend. As the meeting progressed she began to wonder why any of them were there. She checked her watch and glanced over at Sophie who, every so often, seemed to be ticking something off on the pad on her lap. Sophie angled the page for Anna to see she was playing Bullshit Bingo and only needed 'Moving goal posts' and 'Circle back' for a full house.

Anna shook her head and tried to tune back in to the meeting. 'Can I raise one point? We don't want to reinvent the wheel here,' said Roberta, and a slightly indiscreet fist pump from Karl told her he'd beaten Sophie to the Bullshit Bingo full house. This proved to be the high point of the meeting. Another hour of my life I'm never getting back, thought Anna. After the meeting Sophie beckoned for Anna and Karl to stay in the room.

Sophie turned to Karl. 'I wanted you to know before I tell everyone else – I'm pregnant.' She said it like she was breaking bad news.

'Shit, is it mine?' asked Karl, his face serious. Anna's eyebrows darted up involuntarily.

'Karl. Stop being an idiot,' said Sophie. She shook her head at Anna to indicate there was never any possibility of this.

'Sure?' said Karl, giving a thinking pout. 'Because I'm pretty potent, you know. Rubbing up against me in a lift could be all it takes.'

'I think you're okay. I won't be after you for maintenance.'

'Anyway. Congratulations on not being fat,' he said, opening his arms for a faux hug and air kiss. 'I was wondering how Dave got you into bed but I bet it's a piece of cake.' He mimed chomping on a slice of cake and luring Sophie with it. She thumped him, but she was smiling.

'I'm going to tell Roberta and I thought I'd also float the idea of a different working hours pattern when I come back after maternity leave. I want to do five days in four. Do you think it's doable?' Sophie was looking between Karl and Anna.

Anna was pulling a face. These sorts of things always seemed like a good idea on paper but often the person ended up doing more hours overall because nobody else could get their head around when they were and weren't working. 'You'd need to be really strict about your day off but I think it's workable in a role like yours,' she said.

Karl seemed to ponder the question for longer. 'Five days of bugger all in four seems very doable to me.'

'Aerosol,' said Sophie.

'Doesn't Steph in the product team do something similar?' asked Anna.

'Yes. Have you noticed she's lost loads of weight?' said Sophie, with admiration.

'Really?' queried Karl. 'She still has an arse like a pair of space hoppers.'

'You are such a snarky cow,' said Sophie, getting up to leave.

'That's the nicest thing you've ever said to me,' said Karl, wiping away an imaginary tear and following her.

Roberta was ranting her way through the office and they all stood back out of the way. Priya was following in her wake, trying to write on a pad and keep up with a furious-looking Roberta at the same time.

'She makes an impact doesn't she?' said Anna, observing everyone in the open office trying to shrink as Roberta passed.

'Yeah, like a fly on a windscreen,' said Karl.

Sophie swallowed hard. 'Perhaps I'll catch her later.' They all hurried in the opposite direction.

Almost before Sophie had opened her front door she could smell it – the overwhelming stink of garlic. What on earth had Dave been cooking? Then she laughed at herself because when did Dave ever cook? She became like a demented sniffer dog trying to identify the source of the stench. It was a difficult task because the whole house reeked of the stuff. A few steps upstairs told her she was heading in the wrong direction and like the child catcher she turned and crept back downstairs sniffing the air as she tried to follow the garlic trail. Entering the kitchen, it became apparent she was nearing the end of her quest. The pong level had shot past maximum and was off the scale. She held her nose as she rummaged in cupboards and drawers.

At last she flung open the dishwasher, which gave a final killer blow to her nostrils. It started to make her eyes water too. This was the problem. Sophie held her breath and rummaged at high speed until she found the garlic press. She opened it a fraction to reveal the remains of at least two plump garlic cloves that Dave had omitted to remove before merrily chucking the press in the dishwasher where it had been liberally jet washed with hot water. She ran to the back door, turned the key and flung the whole thing into the garden. She took a lungful of fresh air.

'Fudging, bollarding, Arsene Wenger, Dave, you total bumfuzzle!' She felt better for the tirade.

'Hello?' said a tentative female voice from the other side of the fence.

Frigging brilliant, thought Sophie. Now was exactly the moment she didn't want to meet the new neighbours.

Anna spent the evening working on her laptop and was about to turn in when her phone flashed up a text. It was Sophie and she needed to vent so Anna called her.

'You won't believe what he's done now?'

Anna didn't need to ask who; Sophie reserved a special tone for all things Dave-cock-up-related. 'Go, on.'

'He had one thing to do today. *One thing.* He had to take his children to nursery and school. That was it. And did he manage it?'

'I'm guessing not.'

'You guessed right. Because this is mother puffin Dave we're talking about. Arlo has just informed me that Daddy took them to work today. Took them to work! And what's more because Petal fell asleep and he'd let Arlo play on his iPad they were both quiet so he didn't realise until the car alarm went off, with my kids inside!'

It was difficult to know what to say. 'Good job he has a car alarm.'

'Exactly, although their poor eardrums. I only found out because Arlo came home with a slip from school saying he'd been complaining of a headache.'

'Do you want me to come round?' Anna shuffled upright on the sofa. She could do with someone to talk to.

'No, the place smells like a garlic canning factory but that's another story. But thank you. I feel better already having had a rant.'

'It's what I'm here for.'

'See you tomorrow,' said Sophie. 'No, Arlo, you can't sleep in your pirate costume . . .' The phone disconnected.

'Night,' said Anna anyway and put the phone down next to her.

Anna's phone pinged with another text and she snatched it up. She tried to ignore the little bubble of unease at how keen she was to see if the message was from Connor. She was starting to really enjoy their brief exchanges. It was a little man fix without all the other complications. She was quite disappointed to see the message was from Dave.

Any ideas for Sophe's birthday?

It's in 2 days. Please tell me you have something planned. A x.

Nope. I was thinking perfume?

He was a lovely guy but he really was a grade A numpty. Here was an ideal opportunity to shine and what would he do? He would buy her whatever the John Lewis fragrance counter assistant recommended – as usual – and Sophie would add it to the ever-growing collection of perfumes she didn't wear, a collection that was already taking over the bathroom cabinet. Anna knew Sophie was a Dior girl, which was unlikely to change. She texted back.

If you get perfume only get Dior. She really wants an Orla Kiely washbag, so that could be a nice surprise. Or I could babysit while you two have a date night?

Anna winced a little when she pressed send. She really hoped he went for the washbag because those kids were full-on and an evening alone with them always filled her with terror.

You're a star. Date night it is.

'Bugger,' said Anna, out loud.

Is it the pink Dior she likes?

NO. It's J'adore. The one in the slinky bottle.

Got it. Ta 😄

Anna had bought gifts for Sophie weeks ago and they were wrapped and labelled, ready for her birthday. She had two days to gird her loins ready for babysitting. She really was an excellent friend.

Sophie's birthday dawned and she was thankful it was a weekend. At least she didn't have to get dressed if she didn't want to. She was woken by the sound of something smashing downstairs and she groaned into consciousness. 'You all right?' she hollered.

There was no reply. Sophie sprang awake. 'Dave?' She was already getting out of bed.

'Yeah?' he called back languidly.

'Never mind,' she said, and she flopped back into bed. She waited for a bit and was about to give up on hopes of breakfast in bed when the bedroom door flew open as if by magic and a strange presence started to pull at the duvet until Petal appeared. Her rosy cheeks were covered in what Sophie very much hoped was Marmite.

'Hello, darling,' she said, heaving her onto the bed. Petal blew a raspberry and giggled. 'Yes, I love you too.'

'Tea?' said Dave holding a mug out of Arlo's reach as they both came in. 'Happy birthday,' he added giving her a fleeting kiss on her cheek.

'Thanks.' She took the tea and searched for somewhere safe to place it down but there really wasn't anywhere so she rested it on her stomach.

'Happy birthday, Mummy. We made you a card,' said Arlo, thrusting a brightly coloured piece of folded paper into her face.

Sophie studied it. 'Thank you. This is amazing.' She turned it round the other way. 'Tell me what we have here?' she asked, trying to make sense of the red and black squiggles.

Arlo pointed at each item in turn. 'This is you and this is your blood and this is a ninja who has sliced your head off. Your head is on the back.' He pointed to a red circle.

'That's, um, nice.' She glared at Dave who was smiling proudly. Arlo was obviously paying far more attention than they realised when Dave was playing games on the telly.

'And what's this?' She pointed to what looked like an angry sprout.

'The moon,' he said proudly.

'It's very green.' Sophie couldn't help pointing this out.

Dave looked over her shoulder. 'It's from Zelda,' he said.

'Don't you think—' she began but Dave was already thrusting something under her nose as a distraction. It worked.

'Here,' said Dave. 'We got you this.' He handed her a present and a card.

She was pleased with the perfume he'd got her, and amazed it was the right one. She opened the card and a slip of paper slid out. Sophie read it. Then she read it again and then she swallowed hard.

'A personal trainer. You've got me a personal trainer?'

'Yeah, for after you've had the baby. See? It's for ten sessions and it doesn't start until December.' Dave appeared very pleased with himself.

'You think I need to lose weight?' She scanned her lumpy body. Her baby bump was showing now, nestled amongst the extra weight she'd not managed to shed after the other two.

'You're always complaining about wanting to be thinner. I thought this would help.' He honestly looked like he thought it was a good idea to buy his pregnant wife personal trainer sessions. There was no hope for him. She put the offending details back in the card and closed it.

'Very . . . thoughtful. Thank you. And we're out for a meal tonight . . .' she said, trying to focus on the positive. Anna was a star for saying she'd childmind for the evening. There weren't many people Sophie was happy to leave her children with, partly because of the children's welfare but mainly because she worried about being sued. 'Where are we going?'

'Wherever you fancy!'

Sophie let out a little sigh. He'd not bothered to book anywhere, meaning the chances of getting into a decent local restaurant were unlikely and as she wasn't drinking she'd be driving if they went further afield. 'As long as it's not a pub chain, I don't mind.'

Chapter Fifteen

Anna was quickly remembering the horrors of the last time she'd babysat Sophie's children. Memories of the naked FaceTime call Arlo made to Karen and him eating a Christmas decoration flashed through her mind and she shivered. Thankfully the decoration had been made of bread and glitter but she hadn't known that at the time. No, tonight was going to be different. She had planned what she was going to do and she was going to face it like any other project.

'Here you go, Arlo,' she said, passing him his pizza.

'Don't like pizza,' said Arlo.

'Since when?'

'Since Willoughby Newell said it's made from blood and maggots.' He screwed up his face.

'But we know that's not true. It's tomato and cheese,' she said, pointing at the sauce and topping in turn.

'Tomato? That's worse. Eurgh!' He gave the plate a shove and it flew spectacularly across the table and launched the pizza into the pristine white wall, where it stuck for a moment before making a slow descent down to the floor, leaving a wide tomatoey trail in its wake.

'Arlo,' said Anna sternly, trying hard not to shout. But

while she was recovering his dinner from the floor she heard a slight whooshing noise followed by the sensation of something warm landing on her back. She turned to see the remains of Petal's mushed chicken and broccoli dinner dripping off her shirt and Arlo and Petal in fits of giggles. Great, she thought.

After she'd cleaned everything down and fed Arlo fish fingers and Petal the rest of the mush and some fresh pineapple she'd found in the fridge she settled them down with a game on the rug in the living room. There was nothing within grabbing distance, which made her feel at ease for the first time that evening. It was a card matching game and Arlo even started to help Petal, who seemed to be keener to eat the cards than to turn them over, but once she got the hang of it she was turning them all over and clapping at how clever she was.

Anna had resorted to putting her own clothes in the washing machine on a quick wash in the hope of getting out the food stains and was wearing Sophie's dressing gown, which swamped her and dragged on the ground. She hated being short.

Petal started to turn a card over and stopped as if someone had put her on freeze frame. Her eyes widened and her faced reddened.

'Petal?' asked Anna. 'Are you okay?' The child was rigid.

'O-oh, poo time,' said Arlo.

This is fine, thought Anna. She'd dealt with nappies before; it didn't faze her. 'It's not a problem, Arlo. You stay there and I'll get her a clean nappy and the changing mat.' They were in the cupboard under the stairs. She was literally feet away. What could possibly happen in the few seconds she was away?

Anna walked back in to a poo disaster on a mammoth

scale. Petal had stood up and something pungent and yellow had started to ooze out of the nappy in all directions, like an experiment gone wrong, and Arlo was at that moment undoing the nappy. As the nappy tabs parted the nappy fell onto the pale soft-touch rug and exploded like a firework splattering both the rug and Arlo.

Arlo started to cry. Petal started to cry. And Anna really wanted to cry too. The thought of carrying Petal upstairs to the bathroom seemed fraught with risks. If she were to do the SWOT analysis it would be a definite no go. She thought fast and decided the sink was a better option. She scooped up Petal and took her into the kitchen, trying to ignore the trail of yellow gunk she was leaving behind. 'Come on, Arlo, you come too and we'll clean you up.' Anna did the best job she could to clean Petal with the kitchen sponge one-handed whilst keeping a safe hold on her with the other. Arlo seemed to be doing an okay job of cleaning himself up with handfuls of kitchen roll but at least he'd stopped crying and wasn't creating any additional havoc.

Once there was no more yellow and Petal seemed to have finished, Anna decided the clean-up of the children was complete and dumped the sponge in the kitchen bin. Petal was happier now too and was playing with the dripping tap. Anna looked about her for something to dry her with. There was no sign of a hand towel. Anna opened all the drawers and eventually discovered the tea towels, so grabbed the first two on the pile and wrapped them around Petal. It was only when she noticed the oddly shaped chickens that Anna realised these were Orla Kiely tea towels – Sophie's favourites. Anna gulped as she picked Petal up – and with a reluctant and poo-smeared Arlo in tow, she went upstairs to get him bathed whilst praying that Petal really had finished. She'd deal with the rest of the poo apocalypse later, she thought, averting her eyes from the living room as she went past.

Sophie scanned the Wetherspoons menu for a third time. She wasn't a snob but on the rare occasion they were going out without the children, and it being her birthday, she would have preferred somewhere a bit more special. She was wearing a top she'd bought from Boden the first time she was pregnant, back when they still had spare cash, and had traded in her comfy leggings for her not-so-comfy maternity jeans. At least one of them had made an effort, she thought. She observed the families and wondered how they got their children to sit and eat quietly. She struggled to get hers to do either of those things let alone both together.

'This is nice, hey?' asked Dave, closing his menu. 'I'm having the pie.'

She had one last scan at the standard pub offerings. 'Fish and chips,' she said. She should probably have the salad but it was her birthday after all and now she had personal trainer sessions to look forward to she didn't have to worry. She wondered if Dave's mother had suggested the personal trainer but she didn't want to ask, knowing the answer would cause further issues either way.

'You okay?' asked Dave.

Sophie studied him. Her husband. The man she'd fallen in love with eight years ago. And she tried to conjure up what she felt. Trapped was the word that sprang to mind and it worried her. How had she ended up here at twenty-nine years of age? This had never been the plan. At university she'd had ideas of living abroad, somewhere hot and exotic. She had a degree in Media Studies and she'd expected to be working in television by now, brushing shoulders with the stars of the small screen and perhaps even moving into films. She'd had big dreams, but somehow she'd been diverted from them. Dave had got the offer of a good job in Birmingham so they'd moved from Bedford.

The move seemed to be the point at which her career took a back seat, before it had really even begun. Her job at the radio station didn't pay well anyway and there was nothing similar available when they moved so she took a job at the insurance company just to tide them over. That had been six years ago. She wanted a little bit of the life she read about in the magazines – a little smattering of sparkle on her otherwise dreary grey existence was all she was after. Was it too much to ask?

'Did you want another Appletiser?' Dave asked and she shook her head, keeping her eyes firmly on the menu so he wouldn't notice the tears welling up in them.

Anna woke with a jolt from a nightmare where she was being chased by a poo-covered Petal who had a weird resemblance to Liam. She was overheating and quickly realised it was thanks to Maurice who was asleep on her pillow with half his body wrapped around her head like a furry hat. It was Sunday and she was very glad she was single and without children. One day she hoped to feel differently and she was sure if she ever found the right person to settle down with she'd change her mind but for now not having children was a relief. Thankfully neither Sophie nor Dave had been at all concerned when she'd relayed the story of poo-gate; it seemed par for the course in their house.

She'd not had a chance to talk to Sophie on her own

but as she wasn't waxing lyrical about the evening out, Anna guessed it hadn't gone well. She'd probably get the lowdown in the office tomorrow. Right now, a quiet Sunday stretched out before her and she pondered how to spend it. Anna hated wasting time or even the feeling she wasn't maximising every minute. Ever since university she'd had this drive to squeeze the most she could out of life, because life was a fickle thing and you didn't know when things could change. Anna never wanted to be in a position where she regretted wasting a moment, and she also felt she owed it to her sister to make the most of her life, as Lynsey's had tragically been cut so short.

Sunday lunch with her parents was a given. She saw them pretty much every week and she liked that routine about her life. The option to step back into their home and not have to think about anything was like being wrapped in the softest blanket and cuddled, and some Sundays they actually did that when a good film was on and it was a bit chilly outside. She loved her parents. They'd all gone through hell when Lynsey died. A shared sorrow that had united them.

Her relationship with them had changed over the years as she'd moved from childhood to the messy teenage years, and then flown the nest for university, but her parents had never let her down. She'd seen it happen with friends: big fallings-out, people not speaking, family feuds – but not in her house. The odd cross word and the occasional shouting match, of course, but through everything they had been her constant source of strength.

She went for a long run in the park. She'd left it a little later than she'd have liked and the sun was high in the sky and everywhere was warming up fast. A mother duck let out a squawk of a quack as she ran near the pond and too close to a brood of small ducklings for the mother's liking. She loved the freedom of the park. It was a beautiful oasis of calm and Anna wondered what it must have been like for the people who originally had it as their garden. She imagined having all the space to herself, although she would miss seeing the park regulars. There was a wisp of a man who walked his small terrier, Bosco, who was very friendly. A sleek elegant woman who walked a pair of pugs called Gainsborough and Stubbs – Anna always felt Stubbs had an understandably inferior look about him. A tall chap who had a snooty-looking Saluki named Malika. Anna had never seen a Saluki before, but had got to know Malika and warmed to her – she was nothing like her pointy beak-shaped face implied. She had no idea what any of the owner's names were, only the dogs.

The park was a community within a community. Everyone smiled and spoke to each other, and it was like they all shared a secret and one they all held dear. An exclusive group who treasured the park and the time they spent there.

She loved seeing the swans who took little notice of her, the ducks who seemed to laugh at her as she passed, and the array of small wild birds who made the park their home. She marvelled at the butterflies flitting across the wildflowers and making the most of their short existence. Anna headed for her favourite bench, up towards the largest oak tree. It was a good place to finish her run and would give her some cooling-down time as she walked back to the flat. The other reason it was her favourite bench was because of the inscription on it: 'In Loving Memory of Betty Baldwin – The friendliest dog in the park'.

* * *

Lunch at her parents' was the usual entertaining affair with Mum knowing exactly what was due out of the oven when, and Dad trying to help but mainly getting in the way.

'Terry, be a love and open the wine,' asked Claire, giving Anna her long-suffering look. Terry did as he was told and popped the cork on a bottle of Merlot, which had a long backstory to do with a friend's trip to France.

'Anna?' He gestured with the bottle when he'd reached the end of the provenance of the wine. 'It's bostin'.'

'Err, no thanks, Dad.' She busied herself with having a nose at what was written on their kitchen calendar.

Her father poured out two glasses and passed one to his wife. 'You are drinking again, aren't you, Anna?'

'What?' Anna tried to appear blasé. 'Of course. But I never drink when I'm driving.' She hated lying to her dad but he'd only worry if he thought her life hadn't completely returned to normal. How could she tell him she had a feeling that it never would?

Her dad seemed to accept her explanation. 'Very wise, bab,' he said, giving her a kiss on the top of her head as he passed.

Dinner was perfect as always and the apple turnover for pudding was top notch. Her father sat back and rubbed his extended stomach. 'Feels like Christmas.' He gave it a pat. 'I could play Santa.'

'How are you finding it, living on your own?' asked her mother, looking concerned.

'It's fine, Mum. It's the same as living with Liam but without the disappointment.' It was meant to be a joke but the sympathetic expressions of her parents told her otherwise. 'Honestly, I'm okay. I like it. And I'm not on my own, I've got Maurice and thanks to him sometimes we have a mouse come to stay.'

'That's great,' said Terry, and his wife shot him a look. 'I think everyone should live on their own at some point in their life. It's important to understand who you are as a person and put yourself first without thinking about someone else.'

'You trying to tell me something?' asked Claire, her expression amused.

'No, you're okay for a bit longer. Truth be told, I couldn't face training up another one.'

He got a playful slap before she folded into his arms. This was how they were, play-fighting one moment, cuddling the next. This was what Anna wanted. Why was it so incredibly hard to find?

As if on cue her mother stopped gazing at Terry and turned back to Anna. 'Anyone else in your life we should know about?'

'I'm still saving the pennies in the jar,' added Terry, his reference to the wedding fund he had been amassing.

'No. I'm off men for the foreseeable future. You should spend it on a holiday or something for the two of you. I don't think marriage is something I'll be considering any time soon, if at all . . .' She tried not to look sad although it was how she felt. Sad not just for the wedding day she'd lost but for the lifelong plans she'd imagined would follow. And despite everything, she was harbouring a hollow sensation. Perhaps she wasn't cut out to be single, but she also wasn't ready to be hurt again.

Chapter Sixteen

Anna had commandeered a room as her project head-quarters. She only had it for two weeks but it was better than nothing and it was a chance to get the plan up on the wall and get it into a fit shape before it was committed to a document. She was surrounded by walls of brown paper and multicoloured Post-it Notes; it was very close to her idea of heaven. Every strand of the project was represented by a different colour, every task to be completed had a Post-it Note, and every Post-it Note had an owner. There were still loads more to be added as things became clearer but it was a start, and for now it was very much a fluid plan.

'Have you seen Silvie?' Anna asked Karl, when he put his head around the door.

'I've seen her new haircut. Looks like it's been done with a knife and fork.'

'Harsh,' said Anna.

'Do you think she was going for the Will.i.am look?'

'It reminded me more of a Cornetto,' said Anna.

Karl gave an approving nod at her description. As if on cue Silvie strode past. 'Morning, Silvie. Love the new haircut,' said Karl.

Anna daren't look at Karl. 'Yes, really suits you.' She felt she needed to comment now he had. All she could think about was a giant Cornetto.

Silvie preened herself. 'Thanks. Anna, you look well, I almost didn't recognise you.' Silvie's lipstick-caked mouth made a boomerang shape but it most definitely wasn't a smile. The woman had a gift for delivering an insult in a way it was difficult to challenge. Anna wished Silvie was a Cornetto then she could leave her to melt in the sun.

'Can I catch up with you later about dependencies?' asked Anna.

'I'll have to check my diary. I definitely can't do Friday as I'm needed in the city,' she said, turning to leave. 'Send me an invite for next week and I'll see if I can squeeze you in.'

She was barely out of earshot before Karl was spluttering out his laughter. 'Needed in the city? Who does she think she is – Batman?'

'Who knows. At least someone needs her. Soon there'll be lots of vacancies,' said Anna, with a knowing shift in her eyebrows.

'Don't be pessimistic,' said Sophie, announcing her arrival with a giant yawn as she dropped her bag at her feet and slumped against the wall, making Anna dash over and adjust the dislodged sticky notes.

'We'll be fine. Change is the only constant,' said Karl, with a faux wise expression.

'Has Liam spoken to you yet?' asked Anna. Sophie shook her head and Anna noticed she had a blueberry stuck in her hair. Liam had kept a fairly low profile in their area having chosen to start from the top and work his way down. He always told clients this approach was to live and breathe the ethos of the company and ensure it was the key thread running through any revised structure. But the truth was he liked to establish himself with the senior leaders quickly, work out what they were expecting and then ensure whatever he recommended wasn't a million miles off. It also meant he cemented strong contacts for any repeat work. This was a tried and tested approach. It was of small reassurance to Anna that she knew his modus operandi.

'He's booked something in for Friday,' said Karl, checking his calendar. Sophie moved a couple of Post-it Notes to be later in the timeline. Anna stared at them. 'I might cancel. I might be needed in the city,' Karl said, putting his hands on either side of his hair to make a cone shape.

'You okay?' asked Sophie, tilting her head at Anna.

Anna chewed the inside of her mouth. 'My parents were going on about marriage again. They only see the positives.'

'Ah,' said Sophie. 'It's not all plain sailing. A marriage is like a marathon.'

'Sweaty?' suggested Karl, his face deadpan. Sophie glared at him. 'You grease your nipples first and dress like a chicken?'

'No. It's bloomin' hard work and you deserve a medal,' said Sophie, shaking her head.

Anna laughed and flicked round to see Hudson.

'Sorry to interrupt. I wondered if you'd like to come to a party. It's just a few friends coming over for drinks on Saturday, but you'd all be very welcome.'

Anna was already shaking her head whilst returning the Post-it Notes to their original position. Anna wasn't a fan of parties. Sophie, however, had quickly perked up and was beaming at Hudson. 'Yes, sounds wicked. We'll be there. What should we bring?'

'Just yourselves.' He seemed to look at each of them in turn. 'Bye, now.'

Sophie trotted to the doorway to watch until he was out of sight. 'He has the perkiest bum,' she said, with a sigh.

'I bet the bloke I saw him kissing says that too,' said Karl, focusing on his screen.

'When was this?' asked Anna.

'The other night. He was outside a bar in Hurst Street and some guy literally jumped into his arms and kissed him.'

'Life is cruel and unfair,' said Sophie, finally dragging her eyes away from Hudson's distant form.

'He probably disagrees with you if he's got men throwing themselves at him,' said Anna, reaching over and pulling the blueberry from Sophie's hair and presenting it to her.

'Bumfuzzle,' said Sophie, with feeling.

Another day of pointless meetings was starting to get Anna down and when a meeting popped into her diary from Roberta it made her anxious.

'Hudson, can we have a chat?'

'Sure,' he said, leaning back to stretch and pushing today's fitted shirt to its limits thanks to the chiselled abs underneath. 'When?'

'Now? Roberta's called a meeting with both of us and I don't think we're making much progress. And any minute now Liam is going to pounce on this project and we need to be in a fit state.'

'Come on,' he said, grabbing the jacket off the back of his chair and striding off, making Anna follow him at a trot and instantly resent it. Why did tall men do that? They must know small women in heels can't do striding.

The little coffee shop in the square was busy but they found a couple of high stools and Anna managed to climb up on the third attempt. Hudson bought the coffees and joined her. 'Liam had a quick talk with me this morning.' He blinked so slowly it was like watching slow motion.

'Did you find anything out? When's he looking at the project? Any mention of redundancies? Anything?' Anna found she was nearing the edge of her seat with every question, getting precariously near to falling off. She shuffled her bottom back a safe distance.

'Nope. He wanted to talk about my girlfriend.'

'Your girlfriend?' Anna's voice went up at the end in disbelief. It was only a moment ago that Karl was recounting how he'd seen Hudson kiss another man.

'You, Anna. You're my girlfriend, remember?'

'Ah, yes,' she said and an embarrassed snort of a giggle escaped. 'Of course I am. I don't know how it slipped my mind! So, what did he say?' The last thing she needed was Liam and Hudson bonding over her faults.

'He says I need to be careful because you are on the rebound.' He pointed a finger at her and rolled his lips together thoughtfully. 'He says if I'm not careful you'll break my heart.'

Anna huffed. 'I think he's the heartbreaker. Not me.' She was annoyed with herself for dwelling on what Liam had said about her. Yes, she'd turned him down, but only after he'd unceremoniously dumped her in the first place. She wished it didn't bother her what he thought of her but it did. She was thoroughly fed up with everything. 'Did he ask anything else? Anything useful?'

'He asked if I'd met your parents yet.' Hudson leaned forward and rested his forearms on his thighs. 'Why haven't I met your parents, Anna?' There was a twinkle in his eye.

'Do you think maybe we should drop the girlfriend-boyfriend thing?'

'Are you dumping me? Are *you* dumping *me*?' Hudson's voice had hit drama diva level as he clutched at his heart in a dramatic fashion. 'What did I do wrong? Was it that I showered you with too many gifts? Did I do the ironing wrong? Was it the sex?'

'Hudson!' Anna twisted about her to see who was listening. From the descending hush it would appear most of the coffee shop had now tuned in. 'Stop it,' she said in a stage whisper.

'Promise you won't dump me,' he said, giving a cheeky twitch of a smile. Anna shook her head in exasperation. 'Promise?' His voice faltered as if choked with emotion.

'Bloody hell. Okay. I promise not to dump you.' She lowered her voice. 'I didn't realise fake boyfriends could be so insecure.'

'I bet I'm the best fake boyfriend you've ever had. Aren't I?' He was openly grinning at her and she found it hard not to grin back.

'Yes. Yes, you are.' Sadly, he was probably better than some of her real boyfriends. 'Now, shall we go through what progress I think we've made?' suggested Anna.

'You can if you like.' He slung one arm over the back of his chair. Why was he completely relaxed all of the time? It wasn't natural. Maybe he took drugs.

'When Liam gets to us, he's going to tear this project apart,' said Anna.

Hudson leaned forward and reached his hand out and for a moment she thought he was going to touch her. She watched his approaching hand until it swept up his coffee cup and he took a slurp. 'This is worrying you, isn't it?'

'Yes, and it should be worrying you.' She was feeling a little irritated by his laissez-faire attitude.

He sat up a bit straighter. 'Anna, I want you to be happy . . .'

She missed what he said next due to a thrumming in her ears. This was a phrase she'd heard before. Something her dad said to her at certain points in her life when things had been bleak. Her dad was her go-to person, her rock, and it was impossible to disassociate the phrase.

'Sorry, what?' asked Anna, widening her eyes and trying to focus her attention on Hudson.

Hudson looked a tad confused but repeated himself anyway. 'I want you to be happy on this project. We have established what the overlaps of the two companies merging are, we understand the main phases and we're doing it as quickly as is humanly possible. And more than anything I know you and I can make this happen, together.'

Anna was spellbound. Not only did she feel something akin to calm settling on her, she also had a sensation of steely determination gripping her insides. It now felt like this was actually within her grasp. Within their grasp.

'Thanks, Hudson.'

'Hey. We're a team.' He sipped his coffee. 'We're a great team.'

Lunch with Sophie was a welcome break from a frustrating session with the technology team who were struggling to give even a ballpark figure on costs and timescales. There was only so much teeth sucking she could stand. Anna retold the conversation she'd had with Hudson.

'He's just so . . . together,' said Sophie, inspecting the inside of her sandwich.

'Overconfident would be more accurate. I'll admit he's all right but I'm not going to his party.'

Sophie stopped millimetres away from plunging her teeth into her sandwich. 'Anna, I need to go.'

'I'm not stopping you from going but you know I don't like parties.' Sophie gave a slow blink. 'No, don't give those wounded kitten eyes. You are quite literally a big girl now,' she said, with a warm smile.

'Ha, ha. No, I'm serious. I need to go to the party to see him with his partner.' Anna was sure the exasperation showed on her face. 'Seriously, if I see him loved up with his boyfriend, it will set my hormones at ease and I'll be able to move on.' Sophie took a huge bite of her sandwich.

'Total rubbish. How can seeing him with his boyfriend sort out your hormones?' She sprinkled a sachet of black pepper over the contents of her sandwich.

'Please come with me, Anna. I know it will help at least. And don't tell me you don't secretly want to have a nose at where he lives.'

Anna rolled her eyes. 'Not in the slightest bit nosy actually.' Sophie started with the wobbly lip thing. 'But I care about you so I'll come. Though I'm not stopping long.'

'I love you,' said Sophie before releasing a huge burp. 'Shocking indigestion, nobody tells you about all the downsides of pregnancy – the veins, the cracked nipples or the piles . . .'

'Enough!' Anna didn't fancy her sandwich any more.

Hudson strode out of the office buttoning his suit jacket. He spotted them and came over. Anna could feel Sophie jittering next to her, and however comical Anna thought it was, this crush was very real for Sophie.

'Hi Hudson, did you want to join us?' asked Sophie,

jiggling up to Anna and squishing her to make room on the bench.

'No, it's okay. Sim has decided it's now a costume party. Amazon theme.'

'Ooh, brilliant,' said Sophie. 'I can't wait.'

Anna tried to think of something enthusiastic to say but nothing came to mind. She took a bite of her sandwich. Not only was she now going to a party she didn't want to go to, she'd also have to spend money on a sodding outfit.

'You all right, Anna?' he asked, holding her gaze.

'All good, thanks.'

He smiled and headed off towards the shops. Sophie watched him go until he was out of sight. 'My God, he has the most gorgeous bum,' she said.

'So you keep pointing out.'

Sophie gazed off into the distance. 'Do you ever wish you'd done things differently?'

'Blimey, that's deep,' said Anna. 'And you're not even thirty yet. You have a lifetime ahead of you to do whatever you want to do.'

Sophie looked glum. 'I don't though. I've got the kids and my future's mapped out. You can do whatever you want. You don't have to be somewhere at a certain time; your life isn't dictated to you.'

'Nor is yours. It's just trickier, that's all.'

'Tricky. There's an understatement.'

This wasn't the first time Sophie had sounded really down about things and it was starting to bother Anna. Going to the party with her was the least she could do and hopefully it would give Sophie the boost she needed.

Sophie thought her biggest issue was whether her hastily ordered fancy dress outfit would arrive in time for the party but now she was trying to squeeze herself in to it she realised that wasn't the case. The black cat costume, which she was going to tell everyone was a black jaguar, was not exactly generous when it came to sizing. She'd gone for the large, which was the biggest they did. It shouldn't have been a surprise that she might not be able to fit in it with her ever-growing baby bump – but it was. And why on earth were the zips always at the back? It was by far the most inconvenient place to put them.

She struggled a bit more and realised it was tiring her out. That horrid sense of exhaustion was sweeping over her again. Perhaps if she closed her eyes she could have a little nap . . .

'I want a Viking party for my birthday, Mum. Mum?' Arlo was staring at the strange creature on the bed.

'Okay, sweetie,' she said, as she considered dislocating her shoulder to get to the zip.

'Does that mean I can have one?' He came closer and peered at his struggling mother.

'Let's not make a decision right now. We'd need to think about what would happen at a Viking party.' She had a quick think as she wriggled onto the other side and had a try with her other arm. 'We could make Viking hats with horns on. Pin the sail on the long boat . . .' She caught the look in Arlo's eye. 'What did you have in mind?'

Arlo's face lit up. 'Setting fire to things. Pillaging. That's stealing things—'

'How many times have I said you mustn't take the go-cart from next door's garden?'

'Ahhh, Mum!'

'Do you think you could help Mummy and do this zip up?' Sophie spun round and presented Arlo with her back.

When nothing happened she glanced over her shoulder at him.

Arlo pouted. 'I think you've grown out of it, Mummy,' he said, and he ran from the room.

Chapter Seventeen

Anna and Sophie followed an elephant and a rather slap-dash zebra into the building, and saw Hudson greeting people warmly with his usual charming approach. He was dressed as an 'Englishman on Safari' and greeted them both enthusiastically.

'Stunning outfit, darling,' he said in a faux British accent, and placed a fleeting kiss on Anna's cheek. Anna was impressed when she stepped into Hudson's flat. It was a trendy loft-style apartment right on the canal and it had been converted into a magical jungle-inspired world. Swathes of black fabric had been pinned to the ceiling with tiny fairy lights twinkling like a thousand stars. All around were tubs of huge plants with bright green shiny leaves and weeping ferns, which swayed as people passed.

The apartment had a mezzanine level where a rope trapeze and a number of vines hung down from the upper ceiling. Huge fur throws, which Anna very much hoped were fakes, were draped over the sofa and chairs. In two large dome-shaped birdcages two magnificently coloured macaws preened themselves meticulously. She wondered what Maurice would make of them.

A very large, and somewhat frightening, stuffed jaguar

was in attack mode about to pounce on the coffee table. A huge vivarium about eight foot long took centre stage and inside lay the biggest snake Anna had ever seen.

'Sim!' Hudson called and a slim tanned man appeared at his side. 'This is Anna and Sophie from work. Anna and Sophie, this is Sim, my . . .'

'Lovely to meet you at last. Huds talks about you all the time,' said Sim, before air-kissing Anna's ears. Sophie was beaming at the comment. 'Get these gorgeous creatures some cocktails,' Sim instructed. Hudson shook his head good-naturedly and disappeared behind a large plant.

'Wow, this is amazing,' said Sophie, taking it all in.

Sim was grinning from ear to ear. 'I know, it's fabulous isn't it? It is, isn't it?' he gabbled.

'Sim, it's incredible and your outfit's, um . . . great,' said Sophie.

'You like?' he asked doing the obligatory twirl followed by a well-practised crack of his whip.

Anna wasn't sure if he was some sort of Doctor Livingstone meets Madam Whiplash character but thought it rude to ask. Instead, she nodded and said, 'It really captures the party mood.'

'Thank you. You are the sweetest,' said Sim, beaming at them. There was a knock on the door. 'God knows where Huds has disappeared to. Grab yourself a large glass of jungle punch and go mingle,' said Sim and with another crack of his whip he went to greet some new arrivals.

Quite a few people were there already, and they were standing in their twos and threes still at the very early drinking stage and not quite ready to start talking to strangers. A few people had made an effort, Anna spotted a couple of Carmen Mirandas, three Tarzans in recycled tiger fur throws, lots of beachwear and T-shirts with bright green bug-eyed frogs on them.

'Come on, let's mingle,' said Sophie and she started to talk to a random stranger. After a few minutes Anna tuned out. There was a limit to the amount of enthusiasm she could fake about air travel to a member of cabin crew. Flying was Anna's idea of hell but he didn't need to know that. Sophie on the other hand was enthralled. Anna looked about and spotted Hudson sitting alone on a beanbag. He was absent-mindedly stirring his swizzle stick round and round his empty glass. She picked up a bottle of Bud and made her way through the jungle.

'Hi,' said Anna, handing him the bottle. 'Has your man gone and left you?'

'Yeah, something like that. You look fantastic.'

Anna was very pleased with her outfit given she had left it until the last minute. Whilst she was a little short to pull off the Amazonian heroine Wonder Woman it was a fun outfit and she'd quite liked the film when Roberta had insisted on all the woman in the office going to see it.

'Thanks,' Anna replied as she plonked herself down on the beanbag next to him and instantly regretted it as the stuffing shifted and she found herself squashed up against him with her legs splayed in the air. She hastily hoiked her top back into place and wriggled until she was no longer tipping, and was a respectable distance away.

'Why are you skulking over here and not chatting to people?' Anna gestured to a group of four guys all in camouflage hot pants.

'I don't know most of them. They're mainly Sim's friends . . .'

'But why so glum?' she asked, not satisfied with his

lame explanation of such downtrodden body language from the man who was always reeking confidence in the office.

'I've been running around all day collecting this lot,' he said, gesturing at the party props. 'Sim goes into Vicious Dictator mode when he's stressed so I'm beat. You won't believe how many times I've had to move the goddamn trapeze; we'll have to get a plasterer in afterwards to fix up the ceiling because it had to be bolted into the beam each time.'

They both looked up. 'It's worth it though. It's amazing.'

'What can I say? He's a slave to his party people.' He fiddled with his beer bottle and Anna wished she could find a soft drink. This was a very different Hudson. He seemed vulnerable, unlike the invincible presence she encountered daily at work.

A hoot from the doorway made Anna turn around. 'Look Karl is here!'

They both watched as Karl dressed in a cardboard cut-out of the cover of *Fifty Shades of Grey* made an entrance and Sophie whooped liked she'd downed half the punch bowl.

'Why's he dressed like a book?' asked Anna.

'I'm surprised he hasn't boasted to you already about his ingenious outfit. He's Amazon . . .'

'Dot com,' said Anna, as the penny dropped. 'Right, I get it,' she said, rolling her eyes.

'There was always going to be one,' said Hudson.

'And it was always going to be Karl.'

'I should make some more punch,' said Hudson with a lacklustre smile, and he disappeared to the kitchen. Even her fake boyfriend didn't want to spend time with her. He was different around her tonight. She hadn't thought before but obviously he would have to drop the fake relationship façade in front of Sim. It made her question the relationship she thought they were building. Perhaps it was all a charade.

Anna sidled up to Sophie who was guffawing loudly next to a gorilla and a Māori – were people really this geographically uneducated? she thought. When there was a pause in the guffawing Anna leaned in. 'Please can we go now?'

'No way! We've only been here a few minutes and it's a good party, even if I can't have the proper cocktails.' Sophie waved a cocktail glass complete with umbrella and cherry.

'Umbrellas in cocktails?' Anna pulled a face.

'It's ironic,' said Sophie, sucking hard on the straw and stepping away from the Māori and the gorilla. 'Those two are dealers.'

'Drugs?' said Anna, in a hushed but frantic voice.

'No, you numpty. Foreign currency. They used to work with Hudson in London. I'm gathering background information on him.'

'Being bloody nosy more like.'

'Yes, that too.' She encouraged Anna up the stairs into the kitchen area. 'How amazing is this flat?'

Anna gave a cursory look around. It was classic loft living; on trend and immaculate. 'Yeah, it seems nice.'

Sophie baulked. 'Nice? Have you any idea how much a place like this costs? This kitchen is top of the range and gadget loaded, and the loo is lush too.'

Anna shook her head. 'You've checked out the loo already?'

'Err, pregnant lady,' said Sophie, pointing dramatically to her bump. 'I've been twice.' She grinned and had another straw full of her virgin cocktail. 'Getting in and out of this outfit is a nightmare.'

'Are you cured of the crush yet?' said Anna, checking her watch. Had they really only been there twenty minutes? It felt like at least an hour.

'Nowhere near,' said Sophie, stifling a yawn and she headed after Sim. Anna followed reluctantly. She knew she was being churlish; she could probably enjoy herself if she made the effort to talk to a few individuals.

Anna felt like a spare part as Sim and Sophie discussed the miracle of her pregnancy.

'I'd love to be a daddy,' said Sim. 'I love children. They see the world in such a pure way and squeeze every last drop of fun out of life.'

'You are so right,' said Sophie, ignoring Anna's twitching. Sophie leaned in closer to Sim. 'Would you like to touch the bump?'

'May I?' Sim looked thrilled to be asked. It seemed Sophie had another gay crush.

'Does Hudson want to be a father too?' asked Anna.

'He does eventually but he's focused on carving out this big career for himself first. He's got this thing about being more successful than his father.' Anna was interested but Sim had turned back to Sophie. 'Do you know what sex the baby is?'

'No, we've already got one of each so we don't mind.'

'Ooh, any names?' asked Sim and Anna decided it was a good cue to have another search for a soft drink because once you got Sophie on names, you were there for the long haul. Sophie had obsessed over the names of the first two for the full nine months each time, having decided she wanted something different from the norm but not too different that the child would be picked on. Anna

163

wasn't entirely sure Sophie had been successful in her choices; Petal and Arlo were a bit too out there for her but they were lovely kids and she was very fond of them.

Anna went to fill her glass at the virgin punch bowl and Hudson appeared. 'Let me help you,' he said, expertly ladling the liquid into her glass. 'Are you okay? I know you don't know many people here. Would you like me to introduce you to some?'

It was thoughtful, but she was capable of talking to strangers without his help. She just didn't like parties and she knew it showed. 'No, thanks, I'm coping fine. I've already had an interesting chat with a monkey and a flamingo,' she said with a brief grimace. She wasn't sure what effect she'd been going for but grimace was definitely the result. 'Nice flat.'

'Flat?' He was almost laughing.

'What would you call it?'

'Condo or apartment.'

'Nice condo.' It was hard to say without sounding absurd.

'Thanks. It's only rented but I've let out my place in London to balance it out. Have you seen the view?' He gestured to the large window and started to walk towards it – Anna felt she had to follow.

'It's stunning,' said Anna. It was still Birmingham but with the canal below and the Birmingham skyline lit up you couldn't fail to be a little bit impressed with it. 'Or bostin' as we locals say.'

'It's like a whole new language here. It's different to London. Karl asked me for a kipper tie last week. It took me most of the day to realise he wasn't joking and he meant a cup of tea.' Hudson's accent went all Prince Charles at the end of the sentence and she laughed.

164

'He's doing it to wind you up. He's a coffee drinker.'

'I'm surprised by how much I like Birmingham. I guess it gets under your skin . . .'

'. . . and in your respiratory system,' said Anna. She was fond of Birmingham but people who weren't born there always had a more romantic view of the city. 'It's not New York, though. That's top of my wish list, somewhere I've always wanted to go. It looks so alive. Do you miss New York?'

'Yeah, I do. I didn't think I would but I don't visit as much since . . .'

Anna gestured for him to continue. Hudson took a deep breath. 'Since my father moved back there.'

This didn't make a lot of sense to Anna. She figured if her dad had moved there she'd be going more often not less. 'Things okay between you?'

'He named me Hudson, what do you think?'

She laughed at his joke, but he was trying to lighten the conversation and he'd got Anna intrigued now although she didn't want to push him. 'I think it's a good name.'

There was an excruciatingly long pause. He knocked back his drink in one go before looking Anna in the eye. 'He's recently remarried.' He scanned the room as if expecting someone to call him over and when they didn't he pointed at Anna's glass. 'You sure you don't want something alcoholic? If you don't fancy cocktails there's wine.'

'No, I don't drink.'

'Oh, okay. Sorry, I didn't realise. Is there any particular reason?'

Anna would have preferred to avoid this topic of conversation altogether, but tried to keep her cool. She didn't want to draw attention to something she longed to forget. 'I guess I've seen the damage it can do.'

'Sure, fair enough,' said Hudson. When he came back he steered them over to a wooden bench. 'Shall we take a seat?' he asked. Anna sat down and immediately had to budge up as Hudson sat down next to her and his hip connected with hers.

The music changed and 'Dreams' by The Cranberries started. Both Anna and Hudson looked over their shoulders and Sim was pointing at Hudson and mouthing 'for you'. Anna had almost forgotten Hudson was gay until that moment.

'Have you and Sim lived together long?'

Hudson had a think. 'He moved in just before Christmas. What's that? About six months.'

'Not long then?'

'No, it just feels a lot longer.' He gave a long-suffering look. 'He could have stayed in London but he's had a tough time recently so moving away for a while felt like the right option.'

'And you thought Birmingham was the answer? Blimey, remind me not to upset you.'

Hudson chuckled and they both sipped their drinks. 'He makes friends easily and the community here has been really welcoming. Talking of which, Sophie tells me you've got yourself a stalker?'

'His name's Connor.'

'Have you met him yet or does his restraining order get in the way of that?' She knew he was teasing but he looked more jovial than concerned.

'No. It's just a texting thing. But I am tempted to know more about him.'

'Just be careful.' He picked at the label on the beer bottle.

'It's okay, I'm off men. Apart from fake boyfriends.' There was a glimmer in his eyes.

They watched as the music changed and Sim began pogoing around with someone dressed as a parrot. A couple in lion onesies came to admire the view.

'Is it very wrong of me to judge people by their costume?' said Hudson, his voice hushed. 'I don't mean the quality, you understand . . .'

'You mean whether it fits with the Amazon theme.'

'Precisely,' said Hudson, clinking his bottle unexpectedly against Anna's glass.

Anna leaned a little closer. 'I've been doing the same.' He leaned his shoulder against hers and it felt companionable as they sipped drinks and watched the lights flicker over Birmingham.

'Hudson, I'm sorry I'm late,' said Roberta, as she barrelled over spoiling the moment completely.

'Great outfit, Roberta,' said Hudson, and Anna had to concentrate to avoid doing a Cheshire cat impression.

'Oh, I'm glad you approve,' said Roberta, preening herself in her tiger-print shift dress.

'Let me get you a drink,' said Hudson, getting up and giving Anna a conspiratorial look as he disappeared.

Chapter Eighteen

Anna yawned and checked her watch. She scanned the room for the umpteenth time. There was no sign of Sophie. She feared she had left the party although she knew she wouldn't have done without telling her. Being pregnant frequently zapped Sophie's energy and it often happened without warning. Perhaps she was having a nap somewhere. Sim came over and linked arms with her.

'We need you,' he said, raising his eyebrows.

'Sorry, Sim, I just need to find Sophie then I'm off I'm afraid.'

'I think she's locked herself in the loo.'

'What?' Anna followed Sim out of the main room to the toilet door where Hudson and Roberta were standing looking anxious. She joined them. 'What's happened?'

'Sophie's locked herself in and won't talk to anyone. Does she do this sort of thing often?' asked Roberta, with a frown that made her forehead look like a Klingon's.

'No, never,' said Anna. 'Has someone upset her?' she asked, looking from Roberta to Hudson and back again. They both shook their heads.

'She said she was going to the loo about ten minutes

ago and we've not seen her since,' said Hudson, his tone a lot softer than Roberta's.

Anna knocked tentatively on the door. 'Hi hun, it's me, are you okay?'

'You won't get a reply,' said Roberta and Anna gave her a withering look.

'There's a window, isn't there?' asked Anna.

Sim took a sharp intake of breath. 'Do you think she's escaped?'

Hudson ignored Sim's dramatics. 'There is a window but it's too small to climb through,' said Hudson. 'Especially . . .' He made a baby bump motion.

'But we could look in and check she's okay,' suggested Anna. Hudson didn't answer but went straight into action mode. He strode over to the bench seat, ordered the snogging lions off it and headed for the balcony with Roberta, Sim and Anna all trailing behind him. The window was open a fraction, which was enough for Hudson to push his fingers through and carefully open it wider and see inside. Hudson froze for a moment and then turned to Anna.

'I think you need to handle this,' he said, offering a hand to help her up onto the bench. A million things rushed through Anna's head but none of them matched the sight she saw through the window.

Sophie was curled in a ball, with her black cat outfit and pants around her ankles as if she had slumped off the toilet – but she was sound asleep.

'Is she all right?' asked Roberta, trying to get onto the bench.

'She's completely fine. No emergency. She's just um . . . asleep. Sim, could you get Roberta another drink please,' said Hudson, indicating the need for speed with his twitching eyebrows. Sim steered a reluctant Roberta away.

'Bloody hell, Sophie,' said Anna, through the window but she didn't respond.

'I'll unlock the door with a screwdriver,' said Hudson, pulling the window closed. 'Then I'm handing over to you.'

'I get all the good jobs,' said Anna and a little of their rapport seemed to have returned.

Anna opened one eye. It was very early on a Sunday morning after a rather late night and she was about to drift back to sleep when she heard someone open her bedroom door. Half expecting to see a mad axe murderer she sat bolt upright.

'Now aren't you a pretty picture?' said Sophie, shuffling in with two mugs of coffee.

Anna squinted. 'What? Why?'

'I have a key remember?' Sophie swapped the mugs to one hand to pull the key from her pocket as evidence.

'Yes, but it's . . .' Anna checked the clock. 'Eight o'clock on a Sunday morning.'

'I wanted to say thanks for sorting me out last night and to check a few things.' Sophie sat on the end of Anna's bed and bit her lip. Anna reached for one of the coffee mugs but Sophie was staring at her expecting something first.

'Ah,' said Anna, realising what she was asking. 'You want to know more about the whole falling asleep in the loo thing. You're okay, I covered up your dignity. Well, I pulled your pants back up.'

Sophie straightened her shoulders and lifted her chin. 'Thank goodness nobody saw my fairy.'

Anna winced. 'Why do you call it that?' She waved a

hand and pointed at the coffee mug – she definitely needed it now.

'Sorry, it's the kids. You forget.' Sophie finally handed her a mug.

'But of all the things to call it.' Anna took a swig of coffee and savoured the rich flavour. Sophie had put the machine on – her friend knew her well.

'Vagina is too medical and you can't say Lady Garden or muff with the kids or they'll repeat it,' mused Sophie, concentrating hard.

'What's wrong with bottom?'

'Then it all gets confusing – front bottom, back bottom?'

Anna instantly wished she hadn't started the discussion. 'And calling it a fairy is less confusing?'

'Yes. Apart from Christmas time when it's a bit weird. Dave is always like a child when it's time to put the fairy on the top of the tree. And don't get us started with fairy lights.'

They giggled together and sipped their coffees.

'So, I have nothing to worry about at the office tomorrow then? Nothing to think up an elaborate explanation for?' asked Sophie, obviously seeking reassurance.

Anna stopped with the mug at her lips. 'We think you fell asleep on the loo after having a wee and then sort of slumped to the floor.'

'We?' said Sophie in a very small voice as Maurice landed on the bed with a thump.

'Me, Sim, Hudson and Roberta.' Anna didn't look up as she rushed the names out.

'OhMyGod! How on earth do I show my face at work?'

'Don't worry, it'll be fine . . . it wasn't your face they were looking at.'

Sophie put down her coffee and slumped back on the

bed. 'Kill me now.' She sighed heavily. 'I could actually go back to sleep right now. I am so tired I might fall asleep walking home.'

Anna threw a pillow at her face and laughed. 'Don't be dramatic.' Maurice walked over Sophie as if she weren't there and flopped down next to her, lifted a leg and proceeded to wash his bum.

'If you dare make a comparison between me and him, I'll thump you,' said Sophie, pointing at the cat.

'My lips are sealed,' said Anna and she tried hard to hide her grin.

Anna's phone beeped with a message from Connor.

Hi, Anna, I love the texting thing we have going on and I wondered if you fancy meeting sometime? C.

Anna blinked at the screen. A frisson of excitement rippled through her at the thought of meeting her mystery man. She passed the phone to Sophie and she sat up. 'Are you going to meet him?' Sophie's eyes were wide.

'I don't think I should. He could be a nutter.'

'Or he could be totally gorgeous. What is this? Is it destiny knocking and you can't be bothered to open the door?'

'I would like to know who he is. He seems nice from his texts.'

'This could be the best fairy tale ever. A texting error leads to your HEA.'

'HEA?' queried Anna, taking back her phone.

'Happily Ever After,' explained Sophie. 'You read this sort of thing in magazines. It does happen you know. People meet the love of their life by pure chance. I think you should at least check it out.'

'I don't know.' Anna ran her bottom lip through her teeth. She'd reply later when she'd made a firm decision and thought up a suitable response.

'I would. Don't have any regrets, Anna. There's loads I wish I'd done before I settled down. Don't be like me.' Anna wanted to question her further. 'Anyway, hark at me going on. I need to get back to the rabble. I'll leave you in peace. Are you still on for a pub lunch?'

Anna had almost forgotten. 'Yes, I'll take my car because I'll pop over to see Mum and Dad afterwards.' As if on cue her phone sprang to life. 'It's them,' she said, pointing at the screen.

'Okay. See you later,' said Sophie and she disappeared.

'Hi Anna,' said her mother. 'How are things?'

'Good, thanks. How about you and Dad?'

'We're fine. Your father has finished boarding the loft. How's it going with Liam?'

Anna pushed herself up straight. 'How do you mean?' She could tell there was something in her mother's voice.

'I just wondered, what with you working together . . .'

'Mum?' said Anna. She knew there was more to the conversation than a casual enquiry.

Her mother sighed. 'I had a coffee with Liam's mother this week and she said he's split up with his girlfriend and . . .'

'Tabitha?'

'Yes, I think that was her name. And she said he was loving working with you.'

Anna screwed up her face. 'I've barely seen him.'

'Oh.' She sounded genuinely surprised. 'She seemed to think you and Liam might be . . .' She left the sentence open.

'She's got it wrong. There's no me and Liam on any level.' Anna was shaking her head. Maurice opened one eye as if to question her actions and she stopped.

'I'm glad I checked.' Her mother's tone had changed to

perfunctory but Anna sensed some disappointment hidden there. Anna wondered how she, herself, was feeling. Did this change things? Liam was single again and she couldn't help wonder if it had anything to do with her, then she gave herself a shake for being immodest.

The conversation drifted off to general updates and talk of her mother's plans for their pearl wedding anniversary, which was in December. As they had gone on a holiday for their twenty-fifth anniversary they'd decided they wanted a big party for their thirtieth. When Anna ended the call she felt a bit wrong-footed by what her mother had said. She knew she meant well and that she worried about her being on her own. So Anna picked up her phone and replied to Connor.

Yes. Let's meet.

She typed and pressed send before she started to think too much about it.

Sophie was mulling over the previous night as she walked up her front steps. She'd really enjoyed herself, and it had felt like a lifetime since she'd been to a party that didn't involve a ball-pit. It had been fun and it almost saddened her to think she had no idea how long it would be before she felt like that again. She rubbed her bump and sighed as she turned her key in the door. The house was eerily quiet.

'Hiya,' she called.

'Hi,' said Dave, from the living room. 'Did you find out what you wanted to know?'

Sophie went through and flopped onto the sofa. 'My bum will be headline gossip in the office tomorrow, for sure.'

Dave tittered. 'Oh well.' Something exploded on the screen and Dave jerked his head back in frustration.

174

Sophie wasn't sure whether to be pleased that he wasn't bothered about her exposing herself or offended. She glanced about and listened. 'Dave, where are the kids?'

'Huh? Playing upstairs I expect.'

'You expect?' Sophie was already on her feet. 'Arlo,' she called as she took the stairs two at a time and then her body reminded her she was pregnant and she went back to one at a time, as fast as she could. 'Arlo!' She scanned each bedroom and the bathroom but there was no sign of them. 'Wholly crab.'

'Dave! The kids aren't upstairs.' She wished she could move quicker. She was already panting as she reached the bottom of the stairs. 'Dave!' It came out as a screech.

'Okay,' he said, sounding frustrated. 'I'll help you find them. They're probably playing hide-and-seek.'

Sophie was close to whacking him but she couldn't spare the moment's delay. She had to find her children right this second. Dave set about checking cupboards and Sophie ran out into the garden. 'Ar-looooooo!'

She waited and listened. Nothing. Only the sounds of people in the park behind. She ran down the garden, struggled with the bolt on the gate in her haste and when it finally opened she flung herself into the park beyond. She tried to remember what the children were wearing. She came to a halt and scanned the park. It had never looked this huge before and she couldn't see all of it from her vantage point, not to mention all the nooks and crannies it had. The wildflower meadows were in full swing and offered heaps of hiding places. She stared at the lake and a sick sensation washed over her. She couldn't see them but began running again anyway. Her mind was like a pinball. Arlo liked climbing trees; maybe he was in one of the many large oaks. Petal loved chasing the ducks;

perhaps she had gone towards the pond. A sob caught in her throat and she realised she was crying. She blinked the tears away and tried to focus.

'Sophie!' shouted Dave. Sophie turned around so fast she almost fell over. He was standing at their gate waving. A big smile on his face and Petal in his arms. He beckoned her back but she no longer had the energy. Her legs crumpled and she flopped onto the spongy grass and cried with relief.

When things were a little calmer and the children were occupied with Play-Doh Sophie took Dave by the arm and marched him into the utility room. 'What the fuzz did you think you were doing leaving our kids on their own?'

'Calm down, Sophe. They were playing in a wardrobe, that's all.'

'But *you* didn't know that, Dave. They could have been anywhere.'

'I knew they were in the house.' His tone was chilled and it irritated her beyond reason.

'Don't lie. You had no idea where they were!' She knew she was shouting but she wanted a reaction from Dave. Something other than his easy-going, no worries approach.

He straightened his back. 'I knew they couldn't get out of the garden. You are blowing this up out of proportion like you always do.'

Sophie's eyes pinged wide. 'Because I'm always stunned by how plugging useless you are.'

'If I'm so useless, find someone else who'll put up with your shit!'

Sophie was shocked. Dave rarely lost his cool. 'Don't swear, the kids might hear you. And what sh . . .' She couldn't bring herself to say it. 'What do you mean exactly?' She was boiling mad that he'd turned this back on her when he was so clearly in the wrong.

'Nothing's ever good enough. You're out all the time—'

'What?' Sophie could barely believe her ears. 'Last night is the first time in months I've been out.'

'Err, what about the team jolly? It's fine to leave the kids with me then isn't it?'

'You need the practice.'

Dave's expression changed. 'Have you got someone else?'

You could have knocked Sophie over with a paperclip. 'What?' She couldn't stop a squeak of a laugh escaping. As if she had time for someone else.

Dave was frowning hard, his eyes boring into hers. 'You heard. Have you got someone else? Is that what this is all about? Are you building up to leaving me and want an excuse to take the kids?'

Sophie shook her head. She wasn't going to have this stupid conversation. 'You are an idiot, Dave.' She opened the utility room door and stormed out.

Chapter Nineteen

It was rare for Anna to not be at home for Sunday lunch. Anna wasn't even sure how she had slipped into the Sunday lunch at her parents' routine. However, this week she had arranged to meet up with Dave and Sophie at a local pub to celebrate Dave's upcoming birthday.

It was a beautiful summer's day: the sun high in the sky, not a cloud to be seen and hot enough to anticipate the headlines of the next day's newspapers. Anna parked up, made her way through the crowded bar and into the sunshine-filled garden at the back where she spotted Arlo digging a hole in a flower bed with his hands. Dave and Sophie appeared to be deep in conversation and shut up as soon as she approached.

'Happy birthday eve, eve,' she said, handing over a card, Dave gave her a kiss in return and she joined them at a picnic table.

A mud-covered Arlo appeared. 'Daddy can't open any cards or presents until his birthday,' said Arlo before running off towards the children's play area. Petal jabbed her stumpy fingers at her father's iPhone.

'How was last night?' asked Dave, looking at Anna.

'I enjoyed myself,' said Anna, almost surprised by her admission.

'I told you, the party was fabulous. They've got a very trendy place, and they know how to enjoy themselves. Anyway, happy birthday, Dave,' said Sophie, clinking glasses. Arlo promptly knocked over his orange juice.

After a nice meal Dave went to get another round of drinks, whilst Sophie settled Petal down for a nap in her buggy. Arlo was playing Vikings in the play area, which seemed to consist of him running around wildly shouting at other children and declaring a victory if he made any of them cry.

'Dave got cross earlier. I've not seen him like it before.'

'It's school holidays – they're always stressful.'

'It's more than that. He accused me of having an affair.' She chewed on the inside of her mouth.

Arlo charged over brandishing Petal's teddy, which he'd pillaged, and Anna had to raise her voice to be heard. 'Do you not think you should explain to Dave why you have feelings for another man?'

'But I don't know why I have them.' Sophie's eyes brimmed with tears. Sophie turned to Arlo. 'Give it back to her!'

'But I'm a Viking!'

'Then swap it for your sword,' suggested Sophie, her jaw tense. Arlo thrust the teddy back at Petal and proceeded to run around the picnic bench squealing.

Sophie turned back to Anna. 'I think about Hudson all the time.' She was almost at shouting volume to be heard over the kids. 'It's messing with my head.'

Anna took her hand. 'I know it is. But I think you need to be honest with Dave.'

'How can I? He'll never understand. I don't even under-stand it myself. How do I tell him I'm obsessed with Hudson? It's such a mess.'

Anna squeezed Sophie's hand. 'It'll be okay.' She wasn't sure if that was true but she really hoped it was. They watched Arlo herd the other children around the play area for a bit. Sophie's phone pinged a message and she glanced at the screen.

Sophie frowned as she read the message, then her expression changed. 'Wholly crab!' said Sophie, fumbling with her phone. She spun around and frantically scanned the pub garden. She pointed at a tray with drinks appearing to match their order on the table behind them. 'Dave must have overheard us.'

'What?' Anna took the phone from Sophie and read the message – **I knew there was someone else. I'm going to sort this out man to man. You stay with the kids. I love you. D x.**

'We need to warn Hudson,' said Anna, pulling out her own phone. Hudson's phone went straight to voicemail. 'Okay. Plan B. Let's go to Hudson's apartment.'

'But we don't know that's where Dave is.' Sophie was gathering up the kids' stuff at high speed and throwing it all into the pushchair.

'No, but where would Dave go if he was going after Hudson?'

'His apartment,' agreed Sophie.

'Unless he doesn't have the address.' Anna felt a small glimmer of hope.

'Aerosols.' Sophie stopped and bit her lip. 'I gave him the address in case there was a problem with the kids and he needed to come and get me early from the party.'

'Call Dave and try and stop him,' said Anna, almost falling over as she extricated herself from the picnic bench. 'Otherwise we'd better get there before he does.'

* * *

180

As Anna pulled into Hudson's road they spotted Dave's car and she moored hers near the kerb where she hoped it wouldn't incur a fine. They both leaped from the vehicle and ran towards the apartment building, then both suddenly stopped and ran back to the children, who were still in the car. They were both asleep.

'Can we leave them?' asked Anna.

Sophie turned around and they watched Dave pull Hudson out of the lobby of the apartments. 'Yes,' said Sophie in a strangled voice. 'We can see them from over there. Come on!'

They raced over to where Dave now had hold of Hudson by his T-shirt and was pinning him against the main door to the apartments.

Hudson had his hands up in self-defence but didn't appear to be retaliating.

'Dave!' shouted Sophie but he didn't respond.

'Hey, now calm down, fella,' said Hudson, looking quite confused by the position he found himself in.

'I'll calm down when you leave my wife alone.' Dave was right in Hudson's face.

Hudson lifted an eyebrow. 'What?' He looked past Dave's angry face to Sophie who was racing towards them panting like a carthorse.

'Get off him, Dave.' Sophie pulled Dave off Hudson. 'He's gay, you idiot.' She was flushing scarlet.

'Err, no I'm not,' said Hudson in a small voice. All heads turned quizzically in his direction, including Anna's.

'B . . . but you're with Sim?' said Sophie, pushing Dave right out of the way.

Hudson shook his head. 'Sim's my lodger.'

'Karl saw you in a gay bar and you kissed someone,'

said Anna. Was Hudson in denial? He was shaking his head. 'About a week ago on Hurst Street,' she added.

Hudson gave a small frown as if trying to recall the situation. 'You know Sim got a new job?' The group shook their heads in unison. 'Well, anyway. They rang here and left a message. I tried his mobile but the battery is garbage so I went out to find him. That was me telling him. For the record, he kissed me, not the other way around. And it was a theatrical smacker – nothing serious.'

Anna opened her mouth and then closed it again. She had no idea what to say. She may have doubted it at first but she'd got used to him being gay. This was very confusing.

'But you wear that pink shirt,' said Sophie, her expression as if she was trying to work out all the numbers of pi. 'It's very well fitted.' She moved her hands in front of her as if smoothing them over his outline.

'Christmas present from Sim. I did wonder if it was a bit much,' said Hudson, with a brief twitch at the corners of his mouth.

Hudson turned to Anna and she felt she needed to add a justification for her beliefs too. '*You've Got Mail* is your favourite film.' She raised an eyebrow, but the tone of her voice gave away that she knew it wasn't the best proof.

Hudson laughed loudly. 'It's my mum's favourite film too. We watched it a lot after Dad left. I mean A LOT. Okay?'

'Okay,' said Anna, trying to pull all the evidence to mind.

'Any other pieces of this puzzle I should know about, or have I done enough to convince you I'm not gay?' He was facing her square on and embarrassment swept over her.

'Well, yeah. But in our defence it was mainly because Sim told Roberta you were in a relationship.'

Hudson gave a dramatic eye roll. 'Oh man. He's done this before. He thinks he's being helpful if there's a lady that, shall we say, takes a liking to me. He said Roberta was giving off those vibes.'

Anna was trying to understand how this changed things. If this changed anything at all. At first she had settled into an uneasy alliance with Hudson but more recently they seemed to really connect with each other. Anna knew she had let down some of her barriers and she felt Hudson had too. But this somehow put a very different lens on their relationship.

Dave was frowning hard with the effort of keeping up with the discussion. He suddenly joined the conversation. 'So you're not gay?' He pointed a finger at Hudson.

'I am not gay,' Hudson repeated, with a small shake of his head.

Dave took a step closer to him. 'Are sleeping with my wife?'

'No!' chorused Sophie, Anna and Hudson together.

'Well then I'm totally confused,' said Dave, rubbing his hands over his face. 'Is anyone sleeping with my wife?'

'No!' chorused Anna and Hudson again.

'And you're definitely not, after this,' said Sophie, barely able to get her words out through clenched teeth. The red blotches on her neck looked angry, to match the rest of her.

'Dave!' said Sophie, giving Dave a shove to make him start walking. 'You are such a plucking embarrassment. Come on, the kids are waiting.' Dave started walking but Sophie turned back.

'I'm so sorry,' she said, looking longingly at Hudson.

'It's okay,' he said, with a one-shouldered shrug.

'No, it's not,' said Sophie, appearing more sad than angry now as she trooped after Dave.

Anna turned to face Hudson and instantly felt self-conscious. 'I'm sorry if I've offended you?'

'Not at all.' Hudson was grinning. 'I'm flattered. Sim and I got mistaken for a couple once before and he thought it was hilarious. I'm not his type – he likes them beefier.'

Anna would have queried Sim not classing Hudson as beefy but she was overcome with embarrassment and there was something else mixed in, making her feel awkward.

'I'd better go,' she said, pointing in the direction of the car unnecessarily.

'You could come in for a coffee. If you want?'

Anna watched as Sophie and Dave argued in hushed tones by his car. 'Actually I will, if that's okay? I don't think they need me right now. I'll swap the kids to Dave's car and I'll be back.'

'I'll put the coffee on.'

'Great,' she said but she wasn't sure if it was. She was feeling more than embarrassed and her explanations of why she'd believed he was gay hadn't helped the situation. Although as she neared the warring couple, she realised coffee with Hudson was most definitely the lesser of the two evils.

She soon moved the kids to Dave's car, hugged both Sophie and Dave and waved them off, hoping they would be able to sort this out although their stony faces told her otherwise. Hudson had left the door open and the smell of fresh coffee wafted to greet her as she slipped inside.

'Up here,' he called from the kitchen and she went to join him. 'Did you want milk? I've got semi or almond. I like one per cent milk but you can't get it over here.'

'One per cent milk? What's the other ninety-nine per cent then?' she said, pointing at the semi-skimmed.

He gave her a mock glare. 'It's the cream content. Like one per cent, two per cent. That makes sense to me.'

'Only because you're American.' She took her coffee and sat down at the table. Hudson moved a chair right next to her and his knee skimmed her thigh as he sat down. She concentrated on her coffee. The flat was surprisingly tidy after the party although the large plants, animals and trapeze were still in situ.

Anna took a breath. 'Look, I'm mortified about the whole gay thing. Still friends?'

'Hey. I'm cool with it.' And he really didn't seem bothered in the slightest. 'And for sure, we're still friends.'

His confirmation made her happier than she'd thought it would. 'Sorry, about Dave too.'

'That's none of my business. I'm worried I said or did something last night that made him think I'd been inappropriate with Sophie.'

Oh, how to broach this one. 'No. It's nothing you've done. It's just a . . . misunderstanding. They're going through a pissing each other off phase.'

He chuckled. 'We did that.' He leaned against her briefly as he spoke like a slow motion nudge.

Her cheeks flushed. 'I guess we did.' They glanced at each other, the awkwardness palpable, and sipped their drinks in silence for a while.

'Champagne truffle?' he asked, leaning behind him and picking up a round box.

She went to take one and he snatched them away. 'Sorry, I forgot they're alcoholic.'

'Chocolate is okay. I'd have to eat a vat of them before they rendered me incapable.' Anna sunk her teeth into the soft truffle and marvelled at the flavour. 'Ooh they're good.'

'But real champagne isn't?'

'I didn't say that.' She pondered whether or not to elaborate. 'At university my friend . . .' It was harder to say than she realised. Hudson was watching her closely. 'There was an alcohol-related incident that didn't end well.' Her eyes swam with unexpected tears.

Hudson put the lid on the truffles and turned towards her. 'And that's why you don't drink?' His voice was gentle. She nodded. 'You know us fake boyfriends do great hugs.'

Anna snorted a laugh. He was very sweet. 'I'm okay, really.' Although a hug right now would have helped but at the end of the day they were colleagues and she didn't want to overstep the mark. She checked her watch. 'I need to go, I'm going out tonight.'

'Should I be suspicious? Have you got someone else?' He held his hand to his chest and gave her a dramatic eye blink. And he wondered why she'd believed Roberta when she'd said he was gay.

'It's not a date. I'm just meeting my mystery texter for a drink.'

Hudson pursed his lips. 'He's male and you're meeting him for a drink in the evening. You call it what you like but I'm telling you he thinks it's a date.'

Anna shook her head. 'I'm not ready to date yet.' She bit the inside of her mouth as she considered what Hudson had said.

'Then make that clear. And be careful, okay. This guy's a stranger.'

'You sound like my dad,' she said, with a chuckle, although she knew he meant well. 'But I will be careful.' She glanced again at her watch. 'I really must go.'

Hudson straightened his shoulders. 'You come round here, drink my coffee, eat my truffles and then go out with another man.' He tutted and shook his head as they went down to the front door. 'I might only be your fake boyfriend but you can always call me if you find yourself in a fix. Okay?'

Anna wasn't sure why but she spontaneously went onto her tiptoes and kissed his cheek. 'Thanks, Hudson.'

'No problem. I hope your date goes well.' Something about the look he gave her made her feel his sentiments weren't genuine.

Maybe it was Hudson calling it a date or perhaps it was something else, but Anna no longer felt excited about her meet-up with the mysterious Connor.

Chapter Twenty

Anna threw a strappy top onto the bed and Maurice pounced on it. She had a pretty grey shrug to go with it if it got chillier later on. Here she was, choosing an outfit to meet up with a total stranger. What was she even doing? She sat down on the bed and Maurice took the opportunity to abandon assassinating the top and curl up on Anna's lap instead.

'I envy you,' she said, scratching him behind his ears and he closed his eyes and pushed his head against her hand. 'You don't have to make big decisions.' She was surprised by how Hudson's revelation had thrown her off course but it had, and now it felt like she was bobbing about in the Atlantic in a barrel. She was also a bit cross with herself because her first instinct, that he was straight, had been correct but she'd allowed herself to get caught up in the office gossip.

Part of her wanted to think it made no difference to their relationship. Why should things change? They were colleagues; they had built an easy friendship out of a fraught situation. She liked his company and they were now, despite their shaky start, working well together. Her relationship with Hudson was fairly straightforward, though she imagined it would likely dwindle and die once the project ended. She gave a little sigh, closed her eyes and had a think.

Was there anything else? Had he mentioned something when they'd shared the takeaway? She thought back. He'd told her he'd been unceremoniously dumped by someone he thought was the one. Therefore, it was a fair assumption that, like her, he wasn't on the lookout for a new relationship any time soon. He hadn't shown any signs of fancying her because it would have been a dead giveaway that he wasn't gay – even she would have spotted that. She took a deep breath. Hudson is in the 'Friends' pigeonhole; let's look at Liam again, she thought, just to be certain.

Liam had been her future for a long time and while she could think about the situation logically almost all the emotion she had felt had gone. It was good to view it analytically and assess it in simple terms. She no longer had a longing to be back with him and she certainly wasn't ready to compromise. She didn't miss him, specifically, although she did miss being in a relationship and the security and closeness it brought. She put Liam firmly in the 'Exes' pigeonhole. Now she had to figure out what she was doing about Connor, maybe temporarily she'd file him in the 'Potentials' pigeonhole.

Who was Connor? She knew very little about him, but that made it exciting. It didn't feel serious and she definitely needed some fun in her life. Sophie was convinced it could be the start of something magical and Anna's curiosity was piqued. She knew she needed to stop looking at every relationship and assessing it to see if they were 'the one' because statistically she knew it was very unlikely to happen. There was also the effort of getting ready to go out and making small talk. Was it still worth meeting

Connor? She wasn't sure any more. She fired off a text to Sophie: **Not sure why I'm meeting Connor. Think I might give it a miss.**

Sophie was quick to reply: **Don't you dare bottle out now. My life is utter poo and I need to live vicariously, which means yours needs to be amazing. Remember what I said. No regrets.**

'Bugger,' said Anna and Maurice stretched out demanding a full-body massage. Would she regret not going to meet Connor? She picked up the strappy top and started to get changed.

Anna gripped her phone as she stepped into the noisy bubble of the bar. Her heart was thumping as if she'd sprinted there rather than just got off the bus. She stayed near to the entrance and took a deep breath as her eyes frantically searched the mass of faces. She realised she had no idea what he looked like. Her thoughts were broken by the door opening behind her. It made her jump and she spun around in alarm at her exit being blocked. She came face to face with a tall man who looked almost as startled as she did.

'Anna?' he said, with a hopeful smile.

'Yes,' she answered, as she took in his mop of fair hair and light eyes. On first impressions, he wasn't bad-looking. Not on the same scale as Hudson but appealing all the same and there was something reassuringly familiar about him too.

'Connor?'

'Yes,' he said, his face lighting up as he appeared to relax. He rubbed his palm on his jeans before presenting it to shake. 'Great to meet you at last.'

Anna was struggling to hear over the noise. She shook

his hand and noted his solid grip. 'Yes, you too.' She really didn't want to shout but it was hard not to. Anna had picked a busy pub because she didn't want to be somewhere isolated when meeting someone who was basically a stranger; however, this was far busier than she'd been expecting.

'Sorry?' Connor turned an ear towards her.

'You too!' she shouted and she held up both thumbs to get her message across and felt instantly stupid.

Connor grinned back at her. 'Can I get you a drink?' He did the actions of tilting an imaginary glass to his lips. Anna nodded and they both looked across at the sea of bodies.

'Diet Coke, please.'

He leaned in to her shoulder. 'Do you want to find a seat outside? There were some free.'

She agreed and gratefully left him to the din of the bar and stepped out into the warm summer evening. The double doors rocked shut and the noise instantly faded to a dull thrum. There were a few people outside and the obligatory smokers' corner. She found a table near a couple who were deep in conversation. She sent a quick text to Sophie as they'd agreed. She instantly got a reply – **What's he like?**

Seems nice. Very tall.

Everyone's tall compared to you. Is he ugly?

Anna shook her head at the message. **No. He looks good.**

Not anyone famous then?

Sorry. No. Will text when I leave. A x.

At last her pulse was returning to normal. It had been a long time since she'd been on a date and she was out of practice and more than a little uncomfortable. Connor reversed through the doors carrying two drinks and had his mobile wedged between his ear and his shoulder. He gave a grimace as he approached and passed Anna one of the glasses.

'Thanks,' she said quietly not wanting to interrupt what might be an important call.

'Okay, but don't walk home on your own,' he said, into the phone. He mouthed to Anna: 'Sorry, it's my mum.' She nodded her understanding.

'Yes, I know you're not decrepit but there are all sorts of weirdos about at night,' he said, giving an eye roll for Anna's benefit. She sipped her Coke. He mouthed to Anna: 'Sorry. I won't be a minute.' He looked very apologetic.

'Call me when it ends and I'll pick you up . . . Yes, eleven will be fine . . .' He looked to Anna for confirmation. She nodded vigorously. She needed to be on the 10.33 bus anyway.

He wrapped up the call. 'Yes, of course she doesn't mind. Call me. Right. Love you too. Bye.' He pushed his phone to the edge of the table and turned his attention to Anna. 'Sorry. I worry about her because she's on her own. She's at the theatre tonight.'

'Honestly, it's okay.' She was reassured by the care he was displaying to his mother.

'Are you close to your parents?' he asked, and as he lifted his glass to his lips she could see a small tremor in his hand – he was nervous too.

'Yeah, I am. There's just me so I think they fuss more. Do you have any brothers or sisters?'

He was bobbing his head in agreement. 'A sister but she's not nearby, which means it's down to me to keep an eye on Mum.'

There was a pause where they both gave sheepish smiles

and Anna longed for the silence to end. Time to make small talk. 'Where do you live?' she asked. She'd noted he didn't have a local accent.

'Coleshill. You?'

'Walmsley.'

'I like Walmsley. Whereabouts?'

'I've got a flat right next to the park.'

'I bet it's lovely. A bit of nature but close to the city.' It was a good summary and she nodded along. 'Are you okay out here?' he asked.

'Yes, thanks, I'm fine.' She sipped her drink and began to relax into the conversation. Perhaps this was exactly what she needed.

Anna was keeping an eye on the time and just after ten o'clock she started making noises about heading home.

'Can I give you a lift home?' he asked.

'No, it's fine I'm getting the bus.' She could have driven but the bus was less hassle than parking in the city centre.

'Then I'll walk you to the bus stop.' He stood up and once again she could see just how tall he was. There had been the occasional lulls in conversation but she sensed he was a little shy. An evening of gentle chatter had been enough to make her see there was more to life than work and sitting at home with the cat. She'd had a nice evening. They left the pub and walked along in silence until they neared the bus stop.

'Thanks, Anna. I've had a really great evening,' said Connor, followed by a small chuckle. 'That sounds lame, doesn't it?'

'Not at all. I've had a nice time too.'

He looked at her from under his mop of hair. 'You wanna do it again sometime?' He wasn't presumptuous although it did put her on the spot. Anna thought for a moment and Connor's expression changed. 'God, that sounded cocky. Sorry.'

He waved his hands in front of her like he was trying to rub out his words. He was kind of gangly and a bit awkward, which was endearing. 'No, that'd be lovely.'

'You've got my number,' he said, pointing at her phone. As the bus pulled in he checked his watch. 'Take care,' he said, with a brief wave.

As she got on the bus, she was glad there was no clumsy attempt to kiss her goodbye, but they caught each other's eye as the bus drove past and Connor gave her another wave, which made her smile. He was really quite sweet and she was glad she'd made the effort to meet him.

Anna was still thinking about Connor as she walked towards home. He'd been good company and she was pleased she hadn't thought about Liam or Hudson all evening. She glanced up and spotted a light on in her flat and she stopped dead. Her heart instantly upped its rhythm. She hadn't left a light on; she knew that for sure because it had still been light outside when she'd left. There was only one explanation – someone was in her flat.

She pulled her phone from her bag as she tiptoed up to the window. How brazen were these burglars, ransacking her home whilst the place was lit up like Selfridges at Christmas? She dialled 999 as she paced back and forth, hoping Maurice was all right in there. She wanted to think he was probably asleep and oblivious. It was too much to hope that he'd launch an attack and chase the intruders out – perhaps she should have got a large dog. She inched closer. The curtains were open and she peered inside. The 999 operator answered. 'Police, please,' she whispered in answer to their question. A figure moved inside and Anna had to stifle a gasp. Then something made her move closer to the glass and get a better look at her intruder. What she saw was both totally confusing and a huge relief. 'Actually, no. I don't need the police. I'm *so* sorry. I thought I was being burgled but I'm not.' She apologised a few more times and then ended the call as she marched round to the front door and let herself in.

'Bloody hell, Sophie. I thought I had burglars!'

Anna's eyes were drawn to the large suitcase in the hallway. She heard feet running towards her and Sophie skidded to a halt. 'Surprise!' she said, almost doing a star jump. Her arms quickly flopped to her sides and Anna looked at her tear-stained face.

'What's happened?'

Sophie took a deep breath and lifted up her chin. 'I've left Dave.'

Chapter Twenty-One

Anna knew she was blinking more times than was necessary but Sophie's words had stunned her. She never believed Sophie would ever actually leave Dave. Sure, they annoyed the crap out of each other, but that was normal for them. She shut her front door behind her and licked her lips as she tried to think of the appropriate thing to say.

'Well, say something,' said Sophie, fresh tears spilling down her cheeks.

Anna stepped forward and enveloped her friend in a tight hug and held her until the crying had subsided. Anna could foresee it being a long evening where Sophie would offload all her woes about Dave and his PhD-level uselessness whilst Anna nodded in the right places and then Sophie went home to shout at Dave a bit more. Anna held her at arm's length. 'I'm going to make us ridiculously calorific hot chocolates and then you're going to tell me all about it. Okay?'

Sophie bobbed her head. 'I'll finish unpacking while you get the drinks.' Anna looked like she'd stepped into a revolving door the wrong way – confused and slightly stunned. She opened her mouth but no words came out. Sophie disappeared into Anna's spare room.

Anna had a number of conversations in her head whilst she was making the hot chocolate, most of them ending in '. . . but you're not *actually* moving out. Are you?' although the fact Sophie was unpacking her stuff and neatly folding it into Anna's IKEA chest of drawers told her it wasn't going to be straightforward. Anna stared at the hot chocolates and for the first time in a very long while she wished they had been alcoholic. She scattered some mini marshmallows on top, took the laden mugs into the living room and waited for Sophie. Maurice stretched out on the sofa next to Anna and gave her arm a pat with his paw. She absent-mindedly stroked him and he started to purr like a small motor.

Sophie came in and flopped into the chair opposite. 'Right, the case is unpacked. I'll go back for more stuff tomorrow. Thanks for this. Yum,' she said, picking up the mug.

Anna wasn't sure how best to tackle this. 'When you say, you've *left* Dave . . .'

Sophie pursed her lips. 'I've had enough. Causing a scene with Hudson was absolutely the last straw.' Sophie was resolute. Anna hadn't seen her quite like this before.

'But what about Arlo and Petal?'

'Oh, I'm not leaving them.' Anna did a sigh of relief followed by a sharp intake of breath and she almost inhaled a marshmallow. If she wasn't leaving the children was she expecting to move them in too? Sophie continued. 'I'm going to get up early so I'll be there when they wake up and then they're off on holiday with the Kraken for two weeks.'

Anna was hugely relieved about this. She'd forgotten Karen was taking the children away for a while. 'It might do you both good to have two weeks together without the children.'

Sophie was already shaking her head. 'No way. I can't do this any more.' Her voice cracked and she pulled a tissue from her pocket and blew her nose loudly. 'This isn't what I wanted, Anna. I wasn't meant to end up like this. I don't know how it happened.' She looked wretched sitting crossed-legged in the chair with her swollen belly stretching her top to the max. She was six months pregnant and she looked it. 'I had plans . . . big plans. I was going to go places . . . see stuff. Not stay in the Midlands and wipe bums for the rest of my life.'

Anna put down her drink and went and gave Sophie another hug. She hated to see her like this. 'What needs to change to make you happy again?'

Sophie sniffed. 'Swapping Dave for Hudson would be a start.' She gave a hiccup of a laugh.

'You'd soon get fed up with his pretty face and perfect body. Yuk.' Anna gave a pretend shudder, passed Sophie back her hot chocolate and Sophie gave a brief smile. 'And I bet he leaves wet towels on the floor too.'

'If it means he's walking around naked, that's fine with me.' Sophie sipped her hot chocolate and gave herself a creamy moustache. 'Hmmm,' she said contentedly and Anna wasn't sure if it was the hot chocolate or the thought of a naked Hudson making her emit the happy sound.

'Dave isn't all bad, though. I'm sure we can come up with a list of his good points.' Anna scanned the room for a pen and paper. She had various ways to solve problems.

'I'm not workshopping my marriage,' said Sophie emphatically.

'Fair enough.' She had a point. 'How about Relate counselling?' Sophie shook her head. 'Then how do we resolve this?'

'I don't think we can,' said Sophie and she sniffed back more tears.

Anna's phone pinged and she quickly scanned the message. **Thanks for a great evening. Hope you got home safe. C.**

Anna couldn't hide the small smile before her eyes darted back to Sophie. Sophie was watching her. 'It's just Connor. Carry on,' said Anna, gesturing with her hand.

'I'm such a rubbish friend. You had your first date in like forever and I forgot to ask you how it went.' Sophie's forlorn expression reflected her slumped body language.

Anna waved the comment away. 'Doesn't matter.'

'No, come on. I need cheering up. Tell me what you found out about the mysterious Connor.' Sophie seemed to perk up. She tucked her feet underneath her and eyed Anna expectantly.

'He's two years younger than me, he works with mobile phones, lives in Coleshill and is close to his mum.' Anna was pleased with her summary.

'Come on I need more info.' Sophie pouted. 'What's he look like? Did you get a photo?'

Anna pulled a face. 'No, how weird would that have been?' Sophie opened her mouth but closed it again. 'He's tall . . .'

'Everyone is tall from the angle you view them.'

Anna stuck her tongue out and continued. 'He looks younger than he is. He was clean and tidy . . . He was quite shy but he was nice.'

'Nice?' It was Sophie's turn to pull a face. 'Not rip-his-clothes-off sexy? Or pant-wettingly funny? Or awe-inspiringly clever?'

Anna realised it wasn't the biggest compliment. 'I liked him, he was . . .' she paused to stop herself repeating nice '. . . pleasant.'

'Ouch. Pleasant is worse than nice. He sounds as exciting as an out-of-date ready meal. No spark then?' Sophie looked disappointed.

'Not necessarily, but that's not always instant. And even if it is, does it make for a lasting relationship?'

'He was ugly,' concluded Sophie and Anna swiped her with a cushion. Anna had been quite happy with the evening until now but she had to admit there had been little in the way of attraction between them. Maybe it would take a few more dates. Question was, was it worth finding out? They sipped their hot chocolates in silence as their thoughts wandered off.

Next morning Sophie had left by the time Anna stirred. She had a quick squiz around the spare bedroom in the hope Sophie had had a rethink during the night but whilst the bed was made her empty case was still there and her hastily grabbed things were still in the wardrobe. Anna sighed and she and Maurice padded through to the kitchen to get breakfast. Something caught Anna's eye, a small brownish something with a tail balancing on the edge of Maurice's food bowl.

'Maurice,' she whispered, pointing at the mouse. It was completely still, like a tiny statue. Maurice flopped on the floor and rolled over. Then all at once he spotted the mouse and the chase was on. Maurice landed in the food bowl sending the dry food inside catapulting across the kitchen floor. The mouse scurried along the line of the cabinets and disappeared into the hall at lightning speed. Maurice skidded on the laminate floor as he tried to turn quickly and went careering after the mouse. Anna grabbed a tea towel and followed the trail of destruction as cushions flew and vases and photo frames wobbled.

Maurice finally cornered the mouse in the spare room. It was cowering next to Sophie's open case, trying to do a good impression of a luggage wheel. Anna scooped up a surprised and unimpressed Maurice, plonked him in the hall and shut the door. In one fluid movement she dropped the tea towel on the mouse, wrapped it up, bundled it into the case and shut the lid. She'd deal with it after she'd had breakfast and a shower.

As the suds soothed Anna's shoulders, she planned herself a quiet evening in front of the telly and an early night. She needed some time to give the Sophie and Dave situation some serious thought. It worried her that Sophie hadn't relented and gone home last night. This was far more serious than Anna had wanted to admit. They needed their heads banging together. She loved them both and she was convinced this wasn't really the end of their relationship; she just had to work out a way of convincing Sophie that was the case.

A piercing shriek made her jolt. Sophie was back. Anna didn't rush from the shower – she could work out that Sophie must have found the mouse. Uncharitably she wondered if a free-running mouse might be enough to send Sophie back to Dave.

A day of back-to-back meetings was finished off with her one-to-one session with Liam. So far she had failed to get any useful information out of him but she was hoping she might be able to today. Anna brought the coffees and would have liked a little more gratitude than 'Ta' from Liam for the large expensive shop-bought variety with an extra shot and syrup just how he liked it. She answered his first few questions about the programme and while he jotted some notes she decided to ask a few of her own.

'How's Tabitha?' She prepared a lovely sweet smile for when he looked up, which he did very slowly, like a soldier looking over a trench.

'I'm sure she's fine but we're not together any more.'

Anna changed her smile to what she hoped was a surprised but sympathetic guise. 'I'm sorry to hear that. Really.'

'It was fun but you know?'

She didn't and she didn't want to know either. 'You'll be delivering your verdict soon then,' she said. Liam merely glanced up. 'When are you presenting it?'

Liam put his pen down. 'No date as yet.'

'Big changes then, I guess.' She maintained eye contact. 'You'll be looking to move jobs soon, won't you?' he asked.

Anna didn't like the way he said it. Was he trying to imply she'd need to move soon? 'Nope. I love working here. I'm planning on staying.'

Liam's eyebrows twitched up a fraction. Bugger, she thought. She doubted she'd be featuring on any structure charts he was drawing up.

Liam picked up his pen and twirled it nonchalantly as if he was considering something. 'I could give you the inside track if you like?'

This is easy, thought Anna. 'That'd be great.' She leaned forward in her seat, keen to grasp every snippet.

Liam chewed the side of his mouth, gave a slow blink. 'Though I'd need something in return, obviously . . .'

Okay, not so easy after all, thought Anna. She could feel her neck prickle with sweat. Was this a trap to see if she'd reveal something she shouldn't? But then Roberta had said to give every cooperation to Liam and she wasn't aware anything was off limits. Too many thoughts overloaded her brain at once. She snatched up her coffee and took a swig but the lid wasn't on properly and she tipped a slug of it all down herself.

'Bugger!' Anna hurriedly pulled tissues from her pocket and tried to mop up the worst of it. 'How I missed my mouth, I'll never know,' she said, trying to hide her fluster levels.

'You okay?' he asked.

'No, I'm not really comfortable with the whole "I'll need something in return" scenario.' She was feeling brave and she liked Liam's surprised expression.

'Oh, I meant . . . the coffee.' They both swallowed and looked uncomfortable. 'It's nothing prohibited. I just wondered what your thoughts are on . . . us?'

Anna's hand wobbled and she returned her cup to the safety of the table for fear of a second dousing. She narrowed her eyes as she stared at him for a moment. Was he joking?

'Umm, I don't know what you mean, Liam.'

Liam stretched his legs out, dug his heels into the carpet tiles near to Anna and pulled himself and his wheelie chair up close to her. 'I've tried hard to ignore it. But being around you . . . I think we acted too hastily when we said it was over.' He gave a practised smile and Anna almost laughed.

'Now you're joking. Aren't you?' She still wasn't sure.

'No.' His forehead puckered. 'I spoke to Hudson and I didn't get the feeling he saw you as anything more than a fling.' Anna was momentarily offended and then she remembered and gave herself a shake. 'Anna, you and I were great together. I'm willing to give our relationship another go if you are.' There was that smile again.

'Bugger me,' said Anna. Liam gave a lascivious look

and opened his mouth. 'Don't even go there,' she said, her tone harsh.

He leaned a fraction closer and went to take her hand. 'What do you think?'

Derision slid across Anna's face. 'Liam, I think you are a supercilious shit, beyond deluded, and so far up your own bottom you're inside out. And not only is my mind thinking "no", it's screaming it.'

For once Anna had said what she thought and it felt great. Liam's face was a picture but Anna feared she may have just sealed her redundancy. She raised an eyebrow, stood up and left.

Chapter Twenty-Two

Anna was sitting in the communal lounge with Bert. It was good to see him being a bit more sociable rather than shutting himself away in his room. They both had large takeaway cups of coffee and sipped them in unison.

'What's new?' asked Anna.

'These bloomin' chairs for starters,' said Bert, wriggling himself about in the large armchair. Anna realised the room was filled with them. All in dark green, very uniform and inoffensive.

'Are they uncomfortable?'

'Hmm, it's not like the old chair I used to sit in. I liked that one better.' He gave an uncharacteristic pout.

'Us humans aren't good with change. I'm sure you'll get used to it.'

He nodded but was still pouting. 'How's Maurice? Has he brought you any presents?' he asked.

'He's excellent, thanks. He's brought me a few mice.'

Bert brightened. 'Oh, that's just the start.' He chuckled to himself.

'I've bought him some sponge balls to play with instead,' said Anna hopefully.

Anna hadn't been to visit for a while so she had lots to

update Bert on. It was like bringing someone up to speed on a long-running soap opera when they'd missed a few episodes.

When she'd finished Bert nodded sagely. 'On my reckoning that makes three.'

'Three what?'

'Young men who are after courting you.'

Anna shook her head. 'No, just Connor and Liam. And seeing as Liam has already let me down and I am very much over him, it leaves Connor.' She'd only met Connor once, and they'd spoken on the phone a couple of times since. They were taking things very slowly at her request, but so far, so good.

Bert was frowning hard. 'But what about the American?'

'Hudson. He never was in the running.'

Bert relaxed back into his chair and breathed out slowly. 'At first you hated Hudson because he was doing your job.'

'Hate's a little harsh . . .'

Bert gave a slow nod. 'You disliked Hudson at first. Then the two of you clubbed together against Liam. You seemed to be close through the summer until you found out he wasn't in a homosexual relationship . . .' Anna noticed a few heads turn in their direction but Bert was unaware so he continued. 'So how has finding out he's *not* gay put you off him?'

Anna opened her mouth. 'I was never *on* him!' Realising what she'd said and the sound of hearing aids being turned up she decided a more carefully considered reply might be better. Bert did have a good point. 'The thing with Hudson is I liked him as a friend. As a gay friend, I guess. And now he's not my gay friend it all feels a bit weird.' It was the truth. She had relaxed into an easy friendship with him knowing there would never be anything else between them.

It had been safe and comfortable and there was no pressure to be anything other than herself around a very good-looking man without worrying about her behaviour and, if she was being honest, how she looked. Now she wasn't sure what their relationship was. They were still rubbing along okay at work but things did feel different between them. She finished her coffee and put the cup down.

'This Connor chap then. Too good to be true?' asked Bert.

Anna was taken by surprise by the comment and a snort of a giggle escaped. 'I don't know. He seems nice enough.'

'Nice?' Bert pulled a face. He was as judgemental as Sophie over her word choice.

'Yes, nice is a good thing. I like him.'

'Hmm,' said Bert, feeling for the table to put his cup on. 'If I ask you a few questions you have to answer honestly with which of the two men pops into your mind. Okay?'

'Not really. It sounds like being on *Jeremy Kyle.*'

'I can't stand him, the whining West Ham supporter. Come on, humour an old man,' said Bert, shuffling to the edge of the seat.

Anna let out a loud sigh. 'O-kay.' She closed her eyes and concentrated. 'Ready.'

'Going to the cinema.'

'Connor. Hudson and I can't decide on anything.'

'Trapped in a lift together.'

Anna was tempted to ask what floor they were on: if it was high up in one of those glass ones she'd probably pass out anyway so it wouldn't matter who she was with. Connor would be calmer than Hudson but Hudson was a better talker. 'Hudson, if we're going to be stuck for anything over half an hour.'

'Have a row with.'

'Hmm, Hudson. I don't think I could have a row with Connor.' Her lips lifted at the edges as she thought of how easy-going Connor was.

'Dress shopping.'

'Connor. Hudson doesn't have the patience.'

'Be silly with.'

Anna paused. She was going to say Connor again but she couldn't recall laughing with him like she could remember laughing with Hudson. 'Either.'

'No. That's not the game. Choose one.'

'Okay. Hudson, I think.'

'Tickle fight.'

'Tickle fight?' Anna's eyes popped open.

'Yep. Imagine having a tickle fight. Who is it you're fighting with?'

The image was already in her mind and it confused her. 'Hudson. Why?'

A satisfied smile crept onto Bert's lips. 'You know tickle fights always end in a kiss?'

'Err, I think that's the end of that game,' said Anna, suddenly flustered.

'Sorry, I didn't mean to make you feel uncomfortable.' Bert reached out a hand and Anna took it.

'You are cheeky.'

'No point getting old if you don't get crafty,' said Bert, and they both laughed. But he had sown some seeds for Anna to dig about in. 'Now, there's someone I'd like you to meet. Rosie, are you there?'

A perky little lady almost sprang from a nearby armchair and Anna realised she must have been watching them all this time. 'Yes, Bert. Are you okay?'

'I'm fine. I'd like you meet a friend of mine. This is

Anna,' he said, pointing in her general direction and smiling proudly. Anna felt a warm glow of affection for the old man. 'Nice to meet you, Rosie,' she said, shaking the bony hand.

'And you, dear. He talks about you and Maurice all the time. And all the men in your life. It seems very exciting.'

'She exaggerates,' said Bert, a little flushed.

'So does he,' said Anna, wagging a finger at Bert.

Sophie had been having the same conversation for what felt like slightly longer than forever when Anna pulled up. Hopefully she'd be able to make sense of whatever Mrs Nowakowski was going on about.

Mrs Nowakowski was now waving her arms frantically. 'D'ese is not that sort of neighbourhood. You look like you're advertising burdel. Shame on you!'

'What's the matter?' asked Anna, butting in.

They both started to speak at once and Anna held up her hands to stop them. 'Sophie, hang on.' Anna gave her best 'bear with me' face before turning to the older woman. 'Mrs Nowakowski, what seems to be the problem?'

'You make this nice place look like burdel. That is problem.' She crossed her arms and gave a sharp nod of her head.

'I think she means brothel.' Sophie dissolved into giggles and felt the baby kick in response.

'Why? What have we done?' asked Anna.

'The bra hanging in your window.' Mrs Nowakowski pointed round to the side of the building where Anna's lounge window was. Anna walked round and as the laughter died Sophie followed. When they reached the window the three women stopped and stared at the large bright red bra hanging there.

209

Anna looked at Sophie and gave a tip of her head. 'What?' said Sophie. 'It's not mine.'

Anna unfolded her arms and pointed to her chest. 'Well, it's definitely not mine!' Anna was grinning.

'Is it the international symbol for brothel?' asked Anna.

'According to Mrs Nosy-kowski,' whispered Sophie.

As the two friends descended into yet more giggles Mrs Nowakowski shook her head and went home. Eventually they realised they were alone and went inside. Anna tugged down the bra that was hooked over the handle of the window, shook her head and dropped the bra in the dirty clothes bin.

Sophie didn't really understand why Anna had hung the bra up, but it had made her laugh and she had to admit it was like one of hers but she was wearing her big comfy maternity bras at the moment, so it couldn't have been. She thought for a second how funny Dave would think it was, then remembered her situation. Suddenly emotion swamped her and she had to swallow hard to keep it in check. Perhaps the break from Dave was having a bigger impact on her than she cared to admit.

Anna made chicken Caesar salad for dinner and they ate it in silence, interrupted only by the pitiful begging mews of Maurice trying to snag a little chicken. He'd already wolfed down his own meal of Ocean fish in a light gravy but some days it was hard to fill him up. Anna was still smiling to herself about the bra. She had no idea why Sophie had hung it in the window unless it was purely to wind up Mrs Nowakowski. Sophie no longer looked amused. She was violently spearing croutons, making her current mood very apparent.

'What's up?' asked Anna.

'I had to say goodbye to the kids and I know they're going to have an amazing time on holiday with Granny Kraken and it means I don't have to go to Butlins but it still felt horrid.'

'Were they okay?'

'Oh, yeah. I think that made it worse. Arlo had a strop because we made him get out of the car to kiss us both goodbye and Petal happily waved and blew raspberries as she was driven away. They couldn't have cared less. It was horrible.'

'Kids take things in their stride. How was Dave?'

'He wound me up. I came back here to escape and got hijacked by Mrs Nowakowski and bra-gate. I thought she was nice but today she really put the cow in Nowa—'

'Now, now. She might have had a point. What did Dave do to wind you up?'

Sophie dropped her fork and it clattered onto her plate. Maurice gave her a haughty look at the disturbance. 'Arlo brought home all his schoolbooks and I was looking through them. When I was away on the team event, Dave had to check Arlo's homework. It was one sodding line, that was all, and he never bothered to check it.' She was shaking her head.

'What was wrong with it then?'

'Arlo had written, "I love cock!" with an exclamation mark at the end. Which to be honest I thought was really advanced for his age . . .'

'Cock?' asked Anna, her face distorted with the effort of not laughing.

'Yes. Obviously he meant Coke,' said Sophie, giving her friend an old-fashioned look. 'Which, more to the point, Dave shouldn't have been letting him drink either. Anyway, his teacher had corrected it and put a smiley face . . .'

'Dave's a cock,' said Anna, and Sophie nodded her agreement. They looked at each other across the small table and dissolved into hysterics.

When they were all called together for a 9 a.m. briefing they knew it would be Liam's presentation and there he was standing at the front of the room looking smug. Liam watched her walk in but his expression remained fixed. Bugger, thought Anna. She'd already calculated her redundancy. It wasn't a lot, but it should mean she wouldn't have to look for something until the new year, which was a bonus. Perhaps she'd take herself off for a holiday.

Hudson strode into the room, overtook a few meanderers and slotted into the seat next to Anna. 'D Day has arrived,' he said, exuding enthusiasm as always.

'Here,' she said, handing Hudson her phone. 'This is a picture of Liam doing ballet aged eight.'

Hudson held the phone and immediately his shoulders started to bob up and down as he took in the photograph of a small boy in a very tight orange leotard displaying a very obvious lump. 'Where did you get this?'

'I remembered his mum sent me a load of old photos for his birthday last year and I thought it might help if we had this to look at while he delivers our fate.'

Karl took the seat next to Hudson and immediately clocked the photo. 'Someone's excited about ballet. Who's this?'

'Liam,' said Hudson, through splutters of laughter. Liam glanced over and they huddled around the phone and reduced their volume.

'Bloody hell, remind me not dump you,' said Karl to Anna. She tried to snatch her phone back but Karl was already passing it along their row.

'I think everyone's here,' said Roberta, stepping up onto the platform. Liam started fiddling with his laptop and looking anxiously at the projector screen behind him and back to the laptop.

'Is he trying to get something up?' asked Karl, and they all began sniggering. There was something infectious about trying not to laugh in serious situations.

The presentation that followed could have told them they were closing the company down at lunchtime and they would have still had smiles on their faces. As it was, the main focus was on a total process overhaul, with the application of Lean methodologies at both the UK offices and in New York. There was a restructure but as everyone scanned it quickly to find their name, they were reassured nobody was missing from their team. Basically Liam had seized the merger as an opportunity to improve the current processes, which delayed things a bit but made ultimate sense. However, there were predicted reductions in the call centre and processing areas following the implementation of the suggested changes. The big impact for Anna was their programme was getting bigger but Anna saw this as a positive. Liam had taken the approach of 'while we've got the bonnet up, let's see what other improvements we can make'. Yes, there would be plenty of rework but this would definitely be a sizeable deliverable on her CV and excellent experience too.

Roberta gave what was probably meant to be a rousing speech and ended with a quote in large letters on the big screen that read – *The only way to get what you want in this world is through hard work.* 'And do you know who said that?' she asked.

'Minnie Mouse?' whispered Karl.

'Tiana from *The Princess and the Frog*,' said Roberta solemnly.

'So close,' said Karl with feeling.

Anna caught Liam looking at her and he gave a tentative smile before explaining the timescales.

'Timescales are tight,' whispered Anna to Hudson.

'Not as tight as his ballet leotard,' chipped in Karl. Anna was starting to feel bad about sharing the photograph and she snatched back her phone. Liam hadn't stitched her up, which was what she had feared he would do. He had done a good job. In fact he could have recommended a separate project for these changes and left Anna and Hudson to finish the merger but what he'd actually done was give them a significant programme of work and enhanced their current project. He'd also stuck to his word and not said anything about her and Hudson because if he had that would have spread as quickly as only office gossip can. She almost felt like she should thank him.

'Scope now includes New York,' said Hudson, with a broad smile. He'd said he was missing New York – was this his opportunity to go home? There was a natural split for the two of them with Hudson managing the changes in New York and her managing the UK project. In one simple slide she could see logically how things should be managed and it meant them going their separate ways. It would no longer be shared responsibilities; there would be clear deliverables for both of them, which was exactly what she'd wanted from the very beginning, but now it didn't seem such an issue.

Chapter Twenty-Three

'Who do these belong to?' said a grinning Sophie, waving aloft a pair of men's Spider-Man underpants as Anna dashed into the kitchen to avoid the downpour outside.

'What?' said Anna, glancing at the swinging underwear. She kicked off her heels and sighed with relief. It had been a very long day. She gave her toes a wriggle. Maurice was lying in the hall stretched out like a furry road bump.

'Who is Mr . . .' Sophie paused to study the label '. . . large?' asked Sophie.

'Who's *who*?' asked Anna, starting to feel a tiny bit irritated by the silly conversation and the stupid pants.

'The owner of these.' Sophie waved the pants dangerously close.

Anna pulled her head out of the way. 'I don't know what you're on about,' she said, an unpleasant thought dawning on her. 'Unless you're trying to tell me you've had a man in here. Have you hooked up with someone?' asked Anna, now paying full attention to the swinging undies.

'What? No,' said Sophie. 'Do you really think I'd do that?' Sophie lowered the pants to hang limply at her side.

'I hope not. Why are you waving them at me then?'
Anna arched an eyebrow as confusion reigned.

'Fine. Don't tell me. I thought we didn't keep secrets,'
said Sophie, throwing the offending undies at Anna's feet
and stomping off to the spare bedroom. Anna shook her
head. She was totally bewildered by what had gone on. It
was looking increasingly like Sophie was losing the plot.
Anna took the tongs from the drawer, picked up the pants
with them and dropped them unceremoniously into the
non-recycling bin.

Maurice wound himself around Anna's legs. 'Hiya,
Maurice,' she said, giving him a stroke. 'I bet you wonder
what's going on too, don't you.' Maurice did one more rub
round her legs and slunk off.

Anna thumbed through her post. A large envelope
intrigued her and she ripped it open first. Her whole body
jolted. She stared wide-eyed at the contents. There was a
covering letter thanking her for her interest and a glossy
brochure for her old university. Her hands began to
tremble and she dropped the brochure on the countertop.
Why would the university send her a prospectus? She
speed-read the letter again. It had all her details printed
on it; it hadn't been misdelivered. It was definitely meant
for her. But she hadn't requested it. There must be some
mistake.

Her stomach lurched at the familiar buildings on the
brochure's cover. She reached out a finger to trace the
lines of the main hall and unwelcome memories rushed
back. Her mind was reeling. Anna tried so hard to not
think about her time at university but in an instant she
felt herself being sucked back there. She pulled her hand
away. It had been a place that had held so much promise
and opportunity but it had all been shattered abruptly,

spinning her off plan. It seemed like every time she was moving on with her life the past had a way of rearing up and catching her off-guard.

Why had the university sent this to her? Was someone trying to freak her out? Or more specifically was Liam trying to freak her out? If it was him it was a very odd way to go about trying to win her over. Unless he hoped she'd turn to him in crisis. Her mind was a muddle of questions and an uncomfortable sensation was bubbling in her gut. She scooped up the brochure and dropped it into the recycling bin. It would be some silly computer error, she told herself. Those sorts of things happened all the time. It didn't mean anything. The brochure images swam in her mind. She just needed to forget about it. She could do that. She had to.

Anna was distracted by Sophie shouting but by the time she got to the bedroom Sophie had already thrown her phone down in disgust.

'He's gone and got steaming drunk,' said Sophie, folding her arms tightly across her ample chest. 'I leave him and he gets the beer out to celebrate.'

'I'm sure it's not exactly like that,' said Anna. She couldn't imagine Dave was celebrating.

'He's rung me to ask me to come home. Is that all he thinks it takes? I'm so desperate a drunk phone call will have me running ba . . .' She couldn't finish the sentence before the tears came. Anna sat on the bed, wrapped her in a hug and rocked her gently. Dave was thoughtless. Anna was sure he had no idea how much he hurt Sophie sometimes. When Sophie's tears had dried, Anna went and made her a decaf coffee.

'You drink this and settle yourself down with some

reality TV and I'm going to have a word with your feck-less husband.' It was time for some home truths.

Sophie looked surprised. 'Do you think you should?'

'Yes, because I'm his friend too. And when your friend is acting like a prize knob then you call them on it.' Anna smiled and Sophie gave a weak version in return.

It took ages for Dave to answer the door. When the door did finally open the disappointment on Dave's face told her a lot. 'I thought you were Sophie,' he said, a faint slur in his voice and a heavy scent of beer wafting off his breath.

'How many have you had?' Anna followed him inside and shut the door.

He held up one finger. 'One . . .'

'One? Was it served in a bucket?'

'Let me finish.' He stifled a burp. 'One too many.' He nodded wisely and stumbled as he tried to climb over a pile of overflowing supermarket bags in the hall.

'Shall I put these away?' asked Anna, already picking up one of the heavy bags and looking inside. 'Blimey that's a lot of carrots,' she said, seeing *all* the bags were full of carrots.

'Online shopping.' Dave shook his head gravely. 'It took me two hours to place my order and I swear I only ordered twelve carrots.'

'Ah,' said Anna. 'Looks like twelve kilos of carrots. You need to watch that.'

'Sophie usually does it. I've not got a clue.'

This was borne out as they both surveyed the pizza-box-strewn living room. 'Come on, Dave, you need to get yourself sorted. Sophie won't want to come home to this.'

'I'll tidy up,' he said, before slumping back onto the sofa.

'Fine but what else, Dave? What else are you going to do?'

Dave shrugged and then without warning burst into tears. Anna instinctively sat down next to him, put her arms round him and hugged him. His body shook with sobs. This was becoming a habit this evening. Anna held him until he'd got the tears under control. He pulled away and rubbed at his eyes.

'I'm sorry, Anna. I can't believe she's left me and the kids.'

'But it's not permanent, Dave, she will come home. You two just need to sort out your differences.'

'I don't think it's that easy.'

'Yes, it is,' insisted Anna. Although she was keen to have her flat back, she wasn't being selfish – she wanted the best for her friends. It bothered her that Dave and Sophie were doing this. Anyone could see they were made for each other and if they couldn't make it work, there was very little hope for her. Yes, they annoyed the crap out of each other but it didn't mean they didn't make each other happy too. They'd just forgotten how.

Dave hiccupped. 'Did she tell you how I found her last week?' Anna shook her head. 'She had a mini roll in one hand, a slice of ham in the other and a jar of Marmite on her lap,' said Dave, shaking his head.

'Maybe neither of you have been at your best lately but the bottom line is – you love each other. That's got to be worth making some changes for. Maybe start with sorting the house out? A bit of decorating, maybe?'

Dave gave a wince. 'It all costs money.'

'Then spend some money. Do what she wants, Dave. Give her the Hollywood house makeover if it'll make her happy.'

'Sophie knows the stuff in magazines is all fantasy; it's not real. We're on a tight budget. She understands we can't live our lives like that.' He glanced at Anna but her expression didn't say she agreed. 'Come on, we're not the Kardashians!'

'You're both working, you must be doing all right.'

'Have you any idea how much the mortgage on this place is?'

'Your mortgage will still be here in twenty years' time but your wife might not be.'

Dave's eyes widened but his pupils didn't. 'You are aware that statement doesn't contain anything positive?'

'Uh-huh,' said Anna, with a head bob. 'You need to woo her back, Dave. Make her feel special.' He opened his mouth but she carried on. 'It doesn't have to cost loads – she just needs to know you care. That you see her as more than free childcare, cook and cleaner.'

He leaned back against the sofa and Anna pulled her arm free just in time.

'You know I love you, Anna?' said Dave, with a hint of a slur in his words.

She knew it was the beer talking fluent bollocks. 'Really?'

'Yes. Absolutely. But in a completely asexual way. You understand? You're lovely and everything but you're just not my type. I don't find you at all attractive.'

'Right,' said Anna, starting to feel a little insulted. 'Is there anything specific?' she asked. Life in business had always taught her to embrace feedback as a positive thing.

Dave closed his eyes, deep in thought. 'You're very up and down figure-wise,' he said, waving his arm in her general direction.

Anna could live with that. She wasn't ever going to be curvy like Sophie.

'And you wear a lot of make-up. Makes me wonder what you're hiding under it.'

'I just like make-up.' She was starting to feel self-conscious.

'And . . .' Great, thought Anna, there's more. 'You have a weird pursing your lips thing like you've just put lipstick on. And your hair is a bit . . .'

'Okay, thanks, Dave. I think I get the picture. Do you talk to Sophie like this?'

'Why?' His head angled towards her but stayed resting against the sofa.

'Because I'm starting to see why she might be feeling a bit cheesed off.'

'But I love the way Sophie looks. I've fancied her from the moment I saw her and she's funny too. We used to laugh a lot, you know?'

'Yeah, I remember. But neither of you are happy like this.'

'I don't mean to upset her but somehow I constantly say and do the wrong thing. She gets her knickers in a twist over the tiniest thing.'

'And those are mighty big maternity knickers she's wearing at the moment,' said Anna.

Dave grinned. 'They're frigging huge.'

'And don't you think it makes her feel a bit less than alluring?'

'It shouldn't. She's carrying my baby, and that makes her the sexiest woman on the planet to me.' Dave started to tear up again.

'Then you should tell her exactly that,' said Anna. Dave sat forward as if about to spring into action. 'Not now.

But maybe once you've had some sleep, a shower and a shave.'

Dave nodded. 'Thanks, Anna.'

'You're welcome,' she said, giving him a pat like you would a trusted Labrador.

Even though it was August it was chilly outside and Anna was grateful to get back into the warm of the flat.

'Hiya,' she said, kicking off her trainers. She could hear sobbing and she followed the sound until she found Sophie curled up on the sofa seemingly trying for the world record attempt of how many tissues can be extracted from a box in five seconds.

'Hey, what's up?' asked Anna, trying to give her a hug but Sophie pushed her away and blew her nose loudly.

'Pants!' was all Sophie said before she went all blotchy and started crying again. Anna was momentarily stunned. She'd spent a whole hour talking to Dave, in an attempt to get them back together. What had happened now?

'What's the matter?' she said, wondering what hormone had now popped into Sophie's bloodstream.

'Those pants you said you knew nothing about,' said Sophie, blinking as more tears tumbled down her cheeks. 'Where are they?'

'In the bin. Have you suddenly realised you're a Marvel fan?'

Sophie ignored the joke and pulled out another tree's worth of tissues. Maurice tried to help and pulled a few more out for her.

'Sophe, I don't know what you're going on about. Do you want to know how I got on with Dave?' The fact Sophie hadn't asked didn't bode well for an early reconciliation.

'I know how you got on with my husband: a million times better than me!'

'Have you been drinking?'

'When were you going to tell me you were having an affair with Dave?'

Anna laughed involuntarily but then saw Sophie's pained expression and clenched jaw – she was serious.

'Come on, Sophie. You're joking, right?' Although everything about Sophie's body language said she wasn't. 'How on earth have you leaped to such a ridiculous conclusion?'

'I think this text from Dave makes it pretty clear how he feels about you. And I don't blame him. You're so much nicer than me. I'm a horrible person.' She passed her phone to Anna, but Anna was concentrating on her distraught friend.

'Sophie. Don't be like this. I shouldn't have to say it but nothing's going on between me and Dave.'

'Read the message,' instructed Sophie, her voice so choked up it was barely audible.

Anna fumbled with the phone before scrolling backwards through the text conversation, past a number of abusive replies from Sophie and finally she read Dave's message.

Talking to Anna has helped me see things clearly. I wish you were her

Anna blinked then she reread it. 'It's a typo, you pair of goons. It should say I wish you were *here*.'

'What?' said Sophie, sniffing back the tears and snatching her phone from Anna.

'Bloody hell,' said Anna. 'Forget the coffee. I might be forced back to alcohol.'

Sophie scrolled through her phone. 'Hairy potholes. What have I done?'

Anna gave her friend a hug. 'You've made your make-up run and you've probably single-handedly increased the Kleenex share price. But otherwise nothing we can't sort out.'

Sophie put down her phone, hugged Anna back and started to cry again but this time it was interspersed with giggles. 'I bloody love you, Strickland,' she said.

'Are you sure you're not pissed?' asked Anna, as they both began to laugh.

Chapter Twenty-Four

Connor had dropped her a text to say he would be in the city centre and asked if she fancied lunch as he'd really like to see her. It had been a nice message and given her a little boost, and so that was how Anna found herself on an impromptu date. She knew the upset between Sophie and Dave was affecting her more than it should have done but right now there wasn't a lot she could do about it. That being said, she had made a pledge with herself to make it her special project to get them back together before the kids came back from their holiday.

When she reached the coffee shop Connor welcomed her with a beaming smile and immediately went to get food and drinks, taking care to make sure he'd got her coffee order right. He really was very sweet. While he was waiting in the queue she had a chance to have a proper look at him without being too obvious. He was tall – maybe even taller than Hudson. Today Connor was wearing a shirt and tie. Nothing fancy but he looked smart and not quite as young as he had the first time they'd met. He didn't fill his shirt like a certain American she knew, but then who did? His limbs seemed a bit out of proportion making him a little gangly and uncoordinated – and as if to demonstrate exactly what Anna was thinking, he tripped over his own feet as he was called forward to the counter. He apologised profusely to everyone nearby and shot a self-conscious glance at Anna, who turned away.

Connor returned with the drinks and a table number. 'Thanks for meeting me. I just thought I've got a couple of hours free, and you're the person I would most like to spend them with,' he said, averting his eyes.

'Thanks. It was a nice thought. It's always good to escape the office.'

'You're a project manager, right?' He seemed to be testing his memory skills from their first-date conversation.

'Yes, well remembered. And you work with mobile phones.' She couldn't recollect what he did exactly.

'Correct. Here, let me show you something. Do you mind?' he asked, pointing to her mobile.

'Sure.' She unlocked it and passed it to him. His thumbs traversed the screen at speed and then he leaned towards her and showed her the screen was now a spirit level.

'If you're doing any DIY you can use this to check your shelves are straight.'

'Okay. I didn't know it did that.' Connor turned away again, pressed a few keys and then placed the phone face down.

'And now if I send a message . . .' He got out his own phone and within seconds the camera flash went off on Anna's phone.

'Wow, has it taken a photo?'

'No, but it's a way of alerting you to a message instead of beeping or vibrating.'

'I guess it's useful if you're deaf,' she said. She knew he

was being helpful by showing her some features she wasn't aware of but it wasn't the most fun she'd ever had. She gave herself a mental shake. Connor was a decent person, he seemed dependable and there was a lot to be said for that. And she wasn't looking for anything serious and as nice, dependable dateable men went, she could do far worse than Connor. A lull in conversation had Connor glancing about restlessly. A group of young people carrying folders came in and filled the small shop with their laughter.

'Seeing all these students about makes me feel seriously old.'

Anna busied herself with her coffee. 'Well, it was a long time ago now,' she said brusquely. 'Have you got a busy afternoon planned?' she added, keen to change the subject and halt the thoughts in her head.

Connor seemed to falter. 'Err, not too busy.' The silence fell on them again. 'I remember my freshers' week. I was part of the rugby team and had to drink beer out of my boots every night for a week.'

Great, thought Anna. The last thing I want to do is rake over my past. She knew he was just trying to make conversation but it uncovered feelings she struggled to manage. Connor bent forward a little and continued. 'And I won't begin to tell you what I had to dress as for my initiation. How about you?' He picked up his drink but didn't take his eyes off Anna.

She tried to keep herself calm but she knew she had to say something. 'There were a few parties, lots of pizza but I don't remember much else. I guess that was all the alcohol.' She tried to laugh at the end but it was impossible to even fake a giggle. Connor was leaning forwards with interest.

'Anything particularly wild?'

Anna felt a mild panic begin to unfold inside her. She needed to change the subject. Just then the camera on her phone flashed making her jump. 'A message.' Thank the Lord, she thought. She opened the rambling rant from Sophie about Dave getting cupcakes delivered to the office. Anna had an idea. 'Bugger. Crisis in the office. I'm sorry, Connor, but I really have to go.'

'What, this second?' For the first time she saw a flash of annoyance although he quickly recovered. 'Okay. If you have to.'

'I'm so sorry. I'll call you. This was really nice.' She gestured to the drinks, grabbed her jacket and bag and hurried out.

Sophie was still grumbling about Dave when Anna joined them for a team meeting. She flopped onto a wheelie chair making it skid backwards and bump into Karl.

'Sorry,' said Anna.

'Women drivers,' said Karl, with a grin.

'Remind me again why you're still single? It's a complete mystery to me,' said Anna, barely glancing in Karl's direction. 'What's up with you?' she asked Sophie.

'My day started with a prick up my bum.' Sophie wagged a finger threateningly at Karl. 'Not a blooming word.' Karl reversed his chair away whilst holding up his hands in surrender. 'Dave put a rose on the driving seat but I didn't notice and sat on the pigging thing. You'll have to inspect my backside later, I'm sure it drew blood.' Sophie rubbed her bum as she spoke.

'Great, I'm really looking forward to that,' said Anna, with a wide fake smile.

'And listen to this,' said Sophie, holding out her phone

on speakerphone as she played a message. A loud noise came from the phone making Anna wince.

'Is it someone playing a trumpet?' asked Anna.

'Or grating a cat's arse?' asked Karl.

'It's Dave blowing his clarinet,' said Sophie. Karl opened his mouth. 'NOT a euphemism,' she added quickly.

Anna concentrated hard. 'What's the tune?'

'It might be the theme from *Titanic*,' said Sophie, not looking convinced.

'Yes, yes, I think it could be. Ah, he's serenading you. That's sweet of him,' said Anna. She couldn't help feeling pleased Dave was making an effort however madcap it may appear.

Sophie pouted. 'I guess.'

'You really need to stop looking at everything Dave does with shit-tinted spectacles,' said Anna.

Sophie sighed. 'I know.' She offered Anna a cupcake from the box – each of them prettily iced with one letter. Anna studied what now remained:

YOU POO ELVIS

Anna glowered at Karl who was studiously ignoring her. 'What did it say before the cretin played anagrams?'

Sophie mumbled her reply. 'Sophie I love you x.'

'He's trying,' said Anna, taking a bite out of a cupcake.

'He certainly is. In fact I think if you look up "Trying" in the dictionary there's actually a picture of Dave next to it.'

'Is everyone here?' said Roberta, striding into the room and sucking the energy from it like a Gucci-clad dementor.

Part way through the meeting Anna's phoned flashed and everyone turned to look. Bugger! 'Sorry I don't know how to turn it off.' She should have asked Connor to switch it back to vibrate; the flashing thing was beginning to get really annoying. She picked up her phone to see who the message was from. It was Connor.

Shame you had to dash off but I do 100% understand. I had a few minutes so here's a music playlist from your uni years. It's a 'throwback' thing that everyone's doing at the moment. Hope it makes a busy afternoon better. C x.

There was a link attached but Anna was staring at the very last letter. A simple letter that when used in a word means nothing but on its own or on a cupcake it makes all the difference. She wasn't sure she was ready for kisses from Connor. She certainly wasn't ready for the modern-day equivalent of a mix tape. She followed the link anyway and as she suspected the songs on the list did have her mind racing back to her student days. She deleted the playlist quickly and tried to tune back in to the meeting.

The last weekend of the school holidays was looming and Sophie was excited because the children would be coming back from their trip, which from all accounts they were thoroughly enjoying. The thought of her having to go home still troubled her. She liked staying at Anna's; it was peaceful and ordered and she was sleeping really well despite having to get up numerous times for a wee because the baby was using her bladder as a pillow. She'd been there nearly two weeks now and she'd become calmer, more relaxed and generally a nicer person. She wasn't cross all the time. She was still cross some of the time because Dave still managed to annoy her but it was easier to escape here.

Sophie was enjoying her Saturday morning curled up on the sofa munching toast and watching a cookery programme on the telly when Anna came in from a run and put her head round the living room door. 'What are your plans for today?' she asked, taking out her ear buds and pulling them through her running top like a magician producing flowers from a sleeve. Sophie shrugged and pointed the remote at the telly. Anna stepped in between her and the telly and Sophie groaned.

'You say you never have time to do things you want to do. Maybe now is a good time to do something more positive than sit on the sofa watching TV all day.'

Sophie's eyes widened. 'Thanks for your opinion but I'm pregnant and watching telly is what I want to do.'

Anna huffed. 'I'm going for a shower and then I'm going out because it's a beautiful day.'

'Fine,' said Sophie, wrapping her dressing gown around her baby bump and staring resolutely at the TV.

'You know what they say about when life gives you lemons?'

Sophie didn't look up. 'If I wasn't pregnant I'd be grabbing the tequila and salt.'

'Very funny. It's not all bad you know.'

Sophie turned to face Anna. 'I was where you are once. The child-free singleton who can please themselves. And whilst I love my children beyond reason they do change everything.'

'I know.'

'No, you don't. I open your freezer and there's no Mr Bump patches cooling ready for the next banged head. You have an adult bathroom; there's not a toy in sight. There's no danger of sitting on a rubber duck and you don't have a toy pirate watch you take a shower. You don't have nursery rhymes playing in your car; you can have any music or radio station you like. You don't hum the tune to the "Wheels On The Bus" when you are on your own because it's the worst earworm ever. Your kitchen is properly clean and it stays clean. You don't have goblin-like creatures who can just look at something and make it sticky. You don't have to make up words to use instead of swear words to express yourself without your child being excluded from school. You can walk around barefoot without the fear of standing on a Lego brick and trust me, that pain is second only to childbirth. You can forget knob in zipper because Lego brick wins every time.' Sophie took a breath. 'You don't know, Anna, and that's okay because one day if you're very lucky you will and then I will laugh and laugh and . . .'

'Thanks that's really graphic and has probably put me off kids for life.' Anna was blinking at the tirade.

'You're welcome. And I have stair gates to negotiate and locks on every cupboard – basically my house is totally childproof.'

'And somehow they still get in,' quipped Anna, making Sophie chuckle. Anna paused in the doorway. 'Are you at least coming to Roberta's barbecue later?'

'I'd forgotten about that.' Sophie eyed the sunshine outside. It wouldn't be long before the temperature changed. Sunny days were few and far between. She didn't want to go, she hated work things at a weekend but Anna was right: she did need to make the most of her time off from being the responsible adult. 'Okay, I'll come.' Sophie snuggled down on the sofa again. 'No point moving until you come out of the shower though,' she said with a grin and she changed the channel again.

The sun was high in the sky and not being interrupted by the few clouds drifting slowly past. It was a gorgeous day and an afternoon spent outside was beginning to appeal to Sophie even if the thought of what state her house was in troubled her. The kids were due back tomorrow and she didn't want them coming home to a pigsty but she also didn't want to tidy up Dave's mess.

Anna knocked on her open bedroom door, wearing a pretty halter-neck dress and looking rather Audrey Hepburn with her hair pinned up and sunglasses nestled on the top of her head. 'Ready?'

Sophie looked down at what she was wearing. Maternity shorts from when she was pregnant with Arlo and a smock top she'd bought last week because everything she owned made her look like she was smuggling a pair of bongos. Her boobs were the biggest they'd ever been. 'Yeah, I guess,' said Sophie, grabbing her lipstick and putting on an extra coat before zhooshing up her hair. She'd have to do.

As they got in Sophie's car she gave a cursory check for any more roses. There hadn't been anything from Dave so far today but it was still early. Sophie reversed out of the visitor parking space and as she turned the car towards the road she saw it. Someone had tied a large sheet to the park railings and painted across it were the words 'Dave + Sophie 4 Ever' inside a large pink heart. Sophie jumped on the brakes, making them both lurch against their seat-belts.

'I'm guessing that's not your handiwork,' said Anna, pointing at the sheet.

'He is *so* embarrassing.' Sophie could feel her neck prickling with heat.

'I'll get it down,' said Anna, getting out of the car. She soon had the sheet rolled up and she shoved it in the boot of Sophie's car and got back in.

'What does he think he's doing?' asked Sophie, as they set off.

'He's trying to woo you back. I think it's quite lovely to be honest.'

'Really?' Sophie was doubtful. This was not how it happened in the films. Romantic gestures were not pinned to fences and did not spike you in the bum – those things only happened to her.

'Yeah, I think so. What would make you go back to him?'

Sophie indicated and let the ticking noise pulse through her mind as she thought. 'I want something more. To feel like I'm a bit special, you know? Like he's made a bit of an effort for me.'

'The sign was for you,' said Anna.

'I know,' said Sophie with a heavy sigh. 'I know he's not one of life's big romantics but surely he could learn. Maybe whisk me away to a fancy hotel? Or send me flowers and chocolates?'

'Didn't you say money was a bit tight?'

'It's just Dave who's tight.' She spotted Anna's expression. 'Okay. But he doesn't have to spend loads. He could take the kids out sometimes to give me a break. I can't remember the last time I had a bath without Arlo insisting on using the toilet while I was in there. Or even just a cup of coffee in bed. Surely it's not too much to ask?'

They fell silent apart from the sat nav giving them directions. Anna concentrated on doing something on her phone, while Sophie wondered if she'd ever feel special again.

Chapter Twenty-Five

Roberta's house was on the edge of Solihull in a wide avenue where parking on the road was forbidden. Luckily she had a large sweep-round drive and despite the number of cars already parked, there was room for them to get in at the back. The house itself was a modernised 1920s' affair painted in stark white with a slate-grey front door, which matched the double garage. It was impressive, as Anna had expected it to be. A sign directed them down the passage at the side of the house, which wasn't a surprise. There was no way Roberta was going to let them all traipse through her house although Anna had a good nose through the front window as she went past.

The garden at the back was huge with a very new-looking patio area that Anna assumed was what Roberta had specifically wanted to show off unless of course this was the 'anything you can do I can do better' response to Hudson's party. Half the office was there. It always amused Anna to see what different people's interpretation of casual was. At work the dress code was fairly easy to predict but at social gatherings it was fascinating to see older men in T-shirts displaying their favourite bands and ladies who always wore straight skirts dancing with abandon in leather trousers.

Roberta was standing on the edge of the patio looking like the love child of Jackie Onassis and Danny DeVito, her large dark shades hiding a lot of her face. 'Anna, Sophie, hi. Champagne over there, elderflower inside.' She bobbed to the side to greet the next person.

'I fancy elderflower,' said Anna.

'I fancy Hudson,' said Sophie, gazing down the garden where Hudson was swigging a beer.

'Still?'

'Look at him. He's even better now he's not gay any more.'

'He never was gay.' Anna couldn't help point out the obvious.

'He's like an expensive coffee. Dark, hot and I bet he'd keep me up all night long.' Sophie let out a long slow breath.

'You poor thing,' said Anna, although she was inclined to agree with her. Hudson was wearing aviator sunglasses, a white polo shirt, navy shorts and flip-flops. Few men could carry off flip-flops convincingly but he was definitely one of them. She found herself staring and quickly looked away.

They returned outside with their drinks and Anna put on her sunglasses. It was far easier to people watch when it wasn't obvious you had them under surveillance. A quick scan of those assembled told her Liam wasn't there, and she hoped it stayed that way. 'Who's manning the barbecue?' asked Anna, nodding in the direction of a grey-haired man in a checked shirt with the cuffs turned back.

'I think it's Roberta's dad,' said Sophie. 'Yep, I'm pretty sure I saw him pick her up from last year's Christmas party.'

He was poking the coals vigorously and shaking his

head. Roberta ferried out a large platter of meat. 'You should be cooking by now. What are you doing?' she snapped.

'I'm cooking the chicken first, like you told me,' he said, sounding quite like his daughter.

'I don't want you poisoning anyone. I'd never hear the end of it,' said Roberta.

'Nice to see it's not just us who get that treatment,' said Anna, in hushed tones and she and Sophie scooted down the garden whilst Roberta continued to argue with her dad.

'You look stunning,' said Hudson when Anna reached him.

'Thank you,' said Sophie and Anna together and they both looked slightly embarrassed.

Hudson greeted them both. Some music started blaring out of the conservatory and everyone looked round to see Karl waving his apologies and Roberta marched off in his direction. Hudson guided Anna away.

'I've spoken to Roberta about the New York position,' he said, with his trademark bright smile.

Anna had suspected this would be the case. She felt a pang of something deep inside. She knew it was coming but the thought he'd be permanently moving to another continent was still a bit of a blow. He was all right when you got used to him. Possibly even more than all right.

'And when will you know if you've got it?'

Hudson gave a slow and measured shake of his head. 'I'm not going for it.'

'What? Why?' Anna was confused. This was the perfect opportunity for them both to have a significant role.

'Because I've recommended you,' he said, happiness lighting up his features.

'What?' said Anna, although it came out as almost a shout.

Hudson looked taken aback. 'You said you've always wanted to go to New York.'

'Yes, but . . . What?' said Anna, scowling. Why on earth would he do this? Her brain was working overtime trying to work out the angle. What was the benefit to him in staying here? She had to be missing something. They might have grown close but at the end of the day he was an ambitious man and he was always going to put his own career first.

'You would be excellent in the role and it's somewhere you wanted to visit. I thought Roberta would automatically think of me so I figured I needed to tell her you were better placed to run the New York side of things and I would stay in the UK.' He raised his beer bottle to clink a cheers with her glass but she was still gazing at him open-mouthed. What the hell had he done?

'But you know I'm afraid of heights,' she said and swallowed. The thought of them made her uneasy. 'A plane is like thirty thousand feet in the air.'

'Yeah, but flying is different.'

Anna was already shaking her head. 'The thought of flying makes my stomach flip.' She held out her palm. 'I'm sweating now just thinking about it.' She'd not been on a plane since she was a child and panic was already sweeping over her.

'Ah,' said Hudson, running his bottom lip through his teeth. 'Maybe not a great suggestion after all.'

'Have you done this to expose my phobia as a weakness?' The question was out before she could vet it.

'No!' He stepped back and waved his free arm. 'You actually think I'd do that to you?'

'No, it's just . . .' started Anna. She was cross he'd made

238

such a big assumption and spoken to Roberta without consulting her first. She was also more than a bit terrified at the thought of getting on a plane.

Hudson did reply but it was drowned out by a whooshing sound as Roberta's dad threw something on the barbecue and the whole thing caught alight. Hudson and Karl ran towards the fiery scene. Hudson grabbed a tea towel and put the lid on the barbecue, which shut off most of the flames. Karl patted down Roberta's dad putting out the flames on his apron and Hudson took off his flip-flop and used it to put out the patches of lawn that were also aflame. Roberta marched over. 'What the hell is going on?' she demanded.

Karl opened up the barbecue and a plume of smoke bellowed out like an Indian smoke signal. 'I think your chicken is done,' said Karl, spearing a charcoal shape with his fork.

The cooking had been moved inside and the afternoon had been pleasant enough but Anna had spent the rest of it avoiding Hudson. He had tried more than a couple of times to have another conversation with her but she had been too racked with anxiety to have a reasonable discussion. How could he make such a huge assumption and not even consult her on it?

Anna got a message on her phone on the way home and she breathed a sigh of relief. A message pinged on Sophie's phone soon afterwards but she was driving. Anna started rummaging through Sophie's bag. 'I'll get it for you. Shall I? It might be important.'

'It can wait. It'll only be Dave to say he needs directions to the kitchen.'

Anna gave a fake laugh. 'I'm sure it's not.' Anna pulled

out a glossy magazine, rummaged her way through a mountain of receipts and found the phone under a packet of wet wipes. 'Here it is,' she said raising it triumphantly. She quickly unlocked it and read the message. 'It's from Dave,' she began.

'See I told you. Useless plughole. What does he want?'

'He says – **I want to show you how much I have changed. Will you please come round at 7 p.m. Love D x.**' Anna sent up a silent thank you to the heavens above. Her frenzied text earlier had at least got the ball rolling; now all Dave had to do was steer it in the right direction.

'Does he say why?' asked Sophie, briefly taking her eyes off the road.

'Nope but it sounds positive to me. It seems like he's turning over a new leaf. You should definitely go and check it out.'

Sophie was scowling. 'I don't know.'

'Yeah, you do,' said Anna, in a singsong voice. 'Go on, what's the worst that could happen?'

'I could see the state the house is in and feel compelled to sort it all out before the kids come home. So no. I'm not going. When Kraken brings them back tomorrow she can see the state of the place and she can sort it out.'

'No, no, no,' said Anna, feeling her master plan sliding from her grasp. 'You don't have to do anything if it's a mess. You can even point out to Dave that Kraken, I mean Karen, will be there tomorrow, which should get him moving if nothing else does.'

'I don't know.' Sophie sounded unsure.

Anna pounced. 'One last chance, Sophe. After all the years you've been together, he deserves one last chance.' Anna held her breath.

There was a long silence. Sophie turned the car into the driveway at the side of the flats and parked the car in the visitor's space. She twisted in her seat to eyeball Anna who was giving her best attempt at a pleading puppy face. 'Okay, but if the house is a tip I swear I'll lamp him one.'

'And you would be completely within your rights to do so. Let's hope it's not.'

Sophie redid her hair and make-up to make herself feel ready for action. She wasn't sure what sort of action but she was adamant she wasn't going to let the state of her once beautiful house upset her and she definitely wasn't clearing it all up. She checked her watch.

'Right, if I'm not back in twenty minutes send the fire brigade round.'

'Fire brigade?' queried Anna.

'Everyone knows they're hunkier than police and I'll bloomin' well need cheering up before they cart me off to prison for murdering Dave.'

'Okay. But give him a chance, that's all I'm going to say.'

'Hmm,' mumbled Sophie and she left.

It felt odd to knock on her own front door but it also didn't feel quite right to Sophie to let herself in. She saw his shadow at the door a moment before he opened it. A waft of the aftershave she'd bought him for Christmas hit her and made her blink. He was clean-shaven and wearing a shirt. Not a work shirt but one of the good ones he used to wear when they went out BC – before children.

'Hey, thanks for coming,' said Dave, his voice uncertain. 'Come in.'

Sophie stepped inside cautiously, her eyes flickering about for the first thing to moan about – but the hall was tidy. She popped her head into the downstairs loo. Everything was spotless. All the coats were hung up on hooks and she noted the missing hook had been screwed back in place. She raised an eyebrow. She followed him through to the living room, where candles were burning and the cushions had been plumped.

'Right, who is she?' said Sophie.

'What? Who?' Dave seemed thrown by her line of questioning.

'Whoever did this. Who is she?'

Dave's eyes widened. 'I did it.'

Sophie squinted at him, deeply suspicious. 'Who are you and what have you done with the real Dave?' she asked, but there was the faintest hint of a smile on her lips. She forced it away. He wasn't getting around her that easily with a fixed coat rack, a tidy room and a scented candle. She noted it was a new Yankee candle – she approved.

'This is the new me, if you'll give me a chance.' He took a step forward.

Sophie slowly held up a hand to pause him. 'I need to know things will change, Dave. I've given up a lot for us and I know it's what we agreed but now I've had time to think about it, I'm not happy.'

'I know and I want that to change. How about you go and have a bath and then we'll talk over dinner. And before you ask, yes I've cooked something. No, it won't poison you and yes, it's from Waitrose. My only involvement was reading the instructions.' He smiled and Sophie smiled too. 'There's a bath already run for you. Go on, I need to check my chicken,' he said, almost shooing her from the room.

Sophie climbed the stairs and with each step her spirits

lifted a fraction. It was a huge step that Dave had recognised he needed to change and she could already smell the enticing scent of patchouli bath foam and was looking forward to sinking into the bubbles. She'd give Dave a chance. Anna was right: he deserved that much.

She had been soaking for about ten minutes when there was a gentle tap on the door and when Sophie turned her head she saw an outstretched arm holding a champagne flute.

'It's bubbles,' said Dave. 'It's non-alcoholic Prosecco but it's meant to be nice.' He passed her the glass and after shaking off the suds she took it.

'Thanks, Dave, this is really nice. But we need to have a proper chat,' she said, preparing herself for the inevitable argument.

'I know, and we will but for now enjoy some peace and quiet,' he said, with a small tweak of his lips. 'How about you get out in about twenty minutes?'

'Okay,' she said and he disappeared. Sophie took a sip and was pleasantly surprised. She sank back underneath the bubbles and closed her eyes. This was a very good start.

Anna closed the park gate behind her, slid the key fob into the pocket of her joggers and started a brisk warm-up walk. The sun was starting to set as she followed the old Victorian path that coaxed its way past the rockery and through the old sunken garden. The foliage became briefly denser, which added to the anticipation, before ahead of her the lake came into view, now circled by a ring of yellow irises and many other colourful wildflowers she'd need the spotter sheet to name. The surface of the water shimmered as the last of the sun gilded the water. As she reached its edge Anna set off the timer on her watch and started to jog. She soon settled into a steady pace and let her thoughts wander.

She knew she needed to have a proper conversation with Hudson about the two available positions. She wished she knew what his motivations were for recommending her for the New York post. It bothered her that he wanted the UK position because it implied it was the better of the two and logically she should have slotted into the role without any question. There was, of course, the possibility he genuinely believed she would be better in the US role but it felt doubtful. Now she would have to explain why she couldn't be considered for the New York role. She realised she was speeding up and she slowed her pace a fraction; this often happened when she got herself agitated about something.

Hudson was right: she had always wanted to go to New York. She'd seen it in many films and read about it in books and magazines and it always seemed amazingly glamorous. She couldn't deny the thought of working there was a thrill but how could it ever be a consideration if she broke out in a sweat at the thought of getting on an aeroplane? Perhaps she could be tranquillised? It felt a bit extreme. Anna took an untimely deep breath and with it sucked in a troop of minuscule dancing flies. As her lungs violently protested about the intrusion she stopped abruptly to cough and splutter in an attempt to evict the tiny creatures lodged in her throat.

'Are you all right?' asked a familiar voice from up ahead.

Chapter Twenty-Six

Sophie dried herself on what she noted was a *clean* towel – one that had even been warming on the heated towel rail. As she padded through to their bedroom she stopped in the doorway. The room was immaculate. Even better than the standard she tried to keep it at. She tiptoed in almost as if she was snooping in someone else's home. Her basket of cosmetics had been neatly ordered rather than all chucked in as she usually did and the hair bobbles and grips, which frequently littered the surface of the dressing table, were now in a small wicker pot. She picked it up. It was pretty. She wondered where it had come from and again started to worry about who had done all this. Kraken was away. Surely it couldn't have been Dave?

Laid out on the bed was a dress. It wasn't hers. She picked it up and saw it still had the labels on. It was a simple black maternity shift dress with some lace detailing on its short sleeves. It felt good quality and she set about putting it on. She looked at herself in the mirror and was pleased by what she saw. She sat down at the dressing table and redid her make-up and hair.

She heard Dave's footsteps on the stairs before a tap on the bedroom door. 'How are you getting on? Dinner is almost ready.' She stood up as he walked in. 'Wow. Just wow,' he said, his eyes skirting over her appreciatively. 'You're amazing, Sophe.'

Her resolve was rapidly dissolving. 'Come on, let's have this dinner then before it's burned to a crisp. Assuming it isn't crisps to start with,' she said, walking past him.

The dinner table was laid, the lights were dimmed and she spotted the bulb, the one that had been out for months, had been replaced. Sophie settled herself at the table while Dave rushed about and clattered in the kitchen. Eventually he emerged with two plates. 'Chicken breasts with ginger, chilli and lime with a vegetable medley,' he announced, sounding quite proud of himself.

'Great,' said Sophie and her stomach growled its appreciation. They ate the meal in relative silence. The silence itself was a treat. Mealtimes were hectic in their house. It was actually quite a stressful time of arguing with Arlo over why he couldn't have cake for every meal interspersed with his multitude of random questions that made her brain hurt. At the same time she would be trying to feed Petal who swung between screaming because she wasn't being fed quickly enough and wanting to grab and wear her food. She realised Dave was usually oblivious to this because he was either on his phone, answering emails, checking football scores or playing some dumb game. Dave didn't have his phone out tonight.

'This is nice. Maybe we should have some rules around mealtimes when the children get home,' she said.

'Yeah, I'm all for that.'

'I think we should also ban any electronics. That way we set the rule now and when they get mobiles they won't be on those when they should be eating.'

'Completely agree. When I was a kid, dinnertime was family time. We all used to talk about our day,' said Dave.

Trust Kraken to have had the perfect family dinnertime. She doubted they would be able to achieve a Walton's Mountain level of family life but they could make some steps towards it. 'Okay. Dave, if I'm to come home, things need to change.'

Dave was already nodding as he chewed a mouthful of food. 'Look around you. Things have changed.'

She knew this was true. 'But is all this just a one-off?'

'No, because I've hired a cleaner and not just any cleaner – she does ironing too.' Dave raised his glass.

'Can we afford a cleaner?'

'If it's what it takes to save our marriage then we definitely can.'

'Did she do all this?' asked Sophie, taking in the pristine kitchen surfaces and clean floor. Dave nodded. 'Blimey, that's brilliant.'

'I know!' They clinked glasses and grinned across the table at each other.

The conversation relaxed once they had dealt with the elephant in the room and before long they were chattering excitedly as they reminisced. Sophie pushed away her dessert bowl. She was full and she had really enjoyed the meal. It was a good choice but it was more that Dave had taken the time to cook it for her. She loved her food but when you had to cook every day you did lose some of the enthusiasm for it. And with children it became a test of whether she was providing them with all their required nutrients, fibre and latest recommended government levels of fruit and vegetables.

'This has been lovely, Dave, thank you,' she said, reaching her hand across the table and clasping his fingers.

He squeezed her hand in return. An evening with Dave without a disaster or something to spoil it was a rare occurrence.

'Oh, I nearly forgot,' said Dave, jumping to his feet. 'It's a bit belated but anyway.' He rummaged around in the utility before switching off the lights. 'Ha-ppy birth-day to you . . .' he sang as he walked back in carrying a cupcake with a sparkler in it, which lit up his face as it fizzed and sparked. He sung all the way to the end of the song before presenting the cake to Sophie for her to blow out the wildly smoking and glowing sparkler. As Sophie blew on the now drooping sparkler the smoke alarm began to shriek and they both dissolved into laughter.

'Bloody hell!' said Anna through gasps of breath. 'Connor, you scared the life out of me.' She finished her coughing fit and looked about. It was almost dark now and she couldn't see anyone else around. 'What are you doing here?'

'Ah, bit embarrassing actually,' said Connor, going all coy. 'I'm not sure what I said the other day at lunch but I got the feeling I'd upset you. And I texted earlier but you didn't reply.'

'Right,' said Anna, feeling uneasy.

'I know this sounds all stalker-ish and I'm really not.' He waved his hands in defence. 'But I was a bit worried and I didn't want to hassle you by text. I thought if I came over I might be able to see that you were here and you were okay. And now I've said it out loud it does sound all stalker-ish and I'm really sorry.' He pulled a funny face and Anna relaxed. She could see his intentions were good.

'It's okay.'

'Are you sure? Because I'd understand if you wanted to

get a restraining order or something. You're quite within your rights.' He fidgeted about like a puppet on strings and it made her warm to him.

'No, I think we're good. Did you want to come back for a coffee?'

Connor's expression became more earnest. 'I'd really like that. Thanks.'

'Sophie's out but she's due back soon and you can meet Maurice,' said Anna, striding off.

'Great,' said Connor, although he didn't sound quite as pleased as he had about the coffee.

Anna's phone had a pinging session as she reached the flat and a quick glance told her it was messages from Sophie and Hudson. She'd have to deal with those later. She put her phone on the kitchen worktop and took off her trainers. Connor was already removing his shoes and the thought shot through her mind how impressed her mum would be with him doing this without having to be asked.

'Do you mind if I have a quick shower?' She pulled at her running top.

'Of course, not. Shall I make us some coffee? I'm sure I can find my way around the kitchen,' he said, with a silly grin. 'Look, there's a kettle.'

'That'd be great, thanks.' She bounded off to the bath-room.

Once clean and dressed in leggings and a shirt she returned to the kitchen where Connor was leaning against the worktop sipping his drink. 'You are allowed into the living room, you know,' she said.

'I didn't want you to think I was snooping.' He handed her a mug of coffee. 'I did it half milk and microwaved it because you had a latte in the café . . .' He tailed off. He really was incredibly thoughtful.

'It's perfect.' She led the way through to the living room and settled herself on one end of the sofa with Connor sitting next to her. Maurice was in the chair opposite and he stretched and eyed the stranger speculatively.

Maurice jumped to the floor and in two strides he was on Connor's lap. 'Whoa!' he said, almost spilling his coffee and hastily putting the mug on the coffee table. Maurice circled around Connor's thighs, each time swishing his fluffy tail in Connor's face whilst kneading his claws into his jeans and from Connor's expression most likely his flesh too.

'Sorry, are you all right?' asked Anna.

'I'm not great with cats,' he said.

'I see.' This felt like the first time he'd said something negative and she tried not to let it show on her face.

He glanced at her. 'I don't hate them or anything. It's because . . . I'm allergic.'

'I'm sorry. Here, let me take him. Come on, Maurice,' said Anna, trying to pick him up. The cat had other ideas and firmly dug his claws into Connor's thighs.

'Ow!' yelped Connor as Anna pulled Maurice and he held on tight.

'Maurice. Let. Go,' said Anna, giving him a gentle tug with each word, embarrassment swamping her. Maurice gave a mew in protest and finally retracted his claws. She placed him on the windowsill and opened the top window in the hope he'd go out. He turned around, swished his tail about crossly and glared at Connor.

Connor brushed down his trousers as if to rid himself of any signs of the cat although Anna couldn't see any fur there. Maurice flounced up and down the windowsill before leaping onto the edge of the open window, in one fluid movement, and out into the night. 'That's an interesting cat flap,' said Connor.

'I know,' said Anna. 'I need to get a proper one for the front door before the weather changes. It's fine to have it open all night in the summer but it'll be no good once it turns a bit chilly.'

'I could fit one for you.'

'I wouldn't want to put you to any trouble.'

'It's not. I'm no Nick Knowles but I know my way around a screwdriver.'

They spent the next hour chatting. It was mainly small talk but it was getting easier between them. Connor spotted the time and said he needed to call in on his mum on the way home and went to put his shoes back on. Anna followed him to the kitchen.

'Thanks for coming around.'

'Sorry, if I freaked you out in the park. I really didn't mean to.' He looked contrite.

'I know you didn't.'

'Anna?' He bent his head towards her and went all shy. 'You're special and I really value what we've got.'

She felt something stronger than fondness towards him and without thinking she reached up and planted a small kiss on his cheek. Why did she do that? She wasn't sure and was a bit shocked with herself for making the first move.

His reaction was initially one of startle and then he looked pleased.

'See you again soon. I hope,' he said. 'By arrangement next time,' he added, with a chuckle.

Anna shut the door and felt a flutter of something. It wasn't wild passion – she was never going to get that with Connor. But he was sweet, caring and dependable. She picked her phone up from the kitchen drainer and walked back to the living room checking her messages. She opened

Sophie's first. It read – **Dave understands and has got us a cleaner! Am staying the night and moving back home tomorrow. Thanks for being best friend ever x.**

'Halle – bloody – lujah!' said Anna, to the room. Oh, the relief, she felt a little emotional. The world was back on its axis and she could relax again. Feeling happy she'd had a small part in their reunion she treated herself to a hot chocolate before replying to Sophie and checking her other messages.

The next three were from Hudson all apologising for recommending her and ending with him offering to go and withdraw his recommendation. She dialled his number without thinking as the irritation bubbled inside.

'Anna, I am truly sorry . . .'

'Don't go and withdraw your recommendation. What the hell will it look like?' She didn't give him a chance to answer. 'Roberta will think you have a reason why I can't do the New York job and—'

'You do, you've got a fear of heights and flying.'

Anna was pacing the kitchen. 'It's the same thing. It's one phobia. I only have *one* phobia. And it doesn't mean I can't do the job; it means I just can't do it . . . over there.' She gestured with her hand.

'Right. What do you want me to do then?' He sounded as exasperated as she felt.

Anna paused for a second. It was a good question and she didn't know the answer. 'How do we get out of this almighty cock-up?'

Hudson chuckled. 'Bloody hell, Hudson, this isn't funny.'

'Sorry, it's that phrase it always makes me laugh. Cock-up. It's funny. It's so British.' Anna huffed. 'Again, I'm truly sorry I screwed up. Just tell me how to fix things and I will.'

'I wish I knew.'

'Okay. How about we both get in early on Monday. I shout you breakfast and we hatch a plan where you look awesome?'

Anna was annoyed with herself for grinning but how could she not when he said things like that. 'I had better look totally amazing.'

'I promise you will. Okay? Am I out of time-out now?'

'No, but I no longer want to harm you.'

'I'll take that,' said Hudson. 'See you Monday. Seven thirty?'

'Okay. I'm expecting a full cooked English breakfast and no more cock-ups.'

'Absolutely.' And the phone went dead. Anna flopped onto the sofa. She was drained like she'd been running again. Something about a fight with Hudson always did that to her.

Chapter Twenty-Seven

Sophie woke on Sunday with her husband's arm wrapped around her baby bump and the smugness level that comes after lots of sex. It had been ages since they'd been like that in the bedroom. The opportunity to get a bit vocal without worrying about waking the children or being interrupted mid enthusiastic shag had unleashed their passion and the last thing Dave had said before he drifted off into a contented sleep was: 'Remind me tomorrow to fit a lock on the door.'

They had enjoyed such a perfect evening. It had reminded them both why they were together as a couple as well as being parents. Employing a cleaner had been a masterstroke. Who would have thought a cleaner could save a marriage? Dave had also made a real effort by fixing a few things around the house that had been bugging her and had pledged to keep on top of things.

Today they were drawing up a rota for bath time and they were also planning to have date night once a month. After last night's bedroom activity they were hoping to get Kraken to have Arlo and Petal overnight and make it a regular event on their grown-up calendar.

Sophie eyed the clock. Eight thirty-eight. A nice lie-in. Another benefit of Kraken having the kids.

'Morning, gorgeous,' mumbled Dave.

'Hiya, lover boy,' said Sophie.

'I'm not re-enacting *Dirty Dancing* again. I think I might have pulled something. But beg me and I might consider it.'

Sophie turned over and kissed him. 'I love you, Dave Butterworth.'

'I love you too.'

A smile was stuck on Sophie's face and she couldn't help it. 'What time is your mother bringing the kids home?'

'She said about nine.'

The smile slid from Sophie's face. 'Bollards. We've got twenty minutes!'

They raced about not unlike Macaulay Culkin in *Home Alone*, collecting up their discarded clothes, which were strewn up the stairs. They cleared the table and wiped down the kitchen but it was all done in good humour and as a team with them stealing kisses whenever they passed each other. Sophie was about to set the dishwasher off when the doorbell rang announcing their time was up. She straightened her hastily thrown-on dress and opened the door. Dave joined her as Arlo barrelled inside and into his father's arms. Petal was being held by Karen and was grizzling until she saw her mother and immediately beamed a toothy smile and lunged forwards.

'Hi, Mum,' said Dave. 'Come in.'

'I won't stop. We're exhausted,' said Karen, throwing an accusatory look at Sophie. 'These children barely sleep, they don't listen and they don't do as they're told.'

'We know,' said Dave, with a stupid grin on his face.

'Aren't they brilliant?' said Sophie, breathing in the smell of Petal as she jiggled happily in her arms. 'Did you have a nice time?'

Karen shook her head and gave an exasperated eye roll. Sophie noted her usually perfectly coiffured look was very off its best this morning. 'I wanted to bring them home early but your father insisted we stick it out.'

'Thanks for taking them, Mum. We were wondering if . . .'

Sophie gave Dave a nudge to shut him up. Now was not the time to ask for a monthly sleepover. 'We were wondering if there was anything we could do to say thank you and show you how much we appreciated it?' Sophie gave a big cheesy grin, which seemed to make Karen draw back.

'No, of course it was our pleasure,' she said, adjusting her hair and pulling out a lump of dried Weetabix.

'Did you have a good time with Granny and Grandad?' Dave asked Arlo.

Arlo shook his whole body in response. 'They smell funny and Granny shouts more than Mummy.' Sophie failed to hide her smugness whilst Karen blinked rapidly.

Dave's father deposited the children's bags on the door-step. 'You've a right pair of tearaways there,' he said, with a chortle.

'I need to get home and have some camomile tea,' said Karen, appearing to speak more to herself than anyone else, and she headed back to the car.

'Bye, and thanks again,' said Sophie, waving them off. She really hoped they'd soon recover.

For Anna Sunday morning was filled with ferrying Sophie's things back to her house. It was interesting how much she had managed to amass at Anna's in two weeks.

Anna had the bed stripped, the sheets in the wash and had a quick run before she went to her parents' for lunch.

She loved being back at her parents' home. It wasn't a big house, but it was clean and tidy and welcoming. It was like putting on a comfy pair of slippers and in her case it was literally like that because they insisted she keep a pair there. She was sitting in the kitchen, swinging her rabbit slippers and watching her parents serve up the roast as they had both refused any help, which they always did.

'When's the party again?' asked Anna, flicking through her phone calendar.

'Third weekend of December,' said Claire.

'Etched on my brain, it is,' said Terry as his wife took a playful swipe at him.

'You can come, can't you?' asked Claire, seeming to sense something was amiss.

Anna bit her bottom lip. 'Yeah, it should be okay,' she spoke slowly. 'It's just that a new opportunity has come up at work.'

'Work should come first,' said her father.

Her mother was frowning. 'Not at a weekend, Terry. What is it, Anna? What are you not telling us?'

Anna slowly looked up. Her parents were in freeze frame holding saucepans and sieves. 'The new opportunity. It might be in the US.'

'America!' She thought her mother was going to faint. Terry was quick to grab the pan of carrots.

Anna explained about the changes thanks to Liam and how the New York opportunity had come about and how she and Hudson were going to hatch a plan to get her out of it. Even as she explained she was starting to question what she really wanted to do. It wasn't as cut and dried as she'd first thought.

257

'I think you should go,' said her father, sitting down to his roast dinner, spearing an extra roast potato and adding it to the pile already on his plate.

'Terry!' The colour had drained from Claire's face.

He reached over and patted his wife's hand. 'She'll be fine. There is no reason why she wouldn't be fine on a plane.'

'But what about her other problem after what happened at . . .' After all these years her mother couldn't bring herself to say the words.

'Do you not think I should be over all of that by now?' asked Anna, eyes darting from one parent to the other.

'Yes, I do,' said Terry, at almost the exact time her mother started shaking her head.

'No. It's probably something you'll never get over,' said Claire. 'I'm sorry,' she said, noting the looks she was getting around the table. 'Surely it's better to be realistic than to set yourself up for something and then have to admit it's too much?'

She had a point. 'I guess,' said Anna.

'But if you don't try, you'll never know,' said Terry, ignoring his wife's glare.

'That's true too,' said Anna, feeling more confused than ever and she bit into a roast potato and winced as the hot potato burst in her mouth.

Monday morning came around too fast as Mondays often do and despite not having slept well Anna was looking forward to breakfast with Hudson. They met at a café overlooking Cathedral Square. They found a table in the corner, ordered large breakfasts and tucked in.

'How was your weekend?' he asked.

Anna gave him a brief summary and he made the

258

suitable noises in the right places as he munched his way through three jam-laden croissants.

'I could do your cat flap for you,' he said, when she reached that part.

'You?' She failed to hide a snigger.

'Sure. You have to be absolutely precise with the measuring. Have you chosen the sort of flap you want yet?'

'No, I figured a cat flap is a cat flap.'

Hudson shook his head. 'There are different sizes for a start.'

'Then I need a very big one.' Anna bobbed her head as she ate a forkful of perfect scrambled egg and crispy bacon.

'You can get ones that only open for your cat because they read their microchip. You have got him microchipped?'

'Yep, they did it at the rescue centre. I like that idea. I had wondered how I'd keep all the other cats out.'

'No need. Here . . .' He showed her a link on his mobile phone. 'I'll send you this. You can order it and when it arrives I'll pop round.'

'Cool. Now, what the hell are we going to do about New York?'

Hudson took a long drink of coffee and she watched his Adam's apple bob as he swallowed. 'Do you want to go to New York?'

It felt like she needed to be completely honest with him. 'I want to go, yes. But I don't think I will be able to because of my phobia.'

'Your one phobia of heights *and* flying?' His eyes were full of mischief and they crinkled at the edges.

'Yes, my *one* phobia.'

Hudson sat back in his seat and appeared to be thinking. 'How about we both go?'

Anna pulled all kinds of faces. 'There's only one job in New York? And who would run the UK project?'

'Not permanently. I mean how about we both go for a recce? This way we can both see how much work needs to be done. You can see if you can handle the flight. I'll be there if you struggle and in New York I can show you around. We can tell Roberta it's to inform who is best placed to manage it.'

Anna was warming to the idea. She had to admit her fear of flying was greatly enhanced by the thought of going alone. 'It might be worth a try. If I backed out at the airport, you could still go.'

'I'd say you caught kuru disease and couldn't fly.'

'Kuru disease?'

'You die laughing,' he said happily.

'Cheers.' They laughed for a moment until something caught Anna's eye outside. A group of youths were running across the square, vaulting walls and railings as they went.

'Look at them.' Anna was shocked at the speed and recklessness of the group as they jumped over other pedestrians. They both watched as one of them ran at a wall and flipped backwards off it.

'Aren't they cool?' Hudson was nodding appreciatively.

'You're joking, right?' She was horrified he'd think this was cool.

'No. Check out the gymnastics involved. You have to be skilled to do something like that.' One of the group did a handstand on a high railing and a back spring off. 'Wow. They're awesome.'

'No, it's irresponsible. It belongs in a gym, not outside. They could be badly injured or worse still, they could injure someone else.'

Hudson's brow furrowed. 'You can't see the skill in parkour?'

Anna watched them vault and tumble their way across the square. 'I can't get past the stupidity. Why you would risk your safety befuddles me. I've known people who've . . .' She stopped herself. 'People get seriously hurt.'

'Okay.' Hudson held up his hands in surrender and returned to his breakfast.

A thought struck Anna. 'Do you want the job in New York?'

Hudson's expression changed and he leaned his fore-arms on the table, shortening the distance between them, his cornflower-blue eyes studying her closely. 'I do want to return to New York at some stage in my career, but it doesn't have to be now.'

Anna tilted her head. 'What does that mean?'

Hudson blew out a breath. 'I don't plan on staying in England forever. Don't get me wrong, I love it here but my heart belongs in America.' He made a fist and bumped it on his chest twice. 'I've got to sort some stuff out in my head first. Closet skeletons that need archiving. Then I'll be all set to go home.'

Anna desperately wanted to know what skeletons he had in his closet but was too polite to ask. 'So when you go back, you go for good.'

'Yeah.'

They were staring at each other and both quickly looked away. Anna paid particular attention to buttering her toast. She picked up the pepper grinder and liberally ground fresh black pepper onto the toast.

'What the . . . ?' Hudson leaned back in horror.

'I like black pepper,' said Anna, with a shrug as she cut the toast into triangles and bit off a corner.

'I know you do, but on toast? That is wrong. You have peanut butter or jelly on toast or even both. But not black pepper.'

'You don't have jelly on anything but ice cream,' she said, before taking another large bite. 'You can have savoury things on toast like Marmite. I just love black pepper.'

'You're weird.'

Anna didn't disagree. 'So what are we telling Roberta in . . .' she checked her watch '. . . twenty minutes?'

'I think we go with the pitch for both of us to go out for, say, a week and do an initial assessment. Then we can make a call on who wants the job.'

This all sounded a bit too good to be true and Anna's bullshit radar was on high alert. 'It still means me getting on a plane.' She took a large gulp of coffee and swallowed.

'It sure does.'

Sophie and Anna were having a quick drink after work because it was Thursday and, thanks to the new timetable she and Dave had drawn up, it was Sophie's night for doing what she wanted after work. After the baby was born she was planning on making Thursday her gym class night but for now it was socialising with Anna night.

'Everything still good with Dave and the kids?'

Sophie wobbled her head. 'It's a million times better but it's still Dave we're dealing with here. He was very excited to ring me earlier to tell me he'd unblocked the toilet. I questioned which toilet because I didn't know what he was on about. Turns out he'd blocked the en-suite loo and then unblocked it but was after brownie points for doing it.'

'Eww, brownie points sounds wrong in that context,'

said Anna, and they both recoiled. 'At least he unblocked it.'

'Exactly. It's an improvement on before and now we've agreed he'll use the downstairs toilet so it's not like sleeping in a public loo. I am thankful for small amounts of progress,' said Sophie, and they clinked their glasses together. 'I have other news . . .'

'Spit it out then.'

'I think I'm almost over Hudson.'

'Great. No more lusty thoughts?'

'I'm not flustered around him any more but there may still be a few lusty thoughts. I'm only human.' She gave a shrug. 'How about you?'

'How about me, what?' Anna sipped her drink.

'You and Hudson? You and Connor?' Sophie bobbed from side to side as she spoke. 'Bloody men are like bloody buses.'

'Usually late and cost you more than you'd think?' teased Anna.

'You know what I mean. Are you interested in either of them?'

'I'm off men. This stage of my life is all about me living independently and focusing on my career.'

'Blah, blah, blah. Don't go all local politician on me. Any feelings for either of them?'

Anna sipped her drink again and Sophie knew she was giving herself some thinking time. 'I like Connor . . .'

'Because he's *nice*.' Sophie's eyes did a loop the loop.

'Yes. And Hudson drives me slightly crackers. We're just colleagues. He's not even an option.'

'I say, shag them both,' said Sophie.

Anna's eyes widened in surprise. 'I don't think that's a good idea.'

263

'Nor do I but I wanted to see your reaction.' Sophie grinned. 'Do you want to shag either of them?'

'Like I said, Hudson is a colleague so he's off limits and he's never shown the slightest interest in me like that anyway. And what worries me is I could easily shag Connor; when he's being all gawky and vulnerable he's quite attractive. But before I know it I'll be knee-deep in another relationship, which will likely end in bitterness and cake hurling two years down the line.' Anna stared miserably at her empty glass. 'Another Diet Coke?'

'I need salt and vinegar crisps and kippers.'

'The crisps are on me. The kippers you'll have to source yourself,' said Anna and she went to queue at the bar.

'Thanks,' said Sophie, taking the packets when Anna returned. 'I want you to be happy, Anna, and I get the distinct feeling you're not.' She held up a hand to stop Anna replying with platitudes. 'You have proved you can be independent and live on your own. If your preference is to be in a relationship, where's the harm?'

Anna appeared to be pondering this. 'True. It does undermine the whole independent woman thing though.'

'But whatever Roberta and her boiled-in-the-bag feminists say, it's only natural. Human beings are meant to find a mate and reproduce. Mother nature is a bitch like that.'

'But I don't trust myself not to jump at the first half-decent bloke to pitch up. It's what I do. It's what I keep doing. It's time I learned from my mistakes. I need to bide my time and wait for the *one* and I'm not the patient type.'

'But you know what you want. It's a start.' Sophie tipped the remainder of the crisps in her mouth and opened a fresh packet.

'But basically I'm basing my future on luck. It makes no sense. Do you know how my parents met?'

'Nope.' Sophie munched on her crisps.

'Mum's aunt had died. She was visiting relatives and Dad's car broke down outside the house. One look at each other was all it took. How random is that?'

'It's lovely,' said Sophie. She adored such stories.

'But what are the odds of you finding your best match?' Anna looked like she was expecting an answer. Maths had never been Sophie's strong point. She shrugged and Anna continued. 'There are 7.6 billion people on the planet. In my lifetime I'll likely meet about eighty thousand people, which is roughly nought point nought, nought one per cent.' She counted it off on her fingers. 'I have a nought point nought, nought one per cent chance of finding the one! Those are the ridiculous odds I'm facing.'

She had a point. Sophie picked up her last packet of crisps. 'When you put it like that it all seems pretty hopeless.'

'Thanks.'

'You're welcome. Crisp?'

Chapter Twenty-Eight

September arrived bullish and full of wind, which reminded Anna a lot of Karl. It was Saturday morning and she didn't have any plans. She mulled over her Friday night. She'd been pleased to get home to find Maurice's cat flap had been delivered. She'd showed it to him but he fleetingly rubbed around the box and then demanded some food. She'd popped a picture on Facebook of Maurice sitting on the cat flap box with the caption 'I don't think that's how it works,' and scrolled through the photos of her friends out with their partners enjoying a Friday night as most couples do. She'd had a text exchange with Connor, a delivery pizza and a box-set binge. This was her Friday night now.

Hudson had messaged her and she'd had some fun banter with him about her ordering the right cat flap. Perhaps this was how it should work. Friends but without any expectations on either side.

Anna started her Saturday with a shower and gave her hair a quick blast with the hairdryer. It didn't warrant styling when you had no plans. She couldn't find a hair bobble anywhere so she took a clean pair of pants from her drawer and used those to tie it up out of the way. She was pulling on socks when her phone pinged. **Are you up?** It was from Hudson.

No, I'm asleep but my multitasking skills are superb. Why? she replied.

Can you sleepwalk to the door and let me in please?

'Good morning,' he said, his usual beaming smile in place when she opened the door. He held aloft a brightly coloured toolbox.

Anna was quizzical for a moment. 'The cat flap. Brilliant.' She stepped aside and let him in.

'Sim had a guy stay over last night, so I thought I'd give them some space this morning.'

'Thoughtful,' said Anna. 'Coffee?'

'Please.' He picked up the cat flap box and immediately started reading the instructions in depth. She left him to it while she had a quick tidy up of the flat and came back to find him marking measurements on the door.

'Here, check that will you?' he asked, pointing to the instructions and what he'd marked on the door.

Anna crouched down. 'Spot on.' She turned and realised their faces were very close together. She spun away and studied the front door.

'What's in your hair?' asked Hudson. She could sense the smile in his voice even without looking.

Anna stood up quickly. 'Just a big scrunchie . . .'

'Right,' he said, with a knowing nod. 'It says Luva Huva Medium on the label and I'm pretty sure they make panties.'

Anna wrestled the knickers from her hair and stuffed them in the upturned umbrella that was propped by the door. 'Yes, well, like their owner they multitask.' She stuck her tongue out at him. 'And please don't say panties. I know you Americans think it's okay, but it's really not.'

'And cock-up is?'

She had no answer so she went to style her hair. Hudson chortled away to himself whilst rummaging through his toolbox. When the sound of drilling had stopped Anna returned to the kitchen to see Hudson pressing buttons on the top of her newly fitted cat flap.

'Wow. It looks great. Thanks, Hudson.'

'Doesn't work yet. We need Maurice to register his microchip.'

'I'll fetch him.' Anna came back with a sleepy Maurice who didn't seem too impressed with being woken up.

'Hiya, handsome boy,' said Hudson, scratching the top of Maurice's head. The cat seemed to come alive and began pushing his head into Hudson's hand. 'He's got such a lovely nature.'

'He has,' said Anna proudly. Hudson and Maurice shared some mutual adoration while Anna's arms began to ache. 'He's also very heavy so when you're ready . . .'

'I'll take him,' said Hudson, carefully lifting the giant cat from her arms and giving him a cuddle. Maurice began rubbing around Hudson's chest like he was his hero. Cats are so fickle, thought Anna. Hudson crouched down, pushed a button on the cat flap and waved a confused-looking Maurice under the sensor until it beeped. 'Okay. Should be ready to go. What's Maurice's favourite food?'

'Mouse,' said Anna, pulling a disgusted face. 'Were you thinking of getting him a Christmas present?'

'No, I was thinking what would encourage him to come through the flap to test it works.'

'Right, okay.' Anna felt slightly foolish and went to get a tin of tuna. Maurice was immediately snaking around her legs and mewing pitifully. 'I do feed him, honest.'

'They're all like that. My old cat in Port Chester was

268

the same. I'd love another one someday. You know, when I'm properly settled . . .'

'. . . in America.' She finished his sentence and it felt like it burned a tiny hole inside her. They stared at each other for a moment until Maurice meowed a protest at the slow delivery of the tuna and they both gave an awkward half laugh.

'Right, now listen, Maurice,' said Hudson, picking the cat up again. 'You need to show Anna here what a top job I've done with your new door.' He popped Maurice gently down outside and shut the door. Anna placed the bowl of tuna on the kitchen floor and they waited.

Maurice's face appeared at the transparent cat flap and he meowed another protest. 'He doesn't know how to use it,' said Anna, feeling like an anxious mother and wondering if she'd wasted her money. She stepped towards the door.

Hudson put his hand on her arm to stop her and all the tiny hairs stood to attention. 'Give him a minute. He's a smart boy. He'll work it out.' Anna waited and watched.

Maurice complained a bit more, then he put his paw on the cat flap, there was a click and the flap opened a fraction. Maurice instantly put his face on the door, pushed it open and came inside. He wasn't interested in the over-the-top praise he received from Anna and Hudson; he just wanted to eat his tuna. They were standing like proud parents watching him gulp it down when there was a tap on the door.

Anna opened it to see Connor standing outside holding up a screwdriver. 'Hiya, I thought I'd come round and . . .' He tailed off as all eyes went to the newly fitted cat flap.

'Hey there, you must be Connor,' said Hudson, stretching forward to give him a manly handshake. 'I'm Hudson

Jones. I work with Anna. Looks like I beat you to it on the DIY!'

Connor didn't look impressed. 'Come in,' said Anna, feeling flustered. She hadn't actually asked either of them to fit the cat flap but somehow they had both assumed she wanted them to. 'Coffee?' she asked Connor.

'Err, yeah. Okay. Thanks,' said Connor. He rubbed his palms on his trousers as he followed them into the kitchen, which suddenly felt rather small with them all in it together. Connor took off his shoes and put them next to Hudson's. The men looked at each other with an air of awkwardness whilst the kettle boiled. Anna wanted to break the uncomfortable silence but it was always difficult to make conversation while the kettle was boiling without seeming like you were shouting at people.

Once the drinks were made Anna was keen to lighten the mood. 'Let's go through to the living room,' she suggested and led the way wondering what she was going to do now. Both the men sat down on the sofa and she took the chair. It was the first time she'd seen them like that, side by side, and it was hard not to start comparing. Hudson was already relaxing into the sofa like he lived there whereas Connor was perched on the edge staring intently at the contents of his coffee mug. Hudson's outfit implied he'd stepped off the front cover of *GQ* magazine whereas Connor was more ScrewFix but to be honest he had come to do a manual task.

Anna realised she was staring and nobody had spoken. She felt obliged to get the conversation going. What the heck would these two have in common? Apart from her cat flap?

She was saved by a click from the kitchen, which had both Anna and Hudson on their feet in an instant. They skidded into the hall laughing at almost bumping into each other to see the tip of Maurice's fluffy tail disappear through the cat flap. They turned to each other and as Hudson put up his hand to high five her she hugged him. She had no idea why she did it. It was a spontaneous reaction to the delight of seeing Maurice go outside via a more conventional route than the living room window. Hudson was ever the gentleman and gave her a quick squeeze in return. She let go quickly and they held each other's gaze. Anna opened her mouth but had no idea what to say. He gave her his Hollywood smile and something like molten candle wax puddled in her stomach. What was going on? Hudson pointed back to the living room. Anna tucked her hair behind her ear and went back in. No words passed between them; they didn't need to say anything.

'Everything all right?' asked Connor, still perched on the sofa but appearing confused by the sudden evacuation.

'Maurice used the cat flap to go out for the first time,' explained Anna, sitting back down and hoping one of them would leave soon. This was beyond uncomfortable.

'And it didn't fall off,' said Hudson. 'It's only my second cat flap.'

'Then you were the right person for the job,' said Connor. 'I'm not the best at DIY.'

'What is your thing, Connor?' asked Hudson. There was something bewitchingly confident about how Americans used first names.

'Hmm.' Connor took a sip of his coffee. 'I like lacrosse.'

'How interesting. That's where they have the stick with the little net on the end, right?'

'Yeah, it's a good game. Shame it's not more popular,' said Connor. Anna had only ever known one other person who played lacrosse. She pushed that person from her mind.

'What else are you into?'

'I like body boarding but there's not much opportunity round here.' Connor pouted his bottom lip, which was quite cute.

'Man, I love to surf but even though this is an island there's like a handful of places to do it. How crazy is that?'

'True, but the surfing is great in Cornwall. Have you been?'

The conversation continued and Anna took a moment to watch the pair of them. It was the most animated she'd ever seen Connor. Hudson seemed to bring the best out of people. He had a way of putting you at ease and making you feel special. Connor was smiling and it changed his features considerably. Gone was the cautious, slightly troubled look; his face was open and engaging. Anna noticed it was raining quite heavily outside and wondered when she'd get a run in today.

Her thoughts were interrupted by a click and all three of them halted. They watched the doorway all expecting Maurice to appear but he didn't. The sound of paws racing across the floor made the three of them spring up to investigate. This time Connor was first on the scene. Anna looked past the two large men to see Maurice dancing around the shoes.

'What's he doing?' asked Connor.

'Who knows?' said Anna. 'Maurice!' The cat gave her a brief uninterested glance and returned his attention to the shoes. Anna opened the fridge and took out the tin of tuna. 'Maurice?' This time he trotted over to Anna and she picked him up although he was still scowling at the shoes.

'I should go,' said Connor. Anna inwardly let out a sigh of relief. He was sweet but was far better on a one-to-one basis. A trio didn't work.

'Okay. Thanks for coming over. Sorry you had a wasted trip,' she said.

'Not wasted. I got to see you.'

Anna was taken aback by the compliment, especially in front of Hudson. 'Thanks,' she said, because she wasn't sure what else to say. Connor started to put his shoes back on and Maurice started to wriggle.

'Did you fancy dinner this week?' asked Connor, looking at Anna whilst he put on his other shoe.

'Err, yeah. Okay.' She didn't mean to sound as hesitant as she did but she could feel Hudson's eyes scrutinising her.

'Great,' said Connor. His thrilled expression quickly changed. He froze like someone had hit the pause button. He swallowed and when he spoke his voice was barely a whisper. 'Something's crawling up my leg,' he said.

Anna and Hudson both looked at his jeans but there was nothing obvious. 'What do you mean?' asked Anna, as Maurice wriggled free and made a beeline for Connor.

Connor pointed at his left leg. 'There's something inside my trouser leg, heading for my . . . groin.' Maurice sat in front of Connor and stared up at him expectantly.

Hudson coughed out a laugh. 'From the look of Maurice I'm guessing it's a mouse.'

Connor jumped like someone had zapped him with a cattle prod. He leaped in the air flaying out arms and legs as he wrenched open the front door and tumbled outside into the pouring rain.

Connor was wildly shaking his left leg. 'It's not coming out!' His voice was almost a scream. 'How do I get it out?'

'You'll need to take your pants off, Connor,' suggested Hudson, who was failing badly to hide his amusement. All Anna could do was watch in horror. Connor undid his jeans and threw them to the floor as Mrs Nowakowski meandered into view carrying two bags of shopping. Her hands instantly shot to cover her gasp at the sight in front of her and she dropped her bags, which spilled out their contents spectacularly.

'Has it gone?' asked Connor, frantically searching his nether region for any signs of the mouse.

Maurice answered his question as he dashed after the small brown creature when it made a break from the crumpled jeans around Connor's ankles. Connor stood for a moment catching his breath with the rain pelting down on him.

Anna had a flash of inspiration. She grabbed the umbrella from by the door and stepping outside she popped it open and they all watched as her pants sailed through the air. Mrs Nowakowski put her hands on her hips and shook her head.

'What?' said Anna trying to brazen it out. 'They're clean.'

Chapter Twenty-Nine

Bert was holding his sides as the tears ran down his face. 'Stop, stop,' he pleaded, as another burst of hysterics had him rocking in his chair.

'Don't – it's not *that* funny,' said Anna, although she was laughing too. A few days had passed and she could now see the funny side.

'It is,' corrected Bert. 'It's hilarious.' He slowly started to get his giggles under control and took a few deep breaths. 'Maurice definitely has a sense of humour.'

'He's a menace. I thought Connor was going to have a seizure. He was terrified the mouse was going to nibble on . . . stuff it shouldn't be nibbling on.'

'Poor mouse was likely terrified.'

'True.' They had another chuckle.

'Any more underwear presents from Maurice?' asked Bert. When Anna had told Bert about the bra and the Spider-Man underpants, a few weeks ago, he had ended the mystery by explaining that Maurice was literally a cat burglar and liked to bring home presents that he'd pilfered from neighbours.

Anna had a think. 'Not since Sophie has been keeping her utility window closed. But he did bring in a random sock and a cooked sausage a few days ago. It was still warm. The sausage, not the sock.' Anna dreaded to think where he'd found the sausage but she suspected a barbecue had been the source. 'I can't believe I've got a klepto-maniac cat.'

'It's a sure sign he's happy. He brought presents for my wife but never for me.' There was a hint of sadness in the old man's voice.

'I'm sure it was nothing personal, Bert. He's just a ladies' man.'

'Whatever it is, I'm pleased he's settled in well with you. Thank you,' said Bert, reaching for Anna's hand and she realised his eyes must be getting worse as he was nowhere near. She gripped his fingers mid-air and moved herself round to sit nearer to him.

'What did the specialist say about your eyes?' She asked the question she'd been avoiding for the last hour.

Bert moved his jaw in a way only people with false teeth seem to be able to do. 'No hope of recovery. It'll only get worse.'

Anna squeezed his hand. 'I'm sorry, Bert. Anything I can do?'

'No, there's nothing anyone can do. I just wish I could see Maurice again or read a newspaper but that's never going to happen now.'

Anna only had platitudes so she kept quiet and carried on squeezing his hand.

'Hello again,' said Rosie, from the doorway and she wandered in to join them.

'Hi, Rosie. How are you?'

'Never better,' said Rosie, patting Bert's arm as she took the chair next to him. 'I've been for a stroll around the gardens. The roses are stunning. It's beautiful outside and we don't know how many more sunny days we'll have. You should join me out there sometimes.' Rosie directed her words at Bert.

'Not a lot of point if you can't see,' said Bert, failing to hide the grumble in his voice.

Anna wiped a tear from her eye and for the first time was thankful he couldn't see her. He would not want her pity. She couldn't imagine how hard it must be to lose your sight and your independence. 'Do the roses smell nice?' she asked Rosie.

'They smell delightful and so do the freesias and lavender.'

'Might be worth checking them out, Bert,' said Anna.

'I'll think about it,' said Bert and he thrummed his fingers on the arm of the chair.

'Thank you,' mouthed Rosie to Anna.

Sophie had her head in a cupboard and her backside wriggled as she spoke. 'Dave's taken the kids to the cinema.'

'Well done, Dave.'

'Yeah. He can have a nap there and I can have a sort-out. I'm clearing out all the sweets before Halloween when they'll get another truckload of sugar. Dentists the world over must clap their hands on Halloween. They'll never go out of business.'

'You need a hand?' asked Anna, from her spot at the kitchen table. It was nice to see Sophie more relaxed. The new routines they'd put in place for themselves and the children seemed to be helping.

'Actually, yes. Could you sort through Arlo's toy cupboard and pull out anything you think is too young for him?'

'He's six. Nothing's too young for him.'

Sophie sat back on her haunches, making her belly appear more pronounced. 'I've got three weeks to go and after number three shows up we'll be on the countdown to Christmas when another load of toys will arrive and we've got no space now.' Her face was pleading.

Anna didn't need to be asked twice. 'Okay, I'm on it,' she said, getting to her feet.

After about twenty minutes she could see what Sophie meant. Pretty much everything he'd ever been given was shoved in the cupboard. Anna found the same things but in newer slightly more advanced versions like one wooden train set and then a more conventional one, a chunky pirate ship and then a sleeker version. She pulled out a pair of Disney head-phones and went to find Sophie.

'Does Arlo still need these?'

Sophie rubbed her hand across her sweating forehead. 'No, he got some Bluetooth ones for his birthday.'

'Can I have them?'

Sophie gave a quizzical look. 'Really? Are you into Mickey Mouse?'

'No, but I've had an idea.'

'Sure, knock yourself out. There's a whole load of Duplo that needs a home too if you're interested.'

'No, you're okay. I think you need a break. You're looking tired out.'

Sophie looked like she was going to protest and then her expression changed and she hauled herself up onto a chair. 'You're right, I am.'

'I'll get you a drink then I'll finish off here while you tell me how wonderful your new improved husband is and try not to make me feel like a stale husk of a spinster while you're at it.'

'It'll be hard, but I'll try. Can you put some stuff in the loft for me too, please?'

'Sure.'

It didn't take Anna long to get rid of the small sweet mountain and tidy the cupboard. A big box of old toys, all wiped down with wet wipes, was in the hall waiting for Dave to take to the charity shop alongside the box of things for the loft. Anna took it upstairs and pulled down the loft ladder. She took a lungful of air and started climbing. I'm fine. I'm fine, she recited in her head. It was just a ladder; it was the same as the stairs. She was pleased to make it to the top with only a slight quickening of her pulse. She found a place for the box and was about to come down when she noticed a tiny Velux window.

Anna was feeling brave. She knew she was quite safe. A quick look out of the window couldn't do her any harm. She strode over to the window and looked out. Her stomach flipped. She steadied her breathing. She could do this. She opened the window a fraction and leaned out. She could hear the buzz of the mowers doing their annual cut of the park wildflowers. She looked about and a pressure descended on her and her head started to swim. 'I'm fine,' she said out loud. 'It's safe.' She glanced down out of the window and fear seized her insides. She gripped the edge of the window and closed her eyes. This was not good. Nausea swilled around her stomach. Images flashed through her mind. They were all in her imagination but she couldn't escape them all the same.

'You all right?' Sophie called up through the hatch.

Anna swallowed down the bitter taste in her mouth. 'I'm fine. I'll be down in a minute.' She opened her eyes, took one last look and knew there was no way she *was* getting on an aeroplane.

She took a few minutes to calm herself down before shutting the window and going back downstairs. Anna found Sophie settled in the living room reading a magazine. She glanced up as Anna came in. 'There's an article here about what to do with leftover cake. What kind of sick world do we live in where people have leftover cake?' Sophie shook her head and then took a fresh look at Anna. 'You're pale. Are you okay?'

Anna sat down but it was hard to keep her mind off the decision that had been made for her upstairs.

'What do you mean you don't want to go to New York?' Hudson was looking exasperated. 'We agreed we'd both go, and I've pitched our plan to Roberta.' They were standing in the tiniest of meeting rooms, the only one available. It was like being in a cupboard.

Anna rolled her lips together. 'I can't do it. I know I can't get on an aeroplane because I can't spend ten hours not looking out of the window.'

'It's eight hours and you can wear an eye mask.'

'Don't be ridiculous.'

'You're the one being ridiculous. You have to face your fears.'

'What, because you're telling me to?' Anna had to forcibly stop her hands going to her hips.

'No, because if you don't, you'll always regret it.'

His statement and sincerity took the wind out of her sails. 'I'm sorry, Hudson. I really can't. But you should go.' Her voice turned croaky and she cleared her throat. Being in a confined space with the scent of him commanding the small room was not helping.

'Roberta is going to think I've totally lost the plot. She'll probably not give me any job after this.'

'Don't be petulant. I'll speak to her and explain. This is my problem, not yours,' said Anna.

'You know, there's still time to have therapy. It might help.'

Anna shook her head. 'I'm not American . . .'

'I wasn't aware the British way was to chicken out.'

Anna was tired of fighting. 'That's my decision. I'll tell Roberta. I'm sorry,' she said, giving him an apologetic look before she left the room.

They spent the rest of the day avoiding each other until the last meeting of the day had them sitting side by side. Anna had ended up emailing Roberta because she was impossible to tie down for a conversation. The tracker she'd put on it told her it had been read – hopefully that would be the end of it. Roberta was late and came bustling in grinning like the cat who got the gold top. 'Board have just approved our plans and released funds for the next stage of the project.' There were murmurs of positivity in the room. Roberta turned to Hudson. 'We have dates for New York. Last week of November. Report due by Christmas.'

'Yes, boss,' said Hudson. She gave an over-exaggerated eye roll showing she secretly loved it. She turned to Anna. 'Can you prepare a board pack to brief them on the details of your exploration trip?'

'Of course.' She looked to Hudson to check he didn't have an issue with her doing that for what was now his trip and his job going forward.

'Excellent. Priya, can you get details from Hudson and Anna and book their flights.'

'Err, sorry,' said Anna, feeling all eyes focus on her. 'I sent you an email, Roberta. Did you get a chance—'

'Yes. I read your suggestion, Anna. It doesn't matter who you are, where you come from. The ability to triumph begins with you. Always. Oprah Winfrey said that. This is your opportunity to triumph and I want you to seize it,' said Roberta, looking off into the distance as if she was addressing a feminist rally.

'Err, sorry,' said Anna, giving a little wave to get Roberta's attention back. 'I can't go for . . . medical reasons.'

Roberta straightened her back. 'Are you refusing to travel?'

Anna swallowed. 'Well, no. It's just that—'

'Good. Because I think you'll find it's in your job description.' Roberta turned away. 'I want a financial projection for the rest of the project based on Liam's forecast but factoring in any scope changes I've authorised.'

Anna looked at Hudson. He gave a toothy smile and started to mime being on a plane, accepting a drink from an air steward and reclining. It was all his bloody fault. If only he hadn't put her forward for New York in the first place. She glared at him and he pretended to put on headphones and an eye mask. How was she meant to get out of it now and still keep her job?

Anna was trying to fit in more trips to see Bert but it was difficult. She came rushing into the nursing home and almost sent someone flying. Thank goodness she had a lid on the coffee cups. She dashed through the lounge and found Bert asleep.

'Hi, Bert. It's Ameri . . .' She was definitely off anything American. 'It's coffee time, Bert.'

He came to with a start but smiled at the sound of her voice. She placed the cup carefully into his outstretched hands. 'Careful, it's extra hot today.'

'Okay,' he said, shuffling upright. 'What news have you got for me?'

'Bert, I'm really sorry. I can't stop long. I'm out for dinner with Connor later.'

'Oh.'

Anna wasn't sure how he managed to convey so much disappointment in such a small word but he did. 'I'm really sorry, Bert. I've got twenty minutes. Then I need to dash. Okay?'

'Yes. It's fine. I do understand, you know. I was young and had a purpose once too,' he said.

'What's up, Bert?' asked Anna.

He leaned forward and in a voice she suspected was meant to be a whisper he said, 'I don't like old people.'

She didn't like to point out the obvious. 'It happens to us all, Bert, and it sure beats the alternative.'

Bert seemed to ponder this. 'All they do is moan about their aches and pains.' He paused. 'And moan about other people moaning about their aches and pains.' He gave a wry smile.

'They don't all moan,' said Anna. 'I mean, don't tell anyone, but you're all right.'

'I have my moments.'

'I know. And Rosie seems nice.'

A flicker crossed his lips. 'She's the best of the bunch.' They sipped their drinks for a moment. 'Anna, is Rosie in here?'

'Nope,' said Anna, checking the other chairs. There weren't many in the lounge today.

'Super. Do you think you could describe what Rosie looks like? I want to try and picture her.'

Anna pulled in a breath. She hadn't been expecting that to touch her as it did. She blinked to stop the tears. 'Of

283

course.' She cleared her throat. 'She's about my height, which is five foot one. She's got thick white hair with a darker layer of grey underneath and it's cut short but stylish. I can't remember what colour her eyes are but she smiles a lot and has a heart-shaped face. There's a touch of Felicity Kendal about her. Is that okay?'

Bert was nodding. 'Thank you.'

'Right, are you sitting comfortably because Hudson has got me into a right flaming fix . . .' Anna recounted the job situation and Bert nodded and made the right noises in the right places until she got to the end of the story. 'What do I do?' Bert sipped his coffee but said nothing. 'Bert,' she prompted. 'What do I do?'

'Oh, sorry I thought it was a rhetorical question. I don't know. You're in a real pickle.'

Anna slumped back in her chair. 'Thanks, Bert, really helpful.' They sat and sipped their coffees in silence for a minute. 'What would you do?'

'Hmm. You see I don't have any phobias, which makes it hard for me to understand. That being said, Hayling Island is the furthest I've ever been. I would have loved to have travelled. Barbara and I liked to watch the travel programmes years ago. All those exotic places. We never had the money though. There was always something else we needed it for rather than fancy holidays. But now I wish we'd gone. Because now I couldn't see them even if you teleported me there.'

Bert's regrets weren't helping. 'Teleporting, now there's an idea,' said Anna.

'Do you really want my advice?' asked Bert, his tone dour.

'Yes,' said Anna. She was very fond of Bert. He was a lot like her old grandad only not quite as blunt and didn't smell of Old Spice aftershave.

'Find a way to overcome this. The longer you leave it the harder it will become. You have your life ahead of you and who knows how different it could be if you could get on an aeroplane?'

Anna blinked. She was breathing faster just at the thought of what he was saying. It all made sense but unless she was unconscious she couldn't see how she was going to make it through the flight.

'Now, have you got time to read me the newspaper sports pages?' he asked, clasping his hands together in front of him, as if almost in prayer.

'Sorry, Bert, I have to dash but I might have something better.' Bert's expression said he didn't believe her. She placed something in his hands. 'This is my iPod. I don't use it any more because my phone does everything but I think it might be useful to you . . .'

Anna went on to explain about podcasts, talking newspapers and audio books. She showed him how to hold down the main button and use his voice to instruct the iPod to go to the app he wanted. Bert was a little startled when the iPod spoke back to him but seemed to find it funny and tried to have a conversation with the disembodied voice.

Anna set Bert up with an audio book she thought he'd enjoy and said her goodbyes before helping him put on the headphones. He gave her a thumbs up, which was her cue to leave. She got to the door and she waited for a bit and watched as Bert sat nodding away. Occasionally he laughed out loud but the whole time he had a huge grin on his face. The old ladies nearby were also grinning at the sight of Bert wearing his Mickey Mouse headphones with their large black Mickey ears on the top but it really didn't matter because Bert was happy.

Chapter Thirty

Anna decided to make an effort for dinner with Connor. He'd been very good about being usurped by Hudson over the cat flap fitting and the whole mouse up the trouser leg scenario hadn't been mentioned at all, which was probably for the best. Connor had chosen a nice pub in Harborne where the building was clearly from a bygone age but the décor was modern and the food was up to date and tasty. She explained that she couldn't go to New York because of her phobia of heights and immediately wished she hadn't. Connor seemed to go into psychiatrist mode.

'Where do you think this phobia stems from?' he said, putting down his cutlery.

Anna concentrated on her plate. 'I've always had it.'

'I don't think that's possible. Phobias are usually triggered by negative experiences. Have a think – there must be something that happened to make you like this.' She glanced up and he was watching her expectantly. Great.

'I followed a window cleaner up a ladder when I was a toddler. I guess it was that,' said Anna. Connor was shaking his head. 'Yes. It was definitely that,' she added emphatically.

'And yet you live in a block of flats.'

'On the ground floor,' said Anna, pointing her knife and then realising it was quite rude so she put it back to work in cutting up her chicken.

'How do you cope in a high-rise office?'

'I don't go near the windows and try not to think about it. How about we do that now?' She held his gaze.

Connor blinked. 'Sure, sorry,' he said, picking his cutlery back up. 'It interests me. That's all.' They ate in silence for a few moments. 'You ever thought of going on the roof?'

Anna dropped her knife in surprise and the resulting clatter had heads spinning in her direction. 'No,' she hissed. 'That would be crazy. Nobody goes on the roof.'

'Aversion therapy is meant to work.'

'My mum calls it kill or cure, and I'm keen to avoid the former. Can we drop the subject, please.'

'Yes, of course. Sorry,' he said and Anna felt the tension in her shoulders loosen its grip. 'Was that our first fight?' he asked.

'I guess.' Anna's mouth lifted at one side. 'And if it was, it was a pretty mild one.'

'Does it mean we're, you know, seeing each other?'

There was a question she hadn't seen coming. Wasn't it meant to be her who instigated those sorts of conversations? She wasn't ready for this. She wanted some more time to think it through before she answered, but she'd known Connor for a few months now. She should have expected this conversation to arise eventually. Connor was still watching her intently from across the small table awaiting her answer. It felt like she had been sitting in the basket of an old bicycle and rushed at high speed to a crossroads and now she had to decide where she was going.

Connor looked away and started eating. She'd left it too

long. The excruciating pause had gone on so long he'd returned to his meal and now a hideous cloud of awkwardness hung over them both. Anna hunched her shoulders and hacked at her chicken.

She couldn't spend the rest of the evening feeling tense. 'I like you and this . . .' she gestured across the table '. . . works for me. Is that okay?'

Connor's lips tweaked. 'Yeah. It's perfect.'

Sophie waddled round to Karl's desk, straightening her panelled maternity top over her ever-expanding bump. 'What the hell are you wearing?' asked Karl. 'You look like badly laid lino.'

'Fuzz off.'

'You can't say that.' He pretended to be offended.

'I can. It's my last day and I really want to go home, put my feet up and forget about you for six whole months.'

'Fair enough. Let's do your leaving presentation and embarrassing speeches at four o'clock. I'll finish our one to one early and you can have a pee just before.'

'You're too kind.' Sophie pulled a face and frisbeed his mouse mat across the office. She sat down and noted the impact on the chair's suspension. 'I'm fed up being this big.' She flapped her giant smock top. 'Do you know what the next size up to this is?'

'Sleeps four to six people?' he said, his expression deadpan.

She took a swipe at him. 'There isn't a size up after this. This is the biggest they do.' Her lip went wobbly.

'What's up?' asked Anna, joining them.

'Hormone levels it would appear,' said Karl, tipping his head in Sophie's direction. She gave him a whack.

'Ooh, happy last day,' said Anna, giving Sophie a hug.

'Is there cake?' She scanned the tops of the nearby filing cabinets.

'Of course,' said Sophie. 'Cake is the answer to everything.'

'Including the question why is my arse this huge?' said Karl.

'Give over. I'm pregnant and anyway my bum hasn't grown much this time. Has it?' Sophie twisted round to try to have a look for herself. Anna was shaking her head in support.

Karl pretended to answer his desk phone. 'Hello. Yes,' said Karl, putting his hand over the mouthpiece. 'It's the Royal Mail. They'd like to allocate your arse its own post-code.'

Anna left the two of them whacking each other with ring binders.

'Anna. Wait up,' called Hudson as she was heading out of the building at the end of a long day. She almost stamped her feet in protest. She was tired and thanks to the unre-solved New York situation she wasn't sleeping well.

'What?' she said, wrapping her scarf tighter around herself in anticipation of the November cold outside.

'Wow. Someone is grumpy.'

'Yeah. I'm the last dwarf left because I murdered the others for pissing me off.'

Hudson laughed. 'You're funny,' he said, emphasising it with a point of his finger. 'I can't get any time in your diary to talk about New York. Can you free something up?'

'No, because I'm not going. Even if I have to break my own leg. I'm not going.' Anna was resolute. She pulled on her woolly hat.

'Let's hope it doesn't come to that. Your hat suits you, by the way.' His head was on one side as he spoke.

'Thank you,' she said reluctantly.

'I want to talk to you about the meeting schedule for the New York trip. Regardless of who is going we need to know who we're seeing, when and what key info we need from each of them.'

It was a reasonable request. 'I've got some ideas. I'll find you an hour. You're right. You need to have a clear purpose for each meeting otherwise I'll never make head or tail of what you send back.'

'I could video conference you in; it'll be just like you're in the room. Obviously, I'd rather you were actually there but, hey.'

'Thanks.' She wanted to be there too but it simply wasn't possible.

'Apart from anything else you'll be missing out on all the really cool stuff New York has to offer.'

Anna's eyes shot skywards and she turned on her heel. She could feel her resolve crumbling and she needed to get away. 'I've got to go. It's fireworks in the park tonight.'

'Come on, Anna. It'll be fun. I promise you,' he called after her and she waved a hand dismissively. 'See your doctor. They can give you something.' Great, now strangers were gawping at her.

Anna strode out the doors without a backwards glance. She wanted to put all her problems into a rocket, light the touch paper, stand well back and watch them get blasted into space.

The odd firework had popped as the light had faded and Maurice had opened one eye at the interruption but otherwise seemed unfazed by it all. Excited banging on the door, however, had him sitting up looking almost alert.

'It's only Arlo,' said Anna, giving him a ruffle behind his ears. She pulled on her coat and headed out. Arlo was hurtling about as if he'd eaten all his Halloween sweets in one go whilst Petal was standing with her arms forced out at a forty-five-degree angle thanks to the numerous layers of clothing she was wearing topped off with Minnie Mouse ear muffs. She gave a toothy smile at her brother's antics.

'Ready to face the madness?' asked Sophie, waving a flashlight.

'Definitely. I love fireworks night.' Anna pulled a bobble hat from her pocket and made a silly face for Petal's benefit as she put it on. It was a crisp but clear night outside.

Sophie handed her Petal's baby reins. 'Here. The lesser of two evils,' she said, with a knowing smile.

'Err, okay. Where's Dave?'

'Stuck in the office, as usual.' Her shoulders sagged as she said it.

'You have to admit he has been better since you . . .' Anna lowered her voice so the children wouldn't hear '. . . went home.'

'He has.' Sophie gave a resigned pout. 'But it's like training a puppy, it'll take a while.'

They headed off into the park with Sophie shouting instructions at the children not to run off as Arlo disappeared from sight.

Hot dogs seemed to calm Arlo down slightly and as Sophie waddled her way towards the nearest bench everyone on it vacated for her. 'My arse isn't that big,' she said grumpily. This was true although her stomach was now of gargantuan proportions. She wasn't overdue so nobody was really bothered from a medical perspective but she looked like any more growth and she'd no longer be able to defy the laws of physics and would topple over. They ate in relative silence apart from Sophie complaining about persistent heartburn.

They chatted for a bit and watched Arlo throw a light stick in the air repeatedly until it landed on his sister and the game was ended. Eventually the conversation turned to Connor.

'Are you a couple?' asked Sophie, watching Arlo doing a frog impression to make his sister laugh.

'I don't know.'

Sophie narrowed her eyes. 'You don't actually know or you can't decide?'

'The latter. There is absolutely no reason why we shouldn't give it a go but . . .'

'And the "but" says it all. My old nan used to say if it's not a definite yes then it must be a no. Unless you're going to string him along until something better comes along?'

'No, that's not fair. Maybe you're right. Maybe I should end it.' She didn't like to admit to herself that a part of her was hedging her bets. And she feared drifting into another average relationship with someone who was perfectly nice but never going to set her heart alight.

They were interrupted by a shaky announcement through a sound system and people began counting down from ten.

'Anna?' The voice came from behind them and Anna twisted to peer into the darkness, missing the first flurry of fireworks as they leaped from the pontoons anchored in the middle of the pond.

'Hudson?' He stepped forward and as a bright firework burst above them he was lit up, giving him an ethereal glow.

'What are you doing here?' She was also wondering how he'd got into the park.

'I wanted to talk to you.'

'If it's about New York, now is not the time.'

'It's not about New York – I just need to talk to you.'

Another firework burst overhead and Petal squealed with delight and started to bob up and down excitedly as more fireworks tore through the sky and erupted into transient stars.

Anna brushed her hair off her face and looked at Hudson expectantly. He nervously rubbed his chin before taking her hand and trying to lead her away but at the same time Sophie grabbed at Anna's other hand halting her. Hudson started to say something but it was drowned out by both another explosion and Sophie's screams. Anna thought she was overreacting to the display somewhat but the tight squeeze of her hand and Sophie's distressed expression told her instantly what was wrong.

'The baby?' asked Anna, reluctantly pulling her hand free from Hudson's.

Sophie nodded as her face contorted with the pain. 'It's coming. And it's coming quick!'

Chapter Thirty-One

Anna watched Sophie hugging her bump as she panted fast. This was it – she was going into labour in Wildflower Park in the middle of a fireworks display. It was dark and cold and the last place you'd want to give birth.

'Right!' said Anna and Hudson together, both appearing to want to take charge of the situation. Anna raised an eyebrow. 'I'll call Dave. You call an ambulance,' instructed Anna. Hudson didn't argue and got straight on his phone.

'Dave. The baby's on its way. Where the hell are you?'

'Crap. I'm stuck in traffic about three miles from home. It's total gridlock. Tell her to hold on,' said Dave.

'You can tell her,' she said, holding the phone to Sophie's ear for him to repeat his request.

'Hold on? You f—' Thankfully everything Sophie said was drowned out by the stream of fireworks whizzing into the sky.

'Ambulance is on its way,' said Hudson. 'They'll come to the main entrance. I'm guessing they'll take her on a stretcher.' The operator was still on the phone.

'I don't want to go on a stretcher,' wailed Sophie. Anna felt for the ambulance crew; she was a whole lot of person to carry across the park.

Hudson must have been having the same thoughts. He whispered to Anna. 'Can they manage her all the way from here?'

'I heard that, you know!' said Sophie and she started to groan loudly.

Anna swivelled round. 'There aren't many other options.' She surveyed the vast crowd around them as the fireworks continued to crash and bloom above.

Hudson was speaking to the emergency services operator and his expression was grim. He whispered to Anna, 'Ambulance is stuck in traffic. Gridlock. About three—'

'Miles away,' finished Anna. 'Bugger. Dave's stuck in the same traffic jam.' Sophie let out a strangled cry. 'We have to move her,' Anna said, turning to Hudson. 'Either to the main entrance or inside. She can't stay here.' Anna pointed to Sophie's house. 'That's her house.'

Hudson thrust his phone at Anna. 'I've got an idea.' He squeezed his way through the immediate crowd and was swallowed by the darkness.

Anna rubbed Sophie's back whilst listening to updates from the ambulance service and oohing and ahhing at the fireworks with Petal. It was multitasking at its most extreme.

She wished Hudson hadn't left her. Every time Sophie winced she felt frightened and helpless. The fireworks display came to an impressive crescendo and the crowd in the park erupted into applause, including the children. With the fireworks over it was dark again and a wind whipped around them. Anna feared for the baby's safety if it arrived now.

After a few minutes she heard Hudson's voice over the crowd. The people started to disperse and Hudson emerged pushing a very old wheelbarrow. Sophie looked up. 'Bloody hell. You have to be joking.'

'You need to get to hospital,' said Hudson and he pointed at the wheelbarrow. 'Cinders, your carriage awaits.'

'I am not going all the way in that thing.'

'No, but we might be able to get you closer to the ambulance.'

Sophie's face registered alarm. 'I don't think there's time. It's coming.'

Hudson rushed to her with the wheelbarrow, which was full of potato sacks. 'Come on,' he said, like it was the most normal thing to hop in a wheelbarrow. Sophie gave him a murderous glare but with a lot of help from him and Anna she clambered on board.

'If this bollarding thing breaks.'

'All stops to Birmingham hospital,' said Hudson, and he set off across the park at an impressive pace.

'My go next,' shouted Arlo, clapping his hands.

Anna relayed the plan to the operator and they confirmed the ambulance was making progress and should be at the main gates in a few minutes. 'Perfect timing,' said Anna, herding the children after Hudson.

'Arghhhhhhhhh!' screamed Sophie.

'Arghhhhhhhhh!' hollered Hudson hitting a pothole and almost wrenching the barrow from his fingers. 'Don't you dare give birth in the wheelbarrow. I can't push two of you.'

'You're about as funny as haemorrhoids,' said Sophie, clamping her teeth together and making a strangled screech.

They could hear the approaching siren and it spurred them all on. The gates came into sight and blue lights flooded the entrance.

The paramedics quickly took over and within minutes Sophie was safely in the back of the ambulance. Anna went to get in with Petal in her arms and the paramedic stopped her. 'Sorry, love, no children allowed in the ambulance.'

'But they're her children,' protested Anna.

'Doesn't matter. Sorry.'

Anna watched Hudson who had Arlo by the hand and was showing him round the ambulance. 'Hudson, you'll have to go with her.'

'Me?' His eyebrows shot up in alarm. 'I'll take the kids and you go.' He held up Arlo's hand.

Anna was torn. She tried to pass Petal to Hudson but she started to cry and clung to Anna. Anna's expression conveyed exactly what needed to happen.

'Okay,' said Hudson, and he climbed in the back while the paramedics did final checks and started to close the doors.

Anna heard heavy breathing behind her. 'Wait! I'm here, I'm . . . here . . .' wheezed Dave, dashing towards the ambulance.

'Plugging hell, Dave, talk about last minute,' said Sophie, pulling the oxygen mask off her face but the look of relief was evident.

Dave motioned for Hudson to get out but he was already undoing his seatbelt. 'Good luck, buddy,' said Hudson, vacating the spot next to Sophie. She gave a weak wave as the doors shut. The siren whooped into life and the ambulance pulled away. Arlo was shouting and clapping excitedly and Petal was copying.

The siren ebbed away and they were left standing together in the dark. Hudson rubbed sweat from his forehead. 'I had better return this,' he said, motioning towards the wheelbarrow.

Anna frowned. 'How the hell did you get a wheelbarrow over the wall?'

Hudson gave a mysterious smile. 'Buy me a beer and I'll tell you.'

'I have coffee or hot chocolate.'

'Hot chocolate!' shouted Arlo. 'Can I have marshmallows in mine, Anna?'

'What do we say?' asked Anna.

'Now!' shouted Arlo. Anna gave him a hard stare. 'Please,' said Arlo reluctantly.

She took him by the hand. 'Come on, let's get you both in the warm.' And they followed Hudson and the wheelbarrow across the park.

Back in the warmth of Sophie's kitchen, Anna made hot chocolate and sat Petal in her high chair with a sippy cup of warm milk. She sat down at the table near to Petal ready to retrieve her cup when she dropped it. Hudson took off his jacket and joined her.

'You were a bit of a hero back there,' she said, glancing at him over her steaming mug.

'All part of the service, ma'am.' He sounded more American than ever.

'I've got to ask. Why were you even here tonight?' Anna couldn't phrase it any better.

Hudson coughed. 'I feel bad about the whole New York thing. I thought I'd try and straighten things out between us. You said you'd be at the fireworks. It wasn't hard to find you.'

'Must have been fairly hard to get in though. It was strictly ticket only and it was sold out.' The committee members had been on every entrance turning people away. Anna peered at him closely.

'Ah. You got me. I jumped the railings.'

'Jumped!' Anna was startled.

298

'No, no. I mean I climbed up and kinda fell down the other side.' He broke eye contact and sipped his hot chocolate.

They were quiet for a bit – the only noise the vigorous sucking from Petal and her sippy cup.

'How's Maurice?' asked Hudson.

'He's loving having his own door. He's not happy about his balls going through the washing machine though.'

Hudson's eyebrows raised quickly. 'I wouldn't be happy either.'

Anna gave him a sideways look. 'They're toy sponge balls. He chases them and they got caught up with a pile of washing.'

Hudson took a deep breath and Anna watched him. 'There was something I wa—'

Anna's phone sprang into life and she grabbed it up, surprised to see it was Liam calling. What did he want? She held a finger up to Hudson.

'Hello?'

'Hi, Anna. How are you?'

'I'm fine thanks.' She could do without the small talk. 'What's up?'

'Does there need to be something up for me to call you?'

Hudson waved at her and indicated he was going to go; Anna shook her head. 'Liam, I'm kind of busy . . .'

'Anna, we really need to have a proper chat.'

'About what?'

'Us, Anna. We made a mistake. I made a mistake. I know I've said it before but I don't think you realise how serious I am. I want you back.' She couldn't ignore the sorrow in his voice.

'Look—'

'Anna!' shouted Arlo and Anna was out of the kitchen in a flash and into the living room.

'Sorry, Liam. I've gotta go.'

Anna's eyes frantically swept around the room but Arlo was sitting on the sofa with the TV on and everything looked fine. 'What's the matter?'

'Can you put the Zombies on. Pleeeeease.' He grinned at her.

'Nope. Kids' TV or bed. Your choice.'

'O-kay. T-V.'

As she reached the hall Hudson came out of the kitchen putting his jacket on. 'What did Liam want?'

'He wants to get back together,' she said very matter-of-factly.

'Right.' Hudson pressed his lips together tightly.

'It's okay. You're still my fake boyfriend.'

'Phew.' They both looked apprehensively at each other. 'I'm going to make a move.'

'Okay.' Anna had hoped once she'd settled Arlo she'd have some adult company for what was likely to be a long night. 'Actually, could you do me one more favour?'

'Sure.'

'I've not been home to feed Maurice and he's going to be eating the furniture before long. Here's my keys. His food is in the cupboard under the sink.'

'No, problem. Do you need anything else? Nightwear? Toothbrush?'

She did but she didn't want him looking through her stuff. 'No, just the cat feeding would be great. Thanks.'

'I won't go snooping. Cross my heart.' He gave her a butter-wouldn't-melt look.

'Okay. Toothbrush and there's a washbag on the

windowsill in the bathroom with most of my stuff. That'd be great. Thanks.'

Hudson was kicking himself as he left Sophie's house. He had come with a clear mission for this evening and he had been derailed twice. Was it an omen? Was the universe trying to tell him something? He jogged round to Anna's front door and let himself in. Maurice came to see him or more likely to point out that he hadn't been fed.

'Hey, Maurice. Sorry to hear about your balls, big guy.' Hudson gave him a fuss and tried to encourage him to eat. Maurice sniffed the food and on deciding it wasn't poisoned he began to eat. Hudson soon found the washbag and was double-checking the door was properly locked when he was aware someone was standing behind him.

He swung round and came face to face with Connor. 'Hey, buddy, you gave me a start. You looking for Anna?'

'Is she okay?' Connor nodded at the floral washbag in Hudson's hand.

'Yeah, she's fine. Sophie has gone into labour. Anna's babysitting and she needed some stuff.' He held up the washbag as evidence. 'I'm taking it back now.' Hudson checked the door again.

'I'll walk with you,' said Connor, falling in step.

'Did you and Anna have plans tonight?' asked Hudson.

Connor puffed out his cheeks. 'Look you seem like a decent bloke but just so we're clear – me and Anna are in a relationship and things are going great. I'd be grateful if you'd respect that.'

Hudson's eyebrows puckered. 'Right. Of course.'

'You don't mind me mentioning it, do you?'

'No. I mean . . .' He wanted to say more but this wasn't the right time and Connor certainly wasn't the right person. 'I'm pleased for you both.' Hudson gave Connor a convivial pat on the shoulder.

'Thanks. She's something else, isn't she?'

'Yeah. You've got one of the best there.' Hudson was relieved when they reached Sophie's house. 'You know, I don't even need to come in. Here.' He handed Connor the washbag and keys. 'Tell her I'll see at work. Night.'

'Will do. Bye.' Connor waited on the steps and watched Hudson leave before knocking.

Anna opened the door with a beaming smile, which faltered for the briefest of moments. She looked past Connor. 'Have you seen . . .'

'Hudson gave me this,' he said, handing over the washbag. 'He had to rush off somewhere.' Connor shrugged.

'Did he give you my keys?'

'Oh, yeah. Here.' He handed them over. 'Can I come in?'

'I'm actually in the middle of putting Arlo to bed and I can't leave him for one second. Sorry. Can I call you?'

Connor's expression was unreadable. 'Sure. You do what you need to.'

'Thanks.' She gave him a quick kiss on the cheek and shut the door.

'Anna! Anna!' called Arlo urgently from upstairs.

'Yes, Arlo?' replied Anna already heading in his direction.

'I've done a huge poo! Come and see.' There was a long pause. 'Please!'

Anna was feeding a breakfast of mushed Weetabix to Petal whilst simultaneously discussing the career opportunities of being a Viking with Arlo when her mobile began vibrating along the worktop.

'Hi, Dave,' she said, before mouthing to Arlo. 'It's Daddy.'

'Hello, Daddy,' shouted Arlo.

'Hi, son,' replied Dave. Anna put him on speakerphone. 'Any news?'

'Okay. Yes, we have news. Hey, kids, you've got a brand-new . . . baby . . .' there was a long pause '. . . brother.'

'Yay!' shouted Arlo.

'Ay!' shouted Petal and she backhanded her Weetabix bowl sending it flying in spectacular fashion across the kitchen, splattering both Anna and Arlo. Arlo started to laugh.

'Congratulations,' said Anna, wiping the worst of the Weetabix assault off her top.

Arlo was frowning. 'Do I have to share my toys?'

Anna flopped onto the sofa at the end of the longest day of her life. She had been babysitting for twenty-four hours straight. She had no idea how Sophie did it. She was exhausted. She'd taken them both out to the soft play centre, which thankfully had taken up most of the day. Just getting out of the house with two small children needed a project plan.

The play centre was a big eye-opener for Anna. Whilst most of the other women seemed focused on talking animatedly with friends whilst mainlining lattes, their children were running riot like crazed banshees or, as she began to realise, like children at a soft play centre. She'd planned to set herself up with Petal in the baby area while Arlo burned off some of his overflowing energy supplies, but Anna found herself scooping Petal up every other minute as high-speed sweaty children hurdled her. It was incredibly stressful.

They had spent the remainder of the afternoon in the

park kicking up the autumn leaves and looking for squirrels. Oddly enough, despite Arlo shouting 'HERE, SQUIRRELS!' at the top of his voice, they hadn't even seen a whisker.

Anna found her eyes were closing when a key in the door made her come to. She crept into the hall.

'Congratulations,' she said, meeting Dave and Sophie at the door. 'Kids are asleep,' she added, as they slunk inside.

'Thanks,' said Sophie. They all cooed over the tiny baby in the overly large car seat. He was sound asleep, his rosebud lips pouting gently.

'He's beautiful,' said Anna.

Sophie angled her head towards the baby. 'Dave thinks he looks like Churchill.'

Dave chuckled. 'All babies look like Churchill – it's a well-known fact. He's still beautiful though.'

Sophie mouthed, 'At least he doesn't look like the Kraken.'

Anna hid her laughter by pulling her into a hug. 'How are you?' she asked. Sophie was pale.

'Okay,' she said, but her expression told a different story. 'It was probably the easiest of the births, certainly the quickest. But still, no walk in the park. Unfortunately, they had to cut my rings off.' She waved her bare left hand sadly.

'Drinks machine was better this time,' chipped in Dave and he went to get the bags from the car. Sophie rolled her eyes.

'He kept turning the radio up to drown me out,' she said, although Anna could tell she wasn't really cross about it.

'Were you being a bit shouty?'

'You would too if you'd almost delivered your child in a wheelbarrow.' They both laughed.

Dave reappeared. 'I'll put this lot upstairs. You sit down,' whispered Dave.

'Not after what they've done to my undercarriage. I may never sit down again.'

'I'll put the kettle on,' Anna cut in, keen not to hear about an episiotomy again.

'Lovely, and you can update me on everything. Still no caffeine for me, I'm breastfeeding.' Sophie pulled a disgruntled face and shuffled off to the living room.

Anna was struggling to remember anything before the babysitting. Was this what it was like for parents?

She took the drinks through and joined Sophie and Dave in the living room. Anna scooched herself round and peered at the scrunched-up bundle who was now being cradled by his mother. 'Does he have a name yet?'

Sophie smiled at Dave who was eyeing the scene fondly. 'We're thinking of Reuben.'

'I like it,' said Anna, failing to hide her surprise at liking the name. She'd been expecting something more obscure.

'Reuben David Butterworth,' said Sophie, glancing up and giving Dave an indulgent look.

'It was my great-grandad's name,' said Dave proudly.

'It's lovely and it suits him.' Anna stroked the baby's cheek and he screwed up his face and for a moment she could see what Dave meant about the Churchill resemblance.

Chapter Thirty-Two

Anna strode into the nursing home day room. 'Hi, Bert.' Bert didn't respond. He had his Mickey Mouse headphones on. She tapped him on the arm and he jumped. 'Hi, Bert,' she repeated.

'Oh, Anna. Hello,' he said, fumbling off the headphones. 'Let me pause this,' he said, running his thumb over the iPod until he found the home key. 'Sit down,' he said.

'Actually, I've got someone to see you. Wait a minute.' Anna put the coffees down on the table and nipped out of the room. A puzzled-looking Bert tidied up his headphone cable and put them carefully on the floor by his feet.

Anna came back in but before she could put the carrier down or explain, Maurice spotted Bert and let out a loud meow.

'Maurice?' said Bert, tears springing to his eyes.

Anna put the cat carrier on the floor, opened it up and Maurice leaped straight onto Bert's lap taking him a bit unawares.

'Hello, old fellow. How are you?' asked Bert and Maurice's deep purr seemed to ask the same question. Maurice resembled a soldier marching on the spot, lifting

306

up his front paws in turn. Bert was trying to stroke him and wipe away tears at the same time.

Bert and Maurice seemed oblivious when other residents came over to see what was going on. A carer put her head around the door and gave Anna a warm smile at the sight of so many residents on their feet chattering excitedly and all trying to get a stroke of Maurice. Anna put the cat carrier out of the way – the last thing she wanted was someone tripping over it and breaking a hip.

Bert's face radiated happiness and it cheered her deep inside. Maurice was soon over the initial excitement and was now stretched out on Bert's lap rhythmically kneading his corduroy trousers.

'Anna,' said Bert, without looking up.

Anna went to his side and touched his shoulder. 'Yes.'

Bert's voice cracked when he spoke. 'This is the nicest thing anyone has ever done for me.' He reached for her hand and squeezed it firmly. 'Thank you.'

'You're welcome, Bert. Maurice is really pleased to see you too. I swear he's grinning.'

'I can imagine,' said Bert. 'I think I'll have that coffee now, please.'

Anna and Maurice didn't stay too long. If Maurice could have curled up and gone to sleep she was sure they could have stayed longer but it seemed all the residents wanted to come and say hello and eventually Maurice jumped off Bert's lap and started to explore. Anna had agreed the visit with the care home's manager and the friendly carer had made sure all doors and windows and any other possible escape routes were secure before Anna had brought Maurice in but they still didn't want a nosy moggy on the loose.

'Okay, time to go,' she said, lifting Maurice into her arms and putting him on the arm of Bert's chair.

Bert seemed to know he was there and gave him a good head rub. 'Bye, Maurice. It's been lovely to see you one last time.'

'Actually,' said Anna. 'Because you've both behaved yourselves, they've said we can do this again.' She leaned in conspiratorially. 'To be honest they said it's the first time they've seen some of the people in here smile for months.'

'That's marvellous. When do you think you'll bring him again?' Bert's face was alight.

Anna mentally whizzed through her calendar. 'Probably in a couple of weeks.'

'After New York?' asked Bert.

'Err,' Anna faltered, she'd pushed it to the back of her mind although her plan was to call in sick on the morning of the flight. It seemed the easiest get-out approach.

'Anna.' His voice was earnest. 'Sometimes you need to be braver than you think possible. This is one of those times.'

Anna's stomach lurched. It sounded like one of Roberta's better quotes. 'I guess.'

'Then I'll see you and Maurice after you've been to New York.'

Sophie looked at home in Anna's kitchen eating biscuits while Anna went through her post.

'I saw my GP today. He's given me some medication in case I want to give flying a go,' said Anna, feeling the familiar acidic flush in her stomach at the very thought of a plane.

'That's a hugely positive step. Well done, you.' Sophie gave her a hug.

'Coffee?' asked Anna, discarding a pile of leaflets that had been put through with her letters.

'I'm not stopping long but Dave insisted on doing bath time so I thought I might as well pop here for a quick natter and a catch up on all the office gossip.'

'Of course, it's always lovely to see you,' said Anna. 'Not much happening in the office though. Roberta's still spouting Minnie Mouse's best motivational quotes and Karl's still walking up and down while he takes his phone calls.'

'Why do men do that?'

'I have no idea,' she said, opening an ordinary white envelope and pulling out an invitation. For a moment she experienced a bubble of excitement but when she saw what it said a wave of nausea came over her. Everything that haunted her about the past rushed into her mind and she found herself gripping the card tightly.

'You okay?' asked Sophie, peering closer. 'What is it?' She took the card from Anna's sweating palm and read it. 'A university reunion?'

'Is someone playing games?' Anna searched Sophie's face for reassurance.

'No, you're overthinking this. Unis have reunions all the time. People love all the nostalgia it throws up.' Sophie paused. 'You know, maybe you should consider going. Lay some ghosts to rest?'

Anna felt giddy at the thought and had to take a deep breath to control the panic rising inside her. She shook her head. 'I . . . I couldn't. The thought of being there brings it all back.'

'It's all right.' Sophie squeezed her shoulder. 'You don't have to do anything. But until you face it you'll never move on. It's like all the things that scare us in life. You can try ignoring them but eventually they rear up and . . .' Anna was blinking rapidly. 'Forget I said that,' said Sophie. 'What do I know?' She dropped the invitation in the bin and Anna watched it tumble as if in slow motion. 'Tell me all about your New York plans instead.'

Anna knew Sophie was right. How much longer could she go on being afraid of her past, ignoring the damage that still haunted her? She knew something had to change but for now Anna just needed to sit down.

Anna gripped her passport tightly. 'You need to hand it over now,' said Hudson, his voice seeming far away.

'What?' Anna snapped back to the moment. She was standing at the check-in desk at Heathrow Airport. This was her last chance to back out. She'd failed at all the other opportunities. Somehow she felt like she'd made Bert a promise. After this, she *was* getting on an aeroplane. Anna swallowed hard.

'Anna.' Hudson's voice was firmer this time. 'You need to do this,' he said, before lowering his voice. 'Because if you don't there is now a long line of customers who will merrily lynch you.'

Anna nodded more times than was healthy in quick succession. 'Right. Yes. I can do this.' She forcefully thrust her passport forward, taking the zoned-out check-in desk operative by surprise.

'Thank you, have you read the list regarding hand luggage . . .' It seemed to kick-start him off on his recited piece, which he probably repeated hundreds of times a day. Anna answered the questions as if she were in court being charged with something. When the grilling was over he held out her passport and boarding pass and said in a singsong voice, 'Have a nice flight.'

Anna was trying to form a reply when Hudson guided her away. 'Next we are going through security check, then to the champagne bar.'

'I'm going to need to score hard drugs before I can get on the plane. What am I doing?' Anna spun around feeling disorientated by all the jolly people with brightly coloured cases.

'You are getting on a plane to New York if it's the last thing you do.'

Anna stopped walking. 'It was the last thing my sister did,' she said, her face serious.

'What?' Hudson looked shocked.

'Lynsey, my sister. I told you she had undiagnosed epilepsy and had a seizure.'

'Yeah.' He gave a sympathetic head tilt.

'It happened on the flight to Tenerife.' Anna felt wobbly as a sick sensation washed over her.

Hudson rubbed his temple. 'That's why you have a fear of flying.' It was a statement, not a question, but Anna nodded. 'I'm sorry if I've pressured you into this. I didn't realise . . .'

'It's okay. I have to face it one day. Why not today?' She tried her hardest to sound positive.

'Why not indeed.' He linked arms with her and escorted her to security.

The business lounge was like a very swish hotel reception and Hudson checked them both in. Anna was still feeling a little flustered after the security check. She was sitting with an orange juice watching Hudson sip chilled champagne.

'You've done this loads, haven't you?' she asked.

'Yep, I've no idea how many times. It's like taking the train to me.'

'That's good,' said Anna. 'I'll remember that. It's like taking the train . . . apart from being thirty-nine thousand feet up in the air!' She took a gulp from her orange juice and choked.

'Hey, slowly,' said Hudson, taking the glass off her. 'It'll be completely fine. I promise you.' The way he looked into her eyes as he said it made her insides turn to mush. 'Let's get something to eat and then I've booked us in for a massage.'

'Booked *us* a massage?'

'It'll help you to relax.' He tilted his head. 'It's not together or anything weird.'

'Good. Thank you. Nothing weird is good.'

She drank plenty of water at Hudson's instruction, took the medication her doctor had prescribed to help her stay calm and came back from her massage feeling like she couldn't be bothered to do much at all. Before she knew it, Hudson was gathering up their carry-ons and ushering her towards the gate, which turned out not to be a gate at all but another less equipped waiting area.

All was well until Hudson took her over to where three small children had their noses pressed to the glass of a giant window. Anna saw what they were looking at – an enormous plane. Her knees buckled and at the same time Hudson's hand snaked around her waist to keep her upright.

She looked up into his blue eyes. 'I've got you,' he said.

The tunnel down to the plane was the best part. The enormous plane she'd seen through the glass seemed much smaller on the inside. Their seats were near the front and as soon as she'd sat down someone was offering her a glass of bubbly, which she politely turned away.

Hudson made sure she had what she needed from her bags and then stowed them in the overhead lockers and began fiddling with a screen that seemed to have popped up out of nowhere.

'You okay?' he paused to ask.

'Yeah. Are we taking off yet?' She held her eye mask tightly in her hands.

'No. About twenty minutes.'

It surprised Anna how much waiting around was involved. 'It's like airlines want to give you maximum opportunity to get as panicky as possible. If you checked in and went down a chute straight onto the plane it would be far better.'

He gave her a warm smile. 'You could suggest that on your feedback form.'

Her eyes darted about agitatedly. Everyone else was either settling down to read a paper, getting out a laptop or fiddling with their screen. Nobody else was panicking.

'Distract yourself with something. Watch a film.' He pulled out the inflight magazine and handed it to her.

When the plane started to move she hadn't expected it to go backwards. 'What's happening?' Her voice was a squeak. 'We're going backwards.' She didn't remember this bit.

'It's called push back. We are up against the terminal building so they have to reverse away. We'll soon be going in the right direction.'

Or straight to hell, was all she could think. And she closed her eyes and tried to stem the panic. It didn't feel like the medication was kicking in yet. A loud noise engulfed the aircraft and Anna let out a shriek. Hudson's warm hand enveloped her own. She opened her eyes and then quickly closed them. She couldn't speak. Her shoulders were so high they were almost touching her ears. The noise increased and the plane started to speed forward.

'It's okay,' said Hudson. His voice soothing and in total contrast to the unholy racket the plane was making. His thumb tenderly stroked across her knuckles and she fleetingly thought how nice that might be if she weren't having a panic attack.

'Is this normal?' she managed to squeak out.

'Completely normal. And here we go.'

'Argh!' Anna couldn't halt the small scream that burst from her when the front of the plane came up. Her heart was racing. Her eyes were tight shut. She could feel sweat sticking her hair to the back of her neck. She gasped in some air.

'Here, sip some water,' said Hudson, prising her fingers from the arm of the seat and giving her a cup. She opened one eye and took it from him. 'You did it. You're flying. Well done.' He pretend chinked his paper cup against hers.

She glanced over to the nearest window and nearly vomited as the plane banked, dipped down one side and clouds whizzed past to reveal green fields a very long way below. Hudson took back the cup of water.

'This was a very bad idea.' Anna resumed clutching the seat.

'Here's what we're going to do,' came Hudson's dulcet tones. 'You are going to keep your eyes closed. Not scrunched up like used teabags,' he said. His voice was low and methodical and almost a whisper, making her concentrate to hear him. 'Okay?'

She nodded her reply.

She felt him lift the armrest between them and move his body closer. He was now leaning against her shoulder. He spoke softly into her ear. 'You are doing great, Anna. I need you to concentrate on your breathing. We need to slow it down. Deep breath in . . .' He paused. 'And slowly exhale. That's awesome.' They did this a few times and she could feel her pulse returning to the right side of normal.

'Now, let's let the tension out of those shoulders. Imagine they're a Lilo and someone is letting the air out. Let those shoulders drop down. That's great.' She could feel his breath on her earlobe and it made her shudder. 'I want you to think about your favourite place to sleep. Picture it and . . .' Hudson's voice had a soothing rhythm to it and whilst Anna was listening she also wasn't.

Before she knew it a sweet female voice was asking someone near her if the lady would like something to eat. She heard Hudson whisper a reply. Anna smiled when she realised the lady must be her. She opened her eyes and yawned.

'Hello, sleeping beauty,' said Hudson, his eyes twinkling.

For a moment Anna wasn't sure where she was. It was a nasty reality jolt to remember she was sitting on a plane. Her mouth was dry but she checked it for dribble anyway. 'Hi,' she said, looking about her feeling slightly dazed. She was a lot better for her nap and not nearly as anxious as before.

'About fifty minutes to landing,' said Hudson, closing his book.

'What?' Anna was stunned. Had she really slept that long? She checked her watch – she had. 'You're like the horse whisperer but for phobic flyers.'

Hudson smiled. 'Would you like something to eat? You'll need to be quick before they start getting ready to land.' He handed her the menu. It was like reading something from a posh restaurant.

Hudson waved a hand to attract the stewardess and she appeared at his side. 'Yes, sir. What else can I get you?'

'I'd like the crayfish sandwich, please,' said Anna, noting how the stewardess seemed to struggle to drag her eyes away from Hudson. She gave him a fresh look.

He was very handsome; he could easily be mistaken for a film star. She mused over how she'd almost come to accept it.

Anna's sandwich arrived and she was aware Hudson was talking but she could no longer hear him properly. Her ears had gone all fuzzy. She began opening her mouth wide and waggling her head from side to side like she had water stuck in her ears. Hudson was watching her. 'Here,' he said, reaching into his bag and pulling out a lollipop. 'It'll help to clear the pressure in your ears.'

'You think of everything.'

'I do my best. Now don't worry if there's a little bump when the wheels hit the runway. It's perfectly normal. Okay?'

'Okay,' said Anna and it really was. It was okay that she was on an aeroplane at thirty-nine thousand feet and it was okay that it was about to land in New York. A city she had dreamed of visiting since she was a teenager. Everything was a lot more okay thanks to Hudson Jones.

Hudson repeated the breathing exercises with her as they came in to land and Anna had to force herself to concentrate and stop grinning like a lunatic. But something made her act like a teenager every time he whispered in her ear.

Hudson led the way and they trooped off the plane and were soon reunited with their luggage, through immigration and being whisked away from the airport in a yellow cab. It felt very special to be cocooned in the back with Hudson. He had a brief chat with the driver and they were soon speeding towards Manhattan. Anna switched her phone off airplane mode and it beeped as it delivered messages from her dad, Sophie and Connor all asking if she had got on the plane. She was pleased to be able to fire off a few quick replies to say she had survived the flight and was now in New York. She felt like she needed to pinch herself. She was actually here. She'd done it.

'I know I have no right to be, but I'm proud of you,' said Hudson. 'You have conquered your fear of flying. That's remarkable.'

'Only thanks to you and I can't guarantee I won't be a gibbering wreck when it's time to go home.' Although she had to admit she was quite proud of herself too.

'Stay alert, we're going to see a few of the sights on our way into Manhattan.' Was she imagining it or had Hudson's accent got a fraction stronger from being on American soil?

Hudson leaned in. 'Look ahead.' Through the windscreen she saw her first glimpse of New York City. The iconic grey skyline she'd seen many times on TV and in films.

'This is the Brooklyn Bridge,' said Hudson, leaning closer.

Anna nodded; she was dumbstruck. It was like being in a film. From the taxi she saw the Woolworth Building, Chase Bank and One World Trade Center. She almost twisted off her head trying to catch a glimpse of the famous Coke bottle when they whizzed through Times Square. Before long the taxi pulled up outside their hotel. The driver got their cases from the boot and Hudson tipped him.

'I figure until we step inside the office tomorrow our time is our own. So if you don't have any plans, would you like me to show you around?' He looked somehow hopeful.

Anna didn't have any plans. This was due largely to her

not really believing she would ever make it onto the plane. 'No plans. I've not even got a guidebook,' she said, dismayed by her own lack of forward planning. 'Let the adventure begin.'

Chapter Thirty-Three

Their first stop was a street vendor selling pretzels. The taste of the warm fresh pretzel was divine. Anna and Hudson exchanged raised eyebrows whilst they munched. Hudson's phone rang and a frown crossed his face as he answered it.

'Emily? I'll call you back.' He ended the call. Anna was watching him and he seemed to read her mind. 'Emily is . . . my stepmother.'

It shouldn't have mattered to Anna who it was on the phone but somehow it did. Hudson tightened his lips and kicked at an unseen stone. She knew his relationship with his father was strained so it was likely relations with his stepmother weren't a lot better.

'Come on, there's somewhere I want to show you.'

After a fair walk they approached a small coffee shop, stopped outside and took in the frontage with its many long windows and dark wood. Anna suddenly realised what she was looking at. '*You've Got Mail*,' she said, clapping her hands together, recognising the coffee shop from the film.

'Correct. Welcome to Café Lalo.' Hudson was beaming and seemed rather pleased with himself.

Inside was stunning and Anna felt like she was walking onto a film set. Flashbacks of her much-loved movie swam into view while they got their drinks and some macarons, because Hudson insisted they were the best in town, and found some comfy seats.

'I love it. Thank you,' said Anna. She was giddy with excitement. She couldn't have asked for a better introduction to New York than this.

Day two was less exciting but their first day in the office had gone exactly to plan. The office itself was a floor of an impressive building in Lower Manhattan. Although the building was stupidly tall their company was situated on level four, which was a bonus. It was still high but no higher than the UK offices so Anna knew she could cope. They'd spent most of the day in meetings but they were all productive and informative. It surprised her that she could see herself working there but she could see Hudson fitting in well too.

Hudson had disappeared for a bit whilst Anna was typing up the day's notes and when he returned the twinkle in his eyes meant he was fired up about something. 'Are we nearly done here?'

'I think we are,' said Anna, her fingers traversing the keyboard at speed. 'I just need to email this to Roberta so she'll pick it up first thing tomorrow and know we're on schedule.' It was very late but they had packed a lot into their first day.

Hudson was fidgeting. 'When you're done, I need to show you something.'

Anna glanced up and took in the boyish glee in his eyes. It made her want to know what it was straight away. He ignited a curiosity inside her. 'Okay. Two minutes.'

Her phone beeped and distracted her. It was Connor. He had been messaging her a lot. Each message was supportive but she was hoping he'd be asleep by now. She wasn't sure why she wanted that. Did she need a break from him? She felt uncharitable for thinking it. She replied with a smiley face and switched the phone off.

After a brief ride in a yellow cab Anna found herself in what appeared to be a small coffee shop. They chose drinks and Anna looked about for a food menu but there wasn't one. 'I thought you said they did food?' asked Anna, and the waiter raised his chin and eyed her suspiciously making her think she'd said something wrong. She wondered why there were so few people when there had been quite a number ahead of them in the queue.

The waiter checked over both shoulders before leaning forward and in a husky whisper he spoke to Hudson. 'Dial twenty and say Denny sent you.' He jerked his head at a payphone in the corner, which Anna had seen another couple use a minute ago. The couple must have left because they weren't there now. Hudson was grinning. It was like he got the joke but she didn't.

'What's going on?' she asked, with growing unease.

'You'll see,' said Hudson, approaching the payphone and doing as the waiter had instructed. Hudson seemed to get some instructions. 'Yep, got it. Thanks.'

He replaced the old-style phone receiver and they went around the side where the sign said toilets. There were two toilets but Hudson was pushing on the wall. To Anna's surprise another door was revealed and they stepped out of the small quiet coffee shop into a large vibrant restaurant. It was like magic. The room was filled with velveteen furniture, opulent 1920s' décor, elegant chandeliers and ornate mirrors. Someone dressed like an old style gangster greeted them warmly and showed them to a table.

'This is so cool,' said Anna, giggling a little at the silliness and subterfuge.

'Isn't it? This is all for the tourists now but during prohibition this really was a speakeasy. Somewhere you could get illegal liquor.' Hudson's eyes were alight.

'I love it,' said Anna. And she was starting to think New York wasn't the only thing she was falling for. She busied herself with choosing starters and hoped the confusing thoughts that were swamping her brain would disappear. She had Connor waiting for her at home. But he wasn't exactly waiting patiently – he was messaging her every five minutes.

The starters were the size of main courses and she wished she hadn't ordered ribs. Although when they arrived she was sure she could find some room for them. Their conversation was easy: a mix of work and social that flowed naturally.

Hudson raised his glass. 'To you conquering your fear of heights and flying.'

She clinked glasses. 'I think just the flying one was cured today. I'm still not sure about heights.'

Hudson seemed to be thinking. 'I thought it was one phobia?'

Anna thought about brushing it aside like she always did. It was something she never discussed but without much thought she knew she wanted to share a little about her reasons with Hudson. 'It's a very long story but I knew someone who had an accident when I was at university. Her name was Esme and she fell from a balcony.' She fought to keep her mind on the facts she knew rather than the questions that haunted her.

'That's terrible. Was she okay?'

Anna shook her head. 'She's been in a coma ever since.'

'And you witnessed her fall?'

Anna took a drink of cranberry and wished it was something stronger. 'No. It was my party, but I'd passed out in my bedroom. I was woken by the screams when she fell. They were playing some stupid drinking game apparently.' Anna's mind was going over the events of that fateful evening as it frequently did. 'If I hadn't drunk so much, I would have been with the others on the balcony and I might have been able to save her.'

'That's why you don't drink,' said Hudson.

'You got me,' said Anna.

'Please don't tell me you blame yourself for this.'

'Yes. I always have. She was my friend, I invited her, and it was my party . . .'

Hudson took her hand. 'Anna. You are the sweetest thing but you have to let this go. Yes, it was a terrible accident. People make bad choices in a nanosecond. This was not your fault.'

Anna wasn't sure whether to pull her hand away or not. She liked the contact. It seemed to make his words all the truer. 'I can't risk being in the same situation again, which is why I won't drink. And it happened just a few years after we lost Lynsey so I was a mess for a while and it definitely compounded my phobia. But I think coming here has already shown me that perhaps I am starting to move on.'

'I'm pleased. You deserve to be happy, Anna. Are you happy?' he asked, his eyes locked on hers.

What a question. She was momentarily floored. Right now, right at this moment, was she happy? There was only one answer. 'Yes, Hudson. I'm happy.'

*

Anna found herself longing for the office days to be over so she could spend time with Hudson. The combination of the vibrancy and life that flowed through New York and the bond deepening between them were to blame. She loved her job and it was going well but it was what was happening outside the office that was taking up all her thoughts. She spoke to Connor every lunchtime and each time it was like the distance between them was widening. She was calling him because she felt she had to. He was keen and interested, which made her feel guilty for enjoying her time in New York and, more so, her time with Hudson.

Hudson looked up from his laptop. 'I've finished the write-up. Did you track down the finance information Roberta asked for?'

'Yep, all sent. I'm finishing off the actions from the last session and I'm ready to go. Where are we going tonight?' She knew she looked as keen as a puppy.

Hudson's expression changed. 'Actually, I was thinking of heading out of town on my own tonight.'

Anna couldn't hide her disappointment. She needed to pull herself together. Of course he could go off on his own. He didn't have to babysit her every night. She forced a smile. 'Sounds like an excellent idea. You have a good time.'

Hudson had his head lowered. 'It's Thanksgiving tomorrow. I kinda felt I should check in with my father while I'm in town.'

Anna felt relieved. He wasn't ditching her because he was fed up with her; it was a family thing. 'Goodness, I'd forgotten about Thanksgiving. The hotel did push a leaflet under my door about it and I know nobody will be in the office but I figured we could still come in and finish off our overall report.' Thanksgiving didn't mean anything to her. She'd assumed they would carry on working. The fact it obviously meant something to Hudson had passed her by. 'Of course, you don't need to come in. You should celebrate with your family. And then Friday is our last day.' Unexpected sadness crept over her at the thought of going home.

'No, it's okay. I'm not expecting an invite to Thanksgiving dinner from my father. I'll book us in at the hotel restaurant if you like?'

'Great.' She failed to hide her excitement and then thought she really should have shown more compassion for him not spending an important holiday with his father. Wasn't Thanksgiving a lot like Christmas to Americans? She couldn't imagine not being with her mum and dad at that time of year. 'Would you not rather be with your dad?'

Hudson gave a dry cough. 'We don't get on great. Short meetings work best for us. It's all a bit awkward.'

'Families can be like that.'

'Yeah, mine certainly is. Look I'm really sorry about tonight. I would have loved to have shown you where I used to live but with things as they are . . . it's better if I go alone.'

'Of course,' said Anna resolutely. 'I wouldn't dream of intruding.'

Hudson rubbed his palm across his chin. She thought he was going to say something else but instead he stood up and started to pack his things away. She had an odd sensation inside. She was on her own in New York. She could go anywhere, do anything she wanted but all she wanted to do was be with Hudson. She needed to give herself a good talking-to. She had poor Connor at home missing her desperately and it was very clear how he felt about her. Hudson on the other hand was much harder to read. He'd never given her any cause to believe their relationship was anything other than friendship.

'Anna?' Hudson was waving a hand in front of her. She must have looked like a stunned mullet as her mind had wandered off.

'Sorry? Yes.'

He smiled warmly at her. 'I'll see you at breakfast. Okay?'

'Yes. Fine. Lovely. See you at breakfast.' She tried to sound positive. 'I'm going to paint the town red. Go exploring on my own.' She straightened her back. She could do this; she could find her way around New York. She needed to buy a guidebook first then she'd be fine. She almost convinced herself.

Concern appeared on Hudson's face. 'Where are you going exploring?'

'I don't know. I'll see where the wind takes me.'

Hudson almost winced. 'You can't really do that in New York. There's places you shouldn't wander around at night.'

'Then I'll do the Empire State Building and the hotel restaurant. I'll be fine.' She could see he was worried about her.

'I was kind of hoping to show you the Empire State Building tomorrow. But it's fine, you go ahead.'

This was awkward. 'I'll do the Statue of Liberty instead.'

Hudson checked his watch. 'It's closed now and you'd need to book.'

Anna searched her brain for another New York landmark she could visit. 'Rockefeller Center!' As it struck her she almost shouted it at him like she were on a game show. She had no idea exactly what the Rockefeller Center was but she'd seen it feature in many a Christmas film, which meant it was probably worth checking out.

Hudson's expression lightened. 'You'll like it. Top of the Rock is fun.'

'Then that's what I'll do.'

'Night,' he said, slinging his laptop bag across his shoulder.

Anna turned her attention back to her screen. There were a few emails she needed to answer and as she was in no rush now she could get them sorted. Out of the corner of her eye she saw Hudson returning. She paused.

'Look, there's no reason why you can't come with me to Port Chester. I will be literally fifteen minutes with my father, tops. If we have a row I'll be back in two. There's a coffee shop not far from the house. I can drop you there or you can go for a walk through the town. It's quite safe. It's not like the city.'

'If you're sure?' She tried hard not to sound too keen although she really wanted to go. The chance to see a little further out and to see where Hudson had grown up was intriguing.

'Yeah, I'm sure. Come on. We've got a train to catch.'

Chapter Thirty-Four

Anna hadn't been expecting to find herself in Grand Central Station. She was all the more surprised the museum-like building was an actual functioning station. She struggled to walk in a straight line through its vast hall because she was constantly looking up at the high arched ceiling above her. It was utterly beautiful, not like a train station at all.

Anna was excited to travel by train. It gave her a new perspective of New York as they left the high-rise bedlam of Manhattan behind them and raced through an increasingly green environment. They stopped at a few stations and Anna craned her neck to see the small towns they were passing. In less than an hour they arrived in Port Chester. Hudson had been relatively quiet on the journey choosing to check his phone rather than look out of the window. She could sense his apprehension at seeing his father.

They left the station and started walking. 'Has it been long since you last saw your dad?'

Hudson tilted his head in thought. 'About two years.'

Anna knew it was unusual for her parents to still be together and even more unusual that they were happy. It saddened her that Hudson hadn't experienced the same. She valued the security it gave her to face all life threw her way.

'Still, it'll be nice to catch up now.'

Hudson's raised eyebrow conveyed his misgivings. 'We'll see. It's not far to my old elementary school, then I'll show you my house and the church and then you'll be a few strides from town. Okay?'

'Sounds great.' It was dark but the streets were well lit and lots of people bustled about carrying shopping.

'Thanksgiving dinner tomorrow,' said Hudson, following her gaze to a man weighed down with bags.

'Of course. This is a bit like Christmas Eve then?'

'Yeah, a bit. No presents and more pumpkin with this holiday. That's how I used to think of it when I was a kid.' His lips twitched at the memory but it was fleeting and was soon replaced by a tight knotting of his eyebrows.

Hudson pointed out his school, an ordinary brick building that invoked a number of amusing stories and the mood briefly lightened. Anna turned up the collar of her coat against the cold. They walked in silence for a while until Hudson's pace slowed.

'This was my road.'

Anna wasn't sure whether to reach out to him. He seemed vulnerable somehow. 'You okay?' she asked.

'Yeah, I'm fine. I've not been back here for a very long time. We usually meet in the city but he'll be home for Thanksgiving and I wanted to see how things have changed.'

'And have they changed?' asked Anna.

'Not much.'

They both took in their surroundings while they walked along the long wide street. Large wooden-fronted houses stood back from wide sidewalks and big American elms loomed over wide driveways.

Hudson stopped dead. 'What the hell?' He set off again at a much faster pace and Anna had to jog to catch up.

'What's wrong?'

He didn't answer but stopped outside a large cream-painted house with a For Sale sign on the front lawn.

Sophie was looking forward to seeing Dave walk through the door. It had been one of those days. Reuben had been whiny all day, Petal was fully embracing toddler tantrums and ever since she'd picked Arlo up from school he'd not stopped talking about the many things he wanted for Christmas. Trying to do anything of any value was almost impossible as at least one other person was demanding her attention. She could tell Petal had cottoned on to the fact she was no longer the priority with baby Reuben in the fold so every time he cried, she cried louder. Sophie had tried to start dinner but she'd been interrupted so many times she could barely remember what she was trying to cook.

She was changing Reuben's nappy and he was expressing his displeasure by wailing. Petal was lying on the floor a few feet away screaming at the top of her voice and at her shoulder she had Arlo shouting to be heard.

'AND I REALLY, REALLY WANT A CAR THAT GOES ON THE CEILING!'

Sophie thought her eardrums were going to burst. They were definitely buzzing slightly. Was that tinnitus?

'But that's quite a few things you've said you'd like.'

'But I've wanted one of those cars ever since I first saw it.'

'That was yesterday, Arlo. You need to write a list to

330

Santa but remember he only delivers to good boys.'

Arlo's head flopped to one side. 'Willoughby Newell isn't good and he says he always gets *everything* he wants. And Toby Peterson has loads of uncles and they all buy him stuff. Why don't I have lots of uncles?'

There were many things Sophie wanted to say about Toby Peterson and his mother's loose morals but she held her tongue. 'Because all families are different and I'm sure it all works out the same in the end. You got a lovely present from Reuben. Toby Peterson doesn't have any brothers or sisters.'

'He's lucky,' said Arlo, giving the still-screaming Petal a sideways glare.

Sophie picked up the two cuddly rabbits they'd bought when the baby arrived. She gave Petal hers and thankfully it distracted her enough to stop her crying. She handed the other to Arlo.

'Come on, Dildo,' he said to his rabbit and he left the room with Petal toddling behind him.

Sophie wondered where he'd got the name from but knew sometimes it was best to ignore it. She drew a deep breath and took a moment to give Reuben a cuddle. He smelled of baby. A sweet powdery scent that propelled her ovaries into overdrive. She snuggled her face into his neck and he burped loudly in her ear. He was most definitely a Butterworth and she loved him dearly.

The sound of Dave's key in the door didn't bring the wave of relief it would have done a few minutes earlier. The storm had passed as she'd learned it always did.

'Hey, gorgeous,' said Dave, giving Sophie a kiss. 'Hiya, stinky,' he said, giving Reuben's tiny fist a bump. 'How were the tribe today?' He paused waiting for her reply.

'Full on, but bearable. How was your day?'

331

'Supplier has let us down again and the legal team are pulling apart the contract. But the coffee shop had an offer on cereal bars – so bearable.' He smiled. She loved that smile. It was warm and full of love for the family they'd created. Petal came in swinging her rabbit round her head and Dave picked her up and blew raspberries on her neck.

'Daddy. Help!' yelled Arlo. 'There's a rainbow in my willy!'

Dave put Petal down and disappeared into the downstairs loo. Sophie followed him to the hallway still cradling Reuben. There was a moment's silence before he popped his round the door. 'It's okay, it's just a vein.'

Sophie smiled to herself, wondered briefly if the Beckhams or the Kardashians had similar crises, and went to have another attempt at making dinner.

Hudson's reaction had been very controlled. He had stared at the house for a few moments before declaring it was time to leave and now they were walking back to the train station in silence. Anna's mobile rang. She answered it quickly, the chirpy ringtone somehow inappropriate for the current mood.

'Hi, Connor.'

'Is everything okay?' he asked, forgoing any preamble. He sounded concerned, alarmed even.

'Yes, everything's fine. Why?'

'Where are you?'

'I'm still in New York.' She pulled a puzzled face but Hudson was staring at the pavement.

'You are?' He went silent.

'Yes.'

'Right. It's just . . .'

'What's wrong?' She could tell from his tone he was anxious about something.

'Nothing. I had this horrible sensation something was wrong. Are you alone?'

'No, I'm with Hudson.' Although she felt a little guilty, Connor should be expecting them to be spending time together. She couldn't feel too bad about that. Hell, she'd done nothing wrong.

'Where are you exactly? At the hotel?' He sounded tentative.

'No, we went out. Hudson was showing me where he used to live.' The line was silent. 'And I wanted to see something other than the inside of an office.' It was stretching the truth a little. Hudson had been excellent at showing her some of the sights of New York.

'Be careful, Anna,' said Connor. But what he said and how he said it had Anna wondering exactly what he meant.

'I'm quite safe.'

Connor seemed to recover. 'Great. That's all I'm worried about. I love you, Anna.'

The statement hung between them. Anna was aware of how close Hudson was to her. It was something she had often longed to hear but now was not the time and she wasn't sure if she was hearing it from the right person either.

'Connor? Are still you there? Hello?' It most likely wasn't the response he'd been hoping for.

'Hello, Anna. Can you hear me?'

'Hello?' She ended the call. 'Must have lost signal,' she said, turning to Hudson who barely grunted in response. 'Are you sure you don't want to talk to your father about him selling the house? These things are usually better face to face.'

Hudson stopped suddenly. 'I appreciate you trying to help but I know he'll say it's none of my business and he'd be right. It's his house. I'd lose my temper and . . . he'd continue to maintain his low opinion of me for getting emotional.'

'You clearly have an attachment to the property. I think we all do to our first home; it's only natural. It was thoughtless of him not to tell you.'

'He was probably waiting until after it was sold. It's not like I'm going to want to buy it.'

'No, but still.' Anna struggled to understand how his own father could be so heartless, to sell up without even letting Hudson know, but once again she was reminded not all families were like hers and certainly all dads were not as thoughtful and devoted as hers. A pang of homesickness jolted her. She would call her parents the minute she got back to the hotel.

Anna wandered down to breakfast the next morning and was greeted by the usual attentive staff who were wishing her a 'Happy Thanksgiving' like they were on repeat. There was no sign of Hudson so she chose a table near the restaurant entrance, ordered tea and took the opportunity to write a postcard to Bert.

Anna was engrossed in her writing when she tuned in to Hudson's voice approaching. She was surprised by the sharpness of his tone. She felt awkward for listening in to the one-sided conversation but it was hard not to given the volume and timbre of his voice.

'No, you listen. When were you planning on telling me? Don't you think I have a right to know about something like that? . . . I know it's Thanksgiving . . . That's baloney! Since when have we ever been a family? . . . What's it matter to you? I'm spending it with a friend.' After a brief pause Hudson strode purposefully into the restaurant. His tense expression lightened when he saw Anna, who tried hard not to look like she'd been listening.

'I take it you heard that?' He gave a little wince.

'Yes, I'm sorry. It was hard not to. Things not great with your dad?'

'Err,' he hesitated. 'No. No, change there. I kinda hit the minibar last night and sent out a few messages so it was to be expected.'

'Ah, drunk in charge of a mobile is never a good thing.'

'Coffee, please,' said Hudson, when the waitress neared their table. 'I'm going to need kick-starting.'

Anna marvelled at the fact he looked as he always did; if this was Hudson with a hangover he hid it well. He was freshly showered and smelled divine, all soapy and lemony with a hint of something she couldn't quite identify.

'You okay?' Hudson was giving her an odd look, which wasn't surprising given she was staring at him.

'Yes. Sorry. Trying to decide on what to have.' She tapped the closed menu in front of her and then opened it swiftly.

'It's a buffet, like it has been all week.'

'Right. I'll go and choose something.' Anna was flustered and she bumped the table as she stood up. 'Whoops. Sorry.' What was wrong with her?

'Word of warning. You'll want to leave plenty of room for Thanksgiving dinner.'

'Yes. Good advice. Thank you. I'll do that.' She sounded like a 1930s' broadcaster. She shook her head at her own ineptitude.

Anna returned with a bowl of fresh fruit salad and busied herself with eating.

'I've got a few things planned for today if you wanted to get a feel for what Thanksgiving is like?' Hudson seemed unsure of himself when he spoke. 'I know you wanted to get some work done but I figured we've still got Friday and we can work on the plane if we have to.'

'I like your plan much better.' She speared a large strawberry and got ready to embrace Thanksgiving New York style.

She soon found herself wrapped up in her winter woollies and standing on a very busy street waiting for the Macy's Thanksgiving Day parade. Strangers around her were wishing her a happy Thanksgiving and she was now quite naturally returning the wishes to expressions of awe at her "cute British accent".' As the noise increased and a giant balloon loomed into view Anna began to get excited. It took an age for all the floats, marching bands and dressed-up walkers to go by and she felt like her arm was going to fall off from all the waving.

'Did you like it?' asked Hudson, as they weaved their way through the crowds catching a last glimpse of Santa Claus on his sleigh at the back of the parade.

'I loved it. It reminded me of a mix of a seaside carnival and pantomime.'

'Yeah, it is. I guess. Although I've never seen a carnival in the UK.'

'No? We should . . .' She quickly corrected herself. 'You should go.'

She scurried alongside Hudson, wondering at the masses of people and the flurry of steam coming from the air vents at her feet. It was exactly like the films and it made her grin to think of it. She was actually here in New York City, and even better than that she was doing traditional Thanksgiving activities with the most gorgeous man. She stopped herself. She needed to halt the inappropriate thoughts; she was getting as bad as Sophie. Perhaps now she could empathise a little more with what her friend had been through.

They waited to cross a street with a hoard of other wrapped-up folk still wishing random strangers a happy holiday when Hudson took her hand and led her across the road. The jolt of contact startled her. 'Sorry, I didn't want to lose you in the crowd.'

'It's okay,' she said. And it really was.

Chapter Thirty-Five

They walked a bit further before they came to some railings where a line of horses and small carriages were standing. 'Hop in,' said Hudson. 'This is the best way to see Central Park.' He was right. The horse trotted off through the entrance at a gentle pace while Hudson tucked a blanket around their legs.

'We're like a couple of old people,' said Anna, noticing she was close enough to feel the heat from his body.

'Wouldn't that be nice?'

'Would it?' She was shocked by how breathy her voice was.

'Yeah. Wouldn't you like to find someone you could grow old with and one day come back here and take a carriage ride tucked up under a blanket?'

'Yes, I'd like that very much.' Do shut up, Anna, she implored herself.

The trip around the park was chilly but beautiful. It was immense and Hudson was a very good guide, pointing out the things they passed as well as the things they wouldn't be able to see. They saw the Bethesda Fountain, trotted through the tree tunnel of the Mall and Literary Walk, passed the Dairy and Carousel. It was like watching scenes escaping from an open book. Anna couldn't get over how vast the park was. It made Wildflower Park look like someone's back garden. Hudson had a word with the driver, the carriage stopped and Anna reluctantly left the warmth of the blanket behind.

They continued on foot. She'd seen signs for the zoo and was wondering if that's where they were heading but when she saw the huge ice rink her face lit up like a child's. 'Are we going ice skating?'

'We sure are,' said Hudson, breaking into a run. They ran towards the rink with abandon. The chill of the air burned her cheeks. They arrived out of breath and were soon kitted out with skates and making their way tentatively onto the ice.

Hudson gripped her gloved hand tightly. 'Is that for your safety or mine?' she said, with a giggle.

'A bit of both. I'm okay once I get going but to start with I'm like Bambi.'

'Me too.'

They quickly got into a rhythm but continued to hold hands whilst they skated. Anna was soon overheating and skated off to remove layers. She found she was grinning to herself. She was having the best time. Anna turned around and scanned the ice for Hudson. She spotted him on the far side of the rink talking to a woman in a bright red coat. Anna set off towards them. As she approached she could see they were having an animated conversation. A moment before she reached them the woman reached up, cupped Hudson's face in her hands and kissed him. Not a peck on the cheek or an air kiss; this was a full-on, intimate kiss. Anna toppled on her skates and quickly righted herself but a fraction too late and she careered into Hudson, ending the kiss abruptly.

'Oh my God, I'm so sorry,' she said, disentangling herself from Hudson. She righted herself and faced the other woman. 'Hello. I'm Anna.' The woman glared at her.

'Anna, this is Emily Jones. Emily this is my friend Anna.'

Emily looked Anna up and down and Anna took an instant dislike to her. She was very well groomed and her red coat looked expensive.

'It's been wonderful to see you again, Hudson. Don't leave it too long,' said Emily, skating backwards from Hudson. She blew him a sultry kiss, performed a pirouette and continued on her way.

'Wow,' said Anna, skidding slightly. 'She's . . .' words momentarily escaped her '. . . impressive. Is she a close friend?' She had to know.

'Emily is divorcing my father.'

'Hang on. When you spoke to your stepmother on the phone. That was her?' Anna couldn't hide the surprise in her voice. She wobbled when she turned to have another ogle. The pretty woman didn't look like she'd hit forty yet; she was certainly very well preserved if she had. Perhaps she'd had work done.

Hudson pulled his eyes away from Emily's retreating back. 'Yeah. She's the reason they're selling the house.'

'Ah,' said Anna, because she couldn't think of anything else to say. Then she blurted out. 'That kiss was a bit . . . well, not really a stepmum sort of kiss.' It was the sort of thing she really should have kept in her head but it was out before she could censor it.

Hudson's expression was grave. 'It's because before she married my father . . .' he glanced up as if questioning whether to finish the sentence or not '. . . she was engaged to me.'

340

Anna felt her skates slip from underneath her and she landed with a hard thud on the ice.

Anna made the best of the afternoon. The meal at the hotel had been lovely and she'd filled the silences with idle chatter. She could tell Hudson was putting on a brave face but there was an Emily-shaped cloud hanging over them. He hadn't volunteered any further information, which she could understand. Having your fiancée dump you for your father wasn't something you'd want to discuss. It explained why he and his father had such a strained relationship. What he had experienced was deceit and betrayal on a huge scale.

After their meal Hudson took her to the Empire State Building. It was somewhere she had always wanted to go and it didn't disappoint. She was beginning to master the super-fast lifts and was feeling quite brave until they were ushered out onto the chilly viewing platform and she froze. The breeze and the sight of the city stretched out below made her body go rigid. She couldn't move a muscle.

'Anna, it's quite safe.' Hudson held out his hand. She stared at it and marvelled at the speed of her racing heart.

She shook her head. She couldn't do this. She wasn't even sure if she could make it back into the lift.

'Anna.' His voice was soothing. 'You have conquered so much. You can't come this far and then not see the view from up here.'

'I can see it. Thanks,' said Anna, darting a glance behind him and feeling her stomach flip.

'But there's something I want you to see.' He tilted his head onto one side and beckoned her with his outstretched fingers. 'Come on. You can do this.'

Anna closed her eyes. She trusted Hudson. He hadn't

let her down. Logically she knew she wasn't going to fall but the fear was still there. She relived the screams that woke her the night Esme fell. She imagined herself falling as Esme had done. Perhaps this was always to be her punishment for not being sober enough to stop it happening?

Her eyes still shut, she felt Hudson's hand close around hers and grip gently. His thumb bumped over her knuckles. 'Anna? Are you ready? It'll be worth it, I promise.'

No, she was not ready. She would never be ready but if Hudson said it was worth it then her curiosity would pull her through. She opened her eyes and his smile encouraged her further. 'Okay.' Her voice was wobbly.

Hudson pulled her gently forward and she took a tentative step. 'What did you think of the creamed onions with dinner?' he asked. She knew he was trying to distract her because she'd already tried to compare them to bread sauce, which was something her mother always made at Christmas but nobody really liked. 'I preferred the creamed asparagus.' She gave a quick look up and could see a brick wall with diamond-shaped mesh above it and then high metal railings. There was no way she was falling over the side. She kept repeating that in her head in an attempt to convince herself.

'Really? I used to have it on toast as a kid.'

'You're quite posh then. I used to get excited when we had baked beans that weren't supermarket value ones.' She chuckled and realised they had now moved slowly round to the side and were away from the entrance.

'And did you like the pumpkin pie?'

'It was a bit sweet for me. And you can stop trying to distract me with questions about the food because I'm feeling less panicky now.'

Hudson laughed. 'You got me. Just a bit further and then I'll show you what you've faced your fears for.'

It was quite busy but they found a spot to stand in. The light was fading. It wouldn't be long before it was dark; they wouldn't be able to see much then. Not a great time of day to do this, she thought.

'We're going to be here for a while. I want you to lean against me and relax. Can you do that?'

Leaning she was fine with. Resting her whole body against his she wasn't sure about. Her pulse started to increase again and this time it had nothing to do with a fear of heights. She tried to be nonchalant. 'Sure.'

Hudson was standing behind her. She took a deep breath and let her body relax against his. There were a few people about but as the light faded they began dispersing. 'Watch the streets and buildings,' said Hudson, his voice hushed and close to her ear.

She wasn't sure what he meant. She didn't like looking down so she'd focus on the buildings. But buildings weren't going to do anything. This wasn't Disney – they weren't likely to pick up their lower floors and dance a tango. But then she saw it. Just a few at first. Lights were coming on all around them. It was like a show. Her eyes darted about trying to catch each new light when it appeared. She steeled herself and spied the street lights come on below her, followed by more and more.

'Can you see Broadway? It's the one not on the grid system.' Hudson's cheek brushed against hers as he drew a line in front of her.

'Wow. Yes, I see. Why is that?'

'It's believed to be the oldest path on Manhattan. Originally it was called the Wickquasgeck Trail by the Native Americans. It actually ran the entire length of

Manhattan, following an original ridge of land snaking through swamps and rocks. When they introduced the grid system they let Broadway stay as a grand boulevard. Probably to placate those who hated the rigidity of the blocks.'

'I love history like that,' said Anna, stifling a sigh.

'Me too. I wonder about the people who were here all those years ago. If they could even begin to imagine what they were creating when they first started to build Manhattan.'

They both drifted off on their thoughts and watched the lights sparkle below them as the night claimed the last of the day. Anna could feel the warmth of Hudson's body behind her own and she felt safe. It was absurd being eighty-six floors up and yet she did feel safe. It was a sensation she wanted to hang on to.

Anna felt oddly elated to have stood on the viewing deck and apart from her initial wobble she had enjoyed it. Perhaps at last she was leaving the past behind her and with it some of her guilt, fears and insecurities.

Once back on the ground she could barely strain her neck back far enough to see the top of the building and she wondered at having been up that high. Her phone buzzed into life and she almost didn't answer because it was a number she didn't recognise although it was a country code she knew. It was the UK. Most likely a sales call but she took it anyway.

'Hello. Is this Anna Strickland?'

'Yes,' she said, expecting the sales patter to follow.

'Hi, I'm Greg. I'm a nurse from Queen Elizabeth Hospital, Birmingham. Your parents were admitted earlier today and your mother is asking for you.'

Anna struggled to take in what she was being told.

Hudson was looking concerned, most likely at the shock on her own face. 'What happened?'

'They were involved in a car accident. Your mother has minor injuries but we're keeping her in overnight as a precaution. Are you able to visit?'

Anna's eyes scanned around her. Taxis scooted by on one side and a throng of people on the other, the bright lights of New York all around her. 'I'm in New York. I don't know how quickly I can get a flight home.'

'Oh, I'm sorry.'

'No, it's fine. Is my dad all right?' There was a brief pause and Anna's stomach lurched.

'He's in a different unit. I don't have an up-to-date picture for him I'm afraid, but I'm sure they'll tell you more when you get here.'

'Which unit?' Anna struggled to get the words out.

'Critical Care.' Anna stifled a sob.

Hudson was already hailing a cab when she ended the call.

'Let's get you back to the hotel. We can check for flights on the way,' said Hudson, opening the cab door and slipping in behind her.

The next few hours had been a whirlwind. Hudson had got her booked onto a flight out of Newark, helped her pack and came with her to the airport. She'd given him a fleeting kiss before she'd entered security and she'd handled the flight like a pro. Nothing scared her more than the thought of her parents being hurt – getting to them had been all that mattered.

The flight was long forgotten by the time the taxi deposited her at the hospital entrance. Once inside the hospital she was soon in a waiting room feeling like she'd been on fast-forward for the last eleven hours and now everything had come to a screaming halt. She watched the minutes tick by slowly on a white plastic clock. She was about to go in search of someone when a young man with a staff badge came in. 'Anna Strickland?' She nodded. 'I'm Doctor Purcell.'

Even in her distressed state she was still tempted to ask how old he was. Wasn't it a sign you were getting old if doctors and policemen looked young? 'I'm a junior doctor here and I'm treating your father. Firstly, let me say your mother's brain scan results are clear. She'll likely be discharged later today.' Anna didn't even know her mum was going for a brain scan. It was like being in a soap opera. He continued. 'Your father has sustained crush injuries. We're keeping him sedated while we ascertain the damage.'

'What does that mean?'

'There's significant damage to his right leg and he's lost a lot of blood. There's also a possibility of some internal bleeding, and if that's the case we'll need to operate to resolve that first.'

'What are you waiting for?'

'We don't want to operate unless we have to. He has suffered significant trauma. The paramedics had to resuscitate him in the ambulance. And there's still a lot of work to do to save his leg.'

Anna gasped and felt warm tears run down her cheeks. It was the first time she'd cried. 'Is there a possibility he could lose his leg?'

'We hope it won't come to that but we need him stable before we can undertake surgery. Then we'll know more.'

Thoughts buzzed around inside her head like angry bees. 'Can I see him?'

346

'Of course.' He led the way through the warren of corridors.

A swipe of his card had the double doors opening into a large ward. They passed lots of beds before finally stopping. Anna had to do a double take at the man lying motionless on the high hospital bed. It hardly looked like her father. He was surrounded by a great deal of monitoring devices all bleeping at different rhythms. She was overwhelmed with emotion.

'Can I touch him?' she asked.

'Watch out for the cables. Otherwise it's fine. I'll leave you with the nurse – she'll be able to answer any further questions.'

Anna sat on the edge of the chair next to the bed and gripped her father's hand. A young nurse stepped into view. 'Try not to worry about all the machines. They're here to help him. He's doing fine.'

Anna could barely drag her eyes away from her father's pale battered face. It was like a horror film where you don't want to look but something compels you to.

'When will he wake up?'

'He's only asleep because of the medication. We need him to stay still until they've finished all the tests. Then he needs to go for surgery.'

Anna swallowed. She couldn't begin to think about what it might mean if he was to lose his leg. All the things he and her mum had planned for their retirement. She couldn't bear the thought of him not being able to walk or worse.

She stifled a sob and the nurse passed her a tissue box. 'Press the red button if you need me or if there's anything you're concerned about.' Anna nodded. Anything she was concerned about? That would be everything then.

'Actually, my mum is in the hospital too but I don't know where.' Her voice broke and Anna knew she sounded pathetic but she couldn't help it.

'I've got a note about your mother. I'll ring her ward and get an update for you. They might be able to wheel her down.'

'Thank you.' Never before had Anna meant those words more. She was totally helpless and at sea in this situation. Her parents were her rock; they were always there for her. Always the ones she turned to when the seas of life got rough but this was the one time they couldn't help her.

Chapter Thirty-Six

Once Anna had fired off quick messages to Sophie and Hudson she switched her phone off again. She was about to ring the buzzer to get back into the critical care unit when her heart leaped at the sound of a familiar voice. 'Anna!'

'Mum.' Anna couldn't stop herself hurtling up the corridor and embracing her mum.

'Ow, careful, love. I'm a bit sore.' Her mum was in a large black wheelchair that made her seem small. Her temple showed a small graze but otherwise she looked fine.

'Sorry. I'm so pleased to see you.' Seeing her mum in better shape than her dad was a huge relief.

The orderly pushing the wheelchair smiled. 'She's been discharged but she'll need to take it easy for a few days. We're on our way to CCU.' He set off again and Anna walked alongside clutching her mother's hand, which meant she was walking at an odd angle but she didn't care.

'Have you seen Dad?' asked Anna.

Claire shook her head. 'But they've been wonderful at keeping me updated. I know he's not out of the woods yet.'

'But what if . . .' Anna's sentence was lost in fresh tears.

'Now, now. You're not to think like that. He needs us to be positive.'

They reached the ward and the nurse came over to them. 'Hi, Anna. And Mrs Strickland?'

Claire nodded and the nurse crouched down in front of her. 'Don't be alarmed. They've taken your husband down to theatre.' Anna could see the shock on her face and suspected she looked the same.

'What happened?' Claire's voice was croaky.

'His blood pressure took a drop. He'll be in theatre for a while. Why don't you go home and get some rest?'

'No,' said Claire and Anna together.

'We'd rather be here,' said Anna, gripping her mother's hand.

Sophie was busying herself with unpacking the pit that was Arlo's school bag when Dave arrived home, gave her a kiss on the cheek and hung up his laptop bag. 'Dave, you've not shaved again. What's going on?'

He leaned in and rubbed his stubble against her neck.

'Gerroff,' she said with a chuckle. She followed him through to the kitchen where Petal was in her high chair and she swapped an empty yogurt pot for two plastic Peppa Pigs.

Dave blinked at them. 'Two Peppas?'

'In case she loses one. It's okay, she probably thinks one is an evil twin.'

Dave laughed. 'Anything to report from the home front?' he asked, pulling her into a hug and giving her a long slow kiss.

When they pulled apart she had a think. 'I went to buy Christmas cards and while I was choosing some nice family ones Arlo licked and stuck down pretty much every envelope within his reach.'

'Does that mean we're banned from the card shop?' Dave said with a chuckle.

'I think we need to give it a miss for a while at least. And Petal and I made Christmas decorations out of paper plates and foil.'

'Excellent.'

'Shizz,' said Sophie, reading the message that popped up on her mobile.

'Homemade stuff always is but the grandparents love it—'

'No, not the decorations.' She waved her phone at him. 'Anna's mum and dad have had an accident.'

'Shit! Shit! Shit!' shouted Petal happily as she bashed both Peppa Pigs on the high chair. Perhaps that alternative word wasn't far enough away from the real thing, thought Sophie.

Sophie filled up Maurice's bowl and leaned against the cupboard while he ate. She wanted to call Anna to find out what was going on but she knew the last thing she needed in the middle of a medical emergency was people asking for an update. She was pleased to be able to help, even if it was only feeding Maurice. Sophie sat on the kitchen floor and gave the cat a stroke while he crunched on his food.

'Anna will be back soon. I promise,' she told him. He didn't seem interested. She wondered if animals ever worried about anything or if they sailed through life simply living in the moment. She could see the benefits of the latter. When he'd had his fill he climbed onto Sophie's lap and began kneading his claws into her jeans.

'You've missed a bit of fuss, haven't you, boy?' He head-butted her hand in response. 'In case you are worrying, don't. Because—'

She was interrupted by a tap on the door. Sophie lifted Maurice into her arms and tried to stand and realised for the first time how heavy he was. 'Blimey, Maurice, you need to come to slimming club with me. You weigh a ton.' Maurice gave her an offended look as if he understood exactly what she'd said.

Sophie struggled to the door and opened it. 'Liam. Hi.'

Liam didn't appear impressed with how close Sophie was holding Maurice. 'Is Anna in?' He was already peering past Sophie into the flat.

'No, she's away on business.' She wanted to keep things formal.

'Right. I really need to speak to her about . . . some stuff.' He looked cagey and Sophie wanted to know more.

'She's got a lot on right now, Liam. You turning up isn't going to . . .' She watched a lone tear slide down Liam's face. 'What's wrong?'

He hesitated before he spoke. 'I've done something really stupid and I need to put it right.'

'Come in,' said Sophie, staggering backwards with the weight of the cat. 'I'll put the kettle on.'

After a few hours at the hospital Anna's system seemed to run out of adrenaline and the fact she'd hardly slept in the last twenty-four hours made her eyelids heavy. It was dark outside and she could feel herself nodding off in the chair.

She became aware of nursing staff on the move and she came to as a bed was wheeled in. Her father looked the same as he had done before – battered and bruised and with an almost grey tinge to his pallid skin. Claire struggled to her feet and Anna held her steady.

'He's fine,' said a fresh-looking nurse. Anna assumed there had been a shift change at some point but the last few hours were a blur. 'They've removed his spleen. That was what was causing the bleed.'

'What does a spleen do?' asked Claire.

'It helps fight infection and make blood cells but it's not essential. He'll be able to function perfectly well without it. He'll probably never notice it's missing.'

'Thank the Lord,' said Claire, clutching his hand.

'And his leg?' asked Anna.

'Sorry, that'll need to be a separate operation. Let's get him over this first.'

They sat at his bed watching him sleep for another hour, which was interspersed with reassurances from the nursing staff that he was fine and they should go home and rest.

'Would you mind if we got a taxi home?' asked her mother. 'We're both exhausted and they've said they're keeping him sedated so he's not going to wake up and wonder where we are.'

Although it initially felt heartless, she had a point. 'I guess we could,' said Anna, looking tentatively at her father, almost as if she were seeking his approval to leave.

'I'd like to sleep in my own bed tonight.'

'Of course.' Anna knew her mother was right but it felt wrong to be leaving her dad alone, although with nurses popping over every few minutes he was hardly on his own.

They checked the current nurse had their contact details and Anna wheeled her mother down to the taxi rank. The sound of a car approaching at a speed inappropriate for

353

a hospital car park made Anna look over her shoulder. Connor's car raced off the roundabout and then came to a screeching halt next to the row of taxis. Anna was surprised to see him but oddly comforted. She'd only told Sophie and Hudson where she was.

'Anna. Am I pleased to see you!' He flung his arms around her and she tried to reciprocate the hug whilst still hanging on to the wheelchair, the last thing they needed now was for her mother to roll off. 'I was worried so I went to see Sophie and Dave told me what had happened.'

'Hello,' said Claire, raising a hand, her shrewd eyes taking him in.

'Mum, this is Connor.' Mum, please don't ask any awkward questions right now. 'Connor this is my mum, Claire.' Connor, please don't say we're an item or my mum will shoot me for not telling her. Anna watched Connor crouch in front of her mother.

'It's lovely to meet you at last, Mrs Strickland. I've been hoping to meet you for a while now but these aren't the circumstances I'd hoped for.'

'We're off home actually,' said Claire.

'Then let's get you in the car. Are you okay to walk?'

'Oh yes, they fuss far too much in hospitals. They're worried you'll sue them. And you must call me Claire,' she said.

Anna considered protesting but she didn't have the energy.

It was a short journey. Anna was thankful her mum and Connor were chatting in the front. Without having to ask she'd gleaned her dad was driving them to Solihull when his tyre had punctured dramatically sending them into a ditch. Anna wanted to avoid too many details

354

because she didn't want to be able to picture it. She knew she could do this with a few scant details because the sight of Esme falling from the balcony was something she hadn't seen and yet she could imagine it as clearly as if she'd witnessed every second.

Anna helped her mum inside and settled her in the living room. Her parents' home was cold. The weather was feeling decidedly wintry and with the temperature dropping and her dad being an advocate of 'put on another jumper' the house was not that welcoming. Anna turned up the thermostat whilst Connor fussed around her mother who despite her protestations was lapping up the attention.

'I've missed you so much,' said Connor, pulling Anna into another hug. He went to kiss her and she made it a brief one. 'You're tired. I'll take you home.'

'No, I can't leave Mum.'

'Then I'll order us all pizza and . . .'

'Connor, you've been really kind but I think what we both need is a good night's sleep.'

Connor blinked. He frowned for a moment. 'Yeah, of course. You've had a long journey and a terrible shock. You're right. I'll feed Maurice.' He held his hand out for her keys.

'It's okay. I've already asked Sophie to feed him. But thank you, you've been really thoughtful.'

'Right, I'll say goodbye to your mum and then I'll be back tomorrow to take you to the hospital. About nine okay?'

Anna hesitated for a second. She was the one who did the organising. But she was learning that sometimes she had to let go of control. 'That'd be great. Thank you.'

She listened as Connor had a brief chat to her mum

about how he was here for them both if they needed anything before he gave Anna a fleeting kiss and was gone.

'He's lovely,' said Claire, giving Anna an old-fashioned look. 'Where've you been hiding him?'

'Nowhere – I have talked about him.' She knew she was being a little defensive.

'You mentioned him, yes, but he seems pretty serious about you.'

Anna didn't like the way her mother was looking at her. 'I think we both need to go to bed.'

'I need a decent cup of tea and a cuddle with my girl first.' Anna went to put the kettle on and prepare for an interrogation by her mother.

Connor arrived on time the next morning and walking back into the hospital Anna felt like she'd never left. Her mother had come to visit too despite vehemently denying she was in any discomfort even though she was visibly wincing with pain when she walked. Anna had expected Connor to drop them off and go but he'd insisted on staying with them despite her explaining that only two people at a time were allowed at the bedside in CCU.

Anna gripped her mum's hand and braced herself for seeing her dad looking pale and powerless as he had the day before. Her mother's gasp gave her a jolt and they both stared at her father. A nurse was filling in a sheet on a clipboard. Terry was sitting up in bed. It felt like a dream. Her mother let go of her hand and embraced her husband, while all Anna could do was stand and stare as happy tears flowed down her face. She watched him hug her mum. He had more colour and looked alive again, not a hundred per cent but so much better than the wisp of a man he had been only hours before.

Her mother gave him a playful swipe as she wiped away tears with her other hand. 'You gave us a fright, Terence Strickland,' she admonished.

'Anna?' Her father's voice was soft. He held out a hand to her and at last she could move her feet. She sat at the side of the bed and wept. 'Oh, Anna. I'm fine.'

'Apart from the fractured tibia and fibula,' said the nurse, raising an eyebrow at her patient.

Terry waved her comment away. 'That won't stop me. It's our party in a couple of weeks' time and I guarantee I'll be there with my beautiful girls.' He held both their hands.

'And that's how you'll break the other leg,' said the nurse. 'The surgeon will be down later to assess you. Until then, no more promises.'

'Yes, boss,' said Terry, with a weak salute.

'I've already had to put off a surly policeman who wanted to speak to you about the accident, but he can wait too.'

Anna learned he'd come round in the early hours and they were hoping to operate on his leg later that day and it would likely take six months to fully heal. A member of staff had to tell them off twice for being too lively so after lunch they decided they would leave him for what the ward called quiet time. Anna needed to track down Connor and get herself home.

Connor was waiting outside CCU and greeted them with a head tilt and a commiserative smile. Anna beamed back at him and she could see the confusion on his face. 'He's fine. Dad's going to be okay.' She threw her arms around Connor and hugged him tight.

Connor faltered, surprise etched on his face. 'My God, that's brilliant.'

'I know!' Anna couldn't hide her joy.

'Claire, I'm thrilled,' said Connor, giving her mum a hug. She seemed taken by surprise but welcomed the embrace all the same. 'You must come to our party, Connor. Three weeks today, it's our thirtieth wedding anniversary, and we would love you to be there.' Her mum glanced at Anna who nodded her agreement. Of course she wanted Connor to come. He'd proved himself – he'd been there when she'd needed him most. A nice reliable man who cared about her was what she needed.

Anna felt like she was still on a high when she entered the office on the Monday morning. The news of her parents' accident was top of the office discussion list and a small crowd soon gathered round her desk for an update, which she gladly gave now the dramatic story had a happy ending. The operation to pin her father's leg had been successful, so it was now all about him healing. Perhaps that was the difference with accidents: maybe they lodged in your mind if there was no recovery at the end?

'Hudson covered for you,' said Roberta, appearing and instantly breaking the good vibe.

'Great. He said he would.' At the thought of Hudson she realised she had only sent him a couple of texts since she got back. Everything had been overtaken by the accident. 'He's usually in by now,' she said, noting the time.

'Didn't you know?' Roberta pulled back her shoulders. 'He's staying in New York for the time being.'

Anna knew she was blinking fast but it was hard to control. 'Right,' said Anna. She hadn't expected that but of course it made sense. She hadn't specifically thought about it but now she did she wouldn't be going for the New York job. She needed to be here for her father and she had Connor. This was how things were to be. The thought was more upsetting than she'd expected. She swallowed hard. 'When New York comes on stream, I'll give him a call,' she said, checking her watch.

'The most difficult thing is the decision to act. The rest is merely tenacity,' said Roberta. Her expression told Anna it was another quote.

'Princess Jasmine?' offered Anna.

'Amelia Earhart,' said Roberta. Anna gave a little frown. She wasn't sure what Roberta meant but she marched off looking pleased with herself.

'You sure you're okay?' asked Karl, being uncharacteristically sympathetic.

Anna tried to paste on a smile. 'Yes, it's just I'm all over the place what with Dad . . . everything.'

'Or it could be early menopause,' said Karl, and she was grateful for the opportunity to take a swipe at him and forget how she was really feeling.

Hudson had done a good job of finishing off the New York office review; he must have put in a lot of hours since she'd left. It was all factually correct with an unmistakable Hudson edge to it. Despite having loads to catch up on she found she was watching the clock this morning. For one thing her father was being moved out of CCU and she was expecting a call from her mother about which ward he'd moved to but she was also waiting for when she could feasibly ring Hudson without waking him up.

When she figured it would be eight in the morning in New York she sprang on her mobile and dialled his number. He answered straight away. 'Hey, you. How are your folks?'

Hearing his voice made something twist in her stomach.

359

'They're okay. Mum has broken a few ribs and Dad needed a couple of operations but they'll both make a full recovery.'

'That's good to hear. I've been worried for you.'

'Thanks for getting me to the airport and everything else in New York.' Her mind drifted back to ice skating in Central Park and watching the lights come on across Manhattan. They were memories she would always cherish as time spent with a good friend.

'And you flew home on your own. Get you, you're a seasoned flyer now.' There was laughter in his voice.

'Not quite, but I wouldn't be as terrified if I had to go again. I hear you're staying in New York.'

There was a moment's silence before she heard him sigh and then speak. 'I think it's probably for the best.'

What did that mean? 'Really?' It was out before her brain had vetted it.

'I think maybe it's time for me to come home. I'm talking to Dad about buying the old house.'

'You're definitely staying then.' She was shocked. Something in her gut tugged hard at her. She was losing someone she cared about and it hurt.

'I guess. Mom understands my reasons and of course I'll visit.'

'That's good.' She nodded to reassure herself. She might see him again. It just wouldn't be every day. But his life was there and hers was here. She didn't know what to say and was glad when Hudson filled the silence.

'I hear Connor came to the rescue.'

'How did you hear that?' she asked, puzzled by the connection.

'Sophie has been keeping me up to date. I wasn't checking up on you. I was worried . . . Okay, you got me,

I was checking up on you but she said Connor had it all covered and you two were . . .'

Anna clutched the phone. What had Sophie said about her and Connor? She wasn't even sure herself. Connor had been brilliant over the last few days and still something was missing.

'What did Sophie say?' she asked.

Hudson cleared his throat. 'She said he gave you what you needed right now. She said he's reliable and good for you.' The tone of his voice changed. 'He sounds like a keeper.'

A weak smile rested on her lips. 'I guess you're right. I've a few work things I want to go over, do you want to call me back when you're in the office?'

'Sure thing. You have a nice day now,' he said in an American drawl full of overenthusiasm.

'You too.' She was smiling when she put the phone down but that didn't reflect the sadness inside. She couldn't help feeling Hudson relocating to New York meant she was losing something very special indeed.

Chapter Thirty-Seven

Anna left the office just before five and visited the hospital. It was a tonic to see her dad on a normal ward and no longer connected to a myriad of machines. He had more colour to his cheeks and was chatty. He'd turned a corner and a weight had lifted from her. She had never been so scared as when his life had hung in the balance. When visiting hours were over, Anna was tired from a long day but had one more stop to make before she went home.

Juggling two takeaway coffees and a gift bag Anna knocked an elbow on Bert's door. She knew he was inside because she could hear the news blaring out.

'Come in,' said Bert.

'Hiya, Bert, how are—' But Anna didn't get to finish the sentence.

'Anna! You're back. This is the most wonderful surprise. Sit down, and switch off that miserable bugger,' he said, pointing at the newsreader. 'Nothing but doom and gloom. Now tell me all about America.' He shuffled himself upright in his chair.

'Hang on a second, take this,' said Anna, placing a travel cup in his hands, which contained his coffee. She waited a moment until she was sure he had hold of it.

'What's this?'

'It's a travel cup. It says I heart NY on it.' It had a grippy bottom and non-spill top, which she hoped would be helpful too.

Bert chuckled. 'Thank you.'

'I got you this too,' she said, putting the gift bag on his lap. Bert felt for his side table and put down the cup. 'You shouldn't have,' he said, reaching in the bag eagerly. 'It's a key ring,' he said, feeling it carefully with his fingers. 'Does it have a picture of New York on it?' he asked.

'No, but it's in the shape of a big apple. A red one. Press the little button on the side.'

Bert's old fingers fiddled until he located the button. 'It's seven thirty-four. Good evening,' said an automated American voice. Bert jumped and they both laughed.

'That's splendid. I often wonder what time it is. Thank you, Anna.' Bert reached for her hand and squeezed it. She could see he was dewy-eyed.

'You're very welcome. What's been happening here?'

'Not a lot. There was nearly a punch-up over the bingo and Rosie and I had a little walk round the garden together. She was just watching I didn't trip over, you understand.' He gave a little cough and reached for his coffee. 'Right, now I want to hear all about what you've been up to.'

It took Anna a while to go through everything she'd done in her short trip to New York and explaining it all to Bert without the use of her photos on her phone was like reliving every tiny detail. She checked her watch. 'Bert, I have to go, but Maurice and I will visit soon.'

She stood up and Bert reached for her hand. 'I've no right to be, but I'm so proud of you for getting on that plane.'

'Thank you, Bert. I'm pretty proud of myself.'

'And I'm glad you and Hudson had such a good time together.'

Anna was about to protest but Bert was right.

The house was almost peaceful. Dave was in the shower and Sophie was putting the finishing touches to her make-up. She looked good and she felt good too, a little tired from the night feeds but Dave was doing two nights a week, which was definitely helping. Karen was due to arrive for babysitting duty in twenty minutes and they had a dinner reservation at the gastro pub a taxi ride away. Date night had become sacrosanct and they both looked forward to it. The children were generally in a better routine, which made escaping the house easier and Karen took pride in always being able to cope with whatever the children threw at her, even if sometimes that was literally.

Sophie was putting in an earring when the doorbell went and she hurried downstairs. The Kraken was early. She opened the door wide and was surprised to see Liam standing on the doorstep.

'Oh. Hi, Liam.' She didn't want to invite him in but couldn't think of a suitable alternative. 'We're about to go out. I thought you were the babysitter but do come in.'

'Sorry, Sophe. I went to Anna's but she's not in.'

Sophie wondered if he'd come to complain about her not passing on his last message. 'Probably at her parents'. They've . . .' She felt she shouldn't share too much detail about their accident – it wasn't any of his business any more. 'They've not been too well. Did you want me to give her a message?' Sophie fiddled with her other earring. She always struggled without a mirror.

Liam pulled a face. 'It's not really a message, more of a warning.'

364

Sophie stopped fiddling with her earring, straightened her shoulders and gave him her best Paddington Bear stare. 'And what does that mean?'

Liam waved his hand. 'No, it's nothing like that. I opened some of her post, by mistake, and there was an invite to a university reunion. I know how she can be about anything to do with the place.'

'Another one?' Sophie checked her watch. The Kraken was arriving in T minus ten.

'Here it is.' He seemed somewhat reluctant to hand it over.

'Is this you playing games?' Sophie narrowed her eyes and Liam pulled his head back slightly.

'Honestly, Sophe, I wouldn't intentionally upset Anna. I'd like to think maybe one day we could get back together so I wouldn't do anything to jeopardise that.'

Sophie was running out of time. 'Apart from your little confession the other night.'

Liam looked uncomfortable and stared at Sophie's midriff. 'When's the baby due?'

So many reasons why she'd never really liked him. 'Five weeks *ago*. You take care now, Liam. Bye.' And she shooed him out of her house.

It was Saturday night and Anna opened her door to Sophie wearing Dave's large winter coat but with her pyjama bottoms clearly visible underneath. 'I've escaped for an hour,' she said, pulling a can of gin and tonic from the pocket of Dave's coat and opening a cupboard to get out a glass. 'Now I know you've told me some of the New York stuff but I need more details. Did Hudson try and get some booty?'

Anna was shocked. 'No! Sophie, you're outrageous. And your mock American accent is equally appalling!'

'Don't protest too much. You know you want to.'

'I do not. We're just friends and—'

She waved away Anna's protests. 'And now you've missed your chance for wild unencumbered animal sex with him because he's staying put in America.' Sophie sighed.

'I know,' said Anna, feeling downhearted. 'I'm really going to miss him.' The truth was she was already missing him.

'I'm going to miss that tight backside of his and that smile. Oh my, that smile. I can feel my knicker elastic loosening at the very thought of it.' Sophie stared into space.

'You're wearing pyjamas.'

'Pyjamas have elastic too,' said Sophie. 'Come on, one hour of girly chat and then you need your beauty sleep and lots of it. You look like Dot Cotton after an all-nighter.'

'Thanks, pal.'

'Oh and Liam keeps dropping round. He brought you another uni invite.' Sophie pulled it from her pocket and handed it over.

Anna was about to put it straight in the recycling but something stopped her. 'Another one?'

'Yup,' said Sophie, sipping her drink and closing her eyes as she swallowed. 'I love being able to drink again.'

Anna studied the invitation. 'This is different to the other one. Different venue, different date.' It also looked more official than the previous one. Something didn't add up.

Anna didn't get a good night's sleep. Having shown Sophie all her photos and gone through the New York trip again, she was thinking about Hudson. When she closed her eyes he was all she could see. She was groggy with tiredness and although she knew it probably wasn't wise she snatched up her mobile and called his number. She ran her fingers through her bed hair and tucked the wayward bits behind her ear, which was a waste of time because she wasn't FaceTiming him.

'Hey, Anna. You okay?' There was concern in his voice.

'Can't sleep. Thought I'd call the only other person who I know is awake.'

She sensed his smile down the line. 'You want me to sing you a lullaby? I warn you I sound a lot like Kermit the Frog when I sing.'

She giggled. 'No, I don't really know why I called.'

'You don't have to have a reason. It's good to hear your voice.'

She was cradling the phone against her face. 'I miss you.' There she'd said it.

There was a muffled noise on the line. 'Sorry, Anna, what was that?'

Anna could hear someone else's voice in the background. She'd assumed he would be on his own. She checked the clock – three twenty-seven. It was almost eleven thirty at night in New York. 'You're busy, aren't you. I should have checked . . .'

'No, it's fine, it's Emily we're—' Anna didn't wait to hear any more. She ended the call and switched off the phone. She wished she'd never called. She put the phone on her bedside cabinet, nudged Maurice over slightly, hunkered down under the covers and tried to ignore the tears that came.

Sophie loved Mondays. This was a whole new experience for her but since she and Dave had employed a cleaner it was now her favourite day. All she had to do was get herself and the three children out of the house for a few hours and when she returned it was like a fairy godmother had waved her wand and miraculously everything was clean and tidy again. The challenge was getting three young children fed and clothed and out the door in time to deposit Arlo at school before the teacher was shaking her head and locking the gate. But unlike before it was a challenge Sophie relished because there was the big prize of the nice clean house at the end and now she'd found a playgroup for the other two with bearable other mums and tolerable coffee it made for a good start to the week.

'The baby ate my homework!' yelled Arlo, his face turning a violent shade of red as he clenched his fists. If he'd been a cartoon he would have jetted off like a rocket.

'Which one?' Sophie squinted at Reuben who, at barely six weeks old, wasn't capable of much, other than crying, burping, farting and pooping.

'Petal. She ate my homework.'

Sophie was relieved. Petal's digestive system was already well tested having eaten worms and dirt in the garden, sand, a raw potato and a variety of other odd but fairly harmless items. 'If you will leave it lying within her reach then she will eat it. It's how little ones learn.' Almost as an afterthought Sophie added, 'What has she eaten exactly?'

'My pirate's head!' Arlo thrust what was left of the Play-Doh model masterpiece under Sophie's nose. It wasn't recognisable as anything vaguely human anyway so the loss of its head had minor impact.

'Now he's a headless pirate,' she said, whilst trying to shoo him towards the hall. Arlo seemed to consider this, giving Sophie time to scoop Petal from the high chair,

368

remove the piece of blue Play-Doh she was still chewing and deftly deposit her in the double buggy in front of a sleeping Reuben.

'Cool. Willoughby Newell won't have thought of that.'

'Right. Let's go!' said Sophie, triumphantly exiting the house on time.

Sophie dropped Arlo at school with moments to spare. She grinned inanely at the teacher heading towards the gate and took pride in the woman's surprised expression when Petal beamed a blue toothy smile. It was a twenty-minute walk to the playgroup, which was enough time to call Anna and have a quick post-weekend chat, assuming Anna wasn't ensconced in meetings.

Anna answered on the third ring. 'I've messed up, Sophie,' she said, her voice monotone.

'Karl will cover for you. He plays the chauvinist that well you can almost forget there's a decent bloke inside.'

'No, not at work. With Hudson.'

Sophie didn't like the sadness in Anna's words. 'What have you done?'

She heard Anna's sigh. 'I called him in the middle of the night and told him I missed him.'

'Ah. And what did he say?'

'He was busy with his ex-fiancée, stepmother Emily woman. I hung up. He's left a couple of messages but I can't call him back. I'm too embarrassed. Karl has fielded a call for me already today.'

'What now?'

'They're confirming the job appointments next week but it's a formality. Hudson will lead the New York team and I'll lead the UK project.'

'There, what's wrong with that?' said Sophie, gripping the buggy with one hand and manoeuvring it quickly out of the way of someone careering towards her on a bike. 'Get off the pavement!' she yelled. 'Sorry, suicide cyclist.'

'I'll still have to speak to him. The projects are running side by side; we need everything to be joined up.'

'When you said you missed him. Was it like you miss *Love Island* when it finishes or more like someone has removed a vital organ?' Sophie adroitly caught Petal's shoe as she kicked and flung it high above her head whooping with delight.

'I feel like . . .' Anna paused. 'I feel like I've lost something important.'

'Ah, like when you can't find your purse?'

'Sort of, but worse, because I know with Hudson he won't turn up rammed down the back of the sofa.'

'You never know. We once had a sofa bed that was very good at swallowing people whole.'

Anna gave a tinny laugh.

'It sounds like you've made your choice and so has he. Maybe it's time to move on. You've got lovely Connor.'

There was silence from the other end of the line.

Chapter Thirty-Eight

The rest of the week went by in a blur for Anna. Work was manic and she was helping her mother get ready for the big anniversary party but truth was she was keeping herself ultra busy in an attempt to stop thinking about a certain American. She still wasn't convinced her dad was well enough for something as tiring as a party but they were both adamant everything was going ahead. Anna had decided to stop asking and get stuck in to helping them, which was how she found herself in the local pub's back room tying knots in balloons.

'Penny for them?' asked Terry.

'Nothing really. I think Mum's overdone the sausage rolls.' Her lips made a line.

Her father's look told her he didn't believe her. 'You can never have enough sausage rolls. You shouldn't be worrying about us. You know we're both fully recovered.' Anna glanced at the crutches. 'I'm ninety-nine per cent there. These will soon be on the fire.'

Anna paused with a balloon end wrapped around her finger. 'You and Mum. How did you know? I mean really know you were always going to be happy?'

Her mother appeared at her shoulder with a tray of

cling-film-covered crisps. 'He liked Bruce Springsteen and Marmite. Perfect match.' She disappeared again in a flurry of pinny and cling film.

Anna turned to her father and he lowered his balloon pump. 'I'd been out with other girls. Quite a few actually but when I started seeing your mum . . .' He let out a slow breath and his lip curled up. 'She went straight to the top of my to do list.'

'Dad!' She was hoping for a serious answer. Anna let the balloon go and it whizzed off around the room, making a farting sound.

'Not like that.' He rolled his eyes. 'I mean she was the most important thing. Whatever plans I thought I had or whatever I wanted to do with my life I knew she would always be the person I wanted to share them with and if I couldn't share them with her then what was the point?'

'Isn't that more like a best friend than a wife?'

'I fancied her too,' he added quickly. 'She had this low-cut top and when she leaned—'

'La, la, la. Not listening,' said Anna, thrusting her fingers in her ears.

'You and your Connor still going strong?'

'He's coming later.'

'Wasn't what I asked.' Her father fixed her with a stare.

'It's fine. Really.' She patted his arm and hoped he'd leave the interrogation for another time.

By seven o'clock Anna had changed into a simple knee-length black dress. Elderly relatives were arriving as if on a conveyer belt, or perhaps they'd been bussed in, but they were all there bang on the dot of seven. Anna settled them away from the speakers and went to deposit coats on the rail by the toilets.

'Hello,' said Sophie, pulling Anna into a hug. 'You look fab-u-lous!'

'You look . . . happy.' It was obvious Sophie had already been drinking.

'The Kraken collected the kids at four so we've had a bit of a grown-up afternoon.' She added an elaborate wink for good measure.

'Lucky you.' By the way Sophie was swaying she'd be asleep by eight o'clock.

Lots more people arrived and Anna left her mum and dad to it. She got a Coke from the bar and pulled up a chair next to Sophie. Dave was whispering something in Sophie's ear and she cackled with laughter before spotting Anna and sitting up straight like a child caught giggling in class. Anna loved seeing the two of them like this. Well, maybe not quite this drunk but it was great to see them happy together. She looked up to see Liam and his parents standing behind Connor who was handing her dad a card and a bottle. Terry turned and waved her over. She hadn't realised Liam was going to be there but supposed it was inevitable: her parents were friends with his parents. After all, they'd once planned a wedding together, so it was only logical they had been invited.

'You okay?' asked Sophie.

'I think this is going to be an awkward evening. Wish me luck.'

She met Connor near the bar and gave him a perfunctory kiss on the cheek. 'You look smart,' she said.

'You look gorgeous.'

'Thanks. And thanks for getting my parents a gift. That was thoughtful.'

'It's not much really.'

'Hi, Anna,' said Liam, slipping into the space between

her and Connor. He kissed her cheek confidently. 'You look amazing.'

'Err. Liam, this is Connor.' Where to begin?

'Hi,' said Liam, shaking Connor's hand. He turned back to Anna. 'No Hudson tonight?' This was going to be a painfully long evening.

Anna and Connor joined Sophie and Dave and thankfully for a while Dave led the conversation with the day's football highlights.

'I'll get us some more drinks,' said Connor, casting his eyes down when he reached Anna.

When he'd disappeared, Anna flopped against the table. 'This is a nightmare.'

'What?' said Dave, confusion creasing his forehead as he gave a giant yawn and set Sophie off too.

Sophie gave him a friendly pat. 'Go back to sleep.'

'You heard from Hudson?' asked Sophie.

'Only work emails. Why?' Anna was watching Sophie's expression closely.

'No reason,' she said, with a shrug. 'Ooh, I love this one. Let's dance,' said Sophie, pulling Anna to her feet when Bruno Mars started to blare out of the speakers and she let Dave slump onto her seat for a snooze.

Anna watched Connor return to the table with the drinks. He angled his chair towards the dance floor. Sophie was shouting the words out with a slight delay and her dancing was vigorous to say the least but Anna was starting to enjoy herself. At least while she was dancing she didn't have to speak to Connor or Liam. And right there, as if in slow motion, she had an epiphany. She didn't want to be in a relationship with either of them. And more importantly, she didn't *need* to be in a relationship with either of them. She was doing fine on her own. In fact, she was happy. Right then, dancing with her best friend at her parents' anniversary party, she felt together and content. She wouldn't be quite so calm when she had to clearly tell both Connor and Liam that they would not be featuring in her future but that could wait until tomorrow.

She looked away. Her mum and dad were sitting at the edge of the dance floor, her dad's leg up on a spare chair and her mum's arm lovingly draped across his shoulders. Terry raised his glass to her, took a sip and gave her the thumbs up. Anna gave a little wave. It was odd being the only sober person sometimes; it was like you were the one who was acting strangely and everyone else was the norm. At least she'd have a clear head tomorrow, unlike most of the others in the room.

'Here you go,' said Connor, pushing a shot across the table to Sophie when she and Anna returned from the dance floor.

'Ooh, thanks.'

'Here's yours,' said Connor, not making eye contact as he passed the glass of Coke to Anna. 'Down in one?'

Sophie looked at Anna and banged her glass on the table. Anna chuckled. 'Mine's Coke.' But Sophie had already knocked hers back. Anna was thirsty and took a long drink from hers. At the last swallow it tasted slightly odd and she gave the glass an accusatory look.

Connor spotted the gesture. 'It's supermarket brand. I think they've run out of the proper stuff.'

Anna nodded her understanding. Sophie was trying to manoeuvre Dave into an upright position. 'I think it's time we went home.'

'I'll call you a cab,' said Connor, pulling out his phone. Within ten minutes Sophie and Dave had said their goodbyes multiple times and left. Anna and Connor returned to their table. She was thankful for the intrusion of some old friends of her parents joining them for twenty minutes even if their sole purpose had been to brag about how well their children had done and the last three cruises they'd been on.

While they were talking Anna began feeling odd. Her vision was all swimmy. She looked around the table, trying hard to focus on Connor who was nodding along to the conversation. Anna blinked and sipped a bit more of her drink.

'It's been lovely to see you. You must tell us all about your New York trip sometime,' said a woman Anna vaguely recognised, who then moved on to the next table.

'Bye,' said Anna, but her lips weren't moving right.

'You okay?' Connor loomed in front of her looking concerned.

'I need . . .' Something made her lie. 'I need the loo.' She got up, held on to the chair to steady herself and went to the bar.

'Anna, can we have a chat?' asked Liam, popping up as if out of nowhere. Anna shook her head and pushed him slowly away. She couldn't deal with him right now. Liam huffed. 'I'll be outside if you change your mind.' He downed his drink and left.

She managed to order a pint of water but she was aware something was wrong. She downed the water and steadied herself. She needed to sit down, her head was pounding and her legs had turned to jelly. Either she was having some sort of stroke or her drink had been spiked.

Anna wasn't sure how she got in the back of the taxi but the sight of Connor talking to her parents and hugging them goodbye set off a panic inside her. She tried to lift her hand to the window but her dad just waved at her and gave a knowing smile. She went to speak, to shout, but she couldn't. She could only make a slight groan of a noise and could barely keep her eyes open. Connor bounced into the car, gave the driver the address and calmly propped her up against him, waving to her parents as they drove off.

Hudson stepped inside the door and surveyed the room. He wasn't sure why he was here. There had been something in Anna's voice when she'd phoned and now she wouldn't answer his calls. He'd then acted spontaneously and done what had seemed perfectly logical at the time and got a plane to Heathrow. But now, as he surveyed the remains of a family party, he was no longer sure. A smart-looking man was leaning on crutches. He made his way over and offered his hand in greeting. 'I'm Terry.'

'Actually, sir, I don't mean to be rude, but is Anna here?' Hudson gave another cursory glance over Terry's shoulder.

'You've just missed her. She's gone home with her boyfriend.'

'Connor?'

'That's the fella.'

Hudson pulled back his shoulders. This was the reality he was facing. 'Right. Then I'm sorry to have troubled you. And happy anniversary, sir.' Hudson turned to leave.

'She was a bit worse for wear. You know how it is at parties.'

Hudson halted and spun around. 'You mean she'd been drinking?'

Terry guffawed. '*Had* she. Plastered she was. She could barely walk. But she's not used to it you see, she—'

Hudson's face was creased with anxiety. 'Where did he take her?'

'Home to bed I shouldn't wonder . . ?' Hudson didn't wait to hear the end of the sentence.

Anna was aware she was going up some steps and Connor was supporting her. 'Come on. Walk!'

Anna came to as an icy wind hit her in the face. Her whole body shook with the sudden chill engulfing her. She was still groggy and focusing was difficult. Where was she? She licked her dry lips. 'What have you done?' Her voice was slurred and barely a whisper.

Connor snorted a laugh but it dropped away. His eyes seemed dark and she instantly felt afraid of him. 'What have I done? What have *I* done? What have *you* done, Anna? What did you do ten years ago?'

Anna's head hurt. Her thoughts were muddled. It was like living a dream; she didn't feel conscious and yet she was.

'Let me remind you. You were at university.' Anna's eyes widened in alarm. 'But you know that, don't you? Just like you knew Esme . . .'

Anna nodded and tried to focus. Fear was wrapping itself around her and squeezing out her breath. 'Yes.' There was asphalt underfoot and the tips of the trees were level with her. Her brain tried to make sense of it. She was on a roof.

'She was my sister.' Connor stepped back a fraction and watched her.

This was the mother of all coincidences. Fear gripped her guts and hung on tight. 'How did you—' She was trying to say: 'How did you discover the connection between me and your sister?' but there was no way she could coherently form all those words out loud.

'How did I find you?' sneered Connor. 'How could you

be so stupid? You *really* believed that a mobile phone engineer managed to get the wrong number . . . *TWICE*?'

The reality of the person she was dealing with hit her like a physical blow to her stomach. She didn't know this man at all. 'Connor, you're scaring me.'

'Good. You deserve to be scared. You're the reason my sister is dead!'

Connor gripped her arms tightly, making them hurt, and marched her backwards but her feet wouldn't move quickly enough and she lost a heel. He slammed her against the door they'd come through and she heard it click shut.

Anna had so much she wanted to say but forming words was hard. She shook her head firmly. 'No.' She was confused. Esme didn't die. Connor seemed to note her expression.

'Esme's dead. Didn't you know?' Anna shook her head again. She was going to say sorry but decided it might infuriate him further. 'My mother, who, by the way, was a raging alcoholic because of what you did . . .' he leaned in close and she could feel the tiny specks of saliva on her cheek as he spoke '. . . she switched off the machine. She let Esme die. She was no better than you.'

Anna had loads of questions but she knew that getting away from Connor was the most important thing she had to do at this moment. She tried to look about her but it was dark. Then she spotted something familiar. She could see the park gates. Just the tips of them. She got an odd sense of relief to know she was on the roof of the flats. Although being four floors up on a December night when your brain was no longer able to function properly was not a good place to be. 'Connor. I wasn't there when it happened. I—'

'Shut up!' he hissed in her face. 'Don't lie, Anna. I found her diary. It told me everything I needed to know. She worshipped you. She idolised you. She was in *love* with you. And you lured her to the party and to her death.'

Anna was shaking her head but part of what he said was true. Esme was in love with Anna, a fact Anna had found out when Esme had consumed enough Dutch courage to fill an Amsterdam canal and declared it in front of everyone. Anna was young and embarrassed and had tried to laugh it off. When Esme had persisted, Anna had told her firmly that she was straight and had no feelings for her at all. Truth was, she had liked Esme, but not in the way she had wanted. To Anna, Esme had become like a sister. She reminded her of her own sister, Lynsey, and she'd often wondered if Lynsey would have grown up to be like Esme. Anna had felt the closeness of the relationship but not spotted the dangers.

Anna had spent the rest of the party drinking and ignoring Esme until she passed out in her bedroom. From what others had told her, Esme had carried on drinking and on a dare had decided to show off her gymnastic skills by doing a handstand on the balcony railing. The accounts of exactly what happened next were conflicting. Some said she wobbled, some said she relaxed her grip. Whatever happened, Esme went head first over the railing and shouted Anna's name as she fell.

'I was asleep when she fell.' It was a struggle to form the words but she had to make him understand.

'She trusted you. She loved you. She's dead because of you!' His voice rose to a shout and Anna hoped someone might hear and come to help her but she knew it was unlikely: the wind was whistling around them and the flats weren't close to the street.

'No. I liked Esme.' She took in lungfuls of cold air in an attempt to kick-start her foggy brain.

Connor's eye twitched and Anna felt a renewed sense of dread. 'You let her fall,' he hissed. Anna shook her head. She took in a gulp of air and the icy blast burned her lungs. He dragged her away from the door and she gripped the handle, trying to scream as her fingers were ripped away.

'Why now?' asked Anna, trying to buy some time. She dug her remaining heel in as he pulled her towards the edge. Through the darkness she could see the outline of the tallest trees in the park.

'Because you deserve to suffer like Esme did and it takes time to properly destroy things, especially people. I've been sending you little reminders of your old university, so you wouldn't forget. Why should you be able to move on? I wanted you to lose everything. I know everything about you, Anna. I've been tracking your phone. I know where you go and who you see. I've been gaining your trust so I could tear your world apart. But despite my best efforts your parents somehow managed to survive the car crash.' He looked disappointed.

'No!' Anna's eyes widened in alarm and she started to fight. Her limbs were useless against his firm hold and she tired quickly. They were very near the edge. Anna tried to brace her foot against a small ridge but Connor kicked at her shin and pushed her a step closer.

'My whole life revolved around hospital visits. Test after test. Disappointment after disappointment. All the while watching my mother slide into depression and alcoholism until she could take it no more and, without telling me, she switched off the life support. But she's not responsible for Esme's death.' He leaned in to her face and prodded

381

her hard in the chest with each word. 'You. Are.' The words were like shards of ice in her stomach. She stepped back and felt she was at the very edge of the building. There was nothing but air between her and the concrete below. 'Look down, Anna. Are you scared? I want you to be as scared as Esme was that night.'

This was it. She was going to die. She clung to his jacket. 'Connor. Don't,' she pleaded. Searching his face for some reassurance. She filled her lungs and with all her might she forced herself to scream.

Connor shook her and she toppled. But instead of falling backwards she was being pushed towards Connor. It took her a moment to work out what was going on. Someone had come up behind her and pushed her. How? She was four floors up. She seized the opportunity and lashed out at Connor. He retaliated and seemed to pirouette, catching his foot on the ridge. His expression changed as he teetered on the edge. Anna was falling. They were going over the edge together.

A single thought seized her attention: she couldn't let this happen again. She'd missed her opportunity to save Esme, but she wasn't about to let Connor fall too. She hung on to Connor's jacket and twisted her body away from the edge. In what felt like slow motion, both she and Connor fell to the floor. Her head smacked on the concrete ridge of the roof. The pain blossomed across her forehead. She was safe and so was Connor. The cold asphalt was rough against her palms as she tried to get up. A strong arm snaked round her waist. 'I got you, Anna. I got you,' said a familiar voice, but the words were drifting into the night. Darkness was closing in, until everything went black and silence engulfed her.

Chapter Thirty-Nine

Anna had spent a night in hospital and then another couple with her parents, and whilst it was lovely to be cossetted and cared for, two days was enough. Part of her was already starting to worry that if she didn't leave soon she would struggle to ever go back. But she needn't have worried. Mrs Nowakowski had been there to welcome her home and tell her she'd started up a Neighbourhood Watch. Anna told her she couldn't think of anyone better for the job, which had seemed to please her. She was also full of apologies because she'd been out on Saturday night.

It amazed Anna how she had completely lost about twelve hours of her life. The doctors said it was very common and the memories of that night would likely never return thanks to the effects of the tranquilliser Connor had sneaked into her drink. Her parents had told her many times this was for the best but a part of Anna wanted to know what had happened up on the roof.

All she did know was Liam had turned up and not being able to get an answer from her flat he'd panicked and gone and woken Sophie. By the time he'd roused her the emergency services had arrived and they'd found Anna and Connor unconscious on the roof.

She had only been home long enough for her mother to make her a cup of tea when Sophie was knocking at the door.

'Wholly crab, look at the state of you,' said Sophie, pointing at the large colourful bruise on her right temple although Anna could see she was fighting back tears.

'Thanks, mate. You should see the other guy.'

'The son of a bishop. If I could get my hands on him, I'd knit his intestines into a tank top.'

'A tank top?' queried Anna, with a chuckle.

'Because nobody flatters a tank top.' Sophie wrapped Anna in a protective hug and squeezed her tightly. 'Are you really all right?' Sophie let her go and sat on the sofa opposite.

'Fine. I just can't remember anything after you left the party.' She noted Sophie's worried expression. 'It's okay, I know Connor nearly pushed me off the roof. I can't understand why he took so long before he did it.'

'Don't try and work it out, Anna. He's a total nut job.'

'I do pick 'em, don't I?'

'You didn't pick him, Anna. He targeted you. You mustn't assume everyone is a psycho who's out to get you. He spent ages tracking you down. Even renting somewhere in the area and staging the whole misdirected text message. That's what it said in the paper.'

She knew Connor was under arrest and not going anywhere any time soon. And whilst she knew she would have been terrified on the roof, the fact she couldn't actually remember it was most likely playing a part in her recovery. More than anything she felt incredibly lucky to be alive.

'I'm glad you're home. I've some flowers at my house for you from Liam.'

'I know,' said Anna. 'He keeps calling. I'm not ready to see him yet.'

Sophie pulled a face. 'I was meant to tell you ages ago.' Anna lowered her head expectantly. 'He owned up to only recommending they bring New York in to the scope of your project so they would relocate Hudson out there. He was deliberately trying to split you two up.'

'What a shit,' said Anna. Images of Hudson came into her mind. Muddled images.

'I let Hudson know what happened. I didn't want him finding out from work. I hope that was okay?'

'I messaged him too but I've not had a reply.' Anna had sent a couple of messages from hospital but had no response. He was no longer part of her life and she needed to accept it.

Anna ventured out in public for the first time the next morning, and it felt good to be back in control of things. Roberta had been uncharacteristically sympathetic, had reeled off a number of inspirational feminist quotes and insisted Anna didn't rush back. Sophie hadn't had to twist her arm much to get Anna to Arlo's nativity. Anna always missed things he did at school so it was a great opportunity to go while she was still officially off work.

It appeared every other parent had had the idea of getting to the nativity early for a good seat, which relegated them to two-thirds of the way back but they managed to get seats on the end of a row where Sophie could park the double buggy next to her.

'Save a seat for Dave,' said Sophie. Anna couldn't help her surprised expression. 'He's going to try and make it.'

'Wow. He really has changed,' said Anna. Sophie gave a proud smile whilst Anna stuffed her scarf into her woolly hat and plopped them on the chair next to her.

The school hall was noisy and it filled up fast. The head teacher took to the stage to welcome everyone and the room fell silent while he went on about the meaning of Christmas and the hours of rehearsing the children had done. The hall was full to bursting; people were standing at the back. Every seat was filled with a mum, dad, doting grandparent or important person who was there to witness one of life's milestones. It made her feel honoured and at the same time a little broody.

Anna tuned back in when the lights dimmed and music boomed from the state-of-the-art sound system; gone were the days of an old lady on the piano. The doors opened a crack and Dave slipped inside, scanning the room. Anna and Sophie gave him a subtle wave and Petal squealed when she caught sight of him and stretched her arms out as far as they would go. Dave spotted them, slunk over and kissed Petal and Sophie. Anna noted Sophie didn't have a go at him for being late. Anna moved into the vacant seat and Dave sat next to Sophie. 'Hiya,' he whispered to Anna. 'Nice to have you back.'

The nativity got under way and every heart in the room melted a fraction when the children sang 'Little Donkey' despite Joseph flashing his Octonauts pants all the way through it. Anna could sense Sophie getting nervous as Arlo's big stage debut neared. The shepherds filtered on to the stage or more accurately a number of children wearing pillowcases with checked tea towels on their heads. The stage lighting went to full and the angels appeared, one of whom was picking his nose.

Sophie leaned forward to whisper to Anna. 'The nose picker of Nazareth is Willoughby Newell.' Anna wasn't surprised.

Back in the stable Mary had given birth to Jesus who

she promptly dropped and in her haste to gather him up Mary kicked him across the stage. An impromptu rugby scrum broke out amongst the shepherds and a teacher had to intervene to recover the doll and return him to a wobbly-lipped Mary who slam-dunked him face down into the manger. Dave started to chuckle and Sophie gave him a dig in the ribs.

At last the three wise men arrived, bearing their gifts for the baby Jesus. While they sang 'We Three Kings' the first one unwrapped his gift and declared: 'It's not gold it's an empty *Maltesers* box.' But he delivered it to Jesus all the same. The narrator announced that the next gift was frankincense. And Arlo marched forward and proudly presented the baby with a pineapple. Anna leaned forward to catch Sophie's eye.

'What?' hissed Sophie. 'I didn't know what it was for. They said he needed to bring in something exotic.' She wiped away a proud tear and blew her nose.

It was all coming to an end and had gone incredibly well until a fight broke out when the donkey tried to take Willoughby Newell's halo. Arlo waded in, snatched back the halo, returned it to Willoughby and with one shove the donkey toppled and landed on the manger, crushing baby Jesus. The curtains were hastily closed and the audience burst into applause. Anna and Dave were on their feet applauding. It was the funniest thing she'd seen in ages and exactly the tonic she needed.

A week later Anna was facing a new challenge – Christmas shopping without a plan. Thanks to New York, her parents' accident and what her parents now referred to as 'that night' she hadn't even looked at a Christmas gift guide or prepared her usual spreadsheet of possible presents for family and friends. Here she was four days before Christmas engulfed in shopping madness.

Birmingham city centre was full of festive cheer with the traditional Christmas market snaking all the way from the Bull Ring along New Street and around Victoria Square. As dusk fell the Christmas lights sparkled and the mulled wine flowed. Anna had already been back to her car once to deposit full bags. She was determined to get most of it done today. She still had to wrap it all, although that was a part of Christmas she loved – her parcels always had twirly ribbon and bows and matching tags. Anna felt her phone vibrate, readjusted her many carrier bags and hoiked the phone from her pocket.

'Hiya, Sophie,' she said, hoping she was still on for a girly natter later like they'd planned.

'Hi. Where are you, *exactly*?'

'I'm in town doing my Christmas shopping.' She had told Sophie. She'd even asked if she wanted to come along but Sophie had said something about preferring to have Edward Scissorhands give her a back massage than face the city centre at Christmas time.

'Yeah, but where *exactly*?' repeated Sophie. 'Right this second?'

Anna glanced about her. 'Standing between a German lebkuchen stand and the Christmas tree in Victoria Square. Why?'

'The Christmas tree in Victoria Square. Right. Stay there!'

'Why? Sophie?' But the line had gone dead. Around her shoppers all wrapped up against the early bite of winter hurried past. She put the bags down and rubbed her sore fingers and waited. She still needed to get something for Petal and a chocolate orange for her dad because she got him one every year.

She scanned the crowd. Presumably Sophie had changed her mind and decided to join her. Lots of people just went for the evening and to enjoy the hot chocolate, gluhwein and German sausage. A woman began singing carols making it all rather festive. Someone did a shrill whistle, the kind you need your fingers for and Anna glanced over her shoulder and up towards the Council House that stood resplendent facing the square.

At first she didn't see anything other than the mass of shoppers but then she spotted someone in a hoodie wave and leap up onto the edge of what was known locally as the 'Floozie in the Jacuzzi' fountain. They couldn't be waving at her but she was going to watch anyway. The way they were leaping about she feared her first aid skills might be needed. The person then proceeded to forward flip, twist and vault their way down the steps much to the delight of the crowd. When they reached the bottom, they did a double backflip landing so close to Anna she grabbed her shopping and moved nearer to the Christmas tree. A brief but spontaneous round of applause broke out as the gymnast stepped nearer to Anna and pulled off his hoodie.

'Hudson!' Anna dropped her shopping and flung her arms around his neck. Joy engulfed her and she had to stop herself from crying because she knew he'd think she was ridiculous. 'What are you doing here?'

'I came to see you.'

She stepped back to look at him as if needing to check he was real. 'What was with all the acrobatics? You'll get yourself killed.' Although a small part of her was mightily impressed.

He hung his head slightly. 'I didn't tell you the whole truth. I used to be a free runner.'

'What, one of those crazies who jumps from building to building?' The thought of it sent a chill through her.

Hudson gave a lopsided smile. 'Yeah. It comes in handy.'

'What for?'

'Saving people on roofs.'

Anna felt like a whoosh of air had been knocked from her lungs. Sensations shot through her body taking her back to being on the roof. The shove in the back that saved her from falling. The voice. 'You?'

Hudson gave a modest shrug. 'The door to the roof was locked. I climbed up the outside.'

'You could have died.'

'You were about to.' His eyes told her so much.

'Thank you.' Her voice was barely a whisper. 'Why weren't you there when the emergency services arrived?'

'I didn't like to move you but there was no signal on the roof so I had to climb down to call 999. As I was speaking to the ambulance Liam arrived, then a police car showed up real quick and Liam seemed to take over. I guess I felt I was in the way.'

'Did you see what happened with Connor?'

He squeezed her shoulder. 'I heard most of it.'

'I can't remember much.'

'When you're ready I'll tell you.' He beamed and something fluttered in her heart.

Her brain went into overdrive. 'Free running . . . that's how you got the wheelbarrow on bonfire night.'

He nodded and gave a cheeky grin. 'It's also how I got in the park without a ticket.' He looked suitably ashamed but only for a nanosecond.

Anna couldn't stop grinning. She was overjoyed to see him again. 'Are you over here for Christmas?'

'Err, I don't know. I keep jetting back and forth like

I'm on a bungee. Something keeps pulling me back here.'

'Last time I spoke to you, you were with Emily.' She watched closely for his reaction.

He seemed to wince at her name. 'Emily is . . . Emily.' He raised his shoulders. 'She's now in a relationship with Dad's business partner.'

Anna was relieved. 'Is everything else okay?'

Hudson seemed to scan her face making her feel a little self-conscious and she pulled down her woolly hat a fraction. A crease appeared on his forehead. 'You see for *everything* to be okay, you and I would need to be in the same country for a start . . .'

Anna gave a nervous giggle; she wasn't sure where this was going. 'We are.' She held up her hands.

'Permanently. Always. Forever,' he said. There was a wisp of mist when his words hit the chill of the evening air.

She swallowed. It felt like her insides were turning to mush. 'How would that work?'

Anna's eyes were wide. Her breathing was ragged. She saw a spark of something in his eyes.

'Anna, we're great together but there lies the issue – we're not together and I can't for the life of me think why that is.'

Anna's grin was actually starting to make her face ache. 'Nor can I.'

Hudson leaned in and hesitated, which made Anna's heart soar even higher at his trepidation. She closed her eyes and savoured the moment when their lips met. He pulled her gently to him and she was lost in the kiss.

'Hey, you need this,' came a friendly voice and a stall-holder pulled a decoration off the wooden cabin and bounded over waving some mistletoe.

They broke apart and began to giggle. Anna put her fingers to her lips. They didn't feel quite like her own – they were sure, brave and certain. And so was her heart.

'Thanks, buddy,' said Hudson, taking out his phone and pulling Anna in for a selfie. And as the camera flashed, Anna knew this was how it was meant to be.

Chapter Forty

Anna was grateful to Hudson for lugging the cat carrier. She was sure Maurice was getting bigger. She couldn't contain her pride as the carers at the nursing home all did a double take when Hudson walked in. They had finished her Christmas shopping in Birmingham and then spent the best part of the next two days in bed together. Brief interludes between fabulous sex were filled with chatter. All the things they had wanted to say for so long had all tumbled out. And now she was introducing him to Bert.

'I am very pleased to meet you,' said Bert, standing up and vigorously shaking Hudson's hand. 'I've been following Anna's love life closely.'

'Bert,' said Anna with caution in her voice. She let Maurice out of the carrier and hoped that would distract him.

Bert pulled Hudson down a fraction to tell him something. 'I wanted it to be you.'

Anna and Hudson exchanged looks. They doubted Bert was aware of the *You Got Mail* reference and it made them smile all the more.

'I wanted it to be me too, Bert,' said Hudson, taking

the seat next to him, and Maurice instantly jumped on his lap.

Bert felt for the cat. 'And you have Maurice's seal of approval.'

'So, it would seem,' said Anna. 'Which is good because Hudson's applying for jobs locally so he'll be sticking around for a while.' They couldn't stop the grins that spread across both their faces.

Bert leaned in conspiratorially. 'Watch out for other men's underwear,' he said with a chortle.

Hudson looked beyond confused. 'Don't worry, it's mainly Dave's,' said Anna, which did nothing to change Hudson's expression. 'Where's Rosie?'

'She's getting some things from my room.' On cue Rosie appeared carrying a gift bag.

They exchanged welcomes and Christmas wishes and Rosie handed the bag to Bert who immediately passed it to Anna.

'It isn't much but it's something to open on Christmas Day.'

'Thanks, Bert. I got you something too,' said Anna, handing him a large wrapped box.

He brushed his hands along the top of the box and down the sides, establishing its dimensions. 'My, this makes me look like a miser. Can I open it?' he asked, eager as a child.

'Of course.'

He ripped the paper off, pulled open the box and began feeling around inside. 'It's some sort of machine. There's a cable and a lid. You'll have to tell me.'

'It's a coffee machine,' said Rosie, peering over his shoulder.

The excitement faded from Bert's face. 'Oh, I see.'

'No, Bert. It doesn't mean I'm not going visit you. It means you don't have to wait for me to get a decent cup of coffee,' said Anna and the grin instantly returned to his face.

'Thank you, Anna. You know how I love an Americano. And now you do too.'

'Bert!' said Rosie and Anna together.

Later that day they met up with Sophie and her brood and were all playing hide-and-seek in Wildflower Park. It was a bright fresh December day, with a clear sky and a chill in the air.

'Found you!' shouted Arlo, his bobble-hatted head pushing through the bushes.

'Well done,' said Anna. 'Who else have you found?'

'I found Reuben. He was hiding under the bench with Mummy. He's rubbish at hide-and-seek.'

Anna scrambled out from behind the bush and tried to keep up with Arlo who raced off across the park. They had limited the hiding area to avoid any missing-children incidents. Anna thought she'd spotted a flash of bright pink behind the large tree stump and she called to Arlo who stumbled to a halt. She pointed to the stump and they both started running towards it.

'Found you!' shouted Arlo as Petal came into view giggling wildly. Anna took Petal's pink-mittened hand and they went to find Hudson. Sophie was watching them from the safety of the bench and she was pointing towards the wooded area. Arlo charged off but Anna veered off towards Sophie.

'Dave just rang, he's ready for us. If it's a disaster I could always do Marmite sandwiches,' said Sophie, pulling a worried face as they passed.

Arlo hollered, 'Found you! I win!' He was already running back to Sophie before Anna had even reached the trees. Petal chased after her brother.

Anna stepped into the copse. A whistle drew her attention and she looked up. Hudson was sitting high up in a gnarled tree, the picture of chilled-out cool.

'You are such a big kid. Come down.' In an easy fluid movement he bounded down through the tree, swung on a branch and landed effortlessly on the grass. He opened his arms and she fell into them. 'Found you!'

'You have,' he said, kissing her softly.

'Come on.' She tugged at his hand. 'Dave's cooking. It'll be like an initiation ceremony.'

'Awesome.'

'No,' she said with a grimace. 'It's unlikely to be awesome, but it will be fun.'

'Is this some weird British holiday I should be doing something for, like maypole dancing or cheese rolling?'

'Nope. It's just something me and Sophie make a big thing of because after today it's all family focused but Christmas Eve eve has been our mini Christmas for the last few years.'

Sophie came in step with Anna as they left the park.

'How'd it go taking Reuben into the office yesterday?' asked Anna.

'It was fine. Karl was actually quite sweet. He said he could hear women's ovaries creaking into life at the mere sound of a babby.'

'The last of the die-hard feminists is our Karl.'

As they approached Sophie and Dave's garden they could see smoke. 'Plugholes,' said Sophie with feeling.

'Daddy's burning something!' yelled Arlo excitedly. 'Is it a Viking party?'

'Not intentionally, no,' said Sophie, exchanging worried looks with Anna.

The children ran ahead and the adults followed up the pathway with Sophie scanning the house for any signs of flames. Further up the path she could see Dave waving although he didn't seem distressed, but that didn't mean there wasn't any need to be alarmed.

Dave was leaning over the old wheelbarrow. When they got closer they could see he was using it as a barbecue.

'That is the coolest barbecue ever,' said Hudson, reaching out to shake Dave's hand.

'Thanks, mate,' said Dave, puffing up with pride. 'I saw Mary Berry do it on the telly.'

'Can we wheel it round the garden while it's on fire?' asked Arlo, jumping up and down.

'No, sorry, son. It needs to stay put. I've got drinks for you and Petal on the wall.' He indicated two plastic mugs of squash nearby. Anna was impressed: Dave really had changed.

The garden was neat and tidy and swathed in tiny lights, giving it a very festive feel.

'I like your fairy lights,' said Hudson, and Dave and Sophie sniggered.

'I'll explain later,' said Anna, shaking her head at her juvenile friends.

'Here you go. You can man the flames for a bit.' Dave handed the barbecue tongs to Hudson, tapped Sophie's arm and guided her up the garden a little way away from the others.

'I wanted to give you this.' He held out a small black velvet box. 'It's not your Christmas present. It's just . . . Here.' He passed her the box and shoved his hands deep in to his coat pockets.

Sophie was surprised but a thread of excitement spun inside her as she opened the box a fraction and peeped inside. Nestled in the velvet box were two rings. Her engagement ring and her wedding ring, although they looked quite different to the last time she'd seen them. No longer cut in two by the hospital they now sparkled as if under jewellery shop lights.

'You got them fixed,' she said, tears springing to her eyes. It was such a thoughtful thing to have done and she'd not even noticed they were missing. Dave took them from the box and slipped them onto Sophie's finger.

'They fit too.'

'I got them resized at the same time.'

'Because I'm not the skinny person you married?' she said mock reproachfully.

'Because you've changed. We both have.'

She was very happy. She tore her eyes briefly away from the sight of her rings glinting on her finger and looked at her husband. Her stupid, ordinary, brilliant, thoughtful husband. 'I love you, Dave,' she said, pulling him into a kiss.

Anna found she was staring at Sophie and Dave. It was a lovely thing to witness – they'd been through a lot.

'They're a great couple,' said Hudson, butting into her thoughts.

'They certainly are,' said Anna, leaning back into Hudson's arms.

'If we're swapping gifts, I got you this,' he said, pulling a small wrapped package from his pocket.

Anna opened it carefully. 'Strawberry and black pepper jam. I love it.'

'I saw it and thought of you,' he said. 'But then I'm thinking of you most of the time.'

'Anna?' Arlo's voice came from near the house. They all turned to look. Arlo was pointing at Maurice. 'Is he allowed to play with those?' asked Arlo, pointing at the cat who was proudly marching off with a pair of Dave's Batman pants.

And despite the chaos, despite the fact her cat was thieving again, she kissed Hudson. Because right at that moment she had everything she could possibly need.

Acknowledgements

It takes so many people to get a book over the finish line so massive thank yous to my fabulous editors Katie Loughnane and Rachel Faulkner-Wilcocks for doing an amazing job of knocking this one into shape along with all the fabulously talented folk at Team Avon. Thanks too to my wonderful agent Kate Nash for always being on hand to nudge me in the right direction.

Huge thanks to my technical experts and life experience sources: Dr David Boulton for wonderful medical ideas and guidance – any errors are entirely my own. Anna Jennings of Warwickshire Wildlife Trust for answering all my wildflower questions. Cherie Niles for some top corporate phrases. The free runners of Birmingham City Centre for parkour information. Cheryl Bourne for, well, you and I know which bit and that's how it shall remain ;-)

I'd like to raise a gin to the ladies of the RNA party train: Erin Green, Phillipa Ashley, Christie Barlow, Liz Hanbury and Nell Dixon for continued support, laughs and full glasses.

Thanks also to Kearan Ramful for his ongoing support. Special thanks to the custodians of Moseley Park for letting me spend a blissful day there with my family, which provided a lot of inspiration for Wildflower Park.

A special mention to all the people I have ever worked in an office with – you are most definitely *not* in this book; however, you have kept me going for the last thirty years and provided much inspiration – thank you.

And probably the biggest thank you goes to the terrific bloggers, reviewers and wonderful readers that spent their hard-earned cash and precious time on my book – you guys rock! And if you have a minute, a review really does make all the difference and means such a lot – thank you.

Loved your time in Wildflower Park? Then join Daisy Wickens in Ottercombe Bay…

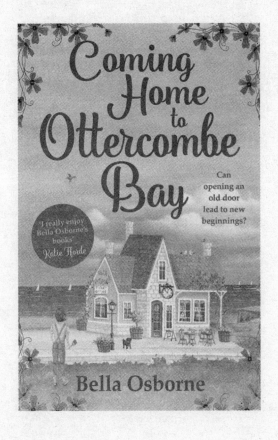

Available in all good bookshops now.

Escape to the Cotswolds with Beth and Leo...

Available in all good bookshops now.

Tempted to read another heart-warming romance by Bella Osborne? Try…

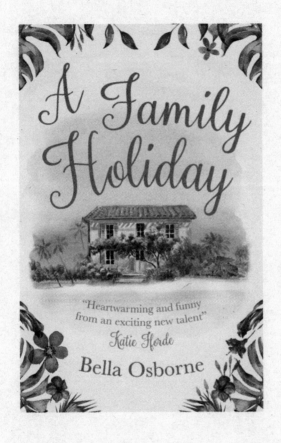

Available in all good bookshops now.

As the sun begins to set on Sunset Cottage,
an unlikely friendship begins to blossom . . .

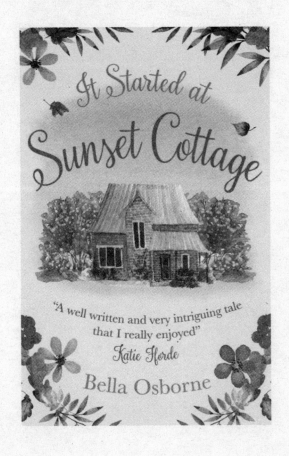